MW01135010

BOOKS BY TIM MCBAIN & L.T. VARGUS

Casting Shadows Everywhere

Fade to Black (Awake in the Dark #1)

Bled White (Awake in the Dark #2)

Red on the Inside (Awake in the Dark #3)

Back in Black (Awake in the Dark #4)

AWAKE IN THE DARK

TIM MCBAIN & LT VARGUS

AWAKE IN THE DARK

OMNIBUS EDITION

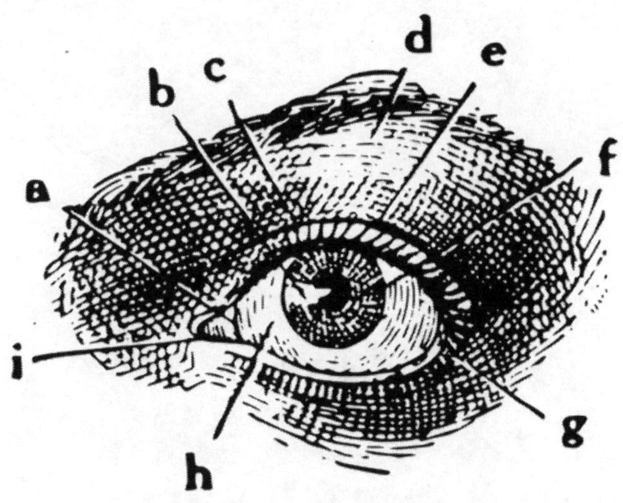

SMARMY PRESS

SMARMY PRESS

AWAKE IN THE DARK

FADE TO BLACK

TIM MCBAIN
L.T. VARGUS

SMARMY PRESS

FADE TO BLACK

BOOK 1

CHAPTER 1

Any minute now a hooded man will come barreling out of nowhere and kill me.

So that sucks.

I know this because it has happened six times before. I wake up in this alley, hung from a post by a piece of rope lashed to one ankle, tied in a hangman's knot. After several minutes of work, I pry my bonds free, and about thirty seconds after I hit the ground, this guy in a black hooded robe gives me a pretty bad case of death.

His hands are cold on my neck. And dry. I try to fight him, to claw at his eyes, but I can't reach. I scratch at his arms. He's too strong. I try to yell at him. I manage more of a gurgle and some clicky noises. I don't even know what I'd say, I guess, but I can assure you that he seems like a real dick.

Everything goes all fuzzy and fades to gray, then black. I die, and then I go… someplace else, I guess.

I don't know. I can't remember that part just now.

Anyway, I guess I should try something different this time. I fold at the waist, my fingers picking at the knot while I think it over. I've tried running out of both ends of the alley. Tried fighting the guy.

All of these failed in spectacular fashion. I'll need to get creative this time.

There's really only one other option I can think of. I get the knot loose enough to slip my ankle free of the rope and plummet to the ground, landing on my feet which immediately slide out from under me to plant my lower back in a mud puddle.

Nice.

I hop up and pop the lid of a dumpster open and lift myself so I'm sitting on the lip. Flies circle near my face before returning to their bacteria buffet. I totter forward, my hands latching onto the metal sides to stop my momentum. My chest heaves in and out with a single deep breath. This may not be the best idea I've ever had, I suppose, but I'd rather avoid getting strangled, so what the hell? I plunge feet first into the pile of trash. I sink and bags shift to flop their limp weight on top of me. Garbage water squishes around me.

It's juicy as hell in here, and it smells like liquid ass.

I can't see the soft mass resting under my hands and knees, but if I had to guess? Dead dog.

I never get a look at his face. The hooded man, I mean. He somehow tucks back into the shadow under the hood. I can make out the outline of his chin, one corner of his wet mouth, but that's it.

For now all I can make out is a little light streaming between the sacks of waste above me and the aforementioned juicy odor. I wait. And wait. I consider poking my head out to breathe some semi fresh air, but I decide against it. It'd be dumb to submerge myself in putrid liquid like this only to get strangled for trying to breathe oxygen that smells like 90% sewage instead of 300% sewage. I can tough it out.

After petting the dog for a few minutes, I hear footsteps

rush into the alley and hesitate. This is it. I feel like I finally appreciate what the cliché "when the shit hits the fan" means, too, because in the dumpster it smells exactly like someone threw a bunch of logs into spinning blades.

The footsteps creep closer, and there's a sloshing sound. I picture his foot sinking ankle deep into a pothole turned mud puddle and almost laugh. Maybe I'm covered in piss and dead dog juice, but he has a wet foot now!

He scampers past the dumpster, pausing at the end of the alley before moving on.

Interesting. This is a new development in our game of cat and guy choking cat. As much as I want to get the eff out of this dumpster, I should wait here a moment longer before I move out. Give him some time to create some distance between us.

I stand, and my head emerges from the debris just enough to get a peek at the end of the alley.

Nothing.

I hold my breath and listen for a moment.

Nothing.

It suddenly strikes me that it really is nothing. No cars going by. No pedestrians around. This seems important, but I can't think of why just now.

I pull myself out of the dumpster, but my foot catches on the rim, and I splat face first on the asphalt.

"Fuck!" I say.

It occurs to me immediately that I've said this altogether too loudly considering I am trying to, you know, not get murdered. I bring my hand away from my cheek bone, and it's bloody with a bunch of sand stuck in it.

I look up, and there he is, standing at the end of the alley.

Just standing there.

I try to think of a name or something to call him, but none of them seem dramatic enough to do this scenario justice. I mean, what can you say to the guy that's about 30 seconds away from snuffing your life out for the seventh damn time? Did I already mention that this guy is a real jerk?

I run. I reach the other end of the alley and bank to the left and keep going. My feet pound the pavement, and I can hear his footsteps echoing mine, drawing closer.

I take another sharp left at the intersection, hoping to gain a little ground with the change of direction.

For the first time I realize how gray everything seems. The sky. The buildings around me. The street. The sidewalk. It doesn't seem right. This place isn't normal. I try to remember what I was doing before I woke up in this alley, but I can't.

I cut left again at the next intersection, I guess out of habit at this point.

His footsteps are much louder now. Close. I sneak a peek over my shoulder just in time to see his outstretched hand reach for the back of my collar. I juke away from him and veer left. He follows, reaches out again.

Just as I think I should probably look where I'm going, I slam into the dumpster and drop to the ground like a bag of sand. I guess that's what four left turns gets you. My fall is so fast, he can't slow down in time and kicks my head, which sends him – Wait, let me rephrase that. I heroically place my head in the perfect spot to trip him, which sends him sprawling into the same mud puddle I fell in earlier.

I can literally see some stars from the cranium kick, but you should see the other guy. He's soaked!

I pull myself to my feet. I'm too wobbly to run, so I lean against the dumpster.

Aw, what the hell? I crawl back into the dumpster, face first this time. If this guy wants to kill me, fine, but let's just say he's probably going to have to touch a dead dog to do it.

I hear him move toward the trash bin, and then there's a familiar metallic sound that I can't quite place. After a very brief lull, I hear what sounds like him jabbing his hand into the garbage. He jabs again and then three more times in rapid succession.

Except I see his hand plunge through the garbage about three inches from the tip of my nose, and it's weird because his hand looks exactly like the blade of a ridiculous combat knife. Like if you had just killed a dinosaur, you would use this thing to skin it. Otherwise, it'd be too big to have any practical purpose I can think of.

So this is yet another new development. He's wielding a knife.

How wonderful.

I watch the knife jabs work their way away from me to the other end of the dumpster and then start their way back. I know I shouldn't move, that if I move he'll see exactly where I am. But once he's within about a foot and a half of me, I can no longer resist the urge to put the dead dog on top of me for protection. Before I can even lift the carcass, though, the knife skims my ear and enters that ball of muscle that connects the neck and shoulder.

This is the opposite of awesome.

He pulls the knife out, and without thinking about it, I lie back, I guess to shrink away from my attacker. I feel the wet warmth surge along the back of my neck. Things suddenly seem quiet, and I realize that I must have been screaming and just stopped.

The knife plunges through the trash once again, this time sinking into my torso two inches lower than my sternum, that soft space between the ribs. I grab his hands around the handle of the knife to try to hold the blade in so he can't keep at it, but he yanks it away without any real trouble.

The place where the knife was in my belly feels empty. A little cold. Like if you hold your mouth open and let the cool air touch everything in there, except a lot more painful.

I really need to figure out how I got here. Who just wakes up in alley that's all empty and shit? Hanging upside down by the foot? Someone must have put me here, I guess, but who? And why? And how do I even keep coming back? Who resurrects in this day and age?

I think I am in shock. Like now, I am out on the asphalt again. I guess he must have pulled me out of the dumpster. I don't know.

It's getting hard to keep my eyes open, and everything is a little blurry around the edges. I see the hooded man swing back into focus, and I realize that he's completely soaked. His robe looks like he's been rolling around in mud. It's a mess.

So that's good.

CHAPTER 2

The first thing that drifts into my consciousness is some soft rock song. It sounds like it's playing far away. I don't know what it's called, but I know I've heard it before.

It blows.

The next thing I'm aware of is a warm breeze tickling my forehead in steady bursts.

"His eyelids are fluttering," a voice says.

Now, this voice is entirely too close to my face. It does not sound like the voice of someone you want close to your face. It sounds like the voice of a guy with a mustache that eats a lot of spaghetti, and it sounds like he's close enough to smear marinara on my cheek with a simple flick of the tongue.

When I first open my eyes, however, it's too bright to make out more than a silhouette hovering over me. I manage to keep my eyes open for a fraction of a second, but I'm left with more questions than answers. Am I in a hospital? Is this a doctor?

I clutch at my belly, but there's no bandage or any other sign of a knife wound.

"I think he's waking up," the voice says.

A murmur of other voices respond. There have to be at least 15 other people gathered nearby. OK, so that seems like a lot for a hospital room, and thinking it over a moment, the mustache voice doesn't sound all that educated.

And then the smell hits me. The warm breeze I've felt on my forehead? Smells like Funyuns. To be more specific, it smells exactly like Funyun breath. So I guess Dr. Funyun is mouth-breathing on my face.

"Are you awake, buddy?" he says.

"Yes."

I open my eyes just in time to see the guy wheel around to face all the ladies standing in a semi-circle around me here in the u-scan aisle at the supermarket, Meijer to be precise.

"He said 'yes,'" he says.

"We can hear him," an old lady clutching a tabloid to her chest says. Her voice sounds like she smokes tubes of actual tar instead of cigarettes.

The man turns back to face me. I sense right away that the grin plastered on his face is genuine. Also, I was right about the mustache, a black Tom Selleck style flecked with gray.

"Name's Glenn Floyd," he says, holding his hand out for me to shake.

"I'm Jeff Grobnagger," I say.

I sit up, and he claps me on the shoulder instead of a handshake. One of those hard shoulder claps usually reserved for awkward encounters between gym teachers and students.

"You scared me, man," he says. "I haven't seen somebody fish out like that since the time Ricky brought a nitrous tank to the party shack back in college."

He lifts the navy blue baseball cap off his head and runs his fingers through his hair.

"Fish out?" I say.

"Oh yeah," he says. "You were floppin' around like a fish, buddy. Trying to bite the floor and stuff. It was wild. Musta been one of them grand mal seizures or something, right?"

A couple of the ladies behind him nod gravely.

A woman strides up on us with a cell phone pressed to her ear. She's wearing pleated front khakis and a fancier version of the Meijer polo shirt, so I take her as some kind of manager.

"Are you feeling all right, sir?" she says.

"Yes, I'm fine."

"I'm glad to hear that. We've called an ambulance, so we'll need you to sit tight until they get here," she says.

I get to my feet.

"What? No," I say. "I'm not getting in any ambulance."

I detect a hint of panic in my voice, so I try to do a nonchalant shoulder shrug to conceal it. Like "I'm not getting in any ambulance *because I'm cool.* Not terrified in the slightest." Glenn squints and gives a nod of approval. I think the Meijer lady buys it as well.

"Sir, it's store policy for us to have you wait here until medical professionals can assist you," she says. "This is in the best interest of your well being as well as our store's insurance purposes."

"Well, I happen to have a very strict policy regarding me not going to the hospital."

Glenn chuckles.

"Oh, man," he says.

I hate to toot my own horn, but I'm getting the distinct sense that Glenn is very impressed with me. Also, I lied earlier. I love tooting my own horn.

I turn toward the door, moving quickly.

"Grobnagger," Glenn says, running to catch up with me. "You almost forgot your wheat grass… and these."

He shoves a little plastic planter of wheat grass and my sunglasses into my hands. So I guess I was here to buy wheat grass. Not sure. I'm guessing the sunglasses popped off when I fell.

I slide them back on. I pretty much always wear sunglasses – inside, outside, daytime, nighttime - doesn't matter. I like to feel covered up, I guess. Plus it's comforting to see the world through lenses that mute all the harshness out there. It's like having a dimmer switch for reality.

For a second I think maybe the old man who says hi and bye to everybody is going to try to physically stop me from leaving the store with some kind of crazy old man neck grip or something. Instead he just tries to guilt me into staying with a dirty look and a slow motion head shake. I cross through the doorway and step away from the building.

In the parking lot, a shriek distracts me – my eyes lock onto a young couple loading groceries into the back of a Hyundai Sonata. The girl has long, scrawny limbs and an equally long face like someone grabbed her by head and foot and stretched all of her out when the bones were still soft when she was an infant. Still pretty, though. The guy has a low brow and muscular legs that suggest a life spent lifting heavy objects for both work and pleasure.

She pushes him in the chest, and he totters backward. Then she squeals in glee as he does a Frankenstein like stalk after her with raised arms. He grips and lifts her in a sort of bear hug, her face going all red in laughter as her frail fists pound at his chest.

Eh…

She could do better.

As I move through the lot, shards of memory start piecing together what all has happened to me here. I had just rung up my wheat grass in the u-scan lane when I overheard Glenn next to me.

"Excuse me, miss," he said to the cashier standing about 15 feet away. "This item won't scan."

He shook a can of Hershey's syrup at her. I watched as the cashier made eye contact with him but didn't help, didn't acknowledge his query at all, in fact, instead turning and walking in the other direction.

"What the fuck?!" Glenn said in a gravelly falsetto that was almost quiet enough to be to himself.

I almost laughed, but he immediately started talking to me.

"Do your cats eat that wheat grass?" he said.

He pointed at the wheat grass.

"That's what I'm about to find out," I said.

"It's supposed to be really good for them," he said. "My cats loved it at first, and now they won't touch the stuff. Figures, right?"

I remember that I tried to respond to this, but it was like my mouth didn't work. First no sound came out even though I was telling it to, and then once I could speak, it was all garbled into stuttering nonsense.

"Whoa. You alright?" Glenn said.

And then everything faded to black. The next thing I knew I was strung up by my left foot in an oddly gray alley.

See, a few months ago I started having these seizures. Sometimes I'm out for a few minutes. Sometimes it's hours. They keep getting more frequent. Actually, the last two were less than a week apart. And each seizure is a one way ticket to strangle city.

Are they just dreams, though? The stranglings in the alley, I mean. Seizure dreams or something? That would make the most sense, of course, but I don't think I believe it. Not all the way, at least.

I don't know.

I move beyond the parking lot and onto the sidewalk. A flame broiled smell emitting from Burger King engulfs this region. It always makes me feel dumb that I think it smells pretty good, and then I remember that some guys in a lab off of the New Jersey turnpike worked very hard to make sure it was an odor I would like.

Yum.

A car with what sounds like no muffler at all pulls up next to me and slows to an idle. I hear the whir of the window going down, and the sound of a familiar voice.

"Hey Grobnagger. Want a ride?" he says. "You probably shouldn't be out walking after your… uh… incident back there."

It's Glenn.

I'm about to say no when I hear the siren in the distance. I picture the old lady releasing the tabloid from her chest to point me out and a couple of hooded paramedics tying me down to a stretcher and forcing me into the back of the ambulance. And though I know this won't actually happen, I just want to get out of here.

"Yeah, alright," I say.

I climb into the passenger seat of Glenn's 2002 Ford Explorer. It's sort of a purpley-red with a pink rear bumper. Bright pink.

"I live close," I say as I close the door. "Like seven blocks from here."

"Oh, that's cool," he says.

I notice that he's sporting some ridiculous wrap around Oakleys that look they were minted in about 1988. I can't say for sure, but I like to think that they are the Jose Canseco signature model.

"You know the Park Terrace Apartments?" I say. "On Kendall?"

"Yep."

"That's where we're headed."

"You got it, buddy."

The oldies station Glenn is listening to is playing "My Baby Does The Hanky Panky." He cranks up the stereo, and we make our way in the general direction of my apartment, the ambulance rushing past us about thirty seconds into the journey.

I watch the city out of the window. All of the grass looks brown and frizzy because it hasn't rained in a while. McDonald's cups and hubcaps huddle with road kill in clusters on the side of the road. The chimney at KFC spews smoke that looks like it's about to congeal into a solid black object in the sky.

And suddenly I realize that we passed the turn to my apartment a while ago.

"You missed my street," I say.

Glenn pushes his sunglasses down to the tip of his nose and regards me.

"I need to swing by to feed my cats and give them their medication if that's cool," he says. "Then I'll get you home."

"Well," I say. "OK."

He pushes the sunglasses back up.

"My oldest, Leroy, has had real bad acid reflux for a while now. I have to feed him small quantities multiple times a day and watch him like a hawk to make sure he doesn't try to steal the other cats' food."

I nod.

"If left to his own devices, he scarfs that extra food and upchucks everywhere."

"Right," I say.

"Thing is, I don't even mind cleaning up the cat vomit. Not really. It just kills me that he's tearing up his esophagus and can't keep any food down, and the poor guy is still hungry after all that, you know?"

"Yeah."

"It ain't right."

After several more blocks of contemplating feline digestive issues in silence, we arrive at Glenn's house, a bungalow that looks in better repair than I had anticipated. I guess I don't know what I expected, really, maybe empty Funyun bags rolling about the lawn like tumbleweed or something.

Glenn cracks the driver's side door open, and then swivels his head at me, trying to force me to lock eyes with those damn Oakleys. I don't take the bait, keeping my gaze focused on the corner of a road map sticking out of the glove box.

"I'll just wait in the car," I say.

"You're probably going to want to come in," he says. "This can take like 20 minutes if Leroy's in an ornery mood and Patches pecks at her Friskies the way she often does."

"It's fine," I say. "I don't mind waiting."

"I have to insist that you come on in, Grobnagger," he says. "I'll fix you something to eat and drink, and you can watch me wrangle these cats."

We're quiet for a time.

"Listen, I'm going to feel like a real dick face if you just wait out here," he says.

"OK," I say, not quite believing the words coming out of my mouth. "I guess."

I open the door and follow him in. I think maybe he had me at "dick face."

Inside, the house is spotlessly clean. There are little Martha Stewart style decorative displays everywhere. Elaborate center pieces. Vases of flowers. Baskets of fruit.

"Do you live here by yourself?" I say.

"Yeah," he says. "Just me and these fuzz bags."

He gestures at the black cat winding around his legs, tilting its head to push its face against the leg of his pants.

"That's Leroy. Leroy, this is Jeff Grobnagger," he says. "But yeah, this is my bachelor pad. Got divorced from the Crypt Keeper four years ago. Thank God. Our daughter is grown, and..."

He trails off, which seems out of character. He seems less the type to trail off into thoughtful silence and more the type to emphasize his point by spraying flecks of Funyun while stating it.

"Anyhow," he says. "I'll get you something to chow on."

I consider telling him that I'm not hungry, but I say nothing. He pulls some Tupperware containers out of the fridge and starts plopping stuff on a plate.

"You mind if I ask how old you are?" he says.

"I'm 27."

"Really?" he says. "You look younger than that. Shit, you could pass for a high school kid."

"That's what people tell me."

"What's your secret?"

I scratch my chin.

"Well," I say. "I avoid stressful shit as much as possible. Keeps you young."

"Interesting," he says. "Real interesting. What kind of stressful stuff do you mean, though?"

"Worrying about money. Working a real job. Talking to people. Stuff like that."

Glenn doesn't say anything for a long moment. He just raises his eyebrows. He puts something in the toaster oven, but his torso shields me from getting a good look at it.

"Fair enough," he says finally.

"How old are you?" I say, not wanting the conversation to stall on such a sour note.

"I am 56 years young," he says. "I know what you're thinking, too. '56? Shit, you could pass for 54 easy, dude.'"

I laugh a little.

"Yeah," I say. I sometimes don't know what to say after people make a joke, so I just say "Yeah."

"Here," he says.

He places a plate piled with Caribbean jerk chicken sauced with mango cilantro salsa, fried plantains, and some kind of black bean and rice concoction that seems to be held together with cheese that is effing delicious.

"Thanks," I remember to say a couple of bites in. "This is tasty as hell."

"I like the leftover chicken better cold, but if you want I can heat it up for you," he says. "Else wise, the four legged lords of the manor await their meal."

He bows at the waist and rotates his hand in a florid gesture between us as though he's a servant bidding my royal leave. I continue to mow the food while he goes about feeding his four cats. It might be the best plate of food I've ever eaten.

He's still standing over the feasting cats when I finish my meal. I guess he's been waiting until I was done to re-establish our conversation as he asks a question seconds after I swallow the last bite.

"Where do you work?" he says.

"I don't," I say.

"Oh?" he says.

"I made a bunch of money playing poker online a few years ago," I say. "I live off of that."

"That's awesome," he says. "So you don't play anymore?"

I shake my head.

"A few years ago, it was so easy," I say. "A bunch of people that didn't know what they were doing flocked to online poker sites and basically wound up letting people like me extract the money from their accounts. The government shut a lot of shit down, though, so a lot less people are playing poker these days. The ones that still do play are pretty good."

A piece of rice is stuck in my molars, and I work at dislodging it with my tongue.

"Plus, I don't have the same drive to make money that I did back then."

Glenn tilts his head and looks at me through halfway opened eyes.

"Seems like it'd be stressful, though," he says.

"Nope," I say. "Poker is a game, you know? And playing online, it almost doesn't feel real. I know I'm up against real people, but there's no confrontation. I just sit alone, stare at a screen and click a mouse button. The chips I'm risking don't even seem like real money. I get the feeling of risk - the exhilaration - but it's not real. It's just a game."

"I guess I can see that," he says.

"Sometimes it starts to feel too real, and I clam up, go on little losing streaks. That's when I have to take a break," I say. "But normally, it's so not real to me that I'm pretty relaxed. I just antagonize the other players with aggression until they start making mistakes."

Glenn laughs.

"It's all artificial, though," I say. "The conflict isn't real. I win because I have a combination of less fear and more discipline than my opponents. But I don't have those traits in the real world. I have them in the game."

I'm not sure what has gotten into me to start ranting like this. We fall silent for a moment.

"So are you epileptic?" he says.

"You mean because of the seizure?" I say. "I don't know."

"You don't know?" he says. "What the hell do you mean you don't know?"

"I've never been to a doctor about it," I say.

I try out the cool shrug again, but Glenn is not having it this time.

"Are you kidding?" he says. "How long have you been having seizures?"

"Six or seven months, I guess."

"How many times total?"

"7."

"Were you rendered unconscious all 7 times?"

"Yes."

"Jesus, buddy. That is what doctors would call 'alarming.'"

"Going to the doctor is stressful. I told you. I don't do stressful shit."

"You know what's stressful? Dying is pretty stressful," he says. "If you don't go to the doctor, you might do that instead."

"We'll see, I guess," I say.

Glenn takes off his hat and splays his fingers through his hair again. I guess that must be one of his go to moves.

"Do you ever even think about seeing a doctor?" he says. "You must."

"I think about it, but then I think about playing video games, and that generally sounds more fun."

He takes my plate and rinses it off in the sink.

"Do you dream?" he says. "When you have one of your seizures, I'm saying. Do you dream when you have a seizure?"

"Yep."

I'm so thankful for the opportunity to get off the topic of doctors that I tell Glenn everything. The hanging. The strangling. Every detail in between.

He is the first person I've told any of this to.

When I finish, he doesn't say anything for a long time. He just looks at me.

"You're not into occult stuff, are you?" he says.

"No."

"I didn't figure," he says. "Wait here."

He comes back with a photo album, a black leather bound

book with a weird silver symbol etched onto the cover, and a metallic sphere in contrasting hues of maroon and gold. Of course, I want to get a look at the sphere first, but he sets it aside. Instead, he riffles through the pages of the photo album until he finds the proper place and sets it in front of me.

"This is my daughter, Amity," he says. "These are the most recent pictures I have. Maybe six or eight months old."

He points to a girl in her late 20s with dark hair and wide set eyes. She is pretty, but she looks sad in all of the photos.

"She's missing," he says. "Nobody has heard from her in 36 days. Not her friends. Not me. Not even the Crypt Keeper, whom she talks to daily."

He places the weird black book in front of me.

"I got the landlord to let me into her apartment where I found this," he says. "It was hidden in the furnace vent next to her bed. Nothing else in the apartment seemed amiss."

I open the book, but it's printed in some ornate looking language I've never seen before.

Glenn picks up the sphere and balances it in his palm between us for a moment before he finally hands it over.

"This I found in one of those long term storage lockers at the airport," he says. "The key was in her top dresser drawer."

Holding the sphere in my hands, I realize it's covered in symbols. Hieroglyphics, maybe. The body is maroon and three gold rings run around the sides and can be rotated around, perhaps to line up the symbols? I tilt the sphere to get a look at all sides, and I hear a ball bearing rolling about inside as I move it. I also spot a gold button on one side that depresses.

"Is it a puzzle?" I say.

"No clue," Glenn says. "I did some Google searches but all

that came up was stuff about the Lament Configuration or LeMarchand's box – the box from the movie Hellraiser."

"Weird," I say.

I twist the rings a few times and press the button. Nothing happens.

"Amity was always into weird stuff, morbid stuff," he says. "She loved horror movies when she was a toddler and started reading Aleister Crowley books when she was 9 or 10. It went on from there. But I never thought her curiosity about these things could actually hurt her."

I don't know what to say. As I open my mouth to tell him I'm sorry to hear all of this, he goes on.

"Like I said, I found no information about the sphere, and reading the book wasn't possible, of course. Asking around, however, I found out that she'd been hanging around some local groups that claim to be into magic and occult stuff. Not devil worshippers exactly, but you could call them cults. Maybe not as organized as a full on kool-aid cult, but you wouldn't be far off. I figured realistically we were talking about con men, maybe a leader assuming some messiah like role to get women and money. Maybe a group that talked her into isolating herself from her family for the good of their phony religion, though I wouldn't think Amity would be susceptible to something like that. I guess anything is possible."

He pauses a moment and drums his fingers on the counter.

"But what you described in your seizure dream? It's a lot like the stuff both of these groups write about. Involuntary astral projection and a series of spiritual tests where failure ends in figurative death. The worthy initiate respawns and tries again until they pass the test and move on to the next."

I swallow in a dry throat.

"Thing is, these guys train for years to try to trigger these astral projections and spiritual tests. They train and train and basically nothing happens. I was actually surprised about how frank they were about that aspect of it on their websites and in their newsletters. I figured there'd be all kinds of outlandish claims, but they're pretty straight forward that none of them have achieved much in terms of paranormal experiences or enlightenment or whatever. They just keep trying."

I run the back of my hand over my lips.

"I think mine are just dreams," I say.

A pained look forms on his face and fades.

"Maybe you're right," he says. "But I'm a desperate man nonetheless. I would do or try anything to find my daughter. And my gut says you could help me with that."

I don't avoid his eye contact this time. I stare straight at him.

"I think we met for a reason. Will you help me?" he says.

"No," I say without hesitation.

An edge creeps into his voice, an anger.

"Why?" he says.

"Look, it sucks about your daughter," I say, "But I don't know you or her. And you obviously don't know me. Cause if you did, you'd know that I wouldn't stick my neck out for the people I do know, let alone a stranger. All I want from the world is to be left alone, ok? That's all. I just want to serve out my time in peace, as much of it as I can find, anyway. Is that so goddamn much to ask?"

His eyes whirl away from me and look to the floor. The silence lasts for what feels like a long time.

"Fair enough," he says.

CHAPTER 3

Glenn offered to give me a ride home, but I insisted I'd walk. I'm not sure if that was out of pride or a fear that I'd somehow get roped into like six more stops along the way. Anyway, I'm walking, so, of course, it's sprinkling now.

I hurry along, hoping that the real rain is a ways off yet. I don't know this part of the city very well. Maybe it's just the dark and the wet, but it seems shitty. A liquor store with duct tape crisscrossing the front window takes shape in the distance, illustrating my point. The majority of the businesses around here seem to advertise that they buy gold, have guns for sale or both. And the locals I've happened across seem like the types that traded all of their gold for guns some time ago.

A man puts his arm around a woman on the sidewalk across the street. She nuzzles against him, like he can keep her out of the rain.

Good luck with that.

I arrive at an intersection and jab a finger at the crosswalk button just as the rain really picks up. Rivulets of water gush down from the side of Lucky's Pawn Shop next to me, pelting the cement with a slap and sizzle. I'm kept partially dry under the awning, but the spray from the ground mists one side of my face. The water seems especially cold.

Yelling down the block catches my attention. I look up to

see a prostitute standing in the doorway of a building to keep out of the wet. A man berates her from the sidewalk.

"I don't give a got damn. Get out there," he says. "Walk between the rain drops if you gotta, but get me that money."

She struts out onto the block, some sass in her walk, which seems extra sad to me somehow since she is doing exactly what the pimp told her to. It's the sass walk of the powerless.

Though the light next to me remains green, a black Lincoln pulls up and stops. The passenger door opens, and a large man in a suit steps out. At first, I think maybe he just has some gold to sell, but he seems pretty focused on me. The world is really sucking at the whole leaving me alone thing lately.

"Ms. Babinaux will see you now," he says.

Now, I have no idea who Ms. Babinaux is. Seems to be of French descent. That's all I've got. My guess, of course, is that she has something to do with one of the groups slash cults that Glenn mentioned, though how they might know about me and my seizures, I couldn't say. Still, my instincts say it's best not to tip off my knowledge or lack thereof. I'm guessing they already know the French part, anyway.

"I assume she's in back," I say.

He tilts his head forward to say yes.

"Well, if she has eyes, I'm sure she will see me," I say.

I give a mock wave and smile at the general vicinity of the backseat of the car.

"Here I am. It's me!" I say in a squeaky voice.

The guy snorts and then laughs. At first I think this is some form of sarcasm, but no. It's real laughter.

"Are you new at this?" I say. "Cause stoicism is like 50% of your job description. You're supposed to look imposing and be stoic. That's it. And you're totally effing it up."

"Just get in," he says, opening the door.

I think about running at first, but this would be a good way to get out of the rain and get home. I can't help but think that it'd be better if this were an actual limo, though, because in that case there would probably be beverages.

I climb into the backseat, which is fairly roomy but certainly not overly impressive. A dark haired woman raises her eyebrows at me. She is slender with facial features I associate with sophisticated rich ladies: sharp cheek bones, arched brows, high forehead. She smiles, but I can't get a read on whether it's a nurturing smile or a cold one.

"Nice to meet you, Mr. Grobnagger," she says, extending her hand.

Her hand feels tiny in mine, and somehow her handshake is dainty without seeming weak.

"Nice to meet you, too," I say. "You can call me Jeff."

It occurs to me that everything she does is hard to read. Like just now, she nods and tilts her head in a way that somehow simultaneously looks like a curious kitten and a buzzard about to peck a dead opossum's eyes out.

Which is it?

I don't know, dude.

"Well, this must be a very exciting time for you, so I'll try not to take up too much of your evening," she says.

"Not a problem," I say.

I turn to the driver.

"Do you know where Park Terrace Apartments are?" I say.

"Oh, we know where you live," she says.

"Great," I say.

It's not great, though. I can already imagine this infringing on my right to be left alone.

"We know quite a bit about you as a matter of fact. You wouldn't know this, but there's been a lot of talk about you in our… circles," she says. "I'm violating an agreement with a powerful ally just in speaking with you."

"Uh-huh," I say.

I came in here planning on giving no information, and I'm sticking with it.

"I'm afraid you're in some danger," she says.

I wait for her to elaborate, but she doesn't.

"And what might that entail?" I say.

"It's hard to say," she says. "Many people are invested in your endeavors. Some of them for less than savory reasons."

"I see," I say.

I don't actually see, though.

"Be very careful in who you deal with for the time being," she says.

I find this ironic considering she just ushered me into the backseat of a car with a stranger to have this discussion, but she goes on.

"One way or another, I think your would-be enemies will be contacting you soon, if they haven't already," she says.

I say nothing.

"I apologize for the vagueness. I'm unable to go into detail at this point for a variety of reasons. But do try to keep a low profile."

"You don't even know how low I want to keep this profile," I say.

We pull up to my apartment.

"I'll be in touch soon, and I should be able to share more with you at that time."

We shake hands, and I imagine how much more regal this all would have seemed if we were sitting across from each other in the back of a limo.

I lie in bed. I can't sleep. My thoughts keep returning to Glenn and his daughter. Yeah, I'm a dick that doesn't rescue damsels in distress. Whatever. My thoughts grow clear, though, as I guess they often do when I lie still for a long while.

Now, don't get me wrong. If I could press a button and save this guy's daughter, I would do that. I have nothing against him. He even seems like a nice guy. It's just that I don't get entangled with people. Not anymore. It only leads to pain, in my experience.

For years and years, I got dragged along by friends or family members, suckered into the middle of various dramas and conflicts. I was the sympathetic ear, the shoulder to cry on, the guy always there to help out. But as time went on, I realized that these were empty interactions. All of them.

I don't think most people want friends. They just want someone to listen when they talk. They don't want a connection, they want an audience. So as it dawned on me that this is what relationships meant to people, I felt sorry for them, but then it also meant that's all any relationship I had could be. Me feeling sorry for someone.

And it hurts to feel like that. Like you're not even an individual to anybody in a way, just the audience to witness their life and their thoughts. To know in your heart that no one really cares. It feels like the world is all one way streets that run away from you.

So I dropped out of all of it. No more friends. No more talking. I keep to myself. It's the code I live by. It keeps me safe.

Selfish? Maybe, but it's not so bad, I think. I mean, I don't hurt anybody. I don't bother anybody. I'm just alone.

In my time on my own, I've realized that I have no interest in reality. I don't really want to be part of it. To me, reality is going to funerals, going to hospitals. It's dead pets and cavities and the way all the possibilities disintegrate as you get older and older. It's nurturing relationships that can never go anywhere, disappointing people, being disappointed by people, various iterations of those same concepts over and over again.

I don't say this out of negativity. I'm not complaining about it. I say this out of acceptance. See, everyone is doing everything they can to escape reality all of the time. They're drinking and smoking weed, reading, watching TV, movies, sports, video games, collecting stuff, obsessing about celebrities, going to conventions, writing fiction and making up their own worlds. Basically every hobby is in some way an escape from reality. It is why everyone does everything they actually like doing.

For a while they get to disconnect and from the pain and death all around us.

Think about a funeral, anyway. For three days or so, a dead person is paraded around. They go through this rite of passage in getting their blood sucked out and some makeup smeared on. They get stuffed in a box and wheeled out for everyone to gawk at. None of this is actually for the dead person, of course. That person is gone. I guess it's for the people left behind. But how so? We gather in uncomfortable situations and stare at a corpse. We try to do them justice in words even though that's impossible, and then we bury them.

Maybe trying to make death a formal custom like a wedding means something to somebody, but it doesn't mean a goddamn thing to me. Maybe it helps someone out there deal with it to put on their Sunday best and pal around with distant relatives. Makes them feel like they aren't facing it alone or something.

To me, it's insane. It makes me feel worse. It makes me feel more alone.

See look, we put makeup on the body and a guy gave a speech. Now we can all feel better about it.

Bullshit. Fuck you.

So I take that premise that escaping reality is why everyone does everything and follow it to its conclusion: the only real and true reality is how I feel. I do not partake in any other forms of reality. I don't go to funerals. I don't go to hospitals. I don't go out to eat with people or feel obligated to make (or answer) social calls of any kind. Hell, I barely even talk to other people. I just keep to myself.

Like I said, I don't save damsels in distress.

Once you accept that escape is all you really want, though, things mostly get easier. It's a big relief in a way. You can say eff it and just try to have fun in whatever manner suits your personality. You don't have to feel guilty or get so anxious about anything. You can look at your time differently and try to find ways to relax and enjoy it and not get caught up in some imaginary chase that everyone else thinks is real.

You can let go.

I might have slept for a while in there but no longer. Now I'm watching the shadows of the rain drops streaking down the window, listening to the periodic cars rolling over the wet streets. I contemplate turning the light on to read for a while, but sometimes reading this late hurts my eyes.

This goes on for a while. Time works differently in the dark. It speeds up and slows down without letting me know, so I'm not sure how long I've been lying awake when I finally rise from the bed. As I step through the doorway, I can tell by the gray light creeping around the edges of the curtains that it's almost dawn.

My elbow brushes something odd as I move past the kitchen counter. It's cool with a little bristle to it. It almost feels like smooth hair. I flip on the light and squint while my eyes adjust. First, all I can see is a green blur in a square shape in the area where the elbow brushing transpired. As my pupils constrict, though, it comes into focus.

The wheat grass.

I set the planter on the floor and rub my index finger against my thumb above it to make an almost silent sound. To my cat, however, this sound is not even close to silent. I may as well have banged a gong. Mardy darts into the room, his eyes meeting mine for a second before he gazes upon the wheat grass and his expression goes half alarmed, half aroused. The gray cat stalks toward the grass, partially circling it and stopping short of it. His feet planted a safe distance away, he leans his face closer and closer until his nose and mouth make contact with the blades along the edge. His eyes narrow into half open slits.

As I'm watching this, waves of bad feelings rush over me.

My head gets heavy. My thoughts get tangled up. It's so subtle at first that I almost don't notice it, but it swells to the point that I feel like I'm about to topple over. I lower myself to the kitchen floor. The cat doesn't even notice. It's familiar, this feeling, but I can't quite place it.

I take a couple of deep breaths and start to gather my wits. I think the worst has passed.

And then everything goes black like someone flipped the switch on my brain.

I hear a creaking sound that somehow reminds me of a sailboat in the movies, like a pirate ship nearly motionless in the doldrums. Everything gets quiet again, and I start to drift back to sleep, but there it is again. The groan of rope straining against wood.

Oh.

That.

I open my eyes to find myself dangling upside down in the alley, rope corded around my ankle as per usual. I go to work untying myself, though I have some doubts as to the usefulness of this activity. Still, it's not like I have much else to do.

I hop down, keeping my feet under me this time. The soles of my shoes skim over the surface of the mud puddles. I move with some urgency. I know I have maybe 30 seconds worth of head start time.

I reach the downspout attached to the corner of the brick office building at the edge of the alley. My hands latch onto the aluminum, and I step up onto the brick wall – one foot and then the other. I dig my toes into the gaps between the bricks the best I can and push off from there, leaning back a little for balance. I bet I almost look like a guy rappelling down the face of a rock wall, but I'm going up. Not as rapidly as I'd like, but up all the same. I keep stepping and maintaining my chokehold on the downspout. I'm 10 or maybe 12 feet up now, but it's a big office building or something, and the roof is another 40 feet in front of me, I figure. Maybe more.

Something rattles beneath me. I glance down, and there he is. I would recognize that hood anywhere. I'm just out of his reach, so he tries to mount the wall the same way I have, but he can't seem to get any grip with his feet.

I can't watch him for long, though. I have to focus. Seeing him down there gives me a jolt of motivation or adrenalin, though. Maybe both. In any case, I'm making better progress now. I'm probably 25 feet off of the ground. My toes slip periodically, but I've gotten faster at recovering and moving forward.

Metal grunts and shrieks below. I look down, and he's no longer trying to climb the downspout. He's trying to rip it down. He jerks at the aluminum, and it gives a little like maybe the bracket is bending. The pained metallic wails assure me that the bracket is fighting back with all of its strength, at least. I thought the thing looked sturdier than most, but on the flipside, I can attest to the man's strength first hand. It's beyond human. There's a loud pop as one of the bolts gives out, and the aluminum tube suddenly moves more freely as he yanks on it.

I move faster, legs churning. The roof isn't so far off now.

Just as I gaze down again, he pulls the downspout free. A good 20 feet of aluminum tumbles toward the ground. I brace for this thing to rip out from under me, for the feeling of everything solid falling away. For a nanosecond, I even consider trying to grip the brick with my fingers or lunging for the gutter above.

Instead, nothing happens. The top half of the downspout is unaffected, the pair of brackets up here still being in tact.

I laugh. I know I should keep moving before he starts throwing knives at me or something, but I can't help it. I stop a moment to chuckle and look down as his shoulders heave in frustration.

And then there are two more loud snaps in rapid succession as the top bracket gives. I'm falling. I'm still holding the downspout. Outwardly I'm screaming like a girl that has just seen Freddy Krueger crawl out of her closet, but inside I think about how you're supposed to land on your side when you fall a long way like this. How that is the only way for the body to absorb this kind of shock without serious injury, and that's if you're lucky. And just as I think about how I can try to rotate myself, I land flat on my back on the asphalt with a sound like two rams bashing their skulls into each other.

Two words burst into my head:

SHATTERED.

VERTEBRAE.

My scream goes full falsetto. Pain shoots up and down me. It hurts everywhere. I can feel it in each of my teeth, and then it changes, and it feels overwhelmingly numb all over. So numb that it kind of hurts worse somehow, an overwhelming absence of feeling from the middle of my back down.

I realize that the blur moving toward me must be him, and I try to focus. I try to pay attention. I know time is almost up.

My scream fades to a whimper. I open my eyes wider. I suck in a big breath and hold it.

He kneels and puts his hand over my nose and mouth. It's like a mercy killing this time. All I can see is his jaw, but it's the clearest glimpse I've gotten yet. He looks younger than I figured. Slender. No trace of stubble. This is somehow more emasculating than ever. I'm getting murdered over and over by an oversized 8th grader.

Things are starting to get a little faded around the edges, so I employ my final breath. Though his hand muffles my words, I'm certain he can hear me:

"See you next time."

CHAPTER 4

I wake on the kitchen floor with the cat hovering over my mouth, his whiskers tickling my top lip. I sit up, and Mardy trills before sauntering away. It looks like he tore into the wheat grass pretty good while I was out. Glenn would be pleased to hear that, I think.

I take a look around at the apartment, or what I can see of it from the floor anyway. Something feels off, but I kind of figure I just have post traumatic strangulation disorder at the moment. The kitchen light is still on. Elsewhere, sunlight streams in every crack it can find, illuminating the living room in half light. Everything appears in order. I stand and stretch. Repeated metaphysical deaths can cramp you right up if you don't stretch properly, so I try to stay limber. I open some blinds and flip off the kitchen bulb, trading artificial light for the real thing.

PTSD or not, waking up at home sure feels a lot better than waking up at the grocery store. I take a deep breath and let it out real slow. Even if I have no idea what the hell is wrong with me, I feel safe for the moment, and that's good enough.

I grind up some coffee beans and toast an apple cinnamon bagel - the breakfast of strangled champions. The coffee is some Sumatran kind I decided to try. Weirdly acidic and bright, but good as hell. I down a mug and pour another.

I pace back and forth across the ceramic tiles in the kitchen during the second mug. It's kind of a habit, I guess. I get a little caffeine in me, and I can't sit still. I swear walking gets your brain going in the right direction anyway, though. Gets the blood pumping to it.

My stimulated mind skips from topic to topic:

This coffee is effing great. It's expensive, but I think I'll have to stick with it. Can't imagine going back to the crappy stuff. I wonder if there are other kinds out there that are even better, though.

What am I going to do to that hooded bastard next time? I'm really running out of options. I should probably try to rip an eye out or something like that.

The wheat grass was a success. This is good. I wonder if it will stay that way or if Mardy will grow tired of it like Glenn's cats apparently did.

As soon as I think of Glenn's name, the image flashes in my head of the black book with the silver symbol he found in Amity's room. Not so great for reading, maybe, but it's a conversation piece. If you put a gun to my head and asked me to pick what language it's written in, I think I'd guess Orcish. Maybe Klingon. Wouldn't that be a kick in the sack, though? What seems like a legitimately mysterious and possibly evil book turns out to be some kind of Star Trek memorabilia?

At this point, my pacing takes me out into the living room. I walk to the far end of the apartment, and as I turn around, I see Mardy sniffing at the triangular opening between the front door and the hallway.

Wait.

There isn't supposed to be a triangular opening there.

I rush to the cat and scoop him up before he can abscond, placing him in the bedroom for the moment. The front door looks like someone took a battering ram to it while I was off in strangle land. The bottom hinge is busted off and the top hinge is barely holding on, so the door dangles at a 45 or so degree angle with the help of the security door chain, which I always keep latched. (Remember that thing about wanting to be left alone? Yeah.) There are cracks and splintered spots all over the place around the door frame. Even the steel door itself is dented pretty thoroughly. This took a lot of force.

Just as I squat to grip the sides of the door to try to finagle it back into the frame to keep the cat inside, glass behind me explodes. I don't think. I belly smack the floor. There are two more glassy bursts, and then everything goes quiet.

I look up and see broken windows behind me and three bullet holes in the door above me. So there goes my security deposit.

Maybe the danger has passed. Maybe not. I crawl toward the bedroom where curtains still obscure the only window to be on the safe side. I feel like I'm having a little trouble processing this. Someone is trying to kill me now? Like, for real?

I grab the wheat grass on my way, and when I get to my destination, I present it to Mardy whom seems unfazed by the gunfire. He cocks his head to the side and closes his eyes while he chews the grass. Looks pretty happy to me.

You know what? Killing me in the dream world is one thing, but killing me in real life?

Dick move.

So much for being safe at home.

As the shock fades a bit, I come to a conclusion: When someone tries to kill you, it feels unpleasant. See, there are these emotions inside of me right now that feel all bad and stuff. I don't know. I'm not that great at describing it. Maybe I should have gone to college.

I watch the cat nibble at blades of grass, running back through the event in my mind over and over again. I have a decent sense of "how" this attempt on my life happened, but the "who" and "why" are totally up for grabs. I also still ask myself "what" pretty frequently regarding this matter, as in: What the eff?

Mardy tires of the plant and jumps to find a resting spot at the foot of the bed, folding his feet underneath his body, so that from the back he looks like a loaf of bread with cat fur stretched over it. I consider going back to bed myself but not seriously. I doubt I'd actually sleep at all.

A fragment of Babinaux's warning in the back of the Lincoln flashes in my head. What did she say, again? I could be in danger. They know about my seizures. Many people are invested in my endeavors, some for less than savory reasons.

I guess it's the only thing that makes sense. Someone is trying to kill me because of my dreams.

Tremendous. These seizures are a gift on so many levels.

I reposition myself, still sitting on the floor to avoid getting assassinated via the window. Upon moving, a tingle spreads across my leg, taint and left nard. Much of my lower body has fallen asleep due to my odd floor seating session. The tingle swells into a widespread prickling that creeps and throbs. The nard area proves to be particularly troublesome.

I cry out and move in slow motion to allow relief to happen

while not jostling it into any strong needle prick type feelings. Still, the feeling lingers longer than what seems reasonable before it finally starts to fade out.

Back to my imminent death, though, what options do I really have? I could wait around for someone to try to kill me again. No real upside to going that route, though it's the path of least resistance, the choice I usually opt for. Or I could work with Glenn who has a similar goal and at least some prior connections with these people.

I guess I shouldn't have said "options" after all. I have one option, which makes it more mandatory.

I start looking around at what I'll need to bring with. It won't be safe here for Mardy either, so he'll have to come along. Before I pack everything up, I scrawl a note and magnet it to my fridge:

"Dudes,

Please stop trying to kill me as soon as possible.

Thank you,

Jeff Grobnagger"

CHAPTER 5

Glenn's front door stands before me, a hulking red thing a man and a half wide that makes me feel small. I've already tried the doorbell a few times to no avail, so now the knocking shall commence. My fist pounds the steel, hesitates, bangs again with a little more fervor. I wait, but there's no response. This strikes me as weird because Glenn's Explorer sits in the driveway, pink bumper glaring in the sun. He doesn't seem like the type to sleep in, either.

I linger on the doorstep another moment, and I pick up the cat carrier and turn to leave. Whatever. Guess I'll have to try again this afternoon.

As I hit the sidewalk six paces later, however, I hear a sound like a muffled bang. I can't be sure, but it seems like it came from inside Glenn's house.

I head back toward the door, leave Mardy on the front step and start walking around the perimeter of the building. I peer in the windows along the way, but most of them are covered, and I can't see anything going on in the ones that aren't. There's another bang, definitely coming from inside Glenn's.

Great.

My first thought is that maybe the same person that just tried to shoot me is now going after Glenn. I don't know how much sense that would make, but none of this makes much sense to begin with. The noise doesn't sound like a gunshot, though. It sounds more like something heavy falling or getting bashed against something.

Another crack erupts and is quickly followed by the sound of a man grunting. The voice has that same gritty texture to it that Glenn's had at the u-scan.

I'm scrambling now, moving into the back yard. The smell of cut grass is everywhere. He must have mowed this morning. I twist the knob to the door leading into the garage. It's locked.

I check the windows along the back of the house, but they're all locked, too. I peel around the corner to find a bathroom window cracked. My fingers latch onto the edges of the screen and rip it away from the frame. I throw open the window and climb in.

How ridiculous is this? Yesterday I would've sworn I'd never be back here, and I'm not only back a mere 12 hours later, I'm actually breaking into the place. I guess the complexion of a situation can change once snipers try to shoot you in the face. I think I saw that inspirational message on a mug once.

The walls in the bathroom are sea foam green, and the toilet matches. What a cute place to take a shit, right? I creep to the doorway and poke my head out to look down the hall.

Nothing.

I slip through the doorway and realize a few steps later that I'm doing a weird exaggerated tiptoe walk with my shoulders all hunched over like Nosferatu. I stop doing that and walk in a more normal fashion, though still on the lighter of foot side.

I reach a corner and stop to listen. Though I was just here yesterday, I don't have a great feel for the layout of the house. I can hear a man's voice. It's definitely not Glenn, but it's too quiet to make out any words. The voice sounds oddly upbeat considering the presumed circumstances. Energetic.

I move into the next room – a dining room worthy of a center fold in one of those magazines that interior designers masturbate to. High back chairs upholstered in cream colored velvet surround a table with a top that appears to be one enormous slice of a tree. The surface is polished to a high sheen so it reflects the crystal chandelier overhead almost like a mirror.

As I move past the dining table, I realize that there's music playing. It's fairly soft, but I can make out a pulsing dance music beat. Now things really don't make sense… unless this music is being used as a form of psychological torture, which I've always felt dance music was well suited for. Either way, the music and talking are coming from a door just ahead.

I stand in the hall and watch through the doorway as Glenn bounces around in a small room with an exercise bike and elliptical machine wedged into it. He dances to the right and throws a jab and dances to the left and throws a jab, mirroring the people on his TV including the man with the upbeat voice.

"Uh… hey," I say.

Glenn moves to the heavy bag in the corner, busting into a flurry of squat and punch reps. The bag thuds with each hit, the final punch slamming it into the wall with a reverberating slap that I imagine sounds more like a crack or bang from outside the house.

"Hey!" I say much louder.

He twirls, lays eyes on me, and his brow crinkles. He pops out an earbud.

"How'd you get in here?" he says.

"I rang the bell, but I heard noises, and I thought maybe..."

I trail off, and his confused expression slowly morphs into a smile and a nod.

"Oh, I get it," he says. "You thought I was... That's flippin' hilarious, man. Nah. I'm just doing some Tae Bo."

"I see that."

I didn't know that men do Tae Bo, but I decide not to mention this to Glenn.

I sit in the living room. The house is quiet. Empty. Glenn freaked out about the complete lack of Oreos on hand, pieced together a short grocery list and ran to the store. He didn't ask if I wanted to go, which was perfect because I did not.

Mardy sits on the couch next to me. The two of us watch Leroy peek his head into the room, lock eyes with my cat and then slowly back away. It's weird. So far Glenn's cats are terrified of Mardy. I thought there'd be more feline friction - a blur of claws and fur and guttural sounds - but so far it's just been a couple of hisses and a lot of submission from Leroy and friends. I probably shouldn't be, but I'm kind of proud. My cat is a bad ass.

Before he rushed off, Glenn offered to clear boxes of junk out of the guest room for me to sleep in while I try to avoid getting killed, but I insisted I'd be fine with a sheet and blanket on the sofa. Getting my own room would freak me out somehow. It'd feel too permanent.

I am motionless, sunk into the couch, arms limp at my sides. After 15 minutes of watching dust motes flit around in the bars of sunlight coming through the windows, I finally stir.

I head into the kitchen looking for something to drink. I figure he told me to make myself at home, so I may as well indulge. Glenn strikes me as the type of man to always keep an assortment of beverages on hand, and I'm a fan of tasty drinks.

A scent wafts around the kitchen, hops and barley. I spot two empty Sam Adams bottles in the sink that seem to be the culprit. I guess Glenn drank a couple of beers after mowing the lawn earlier.

The smell of pretty much any alcoholic beverage reminds me of Allie. When we first started hanging out, we drank a lot. A lot. It was more like nightly races to see who would vomit first.

I remember how hard she laughed when we were walking home from a party and I threw up in someone's front yard on Broad Street and immediately fell in it. And I remember after I moved in with her, whenever we lay in bed together she always said my breath smelled like oranges when I drank.

I bring my hand to my brow, a little light headed. The memories lurch and sway in my brain like if the synapses fire just right, the people and places from the past can become real again, take physical shape in Glenn's kitchen, instead of just being images encoded in the cells in some guy's head.

I sit down at the snack bar to wait for the dizzy spell to pass. The stench hangs in the air all around me now.

But a smell never conjures just memories of events. It dredges up all the feelings of that time, all the hopes and dreams I had when I was young that withered away some time ago, all the doors long closed, and the way that what seems possible slowly shifts into something smaller and smaller as time passes.

I remember lying in bed with Allie, awake in the dark, listening to her talk about love like it was a magical place we could go together. And I know I believed it at the time. I really did.

But we didn't go there, and I don't believe it anymore.

So yeah, the odor makes me think of Allie, and I don't want to think about her right now.

I rinse out the bottles and toss them in the recycling bin.

CHAPTER 6

Glenn leans over the snack bar with a towel slung over his shoulders. His hair is still wet from the shower. I've filled him in on all the details – the gunfire, the busted door, my most recent trip to Chokington Abbey, the meeting with Ms. Babinaux.

"The way I see it, we've got five mysteries of varying importance laid out in front of us," he says. "Where is my daughter? What's going on in your seizure dreams? What's the deal with the book and sphere from Amity's room? How and what do the cult people know about you? And who is trying to kill you?"

I'm wolfing down another serving of cold chicken, also known as the perfect second breakfast, but I come up for air long enough to chime in.

"That sums it up, though you may have buried the lead a little bit," I say.

Glenn smirks.

"The order we put them in doesn't matter," he says. "Not really, anyhow. They're all intertwined."

"You could be right about that, but I suspect I will be less concerned about solving the other quandaries if I'm deceased," I say.

"We've got to talk to these cult people," he says.

"Might that not be safe?" I say. "I mean, it's the only avenue of investigation I see as well, but if one of them is trying to kill me, I may be better served to keep my distance."

"True," he says. "But Babinaux met with you and warned you, right? She could have just as easily tried to kill you or abduct you at that point, couldn't she?"

"I guess," I say. "Well, you asked around about these cults. Did you hear anything about her?"

"Not much," he says. "Her name came up once that I remember. I got the impression that she's an important player with the League of Light. Perhaps we should start with them."

"Perhaps," I say. "So what are they all about? I take it they are fans of light."

"I'll tell you in the car," he says.

We sit in the Explorer outside of Bucky's Diner, a spot where a bunch of these weirdos hang out according to Glenn. Our mission is to observe from a distance, though I'm not sure how incognito we are with that damn pink bumper gleaming the way it does.

The sign for the diner has a marquee on it, with the letters that can be rearranged to spell out the specials or whatever. The letters read CHOCOLATE CHIP PANCAKES $5.45. One of the 5's is actually an "S". I wonder what goes best on a stack of chocolate chip pancakes. Maple syrup? Seems like overkill. Maybe whipped cream. That sounds pretty tasty.

After a few minutes I'm bored with thinking about pancakes and their hypothetical toppings.

"What exactly are we even looking for?" I say. "So far I've gleaned that the people in the diner drink a lot of coffee."

"We've been here for about three minutes, buddy. Have you ever thought about how impatient you are?" Glenn says. "You know that's going to get you in trouble one of these days."

"Whatever," I say.

"The three guys in the corner booth are in the League," he says. "And the man and woman seated at the counter are as well. I'm sure there are others."

I look them over.

"How can you even tell?" I say.

"I recognize two of the guys in the booth from my prior poking around. They struck me as amateurs," he says. "And the guy and girl each have the sigil on their backpacks."

"Oh," I say. "Right."

We fall silent. I watch the waitress tote two carafes of coffee around to give refills, but my mind starts to wander again. My eyes trace up and down the cracks in the brick façade. The building falls just short of what I would call crumbling, but it's getting there.

"Why do they hang out at this diner?" I say. "Seems like a dump."

"The owner is sympathetic to the cause," he says. "Plus the coffee has caffeine in it, and the burgers ain't bad."

"OK, so they're here, and they're eating," I say. "Now what?"

"Now we exercise patience," he says.

I wait and watch, and the minutes drag by. People stab at pieces of pie with their forks and shovel various soups into their faces. They guzzle colas. They gobble French fries. They generally gorge themselves. It's all quite boring.

"Are we going to go in?" I say.

"Not yet," he says.

"What are we waiting for?" I say.

"An opening," he says.

I think about pointing out that the door is just the opening we need to get in there, but I decide against it. Glenn seems to know what he's doing, or at least he thinks he does. I can go with it.

"So weren't you going to tell me about the League and all of that?" I say.

"Huh?" Glenn says, his eyes still fastened to the dining weirdos. "Oh, right. Yeah."

He wiggles in his seat for a second, I think to adjust the angle of his lower back.

"The League of Light started all of this," he says. "They're into your pretty basic occult stuff – Qabalah, Tarot, various forms of unorthodox spiritual development. Eventually a sect splintered off, calling themselves the Disunion of Shadows."

"Disunion?" I say.

He nods.

"The Disunion's premise is that all modern religions, including the League, worship order too much," he says. "They believe that chaos comprises the other half of human nature – sort of a left brain and right brain thing, I guess. In the end, it's a lot of the same stuff – Qabalah, Tarot and so on – but the Disunion people pursue all of it in the interest of finding a balance between chaos and order. An organization based on Chaos is sort of an oxymoron, right? That's why they named it the Disunion."

"I see," I say. "That's kind of interesting, I guess. I just assumed these people were all dumbasses that burn black candles and pretend weird stuff."

Glenn glances at me.

"I've read a couple of the books and all the articles I could find," he says. "Some of it makes you think. Other stuff is about whacking off while focusing on a particular Tarot card."

I laugh.

"See?" I say. "That's more like what I was imagining."

Inside the diner, the patrons seem to be gathering around a man with a shaved head clad in black. He stands at a table in the center of the room.

"This is it," Glenn says, digging around under the seat.

He pulls an unidentifiable piece of flattened blue fabric from the floor and massages it back into the shape of a baseball cap. It's the trucker style with the mesh in the back, and it says in black letters, "My Wife is on The Warpath again."

"Put this on," he says.

"Not a chance," I say.

He huffs.

"Just do it," he says. "We're running out of time."

I look at the hat again for a moment before I take it from him and slide it on. He finds and pulls on his own, which is covered in fake bird poop and says "DAMN SEAGULLS," in all caps. I'm not sure why he feels like that's a better disguise than his normal blue hat, but he does. At least I'm not the only one wearing a hat with a dumb slogan on it.

"Did you have to throw darts at balloons at the county fair to win these?" I say.

His eyes are fixed on the diner, though, and he doesn't respond for a second.

"What?" he says.

"Nothing," I say.

"OK, listen," he says. "Keep your head down. Don't make eye contact. Don't say anything. I'll do the talking. Let's go."

We leave the Explorer and file into the restaurant. The hat makes me a little self conscious, but nobody looks our way when we walk in. All eyes focus on the man in black.

"Here," Glenn whispers, gesturing to a booth in the corner.

We sit. Glenn turns his coffee cup over, and a waitress fills it within seconds. I order some fries and a coke.

Across the diner to my right, a man and a woman hold hands on the table top in their booth. She has dark hair and eyes that perpetually look like she is about to start laughing. He is bald with a beard that's a bit too well kept. Fussy. He looks too serious.

Right away, I think she could do better.

I look over my shoulder to see what the man in black is up to. He clenches a spoon in his fist with his arm fully extended in front of his body. His nose wrinkles as he squints at the spoon, and the crowd watches this, rapt, like he's holding a grenade or maybe a baby elephant instead of a spoon. He's really putting some stank on it, too. His knuckles are all white.

I open my mouth to say "Pretty cool spoon," but Glenn must know I'm about to do this, so he kicks my shin under the table. I gasp in pain, and Glenn shout whispers:

"Stop it!"

Now, this is annoying on a couple of levels. First of all, he's not my grandma, and we're not at church. I'm pretty sure both of those conditions must be met to legally justify the use of the shout whisper. Second of all, his stupid whisper is louder than my gasp, thereby more than defeating the purpose in this scenario. Nobody notices either of them, anyway, so it's a moot point.

I look at Glenn, half tempted to test him a bit out of annoyance, but his face looks a little redder than usual and his mustache is twitching like a squirrel's mouth, both of which I take as signs of grave seriousness. He shakes his head at me, and his cheeks jiggle, however, undermining said seriousness.

I look back at the man in black, and he's slowly uncurling his fingers from the spoon. His face looks all sweaty and flushed, and he's panting not unlike a German Shepherd. His fingers peel back one by one and pretty soon he's not holding the spoon at all, it's just kind of stuck to his palm. And I'm thinking, "Big deal, this guy stuck a spoon to his palm."

Then he pulls his whole hand back, but the spoon stays there, hovering in the air before him. Floating. Levitating. I don't even know why I know the word levitating, but I am witnessing that shit right now.

The crowd gasps. A little kid with curly red hair in the booth in front of ours brings a hand up to cover his gaping mouth, and then I realize that I just did the same thing.

The man in black moves his hand in a circular motion a few times about two feet from the spoon, until the spoon seems to catch on to the motion like a magnet suddenly pulling something close. It's not drawn to his hand, though, it's drawn to the motion and traces it in the air. He hesitates a moment, and then winds up and pushes the spoon without touching it in one violent heave like someone throwing a shot put. The spoon angles up and up, flying across the room and slamming against the spot where the ceiling meets the wall on the opposite side of the diner before clanging to the floor.

The crowd erupts in applause, and we all stand up simultaneously. Goose bumps crawl down the lengths of my arms. Weird feelings swell in my gut like I've just witnessed something special. Almost like a miracle. Part of my brain is asking whether or not that could be real, and the rest of my brain is screaming, "Yes, it's real! Are you kidding, shithead? I just saw it with our own two eyes!"

I can't stop tracing the spoon's flight path with my gaze. The straight line that leads from the hand of the man in black to the wall across the room. It's a good 20 feet or so. Spoon marks pock up and down the wall, and I realize this has happened many times before. It's a routine.

I glance at Glenn, and he's clapping, but he looks a little indifferent.

Wait a minute.

Am I a dumbass that just got duped? It looked real and all, but Glenn seems like the type that would be eating this up. I mean, he was impressed by my cavalier attitude toward the manager at Meijer, which pales in comparison to this robust display of telekinesis. I would have thought he'd at least be dabbing tears of wonder out of his eyes with a Kleenex at this point if not openly weeping.

I turn back just as the man in black stands upright again, and a hush comes over the crowd. He stretches his arms out to the sides, crucifixion-style, and closes his eyes. He stands that way for a long moment, arms open wide.

I scan the faces in the crowd. Everyone that I can see looks like they're experiencing something religious except for Glenn and a girl in a lime green shirt across the room. She even meets my eyes and smiles as I glance at her. This kind of freaks me out, so I look away really fast.

I remember that I'm wearing the hat. Maybe she was smiling because she thinks my wife really is on the warpath.

Veins begin to bulge in the man in black's neck, and his shoulders quiver. His face reddens and slowly darkens toward purple. As spit hisses between his teeth, the lights in the room shut off for a fraction of a second and flip back on. Several people in the crowd moan. I crane my neck to check the lights for a second, and when I look back, the man in black is flickering. There's an electrical buzz as he flickers between what looks like a solid version of himself and a faded, translucent version of himself. A few sparks start flying from the floor beneath him.

I expect him to let up any second, but he hunches down, his whole body quivering now as he looks to dig in and push even harder. The pace of the flicker picks up, closing in on strobe light levels. His lips curl back now, baring clenched teeth. The skin on his face is the color of a yellowed page in an old paperback book.

"Stop," a voice nearby says.

"Stop it!" a lady toward the front yells.

Additional voices rise in a cacophony more or less urging him to quit, some seemingly saying it more to themselves, some screaming at the man, pleading with him.

The buzzing sound builds to a roar. The man looks like he's gone limp, like the electric current in the air around him is the only thing holding him up.

And then he disappears. He's just gone.

The buzzing stops, and the room falls to silence. Nobody moves.

And the lights turn off again. People stir, and the volume cranks back up on the tangled web of voices.

The light comes back on, and the man in black is back, arms crossed over his heaving chest. He smiles, and everyone bursts into applause again, even rowdier than the last time. You can feel all the tension in the room turn into relief and adoration.

He doesn't sit down so much as free fall into his chair with a plop. It gets a huge laugh.

The applause finally starts to die down, and the normal diner sounds start to return as people sit – clinking coffee cups, forks scraping plates, a bus boy dumping piles of dishes in the sink. I remain standing longer than most, though.

"OK," I say. "THAT was fucking awesome."

I realize right after I say this that I'm talking too loud. I guess I wasn't saying it to Glenn so much as addressing the room at large. For a moment, I feel like we were all together in witnessing something awesome, but I know the universe will make me pay for expressing this feeling.

A bunch of heads snap around to look at me. The girl in the lime green shirt laughs really hard. She tries to stifle it by literally biting her fist. The man in black stands up, and I realize that he's also staring at me. He claps twice.

"Uh, sorry," I say.

I sit down. There's a moment of hesitation, and then the man in black turns and walks out the door with about two thirds of the rest of the diners following him. Most technically stand in line to pay their bill rather than walking straight out, but as I look around I see a lot of half eaten meals, abandoned at the behest of two claps from the leader.

Well, this is embarrassing. I feel warmth crawl across my face, settling on my cheeks. I'm guessing they're about as pink as Glenn's bumper just now.

I don't look at Glenn. My plan, at this juncture, is to just never look at Glenn again. I figure this way I should be fine.

I stare at the wall as Glenn sighs heavily three times. The first time sounds angry. I almost want to look to see if his mustache is doing that squirrel twitch again, but I worry that if I lock eyes with him he'll have an Incredible Hulk type reaction and smash me and everything else in the diner.

His second sigh sounds more frustrated than angry. I guess maybe it's like the stages of death. Acceptance slowly creeps in there.

The third sigh sounds bewildered, like when a dog realizes you're not going to give him any of the pizza you're eating.

Glenn rises from the booth and grunts at me. The sound goes up at the end like it's a question. I take it to mean, "Ready to go?"

"Mmhm," I grunt back.

We pay the bill and exit the diner.

We came. We saw. We did not conquer.

CHAPTER 7

We sit in the Explorer outside the diner for a bit, regrouping. Glenn keeps his hands on the wheel in a way that seems a little aggressive, and I can see muscles bulging at his temples and along his jaw.

"How did they know who I was?" I say.

He shrugs.

"Hard to say," he says. "Perhaps if you'd have kept your mouth shut as I specifically requested..."

He trails off.

"It probably wouldn't have mattered," he says. "I could see it in their faces. They knew who you were right away. We never would have gotten anyone to talk to us."

I shudder at the thought of all of these people talking about me and knowing who I am. I mean, I literally shudder, my torso flailing in an involuntary manner. Somehow Glenn fails to notice this.

"So who was the man in black?" I say.

"Riston Farber," he says. "One of the League hot shots."

"You didn't seem that impressed with his performance," I say.

"I wasn't," he says.

I think back to the flight of the spoon and Farber flickering out of existence. I'm not sure if I could have been more impressed. Seriously, even if it was sheer trickery, I would pay money to watch that again. Glenn's expression looks sour enough that I decide not to press him on this one, though.

"So what do we do now?" I say.

Glenn huffs through his nose, a snort of laughter that comes across as bitter as aspirin.

"You tell me," he says.

"Maybe there's some way we can contact Babinaux," I say. "If not, she said she'd be in touch soon."

The creases etched into his face soften ever so faintly.

"True," he says. "Maybe waiting is all we can do for now."

Just then there's a knock at my window. It startles me, and I jump straight up, high enough to bang my head on the ceiling. For a split second all I can think is that I'm going to die here, picturing my blood pooling on the leather seats.

I turn, and it's the girl in the lime green shirt. She's laughing again. I guess because of the way I jumped. She makes me uncomfortable. I want to warn Glenn about her, but he's already putting down the window.

"You guys want to talk?" she says.

"Get in," Glenn says.

He presses the power lock button, a series of loud clicks and clacks ensue, and she climbs into the backseat.

"We shouldn't stay around here. Drive," she says.

We do.

I don't like her being behind me, because she can see me and I can't see her. On the other hand, it'd be too overwhelming – too confrontational - to look back. She's just back there in the growing shadows of dusk. I have to will myself to not shudder again.

"I'm Louise," she says. "Louise Lockhart."

"Name's Glenn Floyd," he says, offering a hand over his shoulder which she shakes.

"I'm Jeff Grobnagger," I say.

I have to turn back. It's like getting sucked into a tractor beam because once you face her, you can't turn away. I'm too nervous to shake her hand, so I give a little wave. She smiles at me, and right away I notice that I like her teeth.

"Oh, trust me, I've heard all about the great and powerful Jeffrey Grobnagger," she says. "After that hilarity in there, I had to see you up close for myself."

I swallow, which somehow is super loud. This sets her off laughing again.

The sky around us dims to purple. The half light softens the edges of everything in the car except for Louise's face. Her creamy complexion glows, the dark making it look an almost lilac shade.

"So you know who he is, and you're still talking to us?" Glenn says.

"Yep," she says.

"Aren't there orders or something to not talk to us?" he says.

"There are, but I'm not one of those wackos. I just play one as part of my day job," she says.

"And what is your day job?" he says.

"I'm a private investigator," she says. "I'd ask you guys to keep that to yourselves, but none of the people that matter will even talk to you, so what's the difference, I figure."

"So someone is paying you to keep an eye on the League," he says.

"That's right," she says. "Of course I wouldn't divulge my client's name, but in this case I don't even know who the client is. Some rich guy wants to anonymously overpay me to watch some wackos perform parlor tricks at a diner and suck down cheap coffee at unbearably dull meetings? No sweat off my cheeks."

"So you think they were parlor tricks?" I say.

I am somehow not shocked when she laughs.

"Farber sells it really well. I'll give him that. I'm sorry to be the one to tell you this, Jeffrey, but there's no such thing as real magic," she says. "If you saw Criss Angel mind freaking at that diner, you'd probably stain your shorts brown."

Glenn lets out a weird clucking laugh, apparently finding all of this amusing. Maybe I'm biased, but I think Glenn was a lot cooler when he thought I was awesome and wasn't laughing when people picked on me.

The Explorer meanders through an industrial neighborhood, taking lefts and rights at whims. As we get farther and farther out of town, more of the factories sport overgrown lawns. The rows of windows still smile as wide as ever, but some of the teeth are busted out.

"So what do you want from us?" he says.

"What do you mean?" she says.

"I mean, you approached us. You want to talk to us," he says. "Must be something in it for you."

"That's fair," she says. "I'm curious to know about Jeffrey's dreams. I've heard a lot of rumors."

"Then maybe we can trade," he says.

"Sure," she says.

I decide to take the reins.

"How do they know about me and my dreams?" I say.

"That's a good question," she says. "I don't know, to be honest with you. I get the sense that all they really know is that you're having these dreams. I don't think they know much about the actual contents of your dreams or anything like that. It's sort of like they can check the box score in the paper, but that's not the same thing as watching the game, you know what I mean?"

"Wouldn't that suggest that they can do more than parlor tricks, though?" I say. "I mean, if they can somehow check the box scores, like you said, and know who is having these kinds of dreams, it has to mean something, doesn't it?"

"Not necessarily," she says. "Haven't you had at least one of these episodes in public?"

"Well, yeah," I say.

"These freaks get around, and word about this kind of crap gets around even faster," she says. "Believe me, they'd claim to somehow have that ability whether they had it or not."

"So are they trying to kill me?" I say.

"No," she says. "They think you're really important. They're all stressed out about not wanting to 'tamper' with you. That's the word they always use. 'Tamper.'"

"See?" I say. "I can respect that. Why doesn't everyone stop tampering with me already?"

"What about the Disunion?" Glenn says. "Could they be the ones that tried to kill Grobnagger?"

"I doubt it," she says. "The whole chaos thing makes them sound scary, but I've spent some time with them, too. Their version of chaos is more like 'Let's do bong rips, eat nachos and sleep on the beach.'"

"So they're hippies?" I say.

"Pretty much," she says.

"This information isn't turning out to be that useful," I say.

Glenn scratches his chin.

"I'm just answering your questions," she says. "You don't like it, ask better ones."

We fall silent. The Explorer juts left on a dirt road. We're well out of town now, so woods line the roadsides. All I can see in the dark is a thick mess of trees and brush that make me uneasy. Gravel flies up and clinks against the undercarriage in a way that somehow accentuates the quiet in the Explorer. Finally, Louise speaks:

"Here's something. They don't talk about it at their general meetings or anything, but I've overheard some of the League higher ups talking about another group. They call themselves 'The Sons of Man,'" she says. "I guess some members of both the League and the Disunion are rumored to secretly comprise this underground group. They're supposed to be the biggest psychos out of all these people. They want to make man divine. While the others want to understand divinity, these guys want to use stuff like your dreams to become all powerful themselves. Sounds pretty ridiculous to me, but I know the League people are scared shitless of this prospect."

"Doesn't seem like killing me would help them achieve their goal," I say.

"Well, nothing will actually help them achieve their goal," she says. "They're lunatics. Who knows what they might be thinking? Maybe they think they need to sacrifice the great and powerful Jeffrey to get what they want, right?"

"I guess," I say.

"Anyway, I can't read their minds, but I happen to think that was some useful info nonetheless, so let's hear about those dreams already," she says.

I look at Glenn, and he nods, so I tell her about the dreams. She laughs frequently, so I start playing up the absurdities and funny qualities. At least we can agree that some of the things that happen as I get killed over and over again are pretty hilarious. I consider holding back some details here and there, but I think the fact that she doesn't even believe in any of this makes that seem pretty pointless. I tell it all.

While I'm talking, we make our way back into the city. It's not long before we're back, and we drop Louise near the diner.

"I'll keep my eyes and ears open regarding those trying to end your life," she says. "In fact, I must demand that you don't die anytime too soon."

"Why is that?" I say.

"Well, there's a new Thai restaurant on Forbes Street, and I'm going to need you to take me there on Saturday," she says. "I assume you'll be at Glenn's. I'll pick you up around 7."

I don't know what to say, so I say nothing.

"See you soon, Grobnagger," she says.

She turns and walks away.

"Nice," Glenn says.

He bashes a semi-closed hand into my shoulder like he's a football coach and I just came up with a fumble recovery.

"I don't know how you pulled that one off," he says. "But I'll tell you what, she's got a tight little body on her."

"Shut up," I say.

To my surprise, I sound pretty defensive about this. I can't decide if I'm offended that he said that about Louise in particular, or if I'm just generally grossed out by this old guy saying sexually charged shit to me.

"What?" he says. "I'm a man. I notice a nice looking lady when I see one. Is that a crime all of the sudden?"

"Well, notice all you want with your goddamn mouth shut," I say.

Glenn snorts in a way that straddles the line between laughter and disgust. It's the kind of sound a particularly arrogant horse would make, I think.

CHAPTER 8

My consciousness fades in all flicker-y like I can feel the electrical charge coursing through my brain. Like I can see it distorting my vision for a moment before the gray all around me comes into focus. I sigh and reach up to start working the knot out of the rope.

You know what? This alley is the goddamn worst.

But I know what I'm going to do this time. No hiding in the dumpster. No climbing any walls. I'm keeping it real simple this time around.

My feet hit the ground, and I sway for a moment but keep my balance. Here's where my big plan comes into play: I stand. I don't run. I don't walk. I stand. I wipe non-existent dust off of my shirt out of some post fall habit. Other than that? Standing, mostly.

I hear footsteps, and the hooded man hustles around the corner into the alley.

"Hi," I say.

He keeps rushing toward me without a word. Not a big talker, I guess, more of the strong, silent type.

"My name is Jeff," I say. "Jeff Grobnagger. I don't know why I'm here. I don't know why you're here. All I know is that some people are trying to kill me in real life, and my friend Glenn's daughter is missing. Amity. I think it all has something to do with me coming here."

The man slows, still moving toward me but with hesitation. This is good.

"Do you know where we are?" I say.

No response. He keeps walking toward me, but he's just barely creeping at this point. I realize for the first time that he's not nearly as big as I always thought. He might even be slightly smaller than me. I guess your perspective changes when people hover over you for a good strangle. They suddenly seem quite substantial.

"Can't we just talk about this?" I say. "Can you communicate with me, or is that forbidden or something?"

He shrugs. This is new.

I start pivoting away from him like a defensive boxer circling the perimeter of the ring to keep the slugger out of knockout range. He seems content to let me stay just out of reach, though he never stops pursuing me completely. He shrugged, remember? We're practically best friends now.

"Holy shit!" I say. "Are you bleeding?"

I point at his belly and turn to run in one motion. As I suspect, he is thrown by all of this and looks at his belly for a moment as I pull away from him. I look back over my shoulder to see his gaze turn away from his stomach. He begins to give chase. This is by far the best lead I've had on him to date.

I fly. My feet have an extra bounce when they come off of the ground. I tell myself I'm the fastest man in all of the damn dream world, and it feels like it. My feet are so light, like if I concentrated hard enough I could burst into the air and never come back down.

No running around the block this time. I move away from

the alley in as straight of a line as I can, though the street I'm on has some curves to it. Straight-ish, in any case.

I glance over my shoulder just in time to see him stumble over a curb. How humiliating. He's so far back there. He looks tinier than ever. The only thing getting strangled today is this poor bastard's pride.

I get to a fork in the road. Both sides look pretty much identical. If I had to describe them, I'd say that they're gray. The buildings are pretty nondescript. The air seems to move, like smoke or something, in the distance. I veer left. I don't know why, really. Left seems cooler.

Another over the shoulder glance reveals the hooded man to have fallen even farther back. Embarrassing. The part of me that could have become a gym teacher wants to yell at him to quit lollygaggin' and/or playing grab-ass back there. The rest of me stays focused on the running thing.

This doesn't seem like him. He's usually an efficient killing machine. Did my talking to him throw him this far off of his game?

I bank around a curve and begin mounting a steep hill. It strikes me that I'm not out of breath. My legs don't feel tired at all. It's almost like all of me knows this isn't all the way real or something, and I don't have to get tired here anymore.

As I summit the top of the hill, I see a wall of fog about a half of a block in front of me. Thick fog. It doesn't look right. It starts too abruptly, and I can see nothing through it. Just dark gray, almost black. The fog wall stretches as far as I can see in both directions. I realize that it likely forms a perimeter around the entire area. It surrounds us.

I reach the fog and stop. It makes me uncomfortable to be

this close to it. I stick my hand in, and it's like it disappears. It's so cold. I pull my fist back, and for a second my fingers look all gray before the color comes back to them.

Great.

I picture myself taking a step into the fog and freefalling out into nothing. That's all I can imagine: nothing on the other side. Not dark. Not blackness. An absence of anything. It seems like that could be worse than getting strangled.

I sit down on the asphalt. I could run, but apparently there's nowhere to go.

The man arrives soon, and he makes quick work of things. He's good at his job. I can respect that.

I wake up in the Explorer with Glenn staring at me. I look around and see the headlights catching on the rose bushes on either side of the big red door. We're in Glenn's driveway.

"Another seizure, huh?" he says.

"Yes," I say.

The events flash through my head. When I remember that fog it makes me feel sad in a way that doesn't really make sense. Like I've lost something. I don't remember things going black this time, which bothers me. I know the seizures are happening more frequently. Maybe they are coming on quicker, too.

"I figured," he says. "You fished out again. Flopped around like a pair of boobs on a treadmill. Got a real sick look about you toward the end there, too. I thought you were going to upchuck on the leather."

He taps and then pets the head rest like it's something precious.

"Yeah, I'm fine," I say. "Thanks for asking."

"Uh… sorry," he says. "Look, this Explorer is my baby. Eddie Bauer edition. I get carried away about taking care of her sometimes."

"It's ok," I say.

I suppress the urge to mention that this is an '02 with a flaming pink bumper.

"Any new developments?" he says. "In your dream?"

"Yeah," I say. "I got to the edge of the world, I think."

"Oh?" he says. "What was that like?"

"Foggy," I say. "It's a wall of fog that drops off into nothing."

He taps on the steering wheel as he mulls this over.

"Well, at least you know that running away isn't the solution to the test," he says.

"I guess."

"We should get some sleep," he says, opening the door. "Tomorrow is a new day. New days bring new ideas."

CHAPTER 9

I sit on the couch in Glenn's living room, twisting and jabbing at the puzzle sphere in my hands. No progress, though. I've tried googling a few of the hieroglyphic like symbols, but I didn't find much of interest. They're not from the ancient Egyptian hieroglyphic alphabet as it happens. I guess that's important to know. It does not get me any closer to opening the damn thing, however.

Knowing my luck, after hours of painstaking research I will figure this thing out only to learn that once you unlock it, you're whisked away to another dimension where a hooded man strangles you to death in an alley. Hardy har har.

After a few more random and failed attempts at popping the sphere open, I nestle it down into the cushions of the couch so it doesn't roll away, and I reach for my Arnold Palmer on the end table. The glass moistens my fingers with condensation, and the ice cubes tinkle within. I take a long drink. Half lemonade + half iced tea = one full awesome. Pretty sure Glenn is some kind of food wizard. Everything he touches turns to delish.

He retired for the evening a little while ago, but I'm not tired yet. It must be weird to get old. Does every day tire you out? I guess I can see how that shift has already started for me. It wasn't long ago that I would stay up until 4 or 5 am watching movies and such. There would be no real ill effects the next day. If I try to pull something like that now, the next day is miserable.

As I set the sweaty glass back down, movement catches the corner of my eye. I turn my head to see lights flickering on and off out the window. Headlights. It's too dark to be sure, but it looks like a dark colored Lincoln. I think I know what this is about.

I gather myself, slide my feet into my shoes, take one more drink of tea-monade and head for the door. As my hand nears the knob, I pause for a moment. I turn back and grab the sphere, lodging it into my hoodie pocket. It bulges, stretching the fabric like my sweatshirt has a small pregnant belly.

As I get outside, a man in a suit stands outside the car. He opens his mouth to speak, but I interrupt:

"Babinaux?" I say.

"Yes," he says, but I'm in the backseat before he can even finish the word.

Ms. Babinaux sports a black blouse that I think sort of looks like something a pirate would wear, all puffy and stuff. The collar winds up around her neck.

Our hands clasp, and we say hi.

"It's good to see you in one piece, Mr. Grobnagger," she says. "I heard about what happened to your apartment."

"Where'd you hear that?" I say, settling into my seat.

She pushes her hair behind her ears before she replies.

"You're OK, though?" she says. "You're staying with a friend?"

"Yeah, I'm fine," I say, though I note that she dodged my question entirely. "Any idea who would want me dead?"

She squints.

"It doesn't make much sense to me," she says and shakes her head.

Again, she fails to answer my query, being indirect. I have no idea if this is any way significant, but it makes me uneasy.

"Are you ready to explain anything to me?" I say.

"It's tricky to know what to tell. There are so many moving parts," she says. "Much remains unclear."

"Sure, sure," I say. "Another productive meeting here in the backseat of your car."

Her eyebrows dart up. I don't think she anticipated my sarcasm. She smiles after that, but I don't quite buy it.

"I can explain things in vague terms," she says. "As far as I know, there'd be no reason to hurt you. There may be a group that would want to use you, but the who, how and why of the matter remain mysterious."

"The Sons of Man?" I say.

The eyebrows jerk again.

"Where'd you hear that name?" she says.

"People talk," I say. "I listen."

"Jeffrey, I really need to know who told you about this," she says.

"I can explain it in vague terms," I say, my tone conveying the faintest mocking lilt. "A carbon based life form may have told me about it, but this being remains mysterious."

She squints in a way that is somehow intimidating. It suddenly occurs to me that this lady may be capable of a supernova level of rage, so I quickly change the subject:

"Oh hey," I say, pulling the puzzle sphere from my hoodie pocket. "What can you tell me about this?"

She looks at the sphere, and I think I detect a faint eye roll, but it's subtle to the point that I'm not sure.

"Are you serious?" she says.

"I never joke around about puzzle spheres. Ever. Have you ever seen one like it?" I say.

"I've seen a whole display of them," she says.

Wait. Am I missing something? I speak slowly. I can almost hear my dumb brain trying to work this out.

"A whole display?" I say.

"The answers you seek are at the mall, Mr. Grobnagger," she says.

I don't know what to say. She taps a fingernail on the sphere, each impact tinkling a high pitched metallic sound.

"They sell those at the Sharper Image," she says. "Or at least they did a couple of years ago. Sort of a novelty item."

"Oh," I say.

I take another look at the sphere. I guess the ornate grooves in the maroon casing do seem like something stamped out in a factory mass production style more than they seem like some hand crafted product from long ago. Glenn is going to be disappointed to learn this.

"I bet you could find Youtube videos about how to open it, if that's what you're asking," she says, handing the object back to me.

"Yes," I say. "That makes sense."

I shove the sphere back into my hoodie pocket. I can't bear to look at the damn thing. I feel the warmth crawl up onto my cheeks, and I can only imagine the shade of red they're achieving at the moment. To go from all of my sarcasm and truculence to this Sharper Image reveal somehow makes me feel so dumb that I just want to crawl under a floppy dead dog and die.

The next morning I turn on the water, tweaking the knobs back and forth in the eternal struggle to find a sweet spot between frigid and scalding in someone else's bathroom. Pretty sure this can't be done. Anyway, the water pressure seems pretty intense to me as I pass my hand through the stream to check the temp. This suspicion is confirmed when I step into the shower for real. It stings and leaves pink marks where it hits my body. Not out of heat – it's actually on the lukewarm side – out of sheer liquid force. It's like cleaning yourself with a fire hose on full blast. And I can't help but think that if the water got a direct nut shot, it'd rip my sack clean off.

How the hell does a man live like this? In America? These are third world, sack ripping conditions.

I crank the heat up a bit, and the bathroom fills with steam and the sound of the water slapping the tub. I accent that soundtrack periodically with gasps and whimpers as the water tries its best to remove flesh from bone. I soap and rinse, but more than that, I endure.

Upon stepping out, however, I realize how clean I feel. Like all the strangling just got washed away. Maybe power washed away is the more accurate way to say it. Either way, it feels like all traces of the alley just got blasted off my being and sent spiraling down the drain even if I know that isn't physically true.

I bury my face in the fluff of a towel and then wrap it around my waist and move toward the sink. The tiles underfoot give off shocking warmth. Heated flooring? This luxury stands in glaring contrast to the abomination Glenn is trying to pass off as a shower head.

I wipe a circle of steam off of the mirror with the heel of my hand. Pink swirls blotch the skin on my chest and neck, but I'm still here, and I am awake.

In the kitchen, Glenn pushes a glass of something green over to me. I lift the glass and examine its contents. It's a thick liquid about the shade of grass, completely opaque. It smells a little familiar. Some type of fruit juice, I suppose, but I can't place it.

"What is it?" I say.

"Just try it," he says. "Then I'll tell."

I take a sip. It's interesting. A very fresh flavor. A little sweet, like maybe there's some apple in there, but nowhere near as sweet as your average fruit juice.

"You like?" he says.

"It's pretty good," I say. "So what is it?"

"The green giant," he says. "My own recipe - a bunch of kale, lettuce, carrots, cucumbers, oranges and apples. Tossed into the juicer and stirred, not shaken."

"For real?" I say.

He nods. I take another sip. I guess I can detect the greens if I really think about it, but it's a tasty beverage nonetheless.

"You're basically taking in a huge salad's worth of vitamins and nutrients right now, Grobnagger," he says. "I try to make sure to have a glass four or five times a week."

When I tell Glenn what Ms. Babinaux said about the sphere, he pinches his eyes closed and exhales deeply. His torso sags like a deflating beach ball.

"The Sharper Image?" he says. "Ugh. The worst."

His eyelids part in slow motion. He picks up the sphere from the counter, paws at it, turns it over in his hands.

"Damn," he says, setting it back down. "That's a kick in the sack."

"There could still be something inside of it," I say. "Something important, you know?"

The right side of his mouth curls into a smirk that reminds me of a child that just found out that Santa Claus is a complete fabrication.

"Maybe," he says.

We move to Glenn's computer. A Youtube search reveals several videos regarding how to open the sphere. One guy takes a titanium drill bit to it - pretty entertaining but probably not the route for us to pursue. Other techniques involve a little more precision and nuance. Interestingly, two of the three golden dials are for show and have nothing to do with cracking the puzzle.

After we watch a few videos, Glenn gives it a go. He seems to do the first couple of steps correctly, but something goes wrong, and when he presses the button and tries to pull the top free, the sphere remains locked up tighter than a clam.

He doesn't say anything. He just hands me the puzzle, and I know it's my turn.

First, I spin the middle dial to the left, slowly and with care, until I hear the ball bearing inside descend with a metallic chirp and clank. Next, I spin the dial back to the right, once again all slow and deliberate, until I hear a second chirp and clank as the ball bearing descends another level. This is where a little muscle comes in. I whack the puzzle sphere on the corner of the desk.

In retrospect, I believe this to be where Glenn's attempt went awry. He tried to merely bang it on his palm. I give it a much stiffer thump.

I depress the shiny button on top, and I hear the ball bearing move again, more of a scrape than a chirp this time. Still holding the button, I ease my fingernails into the seam and pull on the top. It's stuck. I can feel the two halves still grabbing hold of each other like a tick shoulders deep in a dog's ear. It's not going to work after all.

I adjust my fingers and try one more hard pull. The metal moans and then pops as the top and bottom disengage, the half closest to me yanking free before the other side. For a moment I pause with the two halves of the globe about an inch apart and make eye contact with Glenn. His eyes glow, his beach ball abdomen puffed back up into something proud. He nods at me, and I open the sphere.

There's a spring inside the top half, and a metal cylinder with a hole in the bottom. The cylinder must house the ball bearing as it's nowhere to be seen.

The bottom half has a small chamber hollowed out in the center. There's something in it, wrapped in a torn piece of notebook paper.

I set the top half on the desk and hold the bottom half up to Glenn as though serving him an hors d'oeuvre. His mouth is slightly agape as he pulls the object from the shell and unwraps it.

"Another one?" he says, squinting at the item in his hands.

He tilts his palm toward me so I can see. The paper is blank. Inside is a key.

CHAPTER 10

The airport is the worst. The hordes of travelers open their eyes a little too wide and snap their heads around to watch all the moving parts around them. They huddle around in clusters and talk in semi-hushed tones. They check their phones and watches every two seconds, generally struggling to hold still. It all reminds me of insects.

Anxiety is contagious, I think. Perhaps it's transmittable by sweat and/or body odor.

We weave through crowds of fidgety people toward the lockers. They try to press their nervous smell all up on us. They hover too close and stop in our path. They lean in our direction. If it were socially acceptable to smear their pit stains on our persons, they'd probably never stop doing it.

Glenn has a determined look about him, which I guess makes sense since we stand to finally learn something about Amity. He jostles his way in front of me to take the lead. I don't realize at first that he does so with a clear purpose in mind.

He has a new vision for airport maneuvering. Namely this vision entails jabbing his elbow into the lower back of anyone that crowds in front of him and bellowing:

"LOOK OUT."

If ever words were spoken in all caps, these were those words.

And somehow it works. People clear out of his way like cars pulling over to let an ambulance through. He looks quite pleased with himself. Watching him, I almost wish I was older. I feel like if you're over 50 and do something like this, everyone just complies. You're somehow not to be trifled with.

We arrive at the lockers and scan for G-123, find it, pop in the key and turn that shit. Glenn takes a deep breath and pulls the door open all slow. Like this is a game show, and he's revealing the prize behind Door Number One.

Inside sits one of those black and white composition notebooks. We just stare at it a moment before Glenn scoots it toward us and then lifts it. The notebook fall open in his hands. He flicks through a few pages, but I can't see anything.

"A diary," he says. "Amity's diary."

I sit on Glenn's couch while he reads the diary in the next room. He doesn't insist on us being in separate rooms for this. I do. I figure it best to give him some space. It must be weird to read your daughter's private thoughts, right?

On TV there's a montage of a couple falling in love. The girl sports blindingly white teeth. The guy's jaw displays just the right amount of five o'clock shadow. It's a rapid fire offensive of clichés: They laugh in a movie theater. They get stuck at the top of the Ferris wheel. They hold hands on the beach. They dance all slow. I'm just waiting for them to do the spaghetti thing from "Lady and the Tramp."

I keep realizing that I'm staring at the wall instead of the TV screen. I can barely stand to watch this blossoming romance, I guess, so I keep subconsciously subverting my gaze.

I know this is fictional, but… She could do better, anyway.

For real.

Glenn strides into the room and plops the journal down on the couch next to me. He avoids eye contact. I search his face for information, but he plays it pretty stoic.

"Well?" I say.

"Just read it," he says.

He walks off. I stare at the notebook occupying the seat next to mine. I pick it up, shifting its weight in my fingers a moment before I crack it open.

March 19th

This is not my life.

I wake up. I go to work at the lab and run blood samples. I go home. I read. I watch TV. I go to bed.

I rinse. I repeat.

Is this it? Is this my world?

Sometimes I think there must be more. More than what you can see with your eyes and hold in your hands. More to the universe than the physical world. More to life than just flesh.

I've read about ways to experience the more I speak of. They might be bullshit. They might not. I mean to pursue them, and I'm starting this journal to chronicle my findings. My fear, of course, is that this is another avenue to emptiness, another pathway that leads to the Big Nothing. But the way I look at it, I have little to lose.

Because what do I have now? The wake and work and sleep routine?

No. No. No.

This is not my life.

April 4th

In the past couple of weeks, I've made little progress in my quest. Wait. I probably shouldn't conclude that so definitively. I've met a lot of people with similar interests at various meet ups and gatherings, and perhaps that could lead to something. Networking is neither intuitive nor enjoyable for me, but I understand it can have great value. Unfortunately, it's damn near impossible to distinguish the open minded from the crazies from the con men among this lot. By default I trust none of them, but I don't know how far that rigid position will get me.

Everyone treats me with kindness, at least for now. It's been weird to spend so much time with groups of humans. Sometimes I forget that it can be fun to be around people, even if they might be insane.

Some days in the lab I can go an entire shift without talking to another human being. Not if Jackie is working, of course. She spends so much time wandering around socializing, I wonder if she ever gets any work done.

May 6th

I keep forgetting to update this journal. I suppose there wasn't much to report for a while there. I am now translating a book that seems promising, though. It's an ancient text of unknown origin that supposedly made its way through certain circles among both the Egyptians and Greeks, possibly Isaac Newton as well. He apparently had quite a collection of occult books and objects, and he wrote several thousand pages on the subject. Anyway, it took me a long time to decipher what language it was even written in, but I'm making good progress now.

The person that pointed me in the direction of the book gives me the creeps, however. I'm almost afraid to even write his name down here. It feels like he would know somehow. A bit silly, I realize, and yet I'm still not writing the name.

The whole Jackie thing has really been pissing me off. Three times in the past month Lemke has handed me assignments that were already under Jackie's name on the board. Yesterday, it happened again. I'm working twice as hard just to cover for her laziness.

So I decided to do something about it. I did what any reasonable person would and looked it up on the internet (Ha-Ha). I found a pamphlet that suggested I approach Jackie not as an angry or judgmental coworker but as a concerned friend.

During one of her many breaks, I went up to her and said Lemke had given me another one of her assignments and that she seemed stressed lately, was anything wrong? Mistake of the century.

Now Jackie is under the impression that we are Office BFFs, and as such, I am treated to the minutiae of her private life. For example, I now know that her boyfriend has been having issues with erectile dysfunction for the past several months. Then there's her sister, Leah, who is trying to turn their mother against Jackie. Motive was unclear.

Or my favorite, how she spent all weekend disinfecting her mattress, because her Miniature Schnauzer had a nasty bout of diarrhea.

Thank you, internet.

May 22nd

Something happened last night… I think.

It was late. I'd been reading in between chanting and meditation, which I've been at for a week based on a particular incantation in the book. At the end of the last meditation session I felt a weird sting in my nose – an unpleasant tingle. Kind of like when you get hit in the face, and you keep pressing your fingers to your nostrils, waiting for the blood to trickle out. It seemed to spread from my nose outward, but it was gone after a second so I didn't think much of it.

Over the next 20 minutes, though, I found it harder and harder to read. Not because I was tired. I wasn't. At first, it was like my eyes wouldn't quite listen to me. They fell out of focus or just stopped scanning across the lines of text, and it would take me a second to figure out what was wrong. Then, the book seemed distant like I was holding it at arm's length even though I was just about touching my nose to the page as I tried to fix my efforts on reading. I glanced around the room, and it all appeared that way, like I was moving further up into my head with the rest of the world growing farther and farther away.

I lay back on my bed and watched pink and pale green patterns etch themselves onto the white walls around me. They looked like stencils of a three tear drop shape that I perceived as three leaves on a plant. The shape painted itself repeatedly in rows that ran around the perimeter of the room. When I lifted my head, the rows seemed to realign themselves in new spots. They flowed from place to place with a bending, fluid quality to their adjustments. They were like liquid. The colors oozed into each other, constantly changing. Even when I closed my eyes, the plants were still there. Still everywhere, dripping and streaming.

The back of my head started to throb gently. I shifted my body to adjust my shirt, more out of habit than need, and my book slid off of the edge of the bed and slapped onto the floor. The sound echoed in an unusual manner. Then I realized that every sound reverberated in a strange rhythmic pulse – almost like the sounds were slowed down. The fan in my bedroom went whoosh-whoosh-whoosh with a wavering quality.

The tingling returned, this time starting on the top of my head and spreading down from there. It didn't sting so much like the first time. I sensed it as pleasant, like that mild euphoria you experience after you've downed your first or second alcoholic beverage, long before the depressive qualities kick in.

The echoes all around me built into something louder and more forceful. They threatened to drown everything out.

Despite all of these odd sensory happenings, I felt calm. Tranquil, even. Almost mildly sedated. I could move, but I didn't really want to.

The echoes subsided. The volume got turned down on the sound until I could only hear it if I really concentrated. And then the ceiling and walls faded out. Everything went white. My eyes were still open, but apart from the sensation of breathing, it was like I was no longer connected to the physical world. It felt like I was floating, not moving in any particular direction, just drifting in empty space. With every breath, my being inflated and deflated like a balloon.

And then images took shape in the white. A hallway stretched out in front of me. I drifted down it a ways, passing doorway after doorway – peeking into them at the infinite array of other worlds and possibilities. I didn't go through any of them, though. I somehow knew I was just here for this brief visit to get a glimpse.

But for that moment, everything seemed so clear. I had this overwhelming sense of what a miracle it is to be conscious of the universe, just to exist at all.

May 27th

As time passes, I find myself wanting to think that maybe it was all just my imagination. Maybe it was a dream. Maybe nothing really happened at all.

Sometimes I even think maybe he drugged me. I know how badly he wants me to believe in it all. He would do anything.

June 4th

It happened again. My mind separated from my body. There were elements of darkness this time, though. A feeling of dread as to where this would all go.

The walls and ceiling turned white again. But there was no hallway. It was just geometric shapes on the white. Patterns. It all flashed and morphed too fast this time. I couldn't keep up. It started blue, but it turned to red.

And then it seemed to become less geometric and 2 dimensional and more organic and 3 dimensional - stringy red muscle fibers and muted purple hunks of misshapen meat that seemed like inhuman organs. A series of such materialized before me in strobe light like bursts in front of the white background.

And then a disembodied face with no skin hovered inches in front of my nose, all sinew and strands of connective tissue and exposed teeth. The eyes seemed to look in different directions, unfocused.

I wasn't scared so much as disturbed. How could I fit these images into my prior experience when consciousness seemed like such a wonder? How could I reconcile the meat with the miracle?

The face drifted away from me, and the white gripped around it until it was gone all together, the slate before me restored to its blank whiteness.

I had this feeling that information was being transferred to me, but it was too much for my brain somehow. Someone was trying to communicate something, send me some kind of message, but I couldn't comprehend it. It reminded me of the scrolling text in The Matrix. Like whatever useful data this message might contain was being broken down into lines of code that mean nothing to me.

That's one of the worst feelings, I think. To know someone is trying to tell you something that you can't hear or discern at all and maybe never will. I think your imagination automatically assumes that it could be some crucial, life altering piece of information no matter the circumstances. But considering I was hallucinating or traveling in some metaphysical realm, it seems even more important.

Maybe I'll never-

The following page of the journal is torn out, leaving this entry and possibly the next incomplete.

feel cold when he is around. I know it must be my imagination, but...

Oh yeah, good news: Jackie's boyfriend got a prescription for Viagra, so the erectile problems are a thing of the past.

June 23rd

He knows. I don't know how, but he knows what happened to me.

The rest of the pages are blank. I close the diary, walk into the kitchen and set it on the snack bar. Glenn leans on the counter across from me, his forearms balancing on the corner. He makes eye contact and raises his eyebrows at me to ask what I thought of the journal.

"Pretty interesting stuff. Seems like Amity and I have a lot in common," I say. "And I mean to say beyond our… metaphysical experiences."

Glenn squints.

"In some ways, yeah," he says. "I can see that. She lacks your self hatred, though."

Did not see that coming.

"You think I have… You think I hate myself?" I say.

"Oh, big time, dude," Glenn says. "I don't think I've ever known anyone else that harbors such genuine self loathing. Seriously, you should talk to somebody, but yeah… Weird thing is, you seem to have a good sense of humor about it."

He slaps me on the shoulder and chuckles to himself.

"I mean, I imagine most people that feel that way are pretty unbearable to be around," he says. "But you're actually self sufficient, dependable and pretty entertaining. A self loather, yes, but not a self pity-er, I'd say."

"Well…" I say. "Thank you."

I wake in the night to what sounds like rocks bashing into Glenn's house. Thunder rumbles in the distance, and I realize it must be hail. Ice chunks patter on the roof and chime against the windows. Within a minute or two, though, it quiets down to the normal thrum of falling rain.

I lie awake in the dark, my back nestled into the couch. I blink a few times just to watch the gleam angling into the window from the streetlight vanish and reappear.

I remember what Glenn said about me hating myself, and a melancholy settles over me.

And silent movies play in my head without my say so, unfolding in my imagination like blossoming flowers. Fragmented memories I can't erase of the times just after Allie and I broke up.

The first image flashes in my cerebral cortex – through clouds of smoke at a party, I watch Allie kiss some guy she met that night. This is probably three weeks after we broke up and I moved out, after we lived together for nine months and dated for a year.

It cuts all sharp like being stabbed in the gut, but it's fine. It's fine. It's really all for the best.

Because I think for other people, finding someone new is the fun part. The novelty of the beginning, when anything is possible. It's a social thing, and I'm just not cut out for all of that.

The next image unfurls – I sit at my desk alone, empty beer bottles cluttering every surface around me. I lift the bottle in my left hand to my lips for one last kiss. My right hand pins the phone to my ear. It's a silent film, but I don't have to hear her voice to remember the things she said.

It's the middle of the night. You broke up with me, Jeff. You can't keep calling me like this when you're drunk. I have to work tomorrow. Don't call me anymore.

I shift on Glenn's couch, turning over onto my side like physically moving can get me away from the past.

It doesn't.

The next image opens up – I sweep shards of glass from the floor of my apartment, the broom pushing them off of the carpet and into the dust pan. I had woken on the floor to find that during the night I moved my couch across the room for no good reason and smashed my TV screen, possibly with a hammer. Rivulets of dried blood streak my arm like freezing rain on a windshield, so I must have cut myself on the glass. The blood looks thick, gummy. I had no recollection of doing these things. My last memory was sitting alone in the dark, pouring Jim Beam down my throat.

For years I didn't know that drinking alone wasn't normal. All through high school I did so. I had a few shots of whiskey before school in the morning or guzzled down some gin before I had to mow the lawn.

Later, of course, I realized how, for other people, drinking was a social thing to do at parties or with friends. Once Allie and I broke up, I reverted to my old ways, I guess. It always felt like drinking would quiet the despair in me down, but it only turned the volume up. It made all the bad feelings claw and scratch to try to find their way out, but there was never anywhere for them to go, so they just pulled apart my insides instead.

I barely even drink now, because it only opens up all the dark places I just want to keep closed.

And I remember trying to tell Allie about it one night back when we were still together. I tried to tell her about the bad thoughts in my head, the part of myself that attacks me and picks at my wounds so they never heal quite right, the part of me that wants to crash the plane. And she said that everybody has that, and it's OK, but I don't know. I just felt like she wasn't really listening.

So all these years went by, and yeah, I think she was wrong.

Not everybody has it. Not like this. I don't even know if she thought that for real or if she was trying to make me feel better.

And I don't know.

I don't know.

Maybe Glenn is right.

CHAPTER 11

I'm awakened by someone shouting.

"Boom!" the voice says. "Nailed it."

Sunlight streams into the room, but what room? The first thing my eyes land on is a fire place, so I know it's not my bedroom. I pat around at the couch I've been sleeping on as though that might offer clues. Words pop into my head:

Fine Corinthian leather.

For some reason, one part of my brain finds it highly amusing to think such mundane things in stressful moments. The rest of my brain, however, wants that part to die in a fire.

As footsteps close in on me, I remember where I am: Glenn's living room.

Glenn bursts in and squares his shoulders at the couch with his finger shoved into a big hardcover book as a bookmark.

"Manifesting," he says.

"What?" I say. I can hear the sleep making my voice all deep and weird.

"Grobnagger, we've been going about this all wrong," he says. "The answers we seek aren't to be found at some diner or inside of a diary. The answers are in your dreams, and I've come upon a method that will get us exactly what we want."

Suggesting that Glenn seems a bit manic would be an understatement. I think he is about one notch below foaming at the mouth. He flips open the book and starts scanning the page he's marked, and then closes it again.

"I take it breakfast in bed is out of the question," I say.

"Manifesting," he says again.

"What?" I say again.

"Many people ascribe to the notion that there's power in positive thinking, right?" he says. "That projecting positive energy into the universe reflects it back at you, yeah? That picturing yourself achieving your goals helps you attain them. And so on."

"Right," I say.

"Well, in a sense, this concept has existed in occult writing for hundreds of years," he says.

My mind starts to wander away from manifesting toward waffles and pancakes and such. The chocolate chip pancakes advertised on the Bucky's Diner sign sound pretty delicious at the moment. And only $5.45? A steal.

Glenn flips open the book to the page he has been marking.

"This is how we'll pass that test of yours and figure out what to do next," he says. "Manifesting."

He taps a finger at the page and holds the book up to me. I go to take it, but he rips it away in a wild gesture.

"Can't you see?" he says. "All these things going on around us connect to your dreams. We have to solve that problem before we can solve the others. And the passage in this book is like a tutorial for how to use manifesting to do just that."

He holds the book up to me again, and again he rips it away to fling his arms in the air.

"Can't you see how all the pieces connect?" he says.

"First of all, I can't see anything because you keep jerking that book around like a lunatic," I say. "Second of all, just the other night you talked about how you didn't buy Riston Farber's levitating spoon. Now you're talking like my dreams are real, and I need to pass these tests to fix everything. So which is it? Real or fake?"

Glenn sets the book down on the coffee table and sighs.

"Well, that's a pretty big question," he says. "It's hard to sum up what I believe, yeah? Look at quantum physics. The math proves it's true, but classical physics can't find a way to make it mesh with its laws. It's sort of the idea that particles exist in a state of probability until we are conscious of them, at which point they become real. There have been tests suggesting elements of this dating back to Einstein. It's hard to wrap your head around, but it's sort of like time and space aren't even real until we're conscious of them. Or at least that's my simplified way of restating it to try to grasp it. Might not be completely accurate, but that's the gist, do you follow that?"

"Yeah, I think so," I say.

He better find a way to tie this into what's happening to me, because otherwise I'm afraid he's quite a bit more manic than I thought.

"So some scientists are now theorizing that quantum activity plays a role in consciousness," he says. "It's like the missing ingredient. They found evidence that these microtubules in the brain vibrate in such a way that they conduct quantum activity, or at least they could. They also proved that plants use quantum activity as part of photosynthesis. So they're taking steps toward taking that abstract theory – that reality doesn't exist until we're conscious of it – and finding biological structures that back it up."

He takes a breath.

"It's still a controversial theory, of course. The classical scientific view is that consciousness is merely a byproduct of such a complex cluster of cells as the brain," he says. "They think our brain is merely an information processing system that is so intricate that we become conscious as a result. In fact, some philosophers that ascribe to that theory believe that we're just functioning cells with the illusion of having free will. In other words, our brain functions, and that group of neurons controls our thoughts and behavior, but when we look back on it, our memory tells a story that sort of makes us feel like we had choices in the matter. Does that make sense?"

"Yeah," I say. "I mean, I get it, at least. I don't know how much sense it makes in terms of whether or not I believe it."

"Yeah," he says. "See? I don't buy that either. I mean, we already know that certain things exist outside of physics. Quantum theory and relativity already proved that."

He scratches his chin.

"There is even math that proves all matter is connected by some form of energy that communicates faster than light," he says. "Wouldn't consciousness make sense there? Doesn't that sound like the collective unconscious that Jung wrote about a long time ago? That we really are all connected on some level or dimension that we can't and don't understand?"

He takes a deep breath and lets it out all slow.

"They're still testing these theories, though, so who knows?" he says. "I mean, I don't believe any of that absolutely, but I think it adds a plausible scientific backdrop for what's happening to you, right? It doesn't have to be magic or anything."

"Right," I say.

"But all of that has little to do with manifesting. Forget the book for now," he says. "That has the details, but I guess I better explain the general concept first. You know that positive thinking stuff I was talking about? Well, some people think that's literally true. That with your thoughts and energy directed properly, you can sort of will things into being. There are even some scientists trying to study it. You've heard about those studies that suggest the power of prayer is real? Where people who are prayed for are more likely to heal from various illnesses? Some people think that doesn't prove God chooses to save some people over others. They think it proves that human thoughts can have literal effects on the world."

I don't know what to say, so I nod.

"There are slight variations, but the techniques are all about the same. Whether it's for deeply spiritual reasons or if you just want to will yourself to get rich, you think of a specific goal and concentrate on it and repeat it over and over again to yourself until it's planted deeply in your subconscious. You visualize yourself achieving it or having it or whatever."

"That's it? Doesn't seem like this would do anything," I say.

Glenn shrugs.

"It helped Ken Norton become the heavyweight champ," he says. "Or so he says."

"So you think all of this stuff is real, then?" I say.

"Not all of it. Riston Farber is a phony," he says. "His illusions are designed to make people believe. Not to dupe them, but to use their beliefs. See, if people believe his magic powers exists, then they do exist - in people's minds. And with manifesting we now know how things people believe have a way of coming true, right?"

"I guess so," I say. I wonder if I could manifest some of those chocolate chip pancakes.

"Manifesting might not be anything magic. Clarifying goals and visualizing success could make someone more confident and work that way. Look, I don't know if any of it is real," he says. "But I'm more than willing to try it to get my daughter back."

"OK, that makes sense," I say. "So, for real, what's for breakfast?"

I feast on a breakfast consisting of a fried egg over a wilted spinach salad dressed with a vinaigrette. Glenn then trumps that with a second course of French toast made with homemade bread. Unbelievable. I'm sure the chocolate chip pancakes are good, but this meal is fucking outstanding. While I eat, Glenn goes over the ins and outs of manifesting.

"You choose a specific goal," he says. "So you don't say 'I want to be rich.' You say, 'I want to make one and a half million dollars by next Christmas.' A vague goal is a waste of time. I can't hold rich in my hand. I can hold one and a half million dollars in my hand."

"Might need to put that in a sack or something," I say. "I mean, that's a lot of bills to lug around in your bare hands."

He ignores my comment and continues, his eyes tilted up and to the right. I can't tell if he's examining the fern hanging over the kitchen sink or staring off into space.

"You say the goal aloud," he says. "Saying it out loud already makes it more real, more concrete than just having it in your head. This is not a dream. It's a desire. Something you can have or will achieve. Dreams live in your head. Desires live in the real world."

Yolk runs down my chin, and I dab at it with a napkin. Glenn asks if I want a refill by way of hoisting the coffee carafe at me and wiggling it while raising his eyebrows.

"Well, yeah," I say, holding my cup up.

"You tell it to yourself, repeating it over and over," he says. "You make it a ritual to spend 10 minutes at a time focusing on just repeating your specific goal to yourself like a mantra. You do this at least three times a day. Preferably six. Whenever you can, it's out loud. If you're in public or at work, you chant it in your mind with feeling. You hear your voice saying it. You repeat it so much that it wires a place in your brain and seeps into your subconscious. It becomes part of you."

I take a long drink of coffee. It's just hot enough to make my tongue tingle.

"You visualize yourself achieving it," he says. "You picture yourself accomplishing the goal repeatedly while you do your mantra. By the time it happens, it's no surprise. You've watched it a few thousand times in your mind's eye."

"This doesn't sound like magic," I say. "It sounds like a good way to focus yourself on something. I don't know if you need to chant to yourself for an hour a day, but..."

Glenn drags his knuckles back and forth over the granite countertop.

"I told you," he says. "Maybe it's magic. Maybe it's not. A lot of people say it works, and I've got nothing to lose and all to gain."

"So how you do you figure all of this applies to my dreams?" I say.

"I read an article once about dreams," he says. "A lady had all of these nightmares that a shark was attacking her and eating her. So a therapist had her imagine the shark before bed every night, except instead of letting the shark attack her, she would imagine herself tickling the shark and the shark laughing really hard."

"That changed her dreams?" I say.

He nods.

"I know yours might not be regular dreams, but I figure it's worth a shot," he says.

"Yeah, I guess so," I say.

CHAPTER 12

I chant. It's an odd feeling to sit in a room and repeat stuff about how you're going to kill someone in a dream, but I power through it for the good of the team. I considered going the tickle route, like the lady with the shark, but killing seems a lot more efficient. Either way, I feel too dumb to do these chants within earshot of Glenn, so I make him go outside with his headphones on while I blast through my 10 minutes.

I'm in a room he calls his "library" now. I mean, it has a few hundred books, probably, but let's get real. Nobody's trying to acquire a card to come check out your Tom Clancy books, dude. I probably have this many books on my kindle, but I don't call it a "mobile library" or whatever.

When the clock hits 10:26, I cease my chant and head out to get Glenn. I watch through the screen door for a second as he paces back and forth on a sidewalk running through the backyard. His shoulders slump, and his arms dangle limply at his sides in a way that makes him look like a third grader. He thrusts his head forward and back to the beat of the music. This is one of the more embarrassing moves I've witnessed to date.

His eyes meet mine as I open the door, and I give him a wave to come in.

"How'd it go?" he says.

"I don't know what to say," I say. "It was pretty chant-y, I guess."

He smirks as he walks past me into the house.

"How long do you think it will be, then?" he says.

"Till my next seizure?" I say. "I don't know. They've been pretty frequent of late. I'd guess I'll have one within a couple of hours."

He gets a couple of octagonal glasses out of the cupboard and pours some water from a Brita pitcher. He pushes one toward me and chugs from the other.

"Probably should lay low, then," he says, wiping water from his mouth with the back of his wrist.

I nod and take a sip.

We watch movies into the afternoon in Glenn's "den." He has an HD projector and a massive screen on the wall. I think he said it was 73 inches, but I can't remember for sure. Every so often Glenn squints at me as if discerning whether or not I'm about to start flopping around. Not sure if he's more concerned about me or the upholstery on the theatre seats.

Of course, as soon as I want to have a seizure and go to the dream world of my own volition, it doesn't happen. The afternoon fades to evening without so much as a hand tremor. No shimmies. No shakes. No queasy feelings. No fades to black.

I can't remember how long ago the last movie ended, but I realize that I've been watching the LG logo bounce around the corners of the screen in a daze for several minutes when Glenn speaks.

"You think you're psyching yourself out?" he says.

His voice sounds a little more accusatory than I'd like.

"I don't know," I say. "Do you have any tips on how to

induce a metaphysical seizure you'd like to share with me?"

He huffs.

"I figure there's no use getting upset about it," I say. "Nothing we can do."

Glenn brushes his fingers in his mustache.

"You going to take that girl out or what?" he says.

"Louise?" I say. "I don't know."

"Why wouldn't you?" he says.

"Because I don't know her," I say.

"They have this new thing called dating. It's where guys and gals spend time together and get to know each other," he says. "I guess it's pretty crazy."

"I've heard tell of this," I say. "But I don't know how wise it is to partake in such matters when someone is trying to kill you."

"You just watched five movies with me," he says. "But you can't watch a movie with her for some reason? Doesn't make a lot of sense to me, Grobnagger."

"Why does everyone have to badger me about everything like this?" I say. "I don't bother anybody. I'm not hurting anyone. I just want to be alone."

Glenn leans forward in his seat and points a finger at me.

"What the hell happened to you to make you so closed off from people?" he says. "A beautiful girl wants to be around you, and you'd rather watch movies with some old guy? You'd rather just sit in a room somewhere by yourself?"

"What happened to you to make you such a nosy shit?" I say.

"Just answer me this one question, and we can move on. What's the deal with your parents?" he says. "I figure that will explain your issues sufficiently."

"What are you, Dr. Phil now?" I say.

"Let the record reflect that the witness didn't answer the question," he says. "Seriously, dude, where are mom and dad? How do they fit into the picture?"

"They're dead," I say.

He squirms in his seat, and the chair squeaks beneath him.

"What?" he says. "Both of them?"

I nod.

"My dad died when I was six. Cancer. My mom died when I was born," I say. "Stayed with my grandparents, but they've been gone a few years now, too."

For a second, Glenn remains still with his mouth half open. He stares off into space.

"Jesus," he says. "I'm sorry."

I don't know what to say, so I do the non-chalant shrug. Glenn remains in a state I want to call "flabbergasted," so I see I'll have to say something after all.

"It was a long time ago," I say.

"I didn't..." he says. "I didn't know about that."

I try to think of some smooth segue out of this conversational black hole but I can't. Glenn blinks a few times, and his head slowly swivels until his gaze locks on me. The awkward power of this is hard to capture properly in words.

We just look at each other. My skin crawls, presumably trying to get out of this room. I can't blame it for that and decide it best to follow its lead.

"I have to take a leak," I say.

"Alright," he says.

I don't think I would normally say "leak" like that, but I'm rattled pretty good. My self consciousness swells to the point that it makes it feel odd just to put one foot in front of the other at a normal pace. I have to concentrate to walk rather than sprint out of the den. When I get to the bathroom, I lock the door and turn on the ventilation fan for some white noise. I stand at the sink and try to decide how long I should wait before I go back.

My expression in the mirror looks wounded, and I observe for the thousandth time that my face is too long somehow. My chin looks like the Wicked Witch of the West or something. I stare into my eyes and wonder how anyone can look at me and not see it immediately – that I'm a soft thing that will fall to pieces at the slightest touch. I'm an open wound that just wants time alone to heal.

And even if I never can heal, I just want to be alone rather than suffer in front of a live studio audience.

I dream that I'm in a cave, swinging a torch about, trying to fight off the pitch black nothing all around. I know I need to keep going. There's something I need to get in the depths of this cavern, but I can't quite remember what that would be.

The walls around me are the color of rust and dust and blood intertwined. Maybe it's the hue of the stone that makes me know somehow that I'm far from home. This is a cave in the desert somewhere. A doorway etched into the sand that goes down and down.

I descend for a long time. All is silent aside from the hiss and periodic spit of my torch.

After a time the flame dims and burns out, but I feel my way in the dark and keep going. My fingertips graze along the cool stone.

I feel a breeze on my cheek too cold, and then I make out a glimmer of light in the distance. The descent gives way to flat ground as the light gets closer and closer. I enter the large chamber where the illumination emanates from, and I can see the flicker of the torches against the back wall. I halt in the back of the room, struggling to keep my eyes open in the light after so long in darkness.

When my pupils constrict enough, I note that there are four stone doors along the far wall with torches mounted between them. The doors have weird symbols carved into them. At first I think the carvings to be completely foreign, but something about the one on the fourth door looks familiar.

"Choices and consequences," a voice behind me says, and I almost shit myself.

I turn, and Glenn stands in the chamber next to me. Something about him seems different, though. He's dressed all in black, but he seems strange beyond that. It's like he's not himself. The look in his eye is serious and far away, and I don't really know what to make of it. He doesn't walk so much as glide across the room to stand in front of the doors. I notice there are two benches along the walls.

"What?" I say.

He doesn't say anything, doesn't even look at me, but I've gathered that I need to choose a door.

The fourth symbol is the only one that's vaguely familiar, so I move toward that. As I turn the knob, the torch lights extinguish one by one, and the darkness resumes. It's at this moment I realize where I know the symbol from. It was on the cover of the black book in Amity's room. Somehow, I know that this is not great. I want to go back and choose another one, but my hand is stuck to the knob. The door swings open into blackness, and I can't stop it.

The Earth rumbles around me, and I hear shards of rock start to crack away from the ceiling above and topple to the cave floor. I hear Glenn talking, but I can't make out the words over the sound of the rocks. It doesn't sound like he's talking to me, though.

Then I wake up.

CHAPTER 13

I half rotate my torso on the couch and feel Mardy behind me, nestled in the space behind my knees. I give him a pet, and he pushes a paw into the air in a swim move. Gray light gleams in the windows.

I hear Glenn in the kitchen and something sizzling. Breakfast, I presume. I shuffle out to the kitchen, sit at the breakfast nook, and he serves me a plate of blueberry pancakes with sliced strawberries and the faintest touch of syrup on top like he knew the exact moment I'd be up.

"Morning," he says. "No dreams last night?"

I know that he means seizure dreams, but for a split second I contemplate telling him about my normal dream about the four doorways in the cave.

"None," I say.

His lip curls in a manner that I read as disappointment, but it uncurls just as quickly.

"I didn't figure," he says. "Well, let's get some breakfast in us and figure out something to do today. I'm sick of waiting around."

He doesn't need to ask me twice. We eat.

The Explorer zooms over the hilly terrain down by the water. I have no idea where we're going. Glenn said there's someone we need to talk to. I keep picturing myself falling into convulsions en route, jerking and flailing about on the Eddie Bauer edition leather, but this does not happen.

We drive right along the beach, the water lapping up onto the sand and retreating in rhythmic pulses. Clouds block out the sun, keeping everything swathed in silvery light that seems cold somehow. I look out over the water that stretches as far as I can see.

"So what are we going to talk about?" I say.

"We probably won't talk about much," he says. "This guy we're going to see will likely do all of the talking. If we're lucky at some point he'll pause long enough for us to get out of there."

He squints and turns his head to get a better look at something on the side of the road.

"Here we go," Glenn says to himself.

He pulls the Explorer into a little area where traffic has worn the grass down to sandy ground. We get out and follow the similarly beaten trail slashing through the knee high grass. My feet sink into the sand with each step in a way that makes the going slow enough to be frustrating. Glenn's sandals snap like someone chewing gum really loud.

"So where are we going?" I say.

"Up here," he says and points to a little cabin sitting near where the grass gives way to the beach.

It's a rickety building, the wood exterior stained gray and black by years of rain. Yellowed newspaper covers the only window.

We step up onto the porch, and at first I think it's good to be off the sand and back on something solid. The boards groan and sag under foot, however, and that feeling fades. I can't help but imagine my foot sinking through a disintegrating rotten section and getting lodged ankle deep in porch upon my next step. This also doesn't happen.

Glenn knocks without response. After a few seconds, he knocks again, and something stirs inside. I want to ask him who we're about to talk to, but it seems too weird now that they must be right on the other side of the door.

A man with sallow cheeks and a stocking cap opens the door. He looks at Glenn with dead eyes and says:

"Yeah?"

Then his gaze shifts over to me, and his eyes don't look quite so dead all of the sudden. He perks up.

"Oh, hello there," he says. "I didn't know if you'd come by or not."

"Hi," I say. "I didn't know if I would either."

He pulls the hat off and scratches his head. I can't really tell how old he is. His hairline and crow's feet suggest he must be 45 or older, but his demeanor and attire seem much younger than that. He wears a baggy black hoodie, and his hair is styled into spikes which seem remarkably unaffected by the hat. I imagine him doing manifesting chants all day to keep his hair looking perfectly molded.

"Well, maybe you already know, but I'm Duncan," he says and holds out his hand, which I shake.

"I'm Jeff Grobnagger," I say. "And this is my friend Glenn."

"Right, of course," Duncan says, feigning attention Glenn's way for a split second. "Hey, Glenn. You two should come on in."

The inside of the place looks exactly how you'd expect the

inside of a rotting cabin on the beach to look. The two burning candles on top of wood crates turned tables probably provide more of a fire hazard than they do light. Between the candle flicker and the light coming through the newspaper on the window, everything tints a little yellow.

If the floors ever had any finish on them, all evidence of it is erased. There are eight or ten sleeping bags spread out on the floor, though – some currently occupied and some not.

"Have a seat," Duncan says, gesturing to an invisible piece of furniture.

Glenn and I sit on the floor.

"There are others, you know," Duncan says.

"Others?" I say.

"Like you," he says. "Other people having the dreams."

I look at Glenn, whom I realize hasn't said anything this whole time. He looks at Duncan. I can't decide if he has a great poker face or if he's genuinely super bored.

"Not the same exact dreams as you, I'm sure," Duncan says. "But you're not alone is all."

"How do you know that?" I say.

"Word gets around about these things," he says.

It even makes its way to a stoner hut on the beach, I guess.

"How many are there, do you think?" I say.

"Hard to say," he says. "I think probably at least 10 by now in the United States, but I think the number will grow at a faster and faster pace as time passes."

I mull this over, and Duncan pulls a little one-hitter pipe out of his hoodie pocket, fiddles with it and puts the lighter to it to hit it.

"Why faster?" I say.

He sucks on the pipe a moment longer and holds it. When he talks, his voice is all strained and stiff sounding due to the smoke retaining process.

"Well, I have a theory," he says.

He smirks as he exhales a bunch of smoke in Glenn's general direction.

"Human beings only use like 10% of their brains, right?" Duncan says, his voice mostly back to normal. "We know we have all of this untapped potential. Look at how things have changed in human history. For a long time, thousands of years, we were just hunter gatherers. Then we morphed to an agricultural, largely feudal existence. Then we turned into an industrial, urban society. And now computers and the internet and smart phones are changing everything again."

He checks the pipe with his thumb, decides it's cashed and taps it against the floor. The ashes spill out, and he grinds them into the wood floor with sole of one of his Chuck Taylor's.

"So for thousands of years we barely even used language and lived a nomadic life. Now we're building computers that can process unbelievable amounts of information per second," he says. "Each of these societal changes all but eradicated everything about the way of life that came before it. Once we could grow enough crops to sustain life, nobody would go back to being a nomad, right? Nor would anyone give up the internet to go back to working a feudal farm."

Glancing around the room, I wonder how different living in this sleeping bag cabin is from living in the dark ages. I look at Glenn. His poker face hasn't budged.

"I think what's happening to you and these other people having the dream is the next wave," Duncan says. "Maybe another few percent of your brain has been activated. Or maybe it's less scientific than that and more of a straight up spiritual change. I don't know exactly. But I think it will happen to more and more people until we're all changed. Or maybe one of you few will figure out what it's about and bring that nugget back to share with the rest of us, and that will change everything."

For some reason, this particular turn of phrase makes me picture myself bringing the McDonald's chicken McNugget that's shaped like a boot back from my dream to share with mankind. It is unclear whether or not I'd be able to bring barbeque sauce with that.

"Seems like a pretty loose theory," Glenn says through clenched teeth.

Not sure what he's so pissed about. Duncan laughs.

"Was it a loose theory when it was first suggested the Earth rotates around the sun?" he says to Glenn. "That's a pretty specific concept even if the rest of the details about the solar system and the galaxy and the universe weren't fleshed out just yet."

Glenn doesn't say anything.

"I'm not saying I know exactly what's going on," Duncan says. "I just think it has something to do with our next evolutionary leap is all."

Things fall silent a moment as Duncan goes back to fidgeting with his pipe, so I decide to chime in.

"So I take it you're not the one trying to kill me?" I say.

He laughs.

"Nah," he says. "There's nothing out there I really want to kill, least of all someone like you that might have a lesson to teach before long."

His forehead wrinkles up, and his face suddenly looks more grave.

"There are some you should worry about, though," he says. "That's for sure."

As we climb back into the car, a mix of emotions stir up inside me. I'm in some sense relieved to think that what is happening to me may be part of some bigger phenomenon. Even if it's only a handful of other people experiencing this, at least I'm not alone or insane. On the other hand, the way Duncan got all serious at the end about how I should be worried reignited my fear to some degree.

"I don't get it, though," I say.

Glenn cranks the wheel and the Explorer takes a curve into a dip over a steep hill fast enough to make my stomach flutter.

"What?" he says.

"If Duncan and the Disunion people aren't trying to kill me, and Babinaux and the League aren't trying to kill me," I say. "That only leaves the Sons of Man, right? The craziest of the crazies that no one even really knows about?"

"Maybe," Glenn says. "Maybe not."

"What's that supposed to mean?" I say.

"It's not so simple as that. You're taking everyone's word at face value," he says. "And you're also assuming the couple people we've talked to each represent their entire groups. The truth could be somewhere in the middle or something else entirely."

I ponder this.

"So we're getting nowhere," I say.

"There's no harm in talking to people, but as far as I'm

concerned, our situation hasn't changed much. It won't change until we figure out your dreams," he says. "That's the key to everything."

CHAPTER 14

Back at Glenn's, I do my chants, and then we sit around. Glenn makes martinis for himself. I decide to have one in hopes that it may somehow trigger a dream session. It doesn't, so I have another and another. It's been a long time, so this gets me pretty wasted.

At first that entails euphoria, but soon it slows everything down a bit. I start talking.

"I realized something about myself while watching the Price is Right once," I say. "See, the contestants always run up and hug the host and the models, right? No matter who these contestants are, they do this. Fat contestants. Skinny contestants. Old contestants. Young contestants. Doesn't matter. They all do it."

Glenn mixes another drink for himself while my monologue continues.

"And I realized that every time they did this, I cringed as it was happening and then watched in surprise as the host and models smiled and hugged them back each time. Like my subconscious expected, I guess, for the models to frown and pull away like the contestants were disgusting or something. And this wasn't because I found the people disgusting personally. It's because I would never run up and hug someone like that, because I would assume they'd find me disgusting.

"Disgusting isn't quite the right word, though. I don't feel like they'd retch on the spot, but it would be awkward. Everyone involved would feel kind of bad about it. I am not part of that somehow. Touching and all that.

"So I guess that must run pretty deep when you feel that self loathing on behalf of the contestants on the Price is Right, you know? You worry when they aren't bracing themselves for rejection."

Glenn takes a drink and looks at the floor. I figure I should stop talking about this, but I don't.

"There's something about physicality to it, I guess. I don't think it's just my looks, though that's part of it. It's that animal level that we don't understand about ourselves. The way dogs just know who the pack leader is. Some might test it a little, but they somehow know deep down all along who the big dog is like it's a wave in the air, and they obey that. Everyone can see something about me. That I don't belong somehow.

"When I signed the lease to my apartment, I got the same thing in a different way. I went to the manager's office, and there were people there. Office workers and some lady pushing the papers around and explaining everything and making copies and everything. And I was a little nervous. It wasn't too bad or anything, but they had me sign and initial about 10 sheets of paper for credit checks and all of that, and the lady kind of skimmed through them with me. I was sitting in silence with strangers for a decent interval, so it's tense in a way.

"Anyway, I realized that this lady going over the papers with me put her hand on my arm a lot when she talked to me, and she touched my shoulder when handing some papers from behind me. And this relieved me somehow. It made me feel accepted and surprised about it. Not like it was anything sexual or arousing or even slightly stimulating or anything like that. It was more basic than that. Just kindness, you know. I guess I must feel like I'm so repulsive that even someone putting a hand on my arm surprises me. That almost insignificant level of approval astounds me.

"Even thinking back, I start thinking that she must have done it without thinking. Or maybe it's like a customer service or sales skill they've learned, that you can put people at ease by touching them and make the transaction easier. Part of my brain still won't accept it at face value, even though it's nothing of significance.

"Even when I go to the dentist, I feel really thankful afterward. Thankful to the point of being humbled. I feel like they did something for me that they didn't have to do. Like I'm not worth having my teeth cleaned or something, but they performed this stunning act of charity anyway. I have to remind myself that it's just a service I paid for. It's not personal for them. And then in a way that actually bums me out cause I have to think about how they don't actually care. They weren't actually doing me some favor and taking care of me out of kindness or compassion. They're just doing their job. And something is wrong with me to feel this way.

"I guess the way I think of it is that on some animal level I've been rejected. Rejected by the species, I guess. I'm not part of that part of being a human. I can't connect with other people on that level. I am outside of that. I don't mean this in some maudlin 'it's so hard being me' way or anything. It is the order I have observed in the world, and I accept it the same way that I accept that when I drop things they fall onto the floor because of gravity.

"There's no use getting all upset about it and cursing God and moaning to the heavens. I figure none of us will be here for that long either way."

Glenn slurps down the last of his drink. I can see from the lines in his face that he's still processing what I've said.

"Listen kid," he says. "You can't say shit like that. You have to-"

But before he can say what I have to do, I realize that I'm falling off the stool at the snack bar. The world fades to black before I hit the floor.

For once, I know where I am before I open my eyes. I see the alley sprawl before me in my mind before I even regain consciousness. This seems significant. Like now that I've been doing my chants, all of my life force is prepared for this. My willpower is a loaded gun waiting to go off.

I go about untying my foot and lowering myself to the ground. I walk through the mud puddles and stop at the dumpster. I can see what's inside it before I pop the lid. I can feel it.

The lid swings free, and a gigantic axe sits atop the garbage pile. This is no lumberjack axe. It's probably best described as a "video game axe." It's the ornate medieval style battle axe I've been imagining here for the past couple of days. I think I literally got the image from the cover of some role playing game in the closet at Glenn's, and now I have willed it into existence on whatever plane this dream is transpiring.

I lift it, and it has a good amount of heft to it. It feels heavy, but not too heavy. It's about the right weight to take a hooded head clean off, I'd say.

I smile.

Any minute now a hooded man will come barreling out of nowhere and get axe murdered by me.

So that's good.

I wait, though. This seems to be taking longer than normal. I can't help but consider the notion that as soon as I'm armed he won't show for the sake of irony. Or maybe he's one upping me by digging out a couple of sawed off shotguns. That would be just like him.

But no, he comes rambling around the corner just like always. He doesn't slow down when he spies my axe, which is a little intimidating in a way. Pretty brazen.

As he closes in, it's like the whole world goes into slow motion. I wind up, pulling the axe behind my head and bringing my arms straight up. The weapon hovers there a moment, waiting for him to come into range. I uncoil and everything goes back to full speed as I give him a double fisted chop to the chest. The force of this feels insane and brings a violently abrupt stop to his forward momentum. The axe blade buries itself deep in his sternum region. I release the handle, and he drops to his knees, the axe still planted in his chest. His arms dangle as limp as noodles at his sides. I give him a shove to make sure he falls on his back. I can't think of any good reason to do this except that it was how I always pictured it when I did my chants.

He doesn't twitch or writhe in agony. He lies still.

So this is it. I've vanquished the hooded bastard.

I yell a wordless scream. I feel invincible. I feel like no matter what is thrown at me, I will strike it down and crush it.

If someone dares to speak ill of me, I will pluck their words from the air and send them echoing back to destroy their master.

I feel powerful. I feel like the answer to every question I might ever ask is, "Yes."

A jolt runs all through me. I guess it must be adrenalin. A tingle that centers around my chest and courses up and down my arms and legs in waves that somehow feel electric and liquid at the same time.

My breath heaves hot through my teeth, and cold sweat drips from the corners of my brow.

Something isn't quite right, though. I run back through the event in my mind, feeling the force of the axe colliding with the torso again. I look at the body lying motionless in the alley before me.

"Now what?" I say.

I look at the sky and see only gray, though. Not clouds even, just a shapeless gray heaven above. It almost seems greasy somehow. Like if I dabbed a napkin at the sky, it'd come away all orange and heavy with wet.

"Now what?" I repeat, yelling this time.

The hooded man starts quivering on the ground. His arms and legs shake about for a moment and then go rigid. He sits up halfway and hops to his feet in one motion. His fingers latch onto the axe handle and pull at it, yanking it free from his ribcage after three jerks. He tosses it aside and moves toward me.

I don't run away. I accelerate toward him, get low and drive my shoulders into his belly, tackling him. My face grinds into his open chest wound for a moment during the take down, and his blood smears my face and gushes into my eyes like ketchup out of a packet. I blink a few times, but it doesn't help much. All I can see is black blur with a ring of red around it. I feel him under me and find his neck, crushing it with my hands.

He fights at me, clawing and pushing and grabbing, but I've got him good. I squeeze and don't let go.

After a time, he stops squirming. I bring my t-shirt to my eyes and start trying to wipe clear the blood. This doesn't work very well. I can see a little bit, but I need some liquid to flush the blood out.

I crawl toward where I think the axe landed and my hand lands in a mud puddle. Ah. I lean down and scoop handfuls of water to my eyeballs. The blur starts to change shape a bit. It turns more red than black.

Just as my vision is partially restored, something heavy shoves my face into the puddle and bashes my teeth into the asphalt. I scream, but it doesn't sound like much coming from underwater. An impotent gurgle, I guess.

I buck once, throwing him off balance enough to scrabble forward away from the mud puddle and turn over onto my back. I still can't really see, though. I try to feel around for the axe, but it's useless. He's on me again, and this time his hands find my throat quickly. Maybe it's because I can't see, but something about the way his hands feel all hard on my neck reminds me of an insect.

I know he's smaller than me now, though, and I must have a reach advantage, so I reach out for his face. My left thumb gets inside his cheek, and I rip at that as hard I can. He makes weird pained noises that sound like a kid. I want to laugh, but it's hard with the lack of oxygen. I kind of hiss instead. My right hand skims over his cheek and finds his eye. I dig at that, but he arches his neck and back to get away.

I don't even care if he kills me at this point.

The only thing I want in the universe is to pop that fucking eye out.

I reach out again and my fingers brush over his teeth and nose. I find the eye and dig again, but I don't have the strength left to do much. My hand feels too far away to get any power behind it. My fingers feel almost numb, and he slides away from me again.

My chest spasms as my body tries to breathe even though it can't. My lungs burn and feel like they'll explode soon, which doesn't make much sense in a way – to explode from emptiness. This is an unpleasant feeling, but it's one I'm growing used to.

The world fades in and out in black and red pulses now. I reach out once more and get a pretty good fingernail scrape on his eye socket. I can feel his skin wedged under my nails, and I can tell it's effective as he repeats the weird childlike squeal from earlier.

I guess sometimes in life you have to settle for a pretty good eye scrape rather than ripping the eye out of its socket like you might like. Maybe that is my life lesson for today.

And then everything fades into nothing.

CHAPTER 15

I wake on the couch at Glenn's, and he looks up from his newspaper with his reading glasses perched on the tip of his nose. He raises his eyebrows to wordlessly ask how it went. I shake my head, and his eyebrows slowly drift down into disappointment.

Disappointment is not what I feel, though. I think I'm numb to that type of emotion just now. My head is too full of flames for all that. I want blood. I want to rip out that hooded fucker's heart. I want to eat his face. He can kill me over and over again so long as he suffers just the same.

"I manifested a sweet axe," I say. "And I plunged that shit deep in his chest. It killed him, but he came back. I choked him to death, and he came back again. Then he got me."

I bring my hands to my neck to pantomime choking. Glenn looks out at the room in thought, removes the glasses, rubs his t-shirt on the lenses and puts them back on.

"Maybe we've been on the wrong track," he says.

"Is there actually a right track?" I say. "Cause it seems more like someone just wants to torture me. They bring me someplace just to kill me time and again. I can't see how there can be any purpose in it."

"There must be," he says, pulling the glasses off again and squinting at the lenses. "We'll find it."

I don't know what to say, so I stare at the wall. Glenn huffs breath on the glasses, steams them up, wipes them again.

"At least you're starting to learn how powerful your mind is," he says. "I used to box, and I realized after a while that it's not physical strength that separates fighters. It's not quickness or hand speed or athleticism or even skill, exactly, that makes one guy knock out another. Those things matter, but it's more about mental strength. It's will power. The guy that wants it more, hits harder. The guy that won't be denied isn't."

I have a hard time picturing Glenn in the ring.

"When did you box?" I say.

"Just amateur stuff when I was a teenager," he says. "What I'm saying, though, isn't just that whoever wants to win will win. Everybody wants to win. It's the guy that wants to win so bad, he'll do all the things he doesn't want to do to get there. When every fiber of his being is exhausted and wants to quit, he'll keep going. It's toughness, and it's discipline, and that takes a lot of practice and hard work, right? It's just that all of that work is more about the mental than physical is all."

The room falls silent for a beat.

"Not to change the subject or nothing," Glenn says. "But have you ever had a girlfriend?"

"Yeah," I say.

I hear some defensiveness in my voice, which makes me feel dumb. I clear my throat like the defensiveness can be passed off as some kind of throat malfunction.

"Oh, OK," he says. "Just you seemed so freaked out when Louise asked you out the other night that it made me wonder."

"Well, she didn't ask so much as order me to take her out," I say. "How did I seem freaked out, though?"

"You were making this face," he says. "And then you turned all red and stuff. It was pretty funny."

"Oh," I say.

I look down at the wrinkles on my shirt and smooth them out with my knuckles.

"Anything serious?" Glenn says.

"Huh?" I say.

"Your girlfriends," he says. "Were any of them serious?"

"Oh," I say. "Yeah. One."

I keep knuckle smoothing the spot on my shirt even though the wrinkles are long gone.

"So do you want to just tell me about it, or should I pry it out with a series of questions?" he says.

I sigh.

"We lived together for a couple of years. This was a little over five years ago," I say. "Had this shitty little apartment in the ghetto. She picked it out cause she liked the way it was decorated. It had this ornate crown molding, and the color schemes were all antique. It was an old building. Built in the 1840s, I think."

Glenn interrupts me:

"It's great to hear the history of the architecture and all, but did this girl have a name?"

"Oh," I say. "No, she didn't have a name. It was pretty weird. Had to kind of point and grunt to communicate with her. Anyway, my point is that this building was old as hell."

Glenn does this move where his eyes roll and he lets his head fall all limp at the same time. It's a pretty effective display of disgust. Kind of funny, even.

"Alright, fine," I say. "Her name was Allie. Well, Allison,

but everybody called her Allie."

Glenn nods.

"Anyway, we lived together for a while," I say. "When we first met we went to a lot of parties and got wasted and stuff, but we kind of realized over time that we liked staying home more. Watching movies. Reading. Writing. So we got this apartment and mostly did that. It's crazy in a way, cause the world outside was more fucked up than ever in that neighborhood. Our next door neighbor got murdered by a burglar. The cops were around all the time, and it seems like fireworks went off every 15 minutes year round. Maybe that's why we retreated to the inside world more. I don't know. It was a pretty fun time, I guess. I still have a lot of dreams that take place in that apartment."

"So what happened, then?" he says. "Why did you break up?"

"Well, at first we did everything together. We spent a lot of time analyzing the books and movies we read and watched and stuff like that," I say. "But then I started making all this money playing poker, and she kind of got into her own things."

Things get all quiet while I try to think of how to say it right.

"I don't know," I say. "I guess it's probably more my fault, really. I withdrew into the poker world, you know? All I cared about was winning money. Everything else was boring. I don't even know if it was the money or the winning that I liked more."

I shift in my seat and more wrinkles appear on my shirt, so I smooth them out again.

"Once you get started down that path, though, where one

partner withdraws a little bit, it all goes bad," I say. "I realized after a while that she didn't want to have sex with me anymore."

Glenn interrupts me again:

"Let me stop you right there and ask you a crucial question: Was she hot?"

I grit my teeth. I should have known he'd ask this. Whatever, though. It was a long time ago, like it's not even real anymore.

"Well," I say. "Yeah."

"Good," Glenn says. "Good. OK, continue."

"Hmm..." I say. "No, you messed me up. I'm done."

He leans forward in his seat, the newspaper sliding off of his lap.

"No," he says. "Unacceptable. You will finish the damn story."

"Nope."

"Come on," he says. "Maybe I want to offer some fatherly advice or some goddamn thing, right? Can't do it without the details."

Whatever. Probably better to just get it over with, I guess.

"Fine," I say. "I kind of withdrew into crushing people at poker, and at some point she withdrew, too. I sort of realized that she didn't want to have sex with me anymore after a while. I don't know if she was even conscious of this."

Glenn purses his lips.

"See, I don't blame her," I say. "I wasn't mad about it or anything, I mean. I wouldn't want to have sex with me either. But then it was important somehow, too. Like it was broken between us after that. Not that sex even matters that much on some level, but once you feel rejected that way… I don't know."

"You make a habit of finding rejection everywhere," he says.

"I guess so," I say. "So of course I didn't want to have sex with her after that, either. I mean, why would I want to be with someone who doesn't want me, you know? But I had all of these mixed feelings, I guess. I didn't want to hold it against her. It's not like she got to choose that feeling. But it was also the reality of the situation, even if she didn't know it yet. It was the big truth. How she really felt about me deep down on some animal level. What are you supposed to do, you know?"

Glenn's lips part. I expect fatherly advice to come pouring out any second, but all I get is:

"Yeah."

His word hangs in the air, and then things get all quiet again. We sit. I find this silence more frustrating than usual. I mean, what the hell? People pry a bunch of personal shit out of you, and then don't say anything? But of course. Of course. I get it. This kind of rejection is so painful there is nothing much to say about it, yeah? People aren't supposed to actually talk about shit like this, right? They aren't supposed to communicate the things that hurt them. Oh, it makes great entertainment – just the same way that people roll by a car accident real slow because they might get lucky and see some blood or a bashed in skull. But nobody wants to actually talk to me about this. They just want to crane their neck as they drive by, so they have a juicy story to tell later.

That's why I stay at home. That's why I don't fucking talk to people in the first place. Jesus fuck.

By now I'm pretty worked up. My mouth starts talking

again, whether I want it to or not.

"You ever think about how pointless it is to be a man?" I say. "It's like our part in the life cycle is just jizzing. I remember this Rodney Dangerfield joke about how everything in the universe makes perfect sense, how you're surrounded by harmony and happiness… and then you cum. I think there's a nugget of truth in that. We're wired with this built in illusion that if we can just find a mate and have sex, we'll be fulfilled on some religious level or something. And as it's happening, sometimes it feels like something is complete. But it's just another lie. As soon as it's over, you can feel that. It's not even a real connection with someone in a way. It's emptiness. That's our role in humanity. Pumping out sperm. You're always alone no matter what you do, I think."

Glenn clears his throat.

"Why do you have to be so morbid all the time? Or so morose or whatever you want to call it?" he says. "Listen kid, I understand what you're saying, but you're wrong. There are meaningful things on this planet, no matter what you might believe."

He slams his hand on the end table and the ice cubes in his cup shift and make a glassy wet sound.

"It is a goddamn miracle to be alive at all," he says. "To be conscious of the world around you and try to understand its mysteries. Maybe life isn't some grand narrative with a spectacular ending like you might want. It's a series of moments. They might seem too random to add up to mean something huge, but they each mean the world on their own. You listen to the way a child describes a tree frog stuck to a window. You stand on the beach and feel a rush as the wind embraces you and tries to move you out of the way. You spend a long night drinking and talking with friends that know you better than you know yourself. You meet a girl at a party and listen to her talk and let the way she sees the world capture your imagination. You hold your baby daughter in your arms and think about how she'll get to share so many of these moments with you. And every one of these occasions is a world within a world. A little sliver of time where the doors to your imagination open up and anything is possible. You don't worry about yesterday or tomorrow. You just are for a while."

I don't say anything. I think maybe Glenn is getting emotional. Because of the daughter thing.

"But you? It's like your soul is sick from too much time in the dark," he says. "You've got to get out into the light before it's too late, Grobnagger. The meaning of life is all around us, man. You just gotta surround yourself with the people you care about and get lost in a moment for as long as you can. That's all you can do."

CHAPTER 16

I squirm on the couch at night, the blanket twisting around me like a boa constrictor. Instead of sleeping, I can't stop thinking about what Glenn said. I mean, I guess in some ways he's right. For other people, anyway. I am outside of all of that. There is no happy ending in store for me. No family is going to surround me with warmth and love some day.

Nobody hears that, though, when you say it. It's like when a swimsuit model goes on a talk show and says how shy she is and how she hates having her picture taken, and from there it segues to showing a bunch of the latest photos of her in a bikini with oiled up skin and eyes staring into the camera with the same exact look in every photo that I guess is supposed to be sensual or seductive or something. She describes the location that no one actually cares about. (You could just say "the beach," I think. Good enough.) Do these people not realize that there are people who actually don't have their picture taken? Ever. They'd rather just sit in a room for a lifetime and die alone than have their picture taken.

Because they are hurt inside, I guess. Their physical existence is like an injury they can never recover from, and it makes it bleed all the more to have to look at moments of it frozen in time. To even know that the photos are out there and other people might see them.

So there's a difference. A lot of what people say that sounds hurtful toward themselves is false modesty. Deep down, it's just a more indirect, comfortable way of saying: "I am awesome and special. Here are like 20 pictures of me in bikini that I would like you to broadcast on television."

Some people really mean that shit, though. They say hurtful things because they are hurt. It's not manipulative. It's what they believe in their hearts.

Whatever. I sit up and feel around, find my glass of water on the end table, drink, put it back.

I know all of this, and now what am I doing? Getting ready to go on some date with Louise tomorrow. The ultimate pointlessness. It's too bad in a way. You'd think that with me being quite aware that this date will lead nowhere and serve no purpose beyond wasted time, I'd be able to not feel nervous about it. Why feel nervous about something that doesn't matter, right?

But no, no. I get the worst of both worlds. I get overwhelming nervousness – I'd say it's 50/50 that I'll puke an hour or two before the date from nerves – and I don't get any hope of this meaning something down the road.

If I had the guts, I'd cancel, of course. It's too awkward, though. And she could be a source of information for us, and I can't let Glenn's hunt for his daughter fall apart because I wouldn't go out with some girl.

So here I am. Awake in the dark, twisting the knife in my wounds. What a goddamn delight life really is.

I spin and roll around on the couch some more. The blanket cinches around me again, and I kind of wish it would constrict all the way and squeeze the life out of me for real.

CHAPTER 17

I pace up and down the hall. It's 5:45 PM. Soon it will be 6. Then it will be 7. And at 7 I have to take Louise out. Or maybe it's more accurate to say that she will take me out. Not sure.

I haven't puked.

Yet.

"Relax," Glenn calls from the other room.

"I can't," I say.

He may as well tell someone that just got stabbed to "Quit bleeding!"

I hear him go to work on something in the kitchen – running water, pouring liquid into something, opening the cupboard, closing it. The sounds echo down the hall with ever varying levels of reverb. I'm acutely aware of the way the reflections of the sound seem to shift and alter themselves as I walk my beat. I guess adrenalin heightens your senses.

After the brief stir of noise, all goes silent, and I return my focus to pacing. My mind wanders around to other moments of dread such as this. Excruciating waits before other dates a long time ago when I still thought dates could lead to something. Times I spent bouncing my knee for 20 or 30 minutes while the dentist dicked around before finally getting down to drilling holes in my teeth. Sitting motionless for seemingly endless stretches at the breakfast table so I wouldn't be too early for school and have to wait around in even more discomfort there.

"Come here," Glenn says from the kitchen.

"What?" I say.

"Come here," he says louder.

"No, I mean what do you want?" I say. "I'm not going in there if you're just going to tell me to calm down again."

"I made something for you, dick face," he says.

"Oh," I say.

I walk into the kitchen, and Glenn thrusts a mug at me. Steam coils off of the top of it.

"What's this?" I say.

The heat from the side of the cup stings my fingers for a moment before I change my grip to the handle.

"It's an ancient elixir to soothe the spirit," he says.

"For real?" I say.

He nods.

"I got the recipe out of some antique alchemical book during my research," he says. "A blend of various roots and a few… well… rather odd ingredients."

"Like what?"

"I probably shouldn't tell you," he says. "Just drink."

I start raising the cup to my lips, hesitate.

"Maybe you should tell me," I say.

"You really want to know?" he says.

"Well, yeah," I say.

"It's chamomile tea with a little honey, you dummy," he says. "I was just messing with you."

It is at this moment I notice the box of honey vanilla chamomile on the counter. Yeah.

"It will calm your nerves, though," he says. "I can assure

you that the magic of chamomile is very real."

Louise picks me up shortly after I finish my third chamomile tea. (Vomit free. Proud to be.) She drives a black Volkswagen Passat. Part of me thinks of this as a low end rich person car, but I don't know that much about cars, so I could be way off on that.

They're all the same to me. Cars, I mean. Four wheels? Check. Moves from point A to point B? Check. End of check list.

"You ready?" she says as I climb into the vehicle. She seems all smiley now, less sarcastic than when I saw her last.

"I guess so," I say. After I say it, I think about how unenthused that must sound, so I smile and do this head tilt thing that I think seems lighthearted or whimsical or some other more enthusiastic thingy.

She just keeps on smiling. You know how after a while a smile gets almost creepy? Well, let's just say she's flirting with that right now. Hovering smack dab in that danger zone, about a pubic hair away from seeming like an evil clown. I realize I said her teeth were among her good qualities, but this smile is getting outlandish.

She rolls the windows down as we back out of Glenn's driveway, and when we get up to speed, her hair flutters and whooshes around in the wind. Her cat eye sunglasses perform double duty, functioning as hair goggles along with dimming the glare of the sun.

"Do you like Thai food?" she says. She talks all loud so I can hear her over the wind.

"Yeah," I say. I nod an exaggerated nod rather than talking

loud. Less obnoxious, I think.

I bet you can't guess what she does in response.

Yep.

She smiles.

We pull into the lot of the restaurant. The sign says simply, "Thai Cuisine," and it has a rose on it. It looks like a new building – a brick plaza housing a few places of business under green awnings – but the other store fronts are empty as of yet.

Even so, the place is packed. We find a parking spot on the opposite side of the lot.

"Damn. Looks pretty busy," she says.

I nod.

The nervousness builds as we cross the fresh blacktop, my stomach flopping around in my gut like a furious rainbow trout stranded on a muddy bank somewhere. Heat reflects from the surface of the ground, trying to smother us before we can go eat this food. It'd be a mercy.

I never go out to eat. I hate it. I presume other people find some form of comfort in being in a room full of strangers, being waited on and all of that. I guess it's like a social activity for them. When I'm in a room full of random people, though, I'm looking for exits. I'm scanning for a heavy object I could use as a weapon if I'm attacked. For real. I don't know how many times I've pictured myself bashing someone's skull in with a plaque listing recent employees of the month I've ripped from the wall in my imagination, or plunging the pointy end of a mounted sword fish into some poor bastard's throat.

I don't know why these people in my day dreams would even want to mess with me at this point. I can be quite ruthless.

In any case, today I will play along. I will go out to eat

against my better judgment. I'm guessing I will not enjoy it, but I shall march bravely into certain defeat like a good soldier in any case.

To my surprise, the greeter hustles us right over to one of maybe two empty tables in the place. Good timing, I guess. It's even a corner table, and I get to sit in a position where I can see everyone with no one behind me. I won't outright say that this is ideal. Ideal would be not being here at all. Under the circumstances, however, these conditions are favorable.

We order drinks. She opts for Sierra Mist. I stick with ice water.

"Just water, huh?" she says. I think she is teasing me, maybe.

"Well, you basically just ordered a glass of root canals," I say. "All of that acid and sugar."

She laughs at this, probably harder than the comment deserves.

While we're looking at the menu I scan through some weapon possibilities: steak knife, soy sauce bottle and overturned chair look to be the best possibilities, likely in that order, though the circumstances of any impending attack could change that. In an absolute emergency, I guess I could jam a chopstick in some dude's eye. There's not much to speak of on the walls near us, but that's OK. I'm confident I could do a lot of damage with a steak knife.

I order pad Thai, she requests Masaman curry, and the waiter brings the food out fairly quickly.

"How is it?" she says, gripping a wad of noodles in her chopsticks.

"It's good," I say. "It's almost great."

I twirl noodles onto my fork before I finish my thought:

"It tastes like a dish of really good food mixed with about a quarter cup of garbage juice."

She laughs so hard at this and brings a hand up to cover her mouth in case she projectile laughs anything out of there, I guess. Pink splotches form along her jaw, and her cheeks get all red. Her eyes flood with tears almost immediately.

I was being serious, though. In fact, the garbage juice taste reminds me of huddling in that dumpster with the dead dog right before the hooded man stabbed me in the sternum. Compared to going out to eat, those were good times.

Sigh.

"How about your food?" I say as the laughing slows a bit.

She wipes tears from her eyes before answering.

"It's pretty delicious," she says. "Not even a hint of garbage juice."

She reaches across the table to put her hand on my arm before adding another comment more quietly:

"I know what you mean, though, about that hint of funkiness."

She starts laughing, and for a second I think she's going to lose it again, but she reels it in a moment before it gets away from her. Her hand lingers on my arm all that time before she retracts it to resume eating, and a wave of comfort washes over me, though I only partially accept this as really happening.

So now I don't know what to think. Am I the biggest jerk? Thinking about her smile the way I did and everything? An evil clown? Maybe she was just being nice, and I'm a creepy weirdo.

Or maybe this sense of acceptance is the same lie as always, and even if she thinks something between us could be real, she won't think it for long. She will figure out how things really are.

"What do you want to do after this?" she says, interrupting my internal crisis.

"I don't know," I say.

"What does the great Jeffrey Grobnagger do for fun?" she says.

I think about this for a few seconds but nothing springs to mind.

"I don't know," I say.

She chuckles. I wonder if her teeth are getting dry with all this air time.

"You don't know?" she says.

"Just… like… normal stuff," I say. I scratch an imaginary itch on my lip.

"Geez," she says, her eyes going wide. "I didn't mean to make you so uncomfortable."

The smile fades. Something about this seems so stiff now that I can re-detach:

"Well, I didn't know you were going to be grilling me like this!" I say.

The smile rises like the phoenix. And a calm comes over me. With nothing to gain or lose here, I don't need to be so serious. The sillier I am, the more fun she will have, and that makes me feel better.

"So how's life in the private detective business?" I say. "Do you mostly spy on cheating spouses or what?"

"There is a lot of spouse stuff along with background checks," she says. "It's mostly more boring than people might assume."

"Work is work," I say. "But it's not like you're an

accountant or whatever. Look at this undercover thing you've got going now. More exciting than doing eight hours of math a day."

Her mouth is full, so she gestures her hands in a way that I interpret as halfhearted agreement.

"I'll assume you don't need to ask what I do for a living," I say.

Her smile takes on a more devilish quality.

"Oh, I know all about you," she says.

"I hear that with disturbing frequency of late," I say.

We eat for a while.

"From a distance, my job probably seems fascinating," she says. "But ultimately I spend the day digging up other people's dirt. And once you realize that everyone's dirt is pretty much the same, it's nothing to get excited about. We all have more or less the same things hiding behind the façade. And then we judge everyone else for flaws that aren't unlike our own. After a while, it occurs to you that it's more sad than exciting."

"Well said," I say. "Still better than being an accountant, though."

We eat a while.

"So it's kind of weird," I say. "That you have this case watching the cults, but you don't believe any of the stuff."

"Why is that weird?" she says.

"Well, I guess it's not that weird, necessarily," I say. "But I mean, we're here together because of my dreams even though you think they're completely fake."

"I think you're having the dreams," she says. "I just think they're dreams."

"Maybe that's the weird thing," I say. "I kind of feel like a lot people want to believe in my dreams. Even if they have doubts, they intuitively want something in there to be real, yeah? I get just the opposite from you."

She takes a bite of food.

"I believe in what's here and now," she says. "What I can see, what I can touch, those are real. Everything else is wishful thinking."

This reminds me of Glenn's talk of quantum physics.

"So you think consciousness just arises from any sufficiently complex cluster of cells," I say. "You think we're just neurons functioning to process information and nothing more?"

"I guess so, yeah," she says.

"Do we have free will, then?" I say. "Or are we just functioning cells?"

"I don't know," she says. "If science says we're just functioning cells, that seems like the most plausible explanation."

Her eyes fall to her plate. She looks sad.

CHAPTER 18

On the way out of the restaurant, a man in a black suit and sunglasses approaches. He looks vaguely familiar.

"Jeff Grobnagger," he says.

"Yeah," I say.

"Ms. Babinaux needs to speak with you," he says. He gestures an arm toward the cars in the lot. I scour through the vehicles. No limo, of course.

"She's in the Lincoln?" I say.

He nods. I turn to Louise:

"I get this a lot," I say.

This is an exaggeration, of course, but the opportunity seems too good to pass up. I am in a weird mood.

"The lady comes with me," I say to the man.

"Whatever, dude," he says.

So yeah. This guy is a novice.

We enter the backseat. With three of us, it's actually pretty cramped, and I wind up in the middle so I'm smushed between two ladies. Better than being smushed between two dudes? Absolutely. But not that comfortable, even so.

"Hello," Ms. Babinaux says, eying Louise. Her eyelids seem to convey annoyance even though she is smiling. "You must be Jeff's friend?"

She holds a hand out for Louise to shake.

"This is Louise," I say. "She's cool."

I say this last part with that dramatic delivery people sometimes employ when they mean that someone does drugs or is OK with such activities. Lotta gravitas and perhaps a sense of grandeur. Of course I don't mean it about drugs. I mean she knows about my dumb dreams and all of that.

"Louise, this is Ms. Babinaux," I say. "She is a mysterious figure that periodically meets with me here in the backseat of her car to give vague advice regarding my dream situation."

Louise laughs.

"Yes," Ms. Babinaux says. "Yes."

If eyelids could kill. Holy crap!

"Well, I just wanted to check up on you," Ms. Babinaux says. "Things have been so quiet these past few days."

"I'm great," I say. "Everything is normal, so um… Louise is a private detective, actually. Pretty exciting line of work, I'd say."

Ms. Babinaux struggles to find words in response, her mouth hanging open a moment.

"That's… interesting," she says, her eyes flicking to Louise.

The nervous energy in the car is just right. I can't resist antagonizing Babinaux a bit.

"Yep. It would be improprietous to talk about some of the things she has surely seen during the course of her investigations," I say. "Adultery. Embezzlement. Bestialities. So let's just say she's cracked more than a few cases wide open without getting into all the sordid details and leave it at that."

Louise continues laughing. You know what? Unless I explicitly mention that she is not laughing during our time in Babinaux's car, you should probably assume she is. The misshapen pink and red circles splotch her face again, and tears pour from her eyes. A less modest man might even say that the tears gush from her eyes, but that feels a little boastful to me.

"I am more than willing to leave it at that," Ms. Babinaux says. She's a little pink herself by this time.

"Well, great," I say. "So that just about wraps this up from my end."

"Yes," Ms. Babinaux says. "Perhaps that's all for now."

It occurs to me that maybe Louise's presence has bothered her more than I would have guessed. It's not like Babinaux's trust is beyond question, though. Despite her claims of being my ally, she's done little to help me in any practical sense.

I elbow Louise in the ribs to get the process of getting out of here moving, but she sticks her hand out to Babinaux first.

"Nice meeting you," she says.

"Likewise," Babinaux says.

The handshake seems awkward, and it crosses my mind that they could be working together. I think Glenn might even say that they're "in cahoots." I've never actually heard him say this, but I could imagine it somehow. Then again, maybe the handshake is just awkward because I mentioned bestialities and sort of blocked Babinaux from talking to me for real. Hard to say.

Once Louise is out of the car, Babinaux grabs my arm.

"We'll talk soon," she says, her voice hushed and grave.

"Sure," I say.

I step out of the car, and when Louise makes eye contact with me, she begins giggling again. We embark on the trek across the lot to the Passat.

"That was ridiculous," she says.

"Yeah," I say.

I hear Babinaux's Lincoln start up behind us and the creak of the tires turning as the car backs out of its parking spot.

"What do you think she wanted?" she says.

"I don't know," I say. "I should've said lascivious."

"What?" she says.

"Instead of 'all of the sordid details,' I should have said 'all of the lascivious details,'" I say. "It's funnier, I think. Slightly less of a cliché."

Louise shakes her head, and the conversation dies. I can't help but consider the way she was quick to pump me for information, though whether it means anything or not, I'll probably never know.

I trip on the curb and stumble forward into a running fall. After six lunging paces, I slide safely into home base… except on the pavement between two cars and without a base. Immediately at the end of my slide, though, I put my fist under my chin and kind of kick my legs in a lighthearted way like a kid lying on the floor while they watch cartoons.

"Looked like a good place to sprawl out," I say, even though I know that nobody thinks I'm cool.

Louise chuckles.

I gather myself and we move on.

We climb back into the Passat and drive. No destination in mind. Just driving.

I watch the world slide past out the window. Usually I think the city looks like something that should wash down the gutter with a good rain – shattered concrete, crumbling buildings. Flush it all away, I often think. I don't know if we're in a particularly nice part of town or something, but it doesn't look so bad just here. The shadows of the tree limbs stretch across the glint of the sunlit spots in a way that somehow makes this place seem more interesting than usual. Less tired.

Usually the city seems like a dead end street, but tonight it feels like an open road. It's a nice night all around, really. A little humid, I guess.

"I know!" Louise says, and her driving seems to take on a purpose. Her turns get tighter and more aggressive. I can feel the decisiveness.

I try to get some information out of her concerning where we're headed, but she won't budge. It's a surprise, I guess. The thing I hate about surprises is being surprised by them.

The Passat whips around a curved entryway into a small parking lot next to a cemetery. Louise exits the car, and I follow her lead. I scan the horizon for signs of a business nearby for a moment before I realize that we've arrived at our destination. We're going to the cemetery.

"You scared?" she says, leading me through the gates.

"Yes," I say, and I shiver in mock fright.

She smiles. She does not laugh. Can't win 'em all, I guess.

Rows of grave stones populate the expanse of grass on a massive hillside that arcs up and up into the distance. I feel small standing at the bottom of it. Pathways gash brown lines into the green, forming a crisscross that looks like a weird road map on the ground. We follow the widest path, which veers around one of the many massive trees and then heads up the hill.

"You know anyone here?" I say.

"No," she says. "Nothing like that. This place just catches

my eye when I go by. I've always wanted to walk around up here."

I can see the appeal, I guess. It's probably the biggest cemetery I've ever seen in person, and it runs over some rolling hills, which somehow makes it seem even bigger and more impressive.

"It is substantial," I say. I sweep my arms out to the sides in a way that I believe implies immensity.

She laughs.

"Substantial," she says. "Been a while since I heard that one come up in conversation, I think."

I shrug.

The sun's descent hits the point where everything looks like a dimmed, half gray version of itself, which is heightened in certain areas by all of the shade the trees cast. A few strands of sunlight weave through the branches and leaves to shine wavering yellow light onto the face of an Angel statue atop one grave, but I can't decide if the image is more striking or strange.

"Don't you think it's interesting?" she says. "All the graves. All the people. Reading their names."

She gestures at a stone with the last name Junkin on it. Closer inspection reveals a teddy bear etched into the granite. It seems Matthew Allen Junkin only made it from 1986 to 1988, 19 months.

"Yeah," I say. "It's interesting."

Her smile fades out like the light around us. We walk in silence. I think we're both still thinking about the teddy bear.

"Isn't it crazy, though?" I say.

"What?" she says. She sounds far away.

"Somebody's baby died, and the world just kept going like it was nothing," I say. "Doesn't it seem like the world should stop when something that awful happens?"

She doesn't say anything.

"But then you realize it happens every day," I say. "Like the lady on the other side of town that left her three toddlers alone in their apartment last January. The place caught on fire, and there was nobody there to help them get out."

She swallows.

"And the city just carries on like nothing happened," I say. "I mean, I get it, but it still doesn't seem right in a way, you know?"

"Yeah," she says.

Her smile is now an outright frown, and it occurs to me that perhaps alluding to the charred bodies of children wasn't the best first date move.

Some Don Juan I turned out to be.

At the top of the hill, the broader trail forks off into two skinnier paths. We swerve left, deeper into the cemetery. I kind of thought we'd head back, but I guess not. We don't talk for quite a while. The leaves above us hiss in the airflow. It's not a windy day, but I guess there's a little air moving up there. By the time she speaks again, it's almost all the way dark.

"You're right," she says.

"What?" I say.

"The world will move on without us," she says. "But we're here for a little while. That's something."

And then her eyes are closed, and she's leaning, leaning – kissing me. And my eyes close, and our lips part, and her arms wrap around me and one hand moves to the back of my head, fingers riffling through my hair, and I put my hands around her waist and pull her close to me.

Corpses surround us, stretching off into every direction, but we are alive.

And then I think you're supposed to feel something. When you kiss a girl like this, you're supposed to feel something – something for or toward that person, or maybe you can feel something from them - but I don't think I do.

My eyes snap open, and for a moment, I watch her as the kissing goes on. The twilight tints her creamy skin purple. She is very beautiful, and she seems nice, and she seems smart, but I don't know.

I don't know.

I do not know.

My breathing must change because she opens her eyes, and our mouths detach, and she starts laughing.

"What the hell, Grobnagger?" she says. She spits my surname out of her mouth like it's an insult. "Just staring at me with that dead look in your eyes like some kind of wacko."

"Sorry," I say.

She laughs again, and she pushes herself into my side and curls her arm around mine, and maybe part of me wants to believe, but I already know.

I already know how things really are.

"It's getting dark," I say.

"So what?" she says.

A scuffling of leaves emits from somewhere nearby, and we both swivel our heads to find the source. In the half light I can just make out an older couple arriving at the top of the hill. The man sports sunglasses and a do-rag over his long hair, and the lady wears a leather vest. Bikers? Not sure.

After all of this time alone in the graveyard, it almost feels like a violation for someone else to be here. Whatever sense of security or privacy we'd been lulled into feels like it was naïve, and this place feels awkward and sort of unsafe. I can tell by the look on Louise's face that she feels the same.

"Let's get the fuck out of here," she whispers.

And so we do.

CHAPTER 19

As the Passat snakes its way through the dark back to Glenn's, a panic bloats up in my gut. I need to find a way out of this, a way to make it stop permanently. No half measures this time. No skulking away to hide now and deal with it later.

"What are you thinking about?" she says.

I almost swallow my tongue.

"Nothing, really," I say. "Why?"

"You just look all concerned," she says.

"You can see that in the dark?" I say.

"When the moonlight flashes between the trees I can," she says.

I turn to look at her. She's right. I watch the moonlight spill through onto her skin in pulses. She really is pretty. Maybe in some other life…

But I can't. I can't. I need to rip it out by the roots. Before it grows into something big enough to hurt us.

"So how do you know Glenn?" she says.

"He's my friend," I say. It's not until after I say this out loud that I realize it's true.

"So you've known each other for a while?" she says.

"Yep," I say. Not sure why my instinct is to lie about this, but I suppose it will make no difference soon.

We pull up to Glenn's house, the Passat idling in the

driveway.

"I had a really good time tonight," she says. "You're the only Jeff Grobnagger in the universe. You know that, right?"

"I don't know. I guess so," I say.

Her eyes lock onto mine. Her eyelashes flutter and close and she leans in again. One part of me can't believe this is happening, like it's a dream coming true. The other part sees her mouth as a foreign orifice trying to latch onto me.

"Maybe we shouldn't," I say, just as her lips touch mine. I turn my head. "I'm sorry. You seem really nice, but I've got a lot of shit going on right now."

"Oh," she says, pulling back.

Her face crinkles a bit, her chin quivering. I wish I could erase these images from my mind, but I know I can't.

"I'm sorry," I say again and get out of the car.

I walk down the walkway toward that big red front door, the sound of the Passat easing out of the driveway behind me. The light from the headlights swings across the front of the house. The engine's rumble passes me and begins to recede. I look up to watch the taillights for a second.

Even when I know exactly where things are going, it still pains me to arrive.

I stand outside of the doorway for a long time, watching the spot on the horizon where the taillights faded to black. I need to gather myself before I go inside.

I try to forget everything. I try to filter my thoughts down to how I felt when I was with her, without my self consciousness overanalyzing it and clouding my brain with doubts.

She is smart and funny and attractive and all of those things you would list on paper about a girl you'd like. But isn't the true test how I feel around her?

With everything else blocked out, she is exciting to be around. I mean, she can see that I'm a ridiculous man, and she likes me anyway. This is not to imply that I like being around her simply because she seems to like me, though. It's that she can appreciate the humor in humanity without feeling contempt for it. She can disagree with something but still find likeable qualities in it. She can have empathy without either judgment or pity.

And I start to think maybe I think too much. I try to analyze and judge moments like our kiss in the cemetery before they can even breathe and become themselves. I can't shut off that part of my brain, I guess.

So even though I always know where these things will wind up, I continue to change my mind every two seconds along the way. Pretty annoying, right? Yeah. I don't feel that great about it, either.

But just as I start to think maybe I've been too harsh, I turn and lock eyes with my reflection in the dark window by Glenn's front door.

Because I guess I sort of know that the idea part of me and the physical part of me are separate worlds, right? And my thoughts can wind down these paths where I start to think maybe I'm not so bad off. Maybe my imagination and my perspective on the world are intricate and potentially entertaining. Someone like Louise could find something to like there, perhaps. I can be witty. I can be profound and insightful. All of these types of things. Maybe I'm not so awful. Isolating the idea world from the physical world, I start to think maybe romance is still a possibility for me, and I'm just psyching myself out, yeah?

And then I catch my reflection in the mirror, and I watch the worlds collide. When I look in my face, all of that positivity collapses like touching moth wings when they're still wet.

There's not a light on in Glenn's place. I kind of thought he'd wait up for me. He seemed so eager about it.

I turn the knob and push the door, but it's already partially open, so I stumble in. Right away, my feet tangle in some debris. It's too dark to make out, but I know whatever it is, it doesn't belong here. A hardened ball of dread forms in the diaphragm region of my chest.

My hand slaps and scrapes the wall in search of a light switch, fingernails screeching over drywall. No success. I switch to the other side of the door and flail my arm around over there. My fingers brush past the switch, return to it, flip it.

Let there be light. I squint a second while my eyes adjust.

At my feet lies an overturned table, its drawer pulled out and the contents strewn over the ceramic tile of the entryway. The toppled coat rack leans on one table leg, a couple of jackets still clinging to it while others scatter the area in all directions. I step forward, avoiding the shards of a smashed decorative beer stein. The quiet of the place is overwhelming.

"Glenn?" I say, calling out to be heard throughout the house.

I know he's not here. I know no one is here. I can feel it.

"Hello?" I say at top volume as a formality.

I trot over the trash pile into the living room to find more destruction. Framed pictures pock the floor, having been pulled from the walls. A photo of Amity as a child stares up at me, the lower half of her face obscured by a new smile shaped from shattered glass. The couch cushions and pillows have been slashed, feathers and stuffing hemorrhaging from the wounds.

The kitchen suffers the same fate. Every drawer sprawls on the floor, dumped and tossed aside. Utensils mound themselves on top of spice containers and cookbooks.

It couldn't look more violated. It's not my house. I'd never even seen it until the past week or so. But I feel vulnerable as I take in this wreckage. I feel like something soft in a hard world.

Who would do this? And what could they have wanted? It crosses my mind that they could have been looking for me. Then again, the slashing of the cushions might point to an object as the focus of the search. Amity's book, maybe?

More importantly, where the hell is Glenn, and is he OK?

I check the rest of the place, only finding more messes and broken things. As I return to the living room, Mardy wriggles out from under the couch. Here's my eyewitness that can't tell me anything. He presses the side of his lip against my pant leg and smears. I kneel to pet him.

I use the broom to shove junk out of the way and clear a spot on the kitchen floor to feed him. The meat plops onto a saucer, and the animal nibbles at it. This pleases the beast. With the smell of canned cat food wafting about, Glenn's cats come out of hiding, and I serve them the "sea captain's choice" as well. (Spoiler alert: The sea captain chose fish. Again.)

I'm a little worried about Leroy puking, but he evades any such problems for tonight, at least. After eating, the cats move slowly through the suddenly unfamiliar terrain. They sniff and take careful steps, staying low with their bellies tucked almost to the floor. Mardy seems the most brazen of the lot, opting to lie on the tattered couch and clean himself. The others return to their hiding spots somewhere out of sight.

I rinse the plates off, as pointless as it seems considering the mess, and as I shut off the water, I hear a crunching noise near the front door. It's glass, and it sounds like it's being trampled.

By feet.

Feet that are bigger than cat feet, probably shoed and everything. By the sound of it, it's more than one person.

I spin to face the intruders, whom I still can't see but can hear coming closer. In a flash, my mind lists my options:

A. Grab a pair of butcher knives from the floor and prepare to skewer some eyeballs. This could backfire if any of my potential assailants possess a gun.

B. Run out the back door, knowing they'd likely hear me and follow. Assuming I could make it outside, this one is pretty open ended. On the other hand, the Grobnaggers are not known for their sprinter's speed. I believe there's a tortoise on the family crest.

C. Hide. There may not be time to find and nestle into a good spot, but I'm maybe seven paces from the basement. I might be able to cover myself in a pile of beach towels in the closet next to the laundry room down there.

Maybe a single second passes before I decide, but with my adrenalin flowing, it feels much longer. In the end, I opt for none of the above. While the knife idea seems the most promising, I feel a wave of nausea come over me, and I decide to flop around and have a seizure instead.

CHAPTER 20

I hang upside down yet again, the rope coiling around my ankle the way it always does. I look out at the alley through halfway opened eyes, and everything blurs around the edges where my eyelashes obscure my view. My whole life has led to this. The wet asphalt. The dumpster. The bricks. That hooded bastard, wherever he is. This is my fate.

A nagging feeling steps forward from the back of my mind. It wants me to remember where I just was, what I was just doing before I got here. I grasp for it in my memories, but it keeps its distance. Truthfully, though, I don't think it matters. Not now.

I close my eyes and ponder this. After a moment I realize that the usual dread of this place fails to well in my belly like a swollen tape worm this time around. Instead, a calm comes over me. The tranquility one feels when they are completely without fear.

This is new.

There is a peace in accepting your fate, I guess. I start to think maybe I'm even lucky in a way.

My fate may not be ideal, but it doesn't elude me the way it does for most. It doesn't hover just outside the periphery of my vision while I distract myself with a million other tasks. My fate has the decency to grab me by the shoulders and make me look into its eyes. And even if I can find no meaning in it, at least it's there. It's something concrete I can mull over. Most people don't get that. They are left on their own to drift in empty space.

I have a place. It's an awful alley where I get strangled over and over, but it's a place. I am plucked from my life and taken there. It's something. It's a kernel of significance even with the lack of any explanation or discernible purpose.

My eyes open to squinted slits, and I see the hooded man creeping through the mud puddles. He moves in slow motion, his feet skimming over the top of the water with a swishing sound, and his shoulders hunched in a manner conveying suspicion, as though he's waiting for me to spring some trap on him. I so hate to disappoint the guy after all of the quality time we've spent here together.

I close my eyes again, though, and that sarcastic feeling fades away, and the calm wraps itself around me. It makes my torso all warm. I take a deep breath, and as I exhale I feel the muscles in my neck and back let go of their tension a little bit. I inhale another big one, hold it a moment, exhale and feel that sense of relaxation run down the lengths of my arms and legs this time.

It's crazy how much of a relief it is once you finally give up. I realize the faintest smile has curled the corners of my lips. A smile – a real one – in this alley? Part of me wants to protest, but when I search my feelings, I find nothing to object to. At some point, you stop being afraid or upset about the way things are. You just accept them.

I snap back to the reality of the alley around me when it strikes me that the skimming noise of the hooded man moving through the mud puddles ended some time ago. If he were coming straight for me, he would have reached me already, even moving in slow motion like he was.

I peel my eyes a quarter of the way open to see him kneeling five feet from where I hang. One knee touches the blacktop, and the other leg forms a right angle with this hands resting on it. He bends slightly at the waist, his head tilted toward the ground beneath me, though I can't tell if this is out deference or something else. I watch for movement for a few seconds, but he doesn't stir.

The impulse to shrug comes over me, but I don't quite have the desire to follow through on it physically. Instead, my body remains motionless, and I close my eyes again.

So I hold still, and he kneels? I don't know what any of this means, and for once, I don't care. I'm content to hang here a while. The only downside I can think of is that my face feels heavy with the pressure of all of the extra blood gravity drags down this way. It's a mild annoyance, though, and nothing compared to the sense of peace that keeps washing over me every time I close my eyes and choose to stay still.

I try to remember what things were like before all of this, before I started making my periodic trek to this alley, I mean, but it's hard to call it to mind just now. I can't recall what life felt like. What did I do all day? What did I think about? All of my memories of that time seem out of focus somehow.

I struggle to conjure a clear image, but as I pull out an obscure memory of feeding Mardy in a hurry before getting back to playing video games, a feeling comes over me. It's a sick feeling. A queasiness in the belly. A sense of the emptiness that I could never have been aware of at the time erodes my newfound calmness. It's a desperate feeling, like there couldn't have been any point to living before this alley came into my life.

And I sense that it's darker outside now. Even through my eyelids I can tell. I take a breath before I look to see that the hooded man is gone, but that's not what's making it darker. It's the black fog forming a circular perimeter around me about 15 feet out and closing fast. The ebon wall of mist undulates and lurches toward me like a living thing.

I remember the cold of sticking my hand into the fog, and it sends the chill through the rest of me. And now I'm bending at the waist, fumbling to undo the lash at my ankle even though there's not enough time and there's no place to run. The calm is so gone that it crosses my mind that pissing and/or shitting myself from fear is a real possibility at the moment. An ironically detached self critique runs through my mind as my fingers fail to undo the knot:

"Am I the type to stay cool under pressure? What do I do in times of crisis?"

The detached voice in my head answers itself aloud through my lips:

"Pants. Poop them."

Tendrils of black reach out for me now, one brushing my shirt before it hooks back toward the wall. My fingers slip on the rope again, and I know it's no use. I ease my abdominals and let myself hang again, my hands dangling toward the blacktop. So that's it. I give up. The dread feels like a physical object in my stomach that I could projectile vomit every which way at any moment.

The wall of fog swells and sways like an angry black sea. It's only about eight feet away now. Maybe if this were a book with a happy ending, someone or something would swoop in and save me at the last minute, but I'm afraid it's not.

A crazy thought flashes in my head – if I somehow killed myself, I'd get out before the fog could get me, and it'd be like nothing happened. It's genius, except I don't have time to get down nor any weapons handy.

Where is that hooded bastard when you need him, right?

I get a faint whiff of a something, a metallic smell, as the black circle begins to cinch around me. I close my eyes once again, this time not out of any sense of calm or relaxation but out of fear. Wild fear as pure and deep as a child's. I can't bear to watch the black nothing envelop me. Because that's what it is. It's not darkness. It's nothingness. I don't know why I'm sure of this, but I am.

The cold coils around my shoulders first, and then I feel its chill crawl all up and down me. It starts to squeeze icy fingers at the exposed skin along my neck and arms. It stings at first, but within seconds my arms and legs are numb, and the frigidity presses itself against me like a pervert on the subway.

And I feel my breath heave hot between my clenched teeth, puffing wind over lips dried and cracking from the cold, and I know that the black will engulf me any second. It will take me. And the words "fucking terrified" spring to mind. I feel like I should try to brace myself for nothingness, but I don't know how to do that. My fists clench, but I doubt it will help.

And then it's like the lash at my ankle releases, and the bottom of the world drops out, and I'm falling, falling. I open my eyes out of instinct, but I can see nothing. A rapid descent into a black forever. I try to scream and flail my arms, but I can't make a sound nor do I get the sense my arms are doing what I tell them to. I feel the scream churning in my throat despite the lack of sound. I can't see anything to be able to confirm or disconfirm it, but it's like my arms aren't even there.

Down.

Down.

Down.

I leave the alley behind. I leave the world behind. The big shadow swallows me up forever and ever, and I tumble toward some belly that may or may not exist. Or maybe some other terror altogether.

Falling.

Falling.

My thoughts start… fracture… linear monologue… splinter off… fragments… can't follow… maybe the dark… crawling in... blotting out…

I focus hard, almost like flexing my brain, and my thoughts flow back together into a stream that makes sense. For now. It seems important to hold it together for as long as I can.

The plummet stretches on and on, seeming to pick up speed all the while, and I try to stop screaming silence, but I can't. I can't turn it off. It's like that's all I am, I think. A feeling like a scream in a throat, and the consciousness to observe it.

I don't know. Do not know. But yeah. Yep. Better go with it.

So I scream a soundless scream, and I fall and fall and fall into the pitch black nothing.

Apparently, it's a long way down.

CHAPTER 21

I try to open my eyes, but yellow static fills my field of vision. It vibrates inside of my head like a mild electric energy and makes everything sound and appear all fizzled. My jaw clenches in violent, involuntarily bursts like my top and bottom teeth are trying to bite through each other. I can feel my head lolling on my neck, shaking and spasming along with the waves of the energy in my skull.

And then pins and needles ripple up and down my body. I can feel my arms and legs again, but I can't move them. The tingle and prickling sensations swell into full on stabs and slashes, and then that hurt intensifies again and spreads over all of me like the skin is being peeled back from the muscle, like I'm being flayed alive.

Every nerve ending is alive and screaming. I try to scream along with them, but my mouth remains motionless, my vocal cords keep still.

It's pain. It's paralysis. It's blindness and deafness and dumbness. I'm trapped inside myself, inside this flesh, and being tortured. On some level, though, I feel like the physical world is there, just on the other side of the yellow and the flaying, and that's a relief after the black nothing.

Time passes. The isolation and torment almost become a game. A challenge to endure. It doesn't scare me. Not anymore.

I'm trapped within my body, yes, but I know now it's only flesh somehow. It's hard to explain the distinction. It's like how when you're a kid, scary movies terrify you, but as you grow older, you realize "it's just a movie." And once you learn that, it's like on some level nothing that can happen in a movie can scare you anymore. Well, it's "just flesh," and on some level, these matters can't scare me anymore.

Falling into the pitch black nothing scares me. I have stared into the void, have been reduced to consciousness blinking off and on in the face of it.

But the physical plane and the nothing plane are separate I see now, and never the twain shall meet. My physical being will never experience death, not consciously anyway. So the things that happen here don't scare me anymore than a monster in a movie.

That's the funny thing about life – getting over the fear of death is the hard part. After that, it's easy.

The yellow fades to a lesser intensity over time, and I can see through the golden swells and rippled spots. The pain also fades. My limbs tingle more like they're deeply asleep rather than being speared and peeled.

I lie on my back, looking up. The black is gone, nor am I in the alley. In their stead, stone walls surround me. Flame flickers from torches mounted at even intervals around the room. As my eyes trace the rocks upward, the walls give way to an arched ceiling of brick way up there. I hold still and take it in for a moment. While the room is large, I get the sense that it's a single chamber and not part of something bigger. (Or maybe it's an antechamber. I've never been clear on the difference.)

I sit up, my movements slowed by the throbbing and

prickling. The smooth floor spans the 50 or so feet of room in front of me. It's empty from what I can see, but something glints near the far wall. I move toward it, my shuffling footsteps echoing all about me.

As I near the far wall, I see that four stone columns protrude from the floor, standing just higher than eye level. Atop each of these platforms rests an object: a sword, a stick, a cup and a coin. Looking closer, though, I believe the stick to be a wand.

I stop short of the columns and examine them. Apart from a decorative flourish of engravings along the lip, they look basically like the walls – stones mortared together somehow and piled high. The ornate bits cover the top six inches of each column. The carvings appear organic somehow, not geometric shapes, something more chaotic. Each one is unique yet equally striking.

A hushed feeling comes over me like this is important. Maybe it's sacred, maybe it's not, but I know I should proceed with caution. I study each object:

The sword rests next to its scabbard, unsheathed and shiny. There's a curve to the blade. No scuffs. No blemishes. It looks like it's never been used. The carving below depicts feathers and leaves that seem to float about each other.

The cup looks plain and old. A goblet or chalice, I guess you'd call it. It's brownish pottery of some type with a fat stem and fatter top. I can't see whether or not there's anything inside. Underneath, the carving seems to be crafted of coral and shell and shaped into portrayals of swirling fluid.

The wand tapers on one end. It's black and almost fuzzy looking with faint brown stripes that texturally remind me of scars. The carving on this column sports flame wrapping around the charred and pocked remains of something I can't identify. If I had to guess, I'd say that the charred corpse of a possum may have been integrated into the piece. For real.

The coin looks to be thick and gold. A purple bag sits nearby, like an ancient purse some king would tote around. The purse string cinches the top too tight to see for sure, but the bottom of the bag plumps in a manner suggesting more coins within. This carving looks like muscle and blood vessels and connective tissue – all stringy and sinewy and gristly.

So that's it, then. Four objects on display, though what they might mean, I couldn't say. I wonder if I'm supposed to use one to accomplish something.

Out of all of them, the one that seems to draw me in the most is the cup. Don't get me wrong. The sword is awesome, and the wand intrigues me. I figure money has little value here, so the coin won't do me much good. In any case, I find myself wondering what might be in the cup. I'm picturing some kind of kickass merlot in there. I'm not even a wine drinker, but I would take a toot off there. Truth is, I'd be happy enough with grape juice. I'm parched. Or maybe I'm convincing myself I'm thirsty because I'm such a beverage enthusiast. Hard to say, but my mouth is watering nonetheless.

I hoist the goblet, my fingers wreathing around the stem to cup the round part. It's heavy. I ease it toward me, moving slowly – half out of some reverence for this place and half out of the fear of spilling precious liquids. It slides under my nose, and I get a glimpse inside.

Not a drop to drink. The cup is empty.

Out of the corner of my eye, I see the columns jerk into

motion. The grind of rock on rock swells around me. The stone pedestals descend into the floor, moving quite quickly.

"Shit," I say out loud, and the sound of my voice startles me.

It occurs to me that I totally should have taken the sword. I rush to put the cup back on the column, but it totters and when I try to steady it, it tumbles off the other side out of view. Based on the clatter, I figure it's broken. I scramble to grab it, though, and it's fine. No damage.

On the downside, the columns and the other objects are long gone, vanished into holes in the floor that seem bottomless from my vantage point.

Great. So I'm stuck with an empty cup instead of a sweet blade.

Unless...

The cup teetering off of the column and nearly breaking calls forth a notion. If I break the cup, wouldn't this scene reset, and I could make the better choice? Just the same way that I came back every time the hooded man strangled me?

I figure I don't have much to lose, so I whip the cup at the floor as hard as I can. It explodes into a spray of shards, some of it almost disintegrating into powder on impact. The high pitched ring of the breaking pottery bounces around the room for a long moment.

And it occurs to me that perhaps this was a bad idea. Maybe I should have waited. I don't know why I'm always rushing into things.

I stop. I wait. I listen.

Nothing happens. Half of me expects the traditional reset process of a fade to black. The other half anticipates some kind of punishment for breaking the cup, though I don't know what that might involve. I feel like it could be on the loud and obnoxious side of things for some reason. A not so subtle case of pants shitting terror seems about right. Just a guess, though.

I walk over to peer down into the holes, but I see only black. I kneel and pick up one of the bigger cup shards. I rub the sharp edges between my thumb and index finger. It's about like a dog's tooth, I think. A big dog, I guess, like a Rottweiler. I lean forward and drop it into the second dark cylinder from the left.

I wait for the sound of its impact.

And wait.

And wait.

Nothing.

It crosses my mind that I missed the sound somehow, and I should drop another Rottweiler tooth, but I figure it's pointless. Here it's totally possible that the holes are bottomless. In fact, I would call it a strong likelihood.

I go to stand up, but something isn't right. My legs won't get under me to bear my weight. It's hard to explain. It's like my feet can't grip the floor. They slide out when I go to step on them, and I just stay kneeled down.

Oh, wait. I'm very lightheaded. Yep. Almost didn't realize it. That must be what's causing this.

I sit back, dispensing with the awkward leg churns and propping myself against the wall. I take a deep breath and feel the muscles in my neck and shoulders relax as I exhale. My head sinks a few inches, my neck dipping as the muscles let go, and then I take another deep breath, and my cranium rises like a buoy riding a wave. I exhale again, and my head sinks and sinks, and I'm out.

CHAPTER 22

When I wake, the darkness is gone. Sort of. I see blackness fouled only by the light of a blinking VCR clock way in the distance.

Two things occur to me right away:

1. This is not Glenn's living room.

2. Someone is still watching stuff on VHS in this day and age. Hard to believe.

I feel around in the dark. I'm lying on a small cot under a blanket slightly coarser than 80 grit sandpaper. The floor is smooth and cold. Concrete, I think. I lower myself from the cot with care, and I realize that the VCR light is blocked from my vision for a fraction of a second as I move. At first I think someone else crossed in front of the light and get a jolt of adrenalin, but without thinking I reach my hand out. My fingers wrap around steel. A bar. I reach my other hand out with the same result. I am behind bars.

Is this jail? It could explain the VCR. They might force the incarcerated to watch Moulin Rouge on VHS as a form of torture. After maybe 10 minutes of Ewan McGregor singing, I'd tell anyone just about anything to make it stop.

I hear noises drawing closer. Muffled voices. People in an adjacent hall? I hustle back to the cot and grind the skin on my arms down to the dermis by pulling the sandpaper blanket over myself too quickly. I close my eyes just as I hear the sound of the door opening.

"Just put him in there like you were told," a man's voice says. It sounds deep, unfamiliar.

There's the sound of a flipped switch, and after the briefest pause, the hum and glow of florescent lights overhead. Even through my eyelids, it seems insanely bright. It sounds like something large is being wheeled toward me.

"Can't just leave him strapped in here. Can we?" a second voice says. It's not as deep as the first and conveys the faintest Southern accent.

"We can, and we will, because that's what we were told to do," Deep Voice says.

Keys jingle. Something metallic clicks, and there's the groan of a hinge. Now the large rolling sounds seem to move away from me.

"Don't sit right with me is all," Southern Accent says. "Shoot. This fella's not going to make it through the night, I don't expect."

"Are you a frickin' doctor now?" Deep Voice says. "Stop pussyfooting around and lock the door. Last thing I want is to be standing here with you in the middle of the night. Don't you know that?"

Another jingle of keys. Another metallic click. Another groaning hinge. And a clank.

"I don't like it is all," Southern Accent says.

"Duly noted. Now let's go," Deep Voice says.

I hear their footsteps pass me and begin to recede. I decide to sneak a peek before the lights go out. Squinting, I see that I'm in one of three cells, maybe four if there's one next to mine that I can't see from this vantage point, which seems likely. The barred chambers comprise one end of a large room with only a couple of small windows along the ceiling – perhaps a basement. This isn't an official jail, then. A hobby jail? The cells appear to be about eight feet square with poured cement walls for three of the walls and legit jail cell bars for the fourth. Quite a heavy duty project, if this is really in someone's basement. There's a little office type set up on the other end of the room, complete with a desk, TV and VCR. I'd bet money there's at least one Pauly Shore movie in the pile of VHS tapes in the corner.

More significant than all of that, though, is what I spot in the cell across from mine, maybe eight or ten feet away. Glenn lies strapped to a gurney. His face is the color of the ash on the tip of a cigarette. He wears no shirt, and large, blood soaked bandages wrap around his middle.

The lights snap off, and the dark surrounds me once again. Fear courses back through me, that desperate kind of fear that only comes around when death is nearby. It almost has a smell. Death hovering close-by, I mean. Not the decay aspect. The doom aspect. Imminent death has its own odor – a pathetic, powerless animal smell. The sweat and hormones and pheromones of the defeated, they smell like piss and fear.

And I realize that time and life are slipping away from me into the darkness. I try to grab a hold of them with my thoughts, like the words in my internal monologue are my hands. I try to wrangle them and make them hold still for a second, but I can't. No matter how tightly I knit my fingers, it all slides away from me.

The blinking of the VCR clock is the only reason I know

I'm not falling into nothing again.

As the footsteps fade away and the quiet resettles on the room, I realize it's not a complete silence. Glenn rasps air in and out. I try to preemptively fight them off, but it's too late: the words "death rattle" pop into my head.

I focus on that flash of a moment in my memory. Glenn looked so different without the navy blue baseball cap on. I've barely ever seen him without it. That almost made him seem more naked than the fact that he was shirtless. Of course, the wounds to his abdomen were the headline of this story. When I picture it now, the bandages are sopping wet, almost like puddles of red with strips of gauze floating in them, but my imagination might be warping things already.

Anything seems possible in the pitch black nothing. Nightmares come true. You can't see anything to disprove your fears. And so you believe them. In your mind, they are true, and in the dark, what you believe is all that's real.

A whirring noise kicks up, perhaps the air conditioner flipping on. It's a relief to hear a new sound. It confirms that there is a whole world of life outside of this room, billions of people crawling all over each other to try to reach the top of the bucket.

I lie back on the cot and close my eyes. Glenn's breathing grows louder, clicking and scraping back and forth in his throat. I try to imagine what the world will feel like when he is gone. It strikes me once again that Glenn is my friend. That he has been a good friend to me.

Is this why I don't want people around me? Because it will hurt so bad to lose them? Because all of our stories end the same way. We've all got a one way ticket to Deathington

Central.

I roll around on the cot a while before my higher brain finally slows down. I sleep. I do not dream.

CHAPTER 23

I wake in the dark, confused until I turn my head and see the VCR clock blinking away. Glenn's breathing has changed. It sounds more normal.

I hear him fumbling with his bandages in the dark, the peeling of tape and wet sounds. I realize that his stirring must have woken me up. Perhaps he's checking the severity of his wounds.

"How's it look?" I say. I talk just above a whisper, so as not to arouse any attention from whomever is guarding us.

He sighs.

"I think I'll live," he says.

There's a wet plop that I can't place, but it doesn't sound promising.

"So who got us?" I say.

"Hm?" he says.

"I had a seizure and woke up here," I say. "So I have no idea what is going on."

"League," he says. "Shot me in the gut. They roughed up my place pretty good, too."

I hear him pulling at the straps on the gurney a second before he continues:

"Jesus. I hope Leroy is OK."

"He's fine," I say. "Or he was. I fed him right before I

blacked out."

"No puke?" he says.

"None," I say.

"Well, that's good," he says.

"I think I finally… solved my dream or whatever," I say.

"Really," he says. "That's great."

"Yeah, maybe," I say. "Kind of."

I explain all of it – the calm, and the hooded man kneeling, and the black nothing closing in and swallowing me, and the falling, and the cup, and the sword, and the wand, and the coin, and smashing the cup. I even backtrack in the middle to explain the date with Louise and the sour ending.

While I talk, I hear Glenn climb out of his stretcher, lowering himself to the floor. Then he starts scratching at something. I don't know if he's just grinding a rock back and forth on the wall out of boredom or what. I guess that's about what it sounds like.

When I finish, he doesn't say anything for a while. He just scratches.

"You're a bit of a slow learner, aren't you?" Glenn says.

"What do you mean?" I say.

"Look, I know you've had a rough life," he says. "Your parents dying and all, but-"

"OK, wait," I say. "I should probably tell you… My parents aren't dead."

"What?" he says. "Jesus Christ, Grobnagger. Are you mentally disturbed? Why would you ever lie about something like that?"

I rub at my eyes, like that will help me see in the dark.

"It's easier to tell people that they're dead than to tell them the truth," I say.

Glenn is silent, no longer fidgeting or scratching or anything.

"I don't really know my parents. They didn't want me," I say. "My dad was gone by the time I was two. I never saw him again. I guess he has a new family. My mom left me with some friends when I was six and never came back. I've seen her a couple of times since then, but it's been probably 15 or so years now."

It's so quiet in the room that I can hear Glenn breathing again even though it's not as raspy as it was.

"That's the thing, though. You tell people your parents are dead, and they leave you alone about it," I say. "That's something they can grasp somehow. Maybe it's the permanence of it all. Death, I mean. You tell them the truth, though? They don't know what to think. At first, they don't say anything, but before long they want to help you fix it. They want to help you plan some bullshit reunion or something. Like my life is some made for Lifetime movie just waiting for them to come write the happy ending for me. Like they can say 'It's not your fault,' six times and make it all go away Good Will Hunting style."

I hear Glenn swallow.

"So I just give people something they can understand is all," I say. "I don't even think of it as lying anymore."

Glenn goes back to scratching. Neither of us says anything for a time.

"Did you ever think about what the dream was trying to teach you?" he says. "Why you kept going to the alley and how you eventually solved the puzzle? Did you think about what that might mean?"

I think this over.

"I thought about it, obviously," I said. "Though I don't know if it was trying to teach me anything, or if I'd use those words for it, at least. I don't know."

"Patience," he says. "You didn't pass the test until you exhibited patience. Until you accepted your circumstances as fully beyond your control, you were doomed to the same fate over and over. It's counterintuitive to just wait there, yes, but sometimes the counterintuitive path is the only way forward. That's the point of the lesson."

That makes a lot of sense. I don't say anything.

"And the broken cup?" he says. "Any idea what that might mean?"

"None," I say.

"Wands, swords, cups and coins are the four suits of the tarot," he says. "The object you were drawn to represents what's dominant in your life right now, spiritually speaking. Cups hold water. Water symbolizes emotions. Not passions exactly, that's fire which is represented by the wand. With water, we're talking about emotions of the heart – romantic notions and poetry and our connections to other people and loneliness and searching your inner self for the deepest and darkest places."

His speech pauses a moment, and the scratching noise grows more furious. Hearing it in more detail, it sounds like something metal grinding grooves into the concrete floor. The sound dwindles as he begins talking again.

"So if a cup holds those emotions, it symbolizes the heart itself, yes?" he says.

"Sure," I say.

He hesitates to respond. I feel like I'm missing something.

"And what did you do with your cup, Grobnagger?" he says.

"I broke it," I say.

As the words fall out of my mouth, it finally dawns on me what he's getting at. This is everything. All of me. All of my life I have sabotaged relationships, I have withdrawn, I have pushed people away and looked for any reason to separate myself from everyone. I severed all friendships and burned every bridge. I broke up with Allie. Just today, I made sure things with Louise wouldn't work.

I have lived my life as an injured being. Like if I could just be by myself for a while and let this wound heal, maybe I could be okay. If the world would just leave me alone for a little while…

But the world didn't cause my injuries, not in my adult life anyway. Other people are not to blame.

Nobody broke my heart. I broke it myself.

CHAPTER 24

I try to speak, but the words catch in my throat.

"There's much I haven't told you," Glenn says. "I didn't want to complicate things."

I hear him, but my mind keeps picturing the cup shattered at my feet.

"You can lay out lessons with words, but experience is always the best teacher," he says. "The things you learn the hard way carve themselves into you deeper."

I try to focus on the things he's saying, but I have that ache in my gut that you get a couple minutes after you get kicked in the balls. The pain swells and swells, and then you feel sick in a new way, a more pitiful way. And you are just a wretched, helpless thing. And the gonad pain fades, but the sick feeling remains, the powerlessness lingers in your belly for a long time.

"You're a tough kid, Grobnagger," he says. "You might not think you are, but you're more hard nosed than you let yourself believe. Problem is, you let fear motivate your behavior instead of love. That's the path to tragedy, man. Because way deep down under many layers of denial and bullshit, every motivation boils down to either fear or love… and you're on the wrong team."

I climb down from the cot and sit on the cool floor, my knees tucked under me. I stare into the black.

"You're scared of being rejected," he says. "And you're confused about who you are inside and how that fits with who you are in the flesh. Because they are separate entities in a way. I think a lot of people struggle with that distinction."

He hesitates a moment, continues.

"Years ago, I lived in a rough neighborhood. There were crack dealers around the corner, out at all hours, and there were prostitutes a couple blocks down. Well, walking down the street I once heard a pimp chastise another man for kissing his girlfriend on the mouth. The pimp was so offended by that act, his lips curled up like he'd just eaten a wedge of lemon. He felt the guy was going down a road to ruin because he allowed himself to respect a woman enough to kiss her on the lips. He said, 'You don't know what she's doing with that mouth when you're not around.' He wasn't talking about a hooker, mind you. Just a regular girl."

The scratching starts again as he keeps talking.

"Over time, I've realized that people like that can't reconcile the idea of a woman being a real human being and having sexual desires at the same time – they can't fathom the soul and the flesh being of the same being. So to make some sense of it, they have to see the woman as an animal. A weak willed thing that is driven entirely by instinctual urges. Never to be trusted or completely empathized with. Only to be controlled. You've heard pimps and their ilk talk. They often don't call them women or girls or anything like that. They call them 'females,' just like they're referring to a dog. To love and respect a woman as an individual is to shame yourself in that world. Because all women are whores deep down. That's how they see it."

Without thinking about it, I start scratching my thumbnail

on the floor in time with Glenn's scraping.

"They have to whittle what exists between men and women down to control," he says. "They see relationships only in that context – power. That one person has to have the power over the other. And they achieve this, in part, by dehumanizing the girl."

It must be close to dawn now. I sense it's almost imperceptibly brighter in the room, but even when I strain my eyes, I still can't see what Glenn is doing.

"It's not just pimps, either," he says. "That mentality is shared by a lot of people. Way more than most people would realize. It's an attitude that's contagious. It spreads like a disease. Sometimes people preach it. Sometimes it's transmitted wordlessly. People pick up on the cues from those around them and emulate it. It becomes their idea of what it is to be a man."

He stops talking for a second, and it sounds like he's dusting something off with his hand, possibly blowing on it. Then he goes on.

"But it's all wrong. None of those people are ever going to be happy. Not really. Controlling someone else will never make you happy. They do it because they're scared. Scared of being rejected or scared of being unable to keep hold of the girls they might develop feelings for."

My legs are cold from the floor, so I climb back onto the cot and roll over onto my back to stretch my neck, my chin reaching up for the ceiling.

"Control makes you feel powerful and less afraid," he says. "But it won't make you happy. In the short term, it may satisfy some part of your brain leftover from the reptilian era of evolution, but it's not going to fulfill you over the long arc of your life. Because the deepest part of your imagination is looking for a partner. Masculine and feminine are the two incomplete halves of humanity. With the right partner, you're made whole. Carl Jung calls it the anima and animus. You know this intuitively starting when you're an adolescent, I'd say. You know that finding someone to be with is why you exist, and you know that it's not about power or control or sex or flesh at all. You want someone you can respect as your absolute peer, someone to become a part of you, and for you to become a part of them, on a higher level than skin."

The scratching stops, and he coughs. It starts again.

"I remember reading somewhere once that, no matter who you are, you sort of believe that you have secret super powers, and being in love is finding someone else that also believes you have secret super powers and vice versa. I think that's a good way to put it," he says. "So that's what you want. That's what everyone wants. Some people are better than others at blocking their intuition out, though. With the way you go on about being left alone, I'm worried that you may be one of them, Grobnagger."

I don't say anything.

"I'm not saying you're like a pimp or anything," he says. "Your way of managing it is much different than theirs. I'm just saying all that stuff about wanting the world to leave you alone is your way of blocking out what you know you want because you're scared."

The sounds coming from Glenn's area change, and I realize that I can half make him out in that purple pre-dawn light. He stands, and he scrapes something on the wall in a rectangular shape about seven feet tall and a little more than shoulder width. He turns to face me. I can't see his facial features, though, just the vague shape of him.

"I have messed up in my life. I learned that lesson too late, and my family fell apart because of me. But you are still young," he says. "Listen, I will try to come back for you."

"What?" I say.

He doesn't answer. Instead, he pivots back toward the wall, reaches an arm out toward it and pulls. There's a crack, and a white light shines through a crease along the rectangular line he drew. He pulls, and the cement rectangle shifts. He pulls again, and it slides toward him a little bit more. I realize it's opening like a door, swinging open a fraction at a time.

I can't speak. I can't move. I can only watch.

Soon the light spills into the room from the opening, and I shade my eyes. It's an unusual light, somehow unlike sunlight or incandescent or florescent or any normal illumination. It's pure white and bright as hell like that flash when you burn magnesium in chemistry class.

The door continues to open slowly but the progress is steadier now. Smooth and consistent, not so herky jerky anymore, the friction of cement on cement grates out a terrible song. As more and more light enters the cell, I see Glenn's discarded bandage on the floor, still wet with red. He turns right then, rotating with the door and revealing that there's no wound on his abdomen now.

Was there ever a wound? Did he heal himself? Watching this cement block move, I'd believe anything.

The light swells to something just shy of blinding. I watch between my fingers and between the bars. Water pours from my eyes, but I don't look away. It's too bright to see him in detail now. I just see the black silhouette of a fat, shirtless man engulfed in a rectangular flare of white that stings my eyes.

"Take care of yourself, Grobnagger," he says.

He steps into the light and disappears.

"Glenn?" I call out.

No reply.

After a second, the door snaps shut, and I'm plunged once more into darkness.

Still sitting in the dark, I reach inside the feelings part of my brain and fish around to try to get a grip on how I'm reacting to all of this. I feel a mix of things, I guess, but it's somehow more good than bad.

I sit on the edge of the cot with the sand paper blanket draped over my legs. The air conditioned chill hugs itself around my torso.

I remember the doorway into the light, and I remain in awe. Even in the dark, I can still see it. I can still see the bright white blaze through the night. I can still see his silhouette enveloped in a flash.

This raises several questions, of course. Glenn lied to me all this time, though in some ways that part doesn't bother me. He left me imprisoned here, which hurts a bit. Ultimately, these things don't conjure as strong of feelings as I might have guessed.

I think about his speech, too, and I feel some hope. It made a lot of sense.

I broke up with Allie over a matter of the flesh. I see now that I saw it wrong. I looked at things backwards. If I saw us as a linking of partners first and the physical side second rather than jumbling it all together, it could have made more sense to me. I mean, don't get me wrong. I like jizzing as much as the next guy, but what I saw as a huge rejection was really just a symptom of problems in our emotional connection, which I always knew in a way, but I couldn't see it clearly.

I let all of that physical stuff get into my psyche. I let it injure me. But that is what's not real. It barely means anything, no matter how the world around me acts. It's just skin.

When you look into the black nothing, you know how little skin means.

Nerve endings and epidermis are not the miracles of existence. Consciousness is the miracle. You can call it a soul or whatever you want. Or not. Doesn't really matter in a way, I guess. Either way, consciousness is the miracle and the physical body is just the tool to experience it through.

I lie back on the cot and pull the blanket up around me. The cool of the sheet slowly goes lukewarm under me.

I mean, it's not like leaping to these conclusions suddenly heals me. I know I'm not quite right. Maybe I never will be. But I also know that I'm not all the way fucked, either. Not yet, anyway.

And I know maybe I've been wrong about everything all of these years, at least partially. I don't know. I hope I have been wrong.

Because I think I'm going to call Louise when I get out of this place.

CHAPTER 25

When I wake again, gray light streams through the small windows along the ceiling. It's enough to half light the cells and the office with the VCR. Apart from the empty stretcher, nothing looks amiss about Glenn's cell. You can't tell that he cracked a chunk out of the wall like a shard of hardboiled eggshell and walked through it.

I sit up, leaning my shoulders against the concrete. After a moment of silence, I hear a scuffle in the hallway and sit forward.

Ms. Babinaux bursts into the room. Her eyebrows furrow in a way that reminds me of a lioness protecting her cubs. She swivels toward me, and her expression softens.

"Question," I say. "What is the policy regarding conjugal visits in here? Is there a form I need to fill out, or… "

She sighs, perhaps out of disgust, and closes her eyes. After a beat, she hustles over to my cell, resting her hands on the bars.

"I'm so sorry that you're stuck in here," she says. "I'm going to get you out, Jeffrey. I promise."

I see now that she's quite upset, on the verge of tears. I stand.

"I'm fine," I say. "I mean, do get me out of here. That'd be tremendous, but I'm OK."

She reaches a hand between the bars, I guess asking me to come closer. I step forward, and she puts her hand on my shoulder. Her eyes well up.

"I'm sorry," she says, retracting her hand. She looks at the floor. "It's just that you've always reminded me of my son. He's 16. A little depressed."

She pulls a kleenex out of her purse and dabs at her makeup smeared eyes.

"It hurts me to see you in here," she says.

I'm pretty taken aback by this. The emotions on her face are real, and I know I've been all wrong about Babinaux this whole time. All the half good, half sinister facial expressions I couldn't decipher were genuinely good, I think. And my doubts about her motivations were unfounded.

That's the thing about being paranoid. Your suspicions are wrong a lot.

"This is all Riston," she says, making eye contact again.

I mull the name for a second.

"The spoon man?" I say.

"What?" she says. "Oh, right. I don't know what he's planning, but he manipulated all of us into not reaching out to you all of this time so he could abduct you. I think things are about to get really, really bad."

"Sons of Man?" I say.

"Maybe," she says. "Either way, we need to get out of here. I'll get the keys and be back in five minutes."

She turns and looks at the empty gurney in Glenn's cell.

"What happened to your friend?" she says.

I wait a beat before I explain it.

"Oh, he drew a door on the wall, opened it and walked into

white light," I say. "And then the door closed."

She just looks at me for a long moment.

"I'll get the keys," she says.

"Don't worry," I say, plopping down onto the cot. "I won't go anywhere."

About 30 seconds after she walks out the door, though, I realize I'm wrong. The nausea wells up in my belly, and my neck can barely hold up my head. I lie down a few seconds before everything fades to black.

I don't wake so much as fade into being. I am running. I do not start running. I am already running as my consciousness turns on, sprinting over wet blacktop. My teeth clench, and my lips gape. My face feels all hot.

I know exactly what I need to do. I don't know why. I don't think why matters anymore, maybe.

I'm on a street I can't quite place with brick buildings running along both sides. Gray surrounds me. It tints the world like this place isn't quite all the way alive. Like stagnant water, it almost looks right, it's hard to even say what's out of the ordinary about it in particular, but it repulses me all the same.

A thought rattles around in my head just out of reach before I finally grab hold of it: This place is gray for now, but it will bleed all the way white eventually, I think. Maybe I am here to help it bleed, maybe just to watch it.

All of this seems familiar – the gray, the bricks, the wet blacktop. Maybe it's important, but I can't remember why just now.

I don't think about it too hard, though. I run. My legs pound beneath me. I almost feel separate from them. Distant.

Like my consciousness is up in my head, and those things straining and churning below me are more like my employees than part of me.

I wheel around a corner, and it all clicks into place. There it is: The alley. My alley. The mud puddles, the dumpster, it's all just like I remember it. I may not be thinking so clearly, but I remember this place.

And what's that hanging from the post? The hooded man. His robe sags differently being upside down. The reversed draping makes him look fat and weak. The hood hangs way down from his head. I can almost see his face. Maybe as I get closer…

I think he spies me barreling toward him. His torso jerks, and he jolts into action, bending at the waist to work at the lash on his ankle. He'll need to work quickly, because I'm rocketing right at him. And I don't have the best intentions.

I cover the ground between us in a flash. To my surprise, he frees his ankle and drops in front of me right as I'm arriving. He runs. I chase. It's not a long chase. He can't accelerate fast enough to get away, and I'm on him within a few paces.

I'm going to kill him. That is what I'm here to do. I knew this the second I arrived here or materialized here or whatever it was. I feel like I've known it as long as I've existed.

I attack more like an animal than a man. I hurl myself into him, flinging myself chest first and swinging both of my arms in a frenzy of looping hooks. The blows glance off of his head and shoulders. I doubt they do any real damage, but it's a matter of time at this point. As my chest collides with his back, the momentum totters us forward into a stagger, our legs tangle up, and we tumble to the ground, a twisted pile of humanity.

We uncoil our limbs and scramble for position. In the melee, my hood gets pulled down over my eyes. I drive one elbow into his back, using my weight to pin him face down to the asphalt. I use the other hand to fix my hood, my fingers brushing back the flap of fabric. It feels soft and thick, almost like a bath robe type texture. I had been expecting a woollier feel. Part of me wonders why I'm wearing a hood at all, but it can be hard to concentrate on matters of fashion when you're possessed by a homicidal rage.

He squirms, so I lean back, giving myself room to wind up and throw a haymaker with my free hand that smashes him in the back of the neck. Off balance and without my legs under me, I don't know how much power I can generate, though it seems to land solidly with a weird scrape and crack. He whimpers. He always sounds so squeaky, it kind of weirds me out. And then it dawns on me that the scraping noise was the sound of his teeth being driven into the pavement. Maybe shattering, maybe not.

I have no desire to say anything to him. No desire to even make him suffer. I just know he needs to die. It's about all I know at the moment.

I release my elbow from his back. Before he can react, I hook my arm under his throat and cinch it tight, using my other arm to lock it in place and apply max pressure on his neck. He wiggles, but he's so weak. His hands grab at my arm, fingers picking and clawing and prying, but it's no use.

And I lean back a little, trying to make it end quicker. And he stops scratching at my arm. He taps it. Like this is a gentlemanly battle, and he can tap out. Like he can just ask me to stop. Something about it bugs me, makes it feel more real.

He keeps on tapping and tapping.

My arm starts shaking from the strain. My breath heaves through my teeth, little flecks of spit traveling with it. The skin on my face weeps sweat that feels like hot grease. It clings to my flesh in little puddles.

The taps slow down. They grow softer. Soon he's just barely making contact, more like caresses that tickle than a guy fighting for his life. Again, this disturbs me. I wonder, for a second, if he ever had these doubts when he was killing me. Did he ever hesitate? Did he feel any pity for me?

I realize that the taps on my arm stopped some time ago. I release my grip, and the body slumps to the ground. I sit back for a moment, trying to catch my breath.

With the deed done, my thoughts tangle and circle around themselves. I feel no satisfaction. I guess I don't know what to feel.

I sit back, my shoulders colliding with the brick wall behind me and propping me up there. I dab my fingers at the oily patches of sweat on my forehead. There's no relief from the heat I feel.

It suddenly seems a lot more important to consider why I was so hell bent on doing this, but I can think of no good reason. Are there holes in my memories? Was there ever a real reason? I know this man killed me many times over, but this place isn't normal. Things work differently here.

Without standing up, I scuttle over to the body. He lies face down, the fabric of the robe fanned out from the corpse in a way that makes him look tiny. There's almost a feminine quality to the textile encased silhouette of the waist and hips.

I reach a hand toward the shoulder, hesitating for a

moment, my hand floating there just short of my enemy's empty shell. I clench and unclench my fist.

I'm not scared, exactly. I don't wonder if he'll come back this time. I know he won't. Something else makes me pause.

Finally, I grip the shoulder and turn the body over. The hood is pulled down over the head. It takes me a few tries to get a hold of it and unsheathe the face.

At first, I only see the eyes. A twisted web of red covers what were once the whites. The words "petechial hemorrhage" pop into my head, I guess a remnant from some murder of the week TV show. Looking close, it almost appears to be little scarlet vines crisscrossing around the iris, each one with a distinct width and sense of texture.

I let the focus of my vision zoom out after a second, and I feel a tightness in my chest. It's her. Soot scuffs her cheek bones and all around her open mouth, her top teeth sheared off in an almost perfectly straight line all the way across, cleaved on the asphalt, a few shards of broken tooth stuck to her tongue. The injuries and the blank look in her eyes make her seem different, but there's no doubt. It's Amity.

The good news is that I've found Glenn's daughter. The bad news…

The shock constricts my chest so I can't breathe. I try to remember. I try to think back on all of our encounters here in this alley. Was it her all along? I remember all of the high pitched sounds, realizing that the hooded figure was smaller than me, the youthful look to the chin and mouth. I think it was always Amity choking me out.

Did she have the same feeling I did upon arriving this time? Some sense of duty regarding the task of murdering me? Some undeniable drive to do so?

I scoot back, my hand curling to my mouth. I run my knuckles back and forth across my lips. The questions keep coming to me:

Will this reset for her like it did for me? Will she come back someplace else?

And then the gray sky above me dims to black, all the light draining away and away to pitch black nothing, holding me in darkness for what seems like a long time. And just when I think I'm about to be transported somewhere else, the illumination fades back in, the light opening the dark up to reveal the alley once more.

But just as the light gets back to full strength, the dimming begins again. Bright to dim to dark to nothing. The alley fades away, and the black is everywhere. It's everything. And I realize that I'm holding my breath, and I'm almost afraid to breathe, afraid to do anything in the dark.

The light blooms, though, and the brick walls and asphalt and dumpster reform. The world becomes something solid around me once more.

I almost go into a trance as it continues. I feel so numb, so frozen.

The sky dims and brightens, dims and brightens – the dark growing darker with the progression, the light surprising me a little more each time it returns. It pulses everywhere – light to dark to light to dark. Every time the black comes, it's like the nothing surrounds me again. The world vanishes into oblivion. The free fall into blackness seems poised to commence, and then the street and buildings rematerialize around me as the light comes back up like everything is normal.

I crawl to the brick wall and droop against it, just to lean on something solid. The alley inhales and exhales the light, and I feel like I'm bobbing in and out of water, thrust into the cold and dark and returned to the bright repeatedly.

Electricity vibrates all through me when the light comes up. I feel the jolt of current in my head, and I imagine the clump of damaged neurons misfiring in unison to cause the seizures that bring me here. The grand mal sizzle of a bunch of bad connections that I follow down to this place.

Noise builds in my ears, a growl of static. It sounds like heavy machines operating, but distorted somehow, crunchy with a bassy hum. It keeps getting louder and louder, the growl growing more and more furious. I feel it closing in on me, shaking me, rattling my sternum harder and harder.

And the dim comes. And the dark stays too long this time. It holds and holds. And it wraps itself around me, all frozen and dead. And I try to yell, but I feel the dark billow into my mouth like cold smoke and almost immediately congeal into something heavier and wet like a greasy mucus. And the slime cuts off my breath as the cold oozes down my throat and spreads over all of me. And all I can do is gag for breath and listen to the growl.

But the light comes back up, and there's a creaking gasp as the bright vacuums the black smoke out of my lungs. For a second, I feel weirdly empty and a little overwhelmed to see the buildings take shape around me once again. I blink rapidly, my eyes watering a bit. Running crosses my mind, but I know it'd be no use.

I take deep breaths, bracing myself for the dark to return. My fingernails claw into the asphalt like that could somehow anchor me here in the solid world of the light.

The illumination wavers a few times and steadies itself, holding longer than it should. I wait for the worst, my eyes narrowed to half slits.

The dark doesn't come, though. The light holds it at bay. Soon, the growling sound recedes like the slow fade out at the end of a song.

So I lie on my back, taking in this world from my vantage point in the alley, looking up at the buildings that reach out for the sky above. Light shines down from the heavens, a gray light that I don't believe cares much for me, but it vanquishes the dark for now, and that's good enough. Within a few seconds, the growl is gone completely. My breathing slows, progressing toward normal. I watch the sky. The gray mass above me that's not quite like a cloud hovers there, strands of it drifting in slow motion like wispy tentacles.

For a long, silent moment, I stare into the gray.

And then light bursts out of everywhere. It explodes from the brick walls. It erupts from the clouds. It flares. It surges. It ruptures my chest and gushes out of me. Without thinking, I bring my hands to my punctured abdomen, but they disintegrate into light as soon as they cross the beam.

And the bright swells and swells and swells until everything is white light.

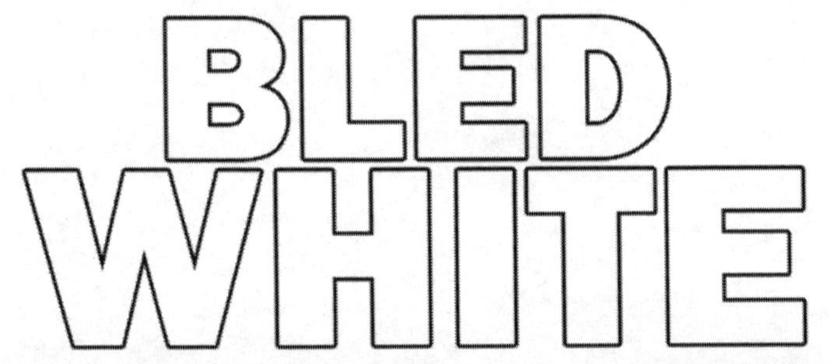

TIM MCBAIN & L.T. VARGUS

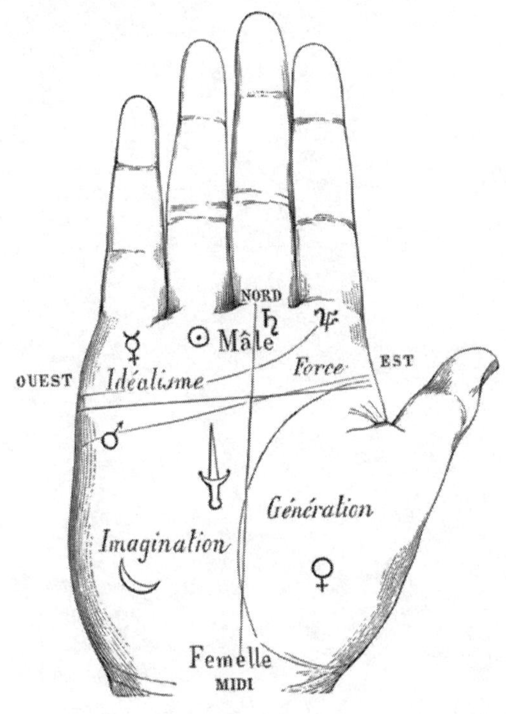

SMARMY PRESS

BLED WHITE

BOOK 2

CHAPTER 1

My consciousness returns and lifts me out of the dark. It feels like I'm rising to the surface of the ocean, floating up and up into the light.

I find myself back in the cell, but it's all different. The walls are pale around me like sickly skin never touched by the sun. It's not just the walls, though. The floor, the bars, the blanket, the ceiling: everything is bled white like the life has been sucked out while I was away. I rub my eyes, but the drained look remains.

And then I notice that my hand is also washed out. My skin sheens opaque white. Texturally it's similar to maggot flesh. Actually, the paleness makes everything look a little bulbous and insect like. I think this is an optical illusion. They say that maggot flesh adds ten pounds.

My hand looks so dead that I wiggle it just to make sure everything still works. My fingers writhe like white worms.

Somehow none of this alarms me. In fact, as I do maggoty jazz hands again, it occurs to me that I'm laughing.

"What's so funny?" a voice says from the hall. The sound echoes and seems far away, but I know it must be close.

I try to sit up.

Fail.

I teeter my head forward, and though my neck feels about

as sturdy as a rubber band, it holds me up long enough to see.

It's Babinaux, picking through keys on a big key ring. She looks all pale as well, though maybe less maggoty than me - must be her bone structure. I forgot that she was here to rescue me.

Pretty sweet.

I wonder if there will be food soon.

I let my rubber band neck snap back, and my head flops onto the cot, bouncing a couple of times, which feels more pleasant than it probably sounds. It's like a trampoline for the brain. I lift my head and let it go a couple more times, my cerebrum rattling against my skull in a nice way. Every time my head lands, it feels like fingers massage the place where my shoulders meet the neck.

"Are you OK?" she says.

"Good," I say. "Good stuff."

"Well then, let's go," she says. "We might not have a lot of time."

Glancing in her direction, I realize the cell door is open and she's standing half in my area. Her posture suggests impatience, like she has been there for a while already.

"Oh," I say. "Sorry."

Not sure what the big rush is. I consider explaining the brain trampoline and decide against it.

I stand up, wobble a moment, and take a step forward. The ground feels squishy underfoot like I'm walking on a layer of marshmallow. I take long, exaggerated steps like that will somehow help me keep my balance. It's hard to feel secure when you're walking on fluff like this.

I shimmy out of the cell and Ms. Babinaux takes my arm to

help steady me.

"Are you sure you're alright?" she says, her lips two flaps of faded meat.

"It's all good," I say. "A little squishier than I might like, but…"

We move through the door into a hallway. The cinder block walls remind me of a college dorm. It's hard to say what all of this might look like without the color being sucked out of everything.

"What is this place?" I say.

"It's an old hospital," she says. "The League bought it years ago. The plan was to rehab it, but the progress has been slow."

I really want to run my hand against the wall, to feel the cool of the painted concrete on my fingertips. But Ms. Babinaux has my arm in a death grip, and she's moving with some urgency, dragging me along like a puppy that wants to stop and smell everything.

I bet there's food wherever we're going. I wonder what it could be. It strikes me that I'm neither hungry nor full. It just seems like food would be pleasant. I like the way it tastes.

Wait. We're in a darker hallway now with smooth concrete walls. It stretches out into the distance so far that I can't see the end, at least not clearly. I think we went downstairs at some point, which would be weird since we were already in the basement.

I kind of want to say "What demonry is this?" but I opt for:

"Where are we?"

"I told you. These are the tunnels under the hospital," she says. "There's a back way out. This way we know we won't run into anybody."

We're quiet for a moment. The only sound is our feet squishing into the marshmallow foam.

"Did they drug you?" she says.

This is a good question. I do feel like I'm walking around in a dream, though I believe it to be real. I try to remember how this all came about, but it feels like some of that stuff was weeks ago. I remember... um...

White. The white is important.

And then the image bursts into my head: beams of white light flaring in all directions. I lie in the alley. My alley. And someone else was there before that. Before the white, I mean. The hooded man. I killed him, but then it wasn't him. It was like a dream where the shapes shift and the scenery changes and the people all change into someone else. The hooded man turned into Amity.

Or wait. Maybe it was always Amity. Glenn's daughter wore the hood the whole time.

Yeah. Yeah, that's right.

Well, that's a little upsetting.

OK, wait again. What did Babinaux just say? Was it something about food?

"Jeffrey," she says. "Did they drug you?"

Damn it. Not food.

She stares at me. Her eyes look like she has milky contacts in.

"I don't think so," I say. "I had a seizure when you left the room. And now everything is bled white."

"Bled white?" she says.

I nod.

"All the life and color got sucked right out," I say. "I feel a little effed up, too, I guess. Hard to remember all the moving pieces."

She presses her lips together, and they look like mating albino caterpillars. It strikes me that the tip of my nose is freezing cold.

The end of the previously endless hall takes shape in front of us. There's a stairway.

"Where are we going?" I say.

"I'm taking you home," she says.

"Won't people just try to abduct me again?" I say.

"I'll have a couple of guys keep an eye on the place," she says.

We climb the staircase and it leads to a steel door. Babinaux opens it, and a rectangle of sunlight glares in the doorway. I squint as we cross the threshold, taking in a grass field that gives way to an empty parking lot in the distance. Turning around, we walked out of what looks like a brick storage shed. You'd probably never guess that it leads down into a weird underground lair if you walked past it.

"Our ride should be here momentarily," she says.

I glance over her shoulder and see the moon in the sky behind her. Even though it's probably mid-morning, the moon is out. Seems weird in a way, but then I guess the moon is always out when Babinaux is around somehow.

CHAPTER 2

By the time the Lincoln pulls into Glenn's driveway, I can make out a red hue to the front door. I swivel my head around, and everywhere I look, the color begins to seep back into things, the white fading away. It's slow, but if I watch it closely enough I can see some progress. It reminds me of something that would happen in a cartoon.

I get out of the car, and my feet don't really squish into the sidewalk as I move toward the front door, at least not like before. It's more like walking on a thick layer of hardboiled egg whites than marshmallow now. It still gives under my weight but in a different way and not as much.

I realize that my state of euphoria is also wearing off. I still feel pleasant, but as I drift back toward normal, I understand how "high" I really was before, for lack of a better term. At the time, I didn't grasp that.

I hesitate outside the door. For some reason, I know Glenn won't be here. The Explorer still sits in the driveway, but I have this sense that when he said he'd try to come back for me, he didn't mean he'd try to come back to the jail cell to get me. He meant it in a bigger way than that.

As I set foot in the doorway, I'm greeted by the mess. Pictures and glass shards and utensils and couch stuffing crowd the floor. I forgot about all of that until I swung the door open.

Yep. The place remains trashed, and these cats didn't lift so much as a paw to do anything about it. Figures.

Against my better judgment, I decide to feed the beasts anyway. The second I lift a can from the stack, Mardy trots into the kitchen. When I pop the lid off, the rest of the pack prowls onto the scene.

Leroy scarfs his food and then tries to steal everybody else's meat, so I have to stand guard until they're all done. Turns out watching cats eat is not super entertaining.

With that out of the way, I get down to business. I rifle through the fridge and take a peek into the cabinets. I even skim through the cans and boxes of food strewn across the floor. There are many viable options here – smoked turkey and honey glazed ham in the form of an expensive brand of lunch meat that I've never tried, Glenn's homemade pickles, a variety of Oreos, some strawberry pop tarts, and an embarrassment of soft drinks.

After much deliberation, I decide to have a glass of orange juice and a blueberry Nutri-grain bar. I realize this is an odd combination, the kind of sweet upon sweet menu building often exhibited by a toddler. Maybe I'm vitamin C deprived or something, but it sounds great to me.

I have big plans to clear a spot on the couch, sit down and really savor this food and drink, but I can't wait. I sip the orange juice as soon as I pour it. I feel the cool fluid wash over my tongue, the acidity tingling on my palate, and then separate waves of sweet and tart hitting at the same time. I guess my senses must be heightened like crazy, because the only way I can describe the flavor is profound. In fact, it is beyond a flavor. It's an experience.

Overwhelmed, I set the glass down on the counter and close my eyes. Time passes. I feel like I can hear the ocean lapping against a beach in the distance. When I open my eyes, it feels like I've gone somewhere else and back again.

I gather my wits along with my drink and breakfast bar and head to the sofa. I scoot piles of couch innards to the left and right and plop down in the middle.

I peel open the foil wrapping on the Nutri-grain bar, the crinkle only adding to the anticipation. I examine it. The bottom looks quite fake, really – the browning and dimpled spots a little too even, too perfect. The smell wafts at me aggressively, all fruit and sweet in my face. My mouth waters.

This is getting pretty intense in a hurry.

I rewrap the bar and set it down on the coffee table, taking a deep breath as I do so. I tell myself to relax. We just got to the pool, Grobnagger. No need to go straight for the damn high dive. Let's wade in and get used to the water first.

I take another sip of juice, and it happens again – the tingle, the waves, my eyes snapping shut involuntarily. I set the glass down and take another deep breath.

As I exhale, I try to relax all of the muscles in my neck and back. It feels like the best massage I've ever had. I slowly lean forward, my eyes droop closed and a calm comes over me. The whole universe is still. I hear that sound again that I know isn't really there, like waves rolling in and out. Within about 10 seconds, I'm asleep.

I start awake a few seconds later, saliva oozing out of the corner of my mouth.

I can't remember ever falling asleep so quickly. I'm usually the guy that rolls around for 45 minutes every night no matter what, but this eating thing is turning out to be kind of exhausting, I guess.

I look over the faintly purple foil wrapper and glass nearly full of pale orange liquid on the table in front of me. They're enticing, but not yet. It's too much. I need to ease into this. I'll just sit for a second, and then I'll eat. Just a second.

A hope wells in me for no good reason that I can think of. It's like a buoy that won't sink no matter how many waves of bad things wash over it.

With my eyes closed, bits of the prior evening come back to me in flashes – the shattered cup, Glenn's speech and exit through the concrete wall, my encounter with Amity in the alley and the white light everywhere. Even as it all comes back to me, I still only feel hope and empathy and a new understanding. Because I know if I get the chance, I will make things right with Louise and see where things might go between us. And something about that makes it feel like everything else will work out fine.

My head tilts forward again, and I'm asleep.

A bell chimes, and I shake myself awake in time to hear the tail end of the sound. The mess of Glenn's living room surrounds me again. I lift my hand to my face, and a swath of couch stuffing clings to my fingers. Sweat beads on the orange juice glass, and the untouched Nutri-grain bar sits next to it. I press my fingertips to the glass and find it's still cool.

Thinking back, though I was asleep, I know the bell chimed at least twice before the one that woke me. I remember hearing it in my dream.

The only clock in the room is smashed, so I have little sense of how long I was out beyond the temp of the juice. More importantly, perhaps: What the eff could the tolling bell have been? I could still hear it trailing off when I woke, so I'm pretty sure it wasn't just a dream.

On cue, it chimes again, and I gaze up at the ceiling as it seems to be coming from up high. From above? Is this another metaphysical test of some kind? A bell is a little ominous, though, right? I mean, for whom does this fucker toll?

There's the clatter of something solid striking metal. It's a familiar noise, but it takes a moment to register. Someone's knocking at the door. I guess that makes the chime a doorbell.

Some genius I turned out to be.

I hustle to the door, wading through the junk pile, and peek through the peep hole. It's her. Her face looks all flushed.

I open the door, and Louise stands before me. The sunlight glints down onto her. It's so much brighter on that side of the doorway. The shade shrouds my side in black. Her face twists into a scowl as she makes eye contact. Her complexion has been splotched with pink before but never looked so uniformly rosy as it does now, and that's with the world still faded a little white for me.

"Hi," I say.

"Listen," she says. "I get it. You're the closed off type, the loner, the outsider, whatever you want to call it. Fine. I understand this premise, alright, but I don't accept it."

"What?" I say.

"I'm not going to let you push me away, Jeffrey," she says. "I know that's how you operate. You push everyone away. You withdraw out of fear, and I won't allow it. I think that we both know-"

Before she can finish her sentence, I lean through the doorway, my face drenched in daylight, and kiss her. The last thing I see before I close my eyes is her eyes going wide and her expression softening.

And then I wonder if my breath tastes like orange juice. I guess there are worse things.

Undaunted by this breathy query, I slide my hands around her waist and pull her close to me, through the doorway and into the shade.

I explain the events of the prior evening as I clear off another spot on the couch and we sit.

"You didn't have to go to all the trouble of cleaning the place just for little ole me," she says as she kicks pieces of a shattered ceramic coaster out from under her seating area.

"Yeah, sorry about this," I say.

"I'm just playin'," she says. "It's hardly your fault a bunch of wackos trashed the place in the name of magic."

I nod. And then I take a sip of the orange juice without thinking about it. I brace myself for an overwhelming taste explosion as the beverage crosses my lips, but it's only mildly orgasmic. I guess I must make a weird face, though.

"You alright, weirdo?" Louise says, laughing.

I look over to see her staring at me out of the corners of her eyes, her head tilted away.

"Huh?" I say. "Oh."

I set the glass down.

"You make the craziest faces, you know that?" she says.

"I guess so," I say.

She opens her mouth to speak again, but a buzz and beep

emit from her purse, interrupting her. She pulls out her phone, taps and swipes the screen. Her brow furrows a moment as she reads, and then the creases unfold and a smile curves her lips.

"Want to see something crazy?" she says.

CHAPTER 3

The charred body stretches before us, blistered and pocked with red and black. Forehead skin pools on the right side of the face, still soft from melting and oozing to gravity's whim. The tissue congeals there, covering one eye. I can hardly tell an eye socket exists underneath.

She doesn't say anything, but Louise puts a hand on my shoulder. Her other hand forms a shield in front of her mouth like she might vomit every which way in a second. I don't think this is what she envisioned when she smiled and asked me about seeing something crazy.

My eyes drift from Louise back to the body. Bone glints where flames ate away the eyelid of the other eye. The lack of flesh makes the eyeball on that side look bulbous like it's about to pop.

Dennis pokes his police baton into the corpse's ribs, and something crunches like an overcooked piece of bacon.

"Jesus Christ, dude," I say.

My feet grind into the gravel as I take a step back and avert my eyes. Dennis laughs, his fingers drumming at his beer belly in delight.

"Aw, he don't mind, Grobnagger," he says, gesturing at the body with the stick.

Louise knows Dennis from her investigations – he's one of

her contacts in the police department - so now I know Dennis as well, which is really too bad.

I look back at the corpse. A few patches of smooth scalp remain, contrasting with the rippled and bubbled swaths. Angry folds and crevices pucker the skin on the neck. My eyes keep tracing over the edge of the mouth where the blackened remnants of the lips give way to the white of the teeth.

The body sprawls in the center of a vacant lot. Judging by the chain link fence around us and some of the bigger pieces of concrete underfoot, I know the building that stood here once was razed to the ground back when the city still tended to such things. Now weeds sprout up in clusters through the chunks of cinder block. A dandelion smears its yellow on the back of my pant leg.

I'm not concerned with the plant life, however. I take a step back and draw my eyes away from the face. The burns leave few identifiable details from the waist up, but the legs suffered little damage. I point to the bottom of the maroon robe draping the ankles.

"That's a League robe?" I say.

Dennis nods.

"A genu-wine ceremonial League of Light robe," he says. "Way I heard Detective Miller sayin', they only bust these things out for initiations and such. Body wasn't burned out here, though. It was burned someplace else and dumped here. That's according to Miller as well."

His lips purse like he's about to spit on the ground, but he stops himself, perhaps remembering that this is a crime scene.

"Figured it was only a matter of time before there was a bunch of dead bodies out this way," he says, gesturing the baton at the land around us. "These damn dirt worshippers ain't but troublemakers and head cases."

Louise turns away. I can't decide where she stands on the vom-o-meter.

"Is ya'll hungry?" Dennis says.

"Uh," I say, glancing away from the crispy body. "No."

Louise shakes her head.

"Damn," Dennis says. "Cause my belly is downright angry. I didn't have no time for breakfast."

"Have the detectives interviewed any of the League people yet?" I say.

"Tried," Dennis says. "They ain't such a cooperative bunch. I guess when you're in the business of savin' souls, it don't look good when one of your people shows up deep fried and all."

We are silent for a moment.

"God, I'm hungry," Dennis says, prodding at the chest with the stick again.

"Stop playing with the goddamn thing!" Louise says, her face all dark now, her eyes open too wide like a boxer moving in for the kill shot after his opponent's knees buckle.

"Huh?" he says.

"It's a human being," she says. "Do you have to keep poking it like that?"

"Oh," he says.

"Not to mention that this is a murder scene," she says. "You're tampering with the victim's body for shit's sake. I mean, who the hell ever let you be a cop?"

Dennis sticks his lips out in a frown. He pulls the baton away from the body and twirls it, almost slapping it into his palm but stopping at the last minute. He kneels to try to wipe the ashy residue off of it in the weeds.

"You know I didn't have to bring y'all out here," he says. "I don't have to give you all the info I give you, miss snippy. I do that as a kindness. For a friend."

Louise's crazy eyes shrink back to normal width. She looks poised to apologize, but Dennis stands and goes on.

"It ain't no thing, though," he says. "Listen, if you're hungry, I'm 'bout to go to Krazy Chicken for lunch once the coroner gets here. Fried chicken. Homemade slaw. Biscuits slathered with honey. It's good as hell."

Louise and I just look at each other.

"Believe it or not, staring at this cooked human body isn't exactly whetting my appetite," I say.

"Whatever, dude," Dennis says. "A man's gotta eat."

As the Passat carries us back to Glenn's house, I stare out the window, letting my eyes go out of focus so all I see is a blur smearing past on the side of the road. The distraction doesn't help. The image of the charred body flickers in my imagination, blur or no blur.

It ranks up there among the worst ways to go, I think - consumed by fire. And the idea that the same people that abducted me could be behind this murder isn't lost on me.

Without meaning to, I imagine the flames crawling over my body, searing, blistering, melting my flesh. I shudder.

"Are you cold?" Louise says, reaching to adjust the AC.

"No," I say. "It's… I'm fine."

She looks at me for a long time.

"OK," she says.

Seeing the blue of her eyes, I realize that everything looks pretty much normal again – no more milky eyeballs, no more faded meat mouths. I hold up my hand and wiggle my fingers, and they look like regular old fingers again.

I guess there's a small amount of relief to the white world thing coming to an end. On the other hand, I was never that upset about everything going maggoty, so the soothing sensation is quite mild. In a way, I think my reaction might be weirder than everything else about it. When your hand looks like a pile of worms, you're supposed to be a little upset, right? I mean, I don't know if laughing is an appropriate response there. At the time, I was pretty pleased with it all, though.

I roll my neck and then lean my head back on the headrest. My eyes drift shut of their own accord. I really should be hungry by now, but I'm not. The last thing I ate was some garbage water Thai food, which feels like it transpired about six months ago. Instead, I'm only sleepy.

I sit up to avoid slumber.

"Did any of them seem like killers to you?" I say.

"What do you mean?" she says.

"You've spent a good bit of time around the League people," I say. "Did any of them seem capable of murder?"

Her eyes point skyward as she thinks a moment, her hands stroking at the wheel of the car.

"None in particular," she says. "But my line of work makes you realize real quick that almost anyone is capable of almost anything."

I scratch the back of my neck.

"I guess that makes sense," I say.

Damn. What the hell? I get locked up in a cell and then a burned body pops up within twelve or so hours? Not great. I wish Glenn was here. He'd know what to make of this.

The Passat glides into the driveway behind the Explorer. I take a deep breath, exhale and look over at Louise. She rubs at the bridge of her nose with thumb and index finger.

"I don't suppose you want to help me clean this mess up?" I say, doing that nonchalant shrug thing that seemed to win Glenn over with such ease.

She narrows her eyes at me.

"I guess," she says.

CHAPTER 4

First, we clear the biggest objects from the living room floor. The shattered bits get thrown out, and the pictures with broken frames get shoved in a closet for Glenn to deal with later. Within a few minutes, we've already made a big difference. With the fallen pictures and broken glass out of way and toppled plants set right, it begins to look like a livable room again.

Then we split up. Louise shoves the stuffing back into the couch cushions and sews them up. I figure we can throw a slipcover over it later and no one will know the difference.

While she does that, I dust bust the areas where soil got ground into the carpet when the plants went down. Once the dirt spots fade away, I broaden my range of attack to sweep up the random debris strewn about the rest of the room. The vacuum keeps finding loads of filth even after the floor passes the eyeball test, and I have to empty Glenn's Dirt Devil three times before I'm through.

After just over an hour, the living room looks to be in order. This is good. Now we just have to do every other room in the house.

I pick up dishes and utensils off of the kitchen floor and throw them in the sink. Louise checks her phone a few times and writes a couple of texts in between picking up various cans and boxes of food from the floor and shoving them back in the cupboard. I think about asking her what the messages are about, but I decide against it.

Once the floor is clear, I start loading the dishwasher, which I will need to run four times to get everything clean. As the first load runs, I move to the dining room to start the process yet again, removing fragments, remnants and scraps on the first sweep.

When I walk by the kitchen again, I see that Louise has butter melting in a frying pan.

"What's this?" I say.

"It's getting late," she says. "We need to eat."

I consider the notion.

"I'm not hungry," I say.

"Me neither," she says. "But I've solved that problem. I'm making something that tastes great whether you're hungry or not."

I nod and get back to work, taking the dust buster to task in the dining area. The Dirt Devil ruffles the fabric of the rug as it passes, spiking it up when I push forward and smoothing it down when I pull it back.

Just as I finish vacuuming, Louise enters the room with two plates each holding one and a half grilled cheese sandwiches.

I wash my hands and sit down at the dining room table that looks like a single slice taken out of a massive tree and glazed with something. In all of my time at Glenn's, this is the first time I've sat at this fancy table under the chandelier. It feels a bit silly, to be honest.

We eat, and she was right about the grilled cheese. It's good.

After the sandwiches, Louise heads home to shower and sleep, and I plan to do the same. I head for the bathroom. And after a glance in the mirror, I dig around in the cabinets until I find an electric razor.

I have this hair that sprouts on the back of my neck and the very top of my back. This is one of the many joys of getting older, I suppose, though I might be partially to blame. Years ago I shaved my head with a razor for a few months, and I shaved this peach fuzz on my neck during that time. Well, it grew back thicker as time went on. I know some people think that that's just a fallacy, that shaving doesn't affect follicles or make hair any thicker. Based on the chia pet thriving between my shoulder blades, I'm pretty sure those people are wrong.

Even worse, it's incongruous. I'm not very hairy elsewhere. I'm not your Robin Williams type. My arms and legs have light, non-offensive hair. This stuff on my neck looks slightly thicker than the stuff that hangs down in a yak's eyes.

Anyway, like I said, now it grows out, this carpet of dark fluff, and I feel like a disgusting troll. Eventually I can't take it anymore, and I go at it with an electric shaver. It's insane how much better I feel after I trim it. The loathsome feeling dies down, and I feel clean. I mean, I feel like a troll still but not a particularly disgusting one.

So I shave and shower, and my skin feels all fresh. The troll meter goes down a little more.

Once I get cleaned up, though, I find myself sitting in the living room doing nothing instead of going to bed. I sip at a tiny glass of orange juice. The flavor doesn't overpower me the way it did earlier, but it seems too acidic to be that enjoyable now, almost bitter. Even so, it's the only food item I find myself drawn to.

I flip through the channels on TV. I stare at the screen, but I can't seem to register the images flashing there nor can I hear what's being said. I imagine this is maybe what it's like for a dog to watch television. Their eyes lock onto the moving pictures, but it means nothing to them most of the time.

Through the window, I see two beams of light slice through the night and swing into the driveway. Headlights. Ah, yes. Babinaux is about due to show up for one of our night meetings, I suppose. The moon is like her bat signal or something.

I head out to meet her in the back of the Lincoln as usual.

"I assume you heard about the body from your investigator friend," she says as I climb into the vehicle.

"Yeah," I say. "I actually saw it, which was… unpleasant."

"I'd think so," she says. "Well, I have some information that your friend wouldn't have. At least not yet. That's why I'm here tonight."

"What's that?" I say.

"It's Farber," she says. "The corpse. It's Riston Farber."

"The spoon man? The one that's trying to kill me?" I say.

"That's the one," she says. "It's a big shock to our community. He had very devoted followers, and they're devastated as you'd expect."

"Who'd want to kill him?" I say.

I actually have an idea on this one, but I'm damn sure not telling her.

"It's hard to say," she says. "His two disciples, Seth Cromwell and Stan Woods, are jockeying to take his place now, and the support seems pretty split. They'd have the most to gain, so it stands to reason that one of them might have done it."

"Crazy," I say.

"The good news for you is that one of them is a moderate," she says.

I assume she's about to elaborate, but when she doesn't I'm forced to ask the obvious question:

"What the hell does the mean?" I say.

"Sorry," she says. "It's been a long day. When Farber kidnapped you and your friend, he was essentially splitting from the League. He had already started the process of making his followers believe he was becoming divine – 'forming,' he called it. I guess he felt you played some role in that."

I nod.

"One of his disciples, Stan Woods, apparently wants no part of that plan," she says. "He wants their group to rejoin the League and let you be. He's a pretty nice guy, Stan."

"I see," I say. "Well, I can get behind that plan, anyway."

She smiles.

"What about the other guy?" I say. "Does he still want to give me the old-"

I pantomime hands closing around my wind pipe.

"I'm not sure," she says, her smile fading. "I don't know him as well, but Cromwell has quite a reputation. There are a lot of stories - nasty stories - but it's hard to say which might be true. I guess I'll say that many in the League fear him. That much I know for a fact."

She scratches her nose before she goes on.

"I think his priority will be the struggle for power at the moment, though, so you're probably safe for now. And I'll still have a couple of men keeping an eye on you."

"I can respect that," I say.

She talks a bit more, but my mind starts to tune out like a dog watching TV again. Because all I can think about is the gut feeling I had when she told me Farber was dead – that Glenn was the one who killed him.

A mix of feelings tumbles inside of me like a load of delicates in the dryer, equal parts alleviation and repulsion and dread. I'm relieved that Farber isn't out there trying to kill me at the moment. For the first time since he walked through the wall, though, I'm worried about Glenn. What might he have gotten himself into? Even if he didn't kill Farber, where the hell is he? I never really felt like he could be in danger, but now it somehow seems more likely than not.

As I start the slow drift to sleep, I keep picturing that burned body laid out in the gravel and weeds. It's hard to even think it was a full grown man once with it all shriveled and blackened like that. It looked so frail like it'd disintegrate if you tried to pick it up. And now to know it was the man I watched hover a spoon? Unreal.

Bad guy or not, what the hell is wrong with the world, you know? Setting people on fire and dumping them out in the boonies? My drowsing mind pries around the edges to try to make sense of it, but it can't.

CHAPTER 5

We sit at the snack bar eating soup. It's a coconut based Thai soup with fish sauce, lime juice, cilantro, shiitake mushrooms, and some shrimp. Sounds weird, right? Well, it's not weird. It's delicious. It's like a crazy awesome version of clam chowder where every bite is somehow light and creamy and acidic and a little fishy at the same time. I think Louise got the recipe from Emeril, but I'm not sure.

"Listen," she says. "My client has been in touch."

"Yeah?" I say.

"Yeah," she says. "It's kind of a good news, bad news thing, I guess. See, he offered me a lot of money to look into the Farber murder."

"That sounds pretty good," I say.

"Right, but the thing is," she says. "He also said that the League people know who I am now. Whether it was you blabbing to Babinaux or not, my cover is blown. They know I'm a P.I. and all, and he has doubts about how useful I'll be going forward, as far as working undercover, anyway."

"That sucks," I say. "If it was me, I'm sorry. What are you going to do?"

"Well, I do have one idea. A way you could make it up to me," she says. "But I don't know what you're going to think about it."

She looks so innocent that I'm pretty concerned.

"What is it?" I say.

"Well, I was thinking," she says. "Maybe you could join the League and be my undercover."

"What?" I say. "It's not like I'm going to fly under the radar over there."

"No. I think you've got the wrong idea, Jeffrey. I was there. I've seen how those people talk about you," she says. "They get Jesus eyes. Most of them would be thrilled to hang out with you, let alone have you join them."

"You mean the ones that tossed me in a cell or the other ones?" I say.

"Look, there are other clients and jobs out there. I'm not trying to pressure you or anything," she says. "Just think it over. I thought you might want to do it to see if you could find out anything about where Glenn is."

Argh. I feel guilty and curious and threatened all at once. Mostly threatened, though.

"I'll think about it," I say.

But what I really mean is that I'll think about how I'll never do it.

Days go by, and to her credit, Louise never mentions me joining the League again. There's also no sign of Glenn. Perhaps the oddest development of all - no seizures. No visions transmitted from heavenly places. No metaphysical activity whatsoever. Maybe breaking the cup was a bigger deal than I thought. Maybe I've been cut off. In any case, I'm not all that concerned about it.

In the downtime, I finish cleaning up Glenn's place,

capping the job with a kickass slipcover for the couch. It's houndstooth and looks like it's from the 70's in an awesome way. I've been reading a couple of the books from Glenn's library. Louise comes over a lot in the evenings, and we get a variety of carryout meals and watch movies. Sometimes we kiss a little. Sometimes we kiss a lot. Kind of depends on how good the movie is, I guess.

Anyway, life is more normal than it has been for a long time, and it's awesome. In many respects, in fact, it is better than my life ever was before all of this.

So I'm sure it will all burst into flames any minute now. If life has taught me one lesson, it's that things can never stay like this for long.

CHAPTER 6

I sprawl on the couch in the living room with my legs draped over Louise's lap. She flips through channels on TV, but nothing is on except the news, which seems particularly unfunny tonight. She turns it off.

"I was thinking maybe we'd go out tonight," she says.

"Go out?" I say, sitting up.

"Yeah. Out. Out of this house," she says. "Maybe we could go to this Mexican restaurant, La Pinata, on Lovell Street. It's supposed to be pretty good, but I rarely go over that way, so I've never tried it."

Fuck.

"Hm..." I say. "I don't know if I really feel like it."

"Well, if you're not in the mood for Mexican, we could get something else," she says.

"No," I say. "I meant I'm not in the mood to go out."

She huffs. She doesn't look at me. Her face twists up into a mask of pure evil, but she keeps her malevolent powers directed at the floor.

The crazy thing is that this could have been so much worse. I could have told her that I'm never in the mood to go out. But I played it cool, so this will blow over, and we'll get back to carryout and a movie on Netflix.

Is she infuriated? Absolutely. Is her face engorged with

homicidal rage blood? You know it is. Could she turn on me faster than a Chow turns on its master? If I pushed it, it's almost a certainty.

But I handled it like a pro. I am in the clear in 5, 4, 3-

"No. I don't accept that, Jeffrey. I know you," she says, wheeling the demon cat gaze straight at me. I feel the evil eyes crawling over my skin, hot like those infrared lamps they keep chicken nuggets under in the school cafeteria.

This would be the perfect time to do one of those cool shrugs and downplay all of this, but I don't do that. I panic and freeze like a groundhog in the path of a minivan, my mouth partially open, my nose possibly twitching.

"This is another one of your quirks," she says. I really want to say "she snarls" there, but it'd be an exaggeration. "You push people away, and you coop yourself up like a weird hermit, and I won't stand for it. It's not healthy for person to live like this. Not all of the time."

My instinct is to scurry under the couch and wait for the bad thing to leave. Instead, I twitch my nose a couple more times, flit my eyes around the room and generally remain fastened to my seat.

"So how about this?" she says. "We'll go out once a week. Go to a restaurant or a movie. You'll see that it's not a big deal. And even if it's a little nerve wracking at first, I bet you'll learn to relax and have fun, yeah?"

How cute. The demon is feigning reasonableness to try to confuse me. I close my eyes like that will make this disappear.

"Jeff?" she says.

I squeeze my eyes and jaw and fists shut as hard as I can.

"Are you OK?" she says.

I squeeze and squeeze and squeeze. And something inside my head pops. It feels wet somehow and like a sudden release of a lot pressure, like a cyst bursting in my brain and gushing goo everywhere. I gasp and exhale, and as the air rolls out of me like a receding wave, time slows down a little bit, and I grow more and more relaxed.

The warmth starts at the place where my head meets my neck and spreads outward from there in all directions. What starts as an alleviation of anxiety and tension quickly turns to a tidal wave of bliss washing all up and down me. Every nerve ending, every cell radiates maximized physical pleasure. I guess the only thing I can compare it to is sexual pleasure, but it's more pure than that. Every atom in my body is happy.

It dawns on me that this is a familiar bliss, in fact. I didn't consciously feel it come over me like this on the cot back in the cell, but it surely started this way. I guess with experience I've developed a sensitivity to the process.

I open my eyes to see the world gone white again. My first reaction is to focus right in on my hands. My fingers look like a cross between bratwursts and white caterpillars. I hold them in front of my face and do my jazz hand routine.

Yep. Still hilarious.

Surveying the rest of the room, though, it's not quite the same as it was back in the cell. The walls here almost look like they have a layer of woven spider web stretched across them. Pieces glisten when the light hits the right angle. I swivel my head around to get the full effect.

I glance over at Louise, and she stares back through milk white eyes. Even with all the color drained from her flesh, she doesn't look bad. It's weird. A girl can still be pretty when they turn all white somehow, while I basically look like the great white worm.

"I guess," I say.

It takes a moment for her to respond. I think she senses that something is different about me. Perhaps the jazz hand bit and ensuing fit of giggles were a giveaway. Hard to say.

"You guess?" she says.

"I guess I'll go out to that Mexican place with you," I say.

Truth is, I'm pretty much down to do whatever now that the white world throbs both inside me and outside me. I'm guessing we could walk around the parking lot at a McDonald's, and I'd be thrilled to experience the assortment of sights and sounds.

"OK," she says. "Great. That's great."

She's doing that look again, though, where she turns her head away and squints at me from the corner of her eye. It's a mischievous expression. It reminds me of a Chihuahua that's about two seconds away from latching on to some poor bastard's nose.

I wonder what's going to be on the menu at La Pinata. I bet they'll have Mexican Coca Cola that's made with real cane sugar instead of high fructose corn syrup.

Good.

As.

Hell.

I'm sure they serve burritos, but I bet they have a bunch of other authentic Mexican entrees I've never tried in addition to that. This could get crazy. I'm usually not one to take a chance on something unknown in a restaurant. I play it safe. Maybe it's the chemical bliss beamed into my head from Christ knows where, but today is the day to get a little adventurous, I think.

CHAPTER 7

The restaurant's décor sends mixed messages. The TVs all play soccer with frantic announcers yelling in Spanish while English closed captioning fights to keep up. There's a giant Mexican flag tacked to the back wall, and a few cacti wave hello from behind the counter. On the wall above our booth, however? One of those cardboard Precious Moments cartoons – a very European looking girl with giant blue eyes holding a stuffed rabbit.

I don't get it.

"What do you think?" Louise says. "Seems like a pretty low key place."

I look around, and she's right. It's not super busy. The lighting is dim, which is relaxing, I think. The waitresses are all dressed as casual as possible.

"Yeah," I say. "I can respect that."

The waitress comes to get our drink order. I ask about the Coke. It's legit Mexican, sugar cane and all. Upon confirming this, I do a fist pump like a guy that just scored a touchdown in the Super Bowl.

I start to feel like I'm maybe too excited about this beverage, but then I remember reading that Hitler used to ejaculate during his speeches, and I feel better knowing that there are much weirder people than me out there getting excited about much weirder things. Really excited. I mean, I like a tasty drink, but I've yet to cream my shorts over one.

As I ponder all of this, the waitress returns with the drinks. The fizzy beverage sits before me, looking much paler than usual, naturally. I tear open my straw and shove it down into the bubbly.

Recalling the orange juice incident, I brace myself as I lift the glass toward my mouth and sip at the straw, but I'm still unprepared. The acid stings my tongue, and the carbonation pelts its bubbles at every surface in my mouth. Then the tsunami of sweet hits, and I swear I see rectangles of color imprint themselves on my vision in violent bursts. Every time the colors hit, all sound fades out. Everything returns tinted blue, slowly receding back to white, and I feel like there should be scrolling text at the bottom of my field of vision alerting me to the technical difficulties I'm experiencing. I'm waiting for a disembodied voice to tell me that this is not a test of the emergency broadcast system.

Louise gives me a look as I shake my limp hand out to the side of the table. It's a move I associate with the hero in a movie shortly after he's knocked out the bad guy, but it seems to make sense here all the same.

I point the straw in the Coke away from myself as a precautionary measure and pick up the menu. My eyes pore over every photo, and I read all the descriptions multiple times. I study it like there's going to be an exam when the waitress comes back.

"What are you getting?" I say.

"Chiles Rellenos," Louise says.

"What's that again?" I say, scanning the menu once more.

"It's a roasted poblano pepper stuffed with cheese," she says.

"Oh," I say.

Lunacy!

I order the Bistec Encebollao, which is a Latin style steak in an adobo marinade. I don't know if this was the best choice, but I'm a gambler.

I lose myself watching the text pop up rapid fire at the bottom of the TV screen, and I guess many minutes pass, as the next thing I know, the waitress moves toward us.

The food comes, and steam rises off of everything in dramatic fashion. The waitress sets our meals in front of us and warns us that the plates are hot. Immediately I press the heel of my hand on my plate.

No damage.

My dish looks really good considering the white worm quality and all. After the Coke incident, unfortunately, I'm quite reluctant to eat any of it. I go to work dicing up my meat, so I can at least keep it moving around on the plate. My knife dances it this way and my fork drags it that way. It's like a meat ballet.

"Is everything to your satisfaction, sir?" the waitress says.

"It's great," I say. "Everything's perfect."

I watch her eyes snap to my barely touched plate of food and shift back to me, accompanied by a smirk forming on her lips.

"I'm not feeling well is all," I say.

The waitress nods and shuffles off to refill drinks at the next table.

"You know, for a guy that supposedly doesn't feel well,

you're kind of smiling like a psychopath," Louise says.

As she speaks, I notice something fluttering out from behind her chair. At first I think it's two birds loose in the restaurant, but their flight patterns aren't right, twisting and veering in the air in a way that's unlike the smooth flight pattern of a bird. It's familiar, though.

Bats. They're bats.

Oh shit, I should say something in response to what she said:

"It's hard to explain," I say. "I need to use the restroom, actually."

I watch the bats flutter above me as I stride toward the men's room. They both fly through the ceiling, but I can still see them, if that makes sense. It occurs to me that they're somewhat translucent. Wherever they're flying, there is no ceiling there.

Am I hallucinating now? I must be.

Other shapes start to form around me – trees and bushes leaning and quivering as though the wind is blowing through them, partially translucent like the bats. I don't feel the wind, but I can hear it.

I hustle to the sink and splash cold water on my face like it can wash these visions away. When I open my eyes, however, nothing has changed. I stare at my white worm face in the mirror. I think the bliss alone prevents me from vomiting. My eyes look insane, in any case.

The bathroom door swings open, and an old man walks through, making his way to the urinals. As soon as his back is to me, I rush into a stall and latch the door behind me.

I stand in the poop cubicle, all silent and still. I'm bursting with energy. I want to pace around, but I'm worried this old dude will notice me walking around in the stall and get freaked out. I need to keep a low profile until these visions pass.

So here I am, feigning a deuce in the men's room at La Pinata. I bet this wouldn't have happened if we just stayed home and watched Netflix. Maybe I was right all along about never going out to eat.

The wind noise grows louder, and the leaves on the see through trees and bushes around me kick up again, and it makes an idea pop into my head. Could I be looking into some other dimension? It'd be like being able to see into the alley. My alley, I mean. Almost like I'm half here and half somewhere else.

The flush of the urinal interrupts my thought, followed by the clicks of the soap dispenser and then the water pouring in the sink. After a split second of quiet, the blow dryer kicks on. When that clicks off, silence descends on the room. I hold my breath and listen for a moment.

Not a peep.

Is he gone?

A wet sounding fart rips through the evening and bounces off of every ceramic tile in the room in a tremendous cacophony of fart reverb. And then the bathroom door squeaks open and closed, and the old man ventures off into the night.

With him gone, I'm free to pace in the 15 square foot stall space. It's handicap accessible, so it's roomier than most, I guess.

I walk back and forth, back and forth, my feet following a particular diagonal pattern on the floor tiles. I close my eyes every few seconds, trying to give the ghostly plant life around me the perfect opportunity to fade out discretely. But they don't take the hint. Every time I check, the bushes are still there, waving leaves at me with as much enthusiasm as ever.

I scratch the back of my arm, and after a few swipes, I realize that it feels great. With every nerve ending already singing divine praises, even a touch as basic as a scratch takes it up another notch. I close my eyes and let the scratching move up and down my arm, setting off a million pin pricks of euphoria. I move my fingernails to the back of my neck and go to work on that sensitive spot where the hairline falls. Unbelievable.

My hand slides down my spine, and I scrape and claw and chafe myself to nirvana, the tingle spreading over all of me. I feel like a Christmas tree with all the lights lit up.

And just then I think about Louise sitting out there by herself with my untouched plate of bistec, and I know I can't hang out in here for much longer.

Shit.

I take a couple of deep breaths. I'm not exactly scared, probably thanks in part to the complete and utter bliss. I'm a little overwhelmed, though, almost like the same sensory overload I got from drinking the Coke. When I think about it, there's nothing to indicate that the bats or anything in the tree world can even see me let alone hurt me. I exhale all slowly, counting backward from 10.

I ease open the latch and exit the stall. I stop at the sink for one more face splash of water. As I dab a paper towel across my brow, I hear a whispering voice say:

"Grobnags!"

I freeze, the brown paper still pressed to my forehead. The

voice, definitely a man's, whisper yells again:

"Grobnagger! It's me!"

I lift the paper towel from my face, and it slowly slides out of the frame of my vision like the curtain rising at the start of a play. I gasp as I take in the translucent figure standing in front of me.

It's Glenn.

CHAPTER 8

Glenn squats among some of the see through bushes. Is he hiding? His torso appears noticeably thinner, and an overgrown beard sprouts along his neck and jaw. The disheveled state makes it look like he's right in the middle of morphing into a werewolf.

I wait a second to be sure. He is not morphing into a werewolf.

"Where are you?" I say.

"That's a good question," he says, running his fingers through the new hair under his chin. "I don't have a great answer, and I also don't have long to talk, so let me ask you one instead."

I nod.

"How much time has passed there?" he says.

"Since you walked through the wall?" I say, tilting my head as I tally it up. "Nine days."

"OK, good," he says.

"Why is that good?" I say.

"Well… Time runs differently here," he says. "It's been… a lot longer than that for me, I think. Listen, you need to join the League."

"What?" I say.

"It's important. The League can keep you safe for now," he

says. "And I'll be back… eventually."

As I'm about to ask him if he killed Farber, a kid runs into the restroom followed a few paces later by his dad. I wash my hands and play it all cool. When I look back, Glenn is gone, and the trees and bushes are beginning to flicker in and out.

I run my hands under the blow dryer. It feels awesome. Not quite as good as scratching but close.

I head back out toward the booth where Louise sits. By this time, the trees and the bushes and the wind have all died out. The white world still rages fierce, though, and the euphoria is as strong as ever.

When I get to the table, I see that she already has our leftovers in doggie bags. Really, they are in little plastic containers. It's neither a bag nor in any way affiliated with a dog, but whatever.

The man that feeds his dog leftover food from a Mexican restaurant is the man who deserves to clean up the hurricane of doggie diarrhea headed his way.

She stands as I approach, a somber look occupying her face and mouth. I hug her. I squeeze her close to me and talk softly in her ear:

"Thanks for making me do this."

As I pull back, she smiles a little.

As the Passat nears Glenn's, I stare out the window, so blissed out I almost can't see straight.

"I've been thinking," I say. "About joining the League."

"Really?" Louise says.

I nod.

"It would make a lot of sense, I guess," I say. "I hate to do it in a way, but…"

I don't know why I avoid telling her about talking to translucent Glenn in the Mexican restroom. Aside from the 15 obvious reasons why I would never tell anyone about that, I mean.

I glance toward the driver's seat, and it takes my eyes a second to focus on her face. She has that psychotic look in her eye again.

"You need to make a spectacle of yourself right away," she says.

"Huh?" I say.

"Listen, I know how these people think," she says. "They want something to believe in, something big and dramatic. Just look at Farber with the spoon trick. He had that crowd fawning all over him. They want miracles, Jeffrey, and you're the guy with the divine dreams. You're already just about a legend to them. If you make some dramatic spectacle early on, they'll worship you, and you'll have an easy time getting information."

She's an ambitious lass. I can respect that.

As I brush my teeth and prepare for bed, the color starts to seep back into the world. I'm glad in a way. As it turns out, euphoria can be very tiring.

Plus, as my thoughts begin to clear, I have this weird sense that not knowing how I feel about anything is messing me up. Usually I let my feelings guide me in many ways. When all I feel is unending happiness for hours and hours at a time, it makes it hard to figure out what the hell is going on.

I lie down on the couch and pull the sheet and afghan up to my shoulders. In the half light, I see the covers puff into a bubbled dome that slowly settles on me. Awake in the dark, I keep my eyes open and feel the cool of the sofa slowly warm under me.

As soon as I do close my eyes, a projector rolls in my head and images stream on the insides of my eyelids. Not dreams, exactly, since I'm not asleep, but vivid memories and imaginary bits all mixed together.

I see Glenn huddled in the bushes again. Was he in danger? He didn't say much, really: Time is different wherever he is, and that I should join the League. It was good to see him. I wish he was here to help me.

I never got a chance to tell him about seeing Amity in the alley. I guess it didn't feel like the right time. It's kind of a lot to explain.

The image of Glenn dissolves, and I see my feet walking the diagonal pattern on the ceramic tiles in the bathroom, except with every step I take, the tile lights up as my foot hits it and darkens when I step off. It looks like something in an old music video.

That fades out, and I see Louise at the Mexican restaurant, sitting across the booth from me. She looks bored. It's funny. We sat together, but we were a million miles apart. When I drank that Coke, reality flashed in and out of existence for me, and she had no idea even though she was two feet away. It doesn't seem right in a way, but I don't know what's right, I guess.

The divide between people is weird. We can be close. We can touch, but we're always separate. It feels like we should be able to connect more than that, you know? I don't know. Maybe I just feel this way because I'm messed up at the moment.

For one of us, bats were flying out of the ground and through the ceiling. For the other, it was just a restaurant and a meal.

I don't know. It seems important just now, but I can't say why. Maybe if I knew how I felt about it all the way…

Sometimes I think all of these things, and I wonder if I could be going mad.

CHAPTER 9

In the gray half light of morning, I stand in the front window of Glenn's living room, sipping coffee. Little clouds of fog roll along just above street level. They're only visible in the circles of light beaming down from the street lamps.

Maybe it's some withdrawal symptom now that the white world has left me, but it strikes me as more drab than ever. Weird, right? That the world seems more drab when it returns to full color? That's how it is, though.

Babinaux's Lincoln pulls into the driveway. I'm prepared for once. I went out first thing in the morning and told the dudes in the Impala that follows me around to get a hold of her.

It's weird how silly it seems to demand a meeting like this. It feels like we're all in on a game of pretend spies or something, but then I guess everything about a cult is sort of pretending, right? Or is everything in the world pretending? I guess once someone believes something, it becomes real in a way no matter what it is.

I don't know. Shit starts seeming a lot more real when a burned corpse shows up. I can tell you that much.

I exit the house and patter over the sidewalk to the Lincoln. En route I note that the moon still hangs in the air. It's the shape of a slice of lemon, low on the horizon.

I slide into the backseat. Babinaux wears some kind of black skirt suit with a satin blouse the color of eggplant underneath. She always looks ready to cross-examine a witness or something.

"Good morning, Jeffrey," she says.

"Hi," I say. "I want to join the League."

She tucks her chin into her neck, I guess out of surprise. It makes a bunch of weird folds in the under chin region, and it looks like she has no chin. She should avoid doing this. Maybe everyone should.

"Really?" she says.

"Yes," I say.

"Can I ask why?" she says.

I splay my fingers over my mouth as I consider the best words to spin this answer into a positive light.

"Because something is happening to me, and the League probably knows more about it than anyone else," I say. "Plus, I think you guys could protect me."

She hesitates, nods.

"I can let the right people know and make the proper arrangements," she says, her chin slowly reappearing. "How are you, though? You look a little puffy around the eyes."

I feel around my eyelids. I do feel a little swollen.

"I'm fine," I say. "Things have been a little weird, I guess. You remember how I told you that the world was bled white while I was in the cell? It happened again last night."

"Interesting," she says. "Is it scary?"

"Not really," I say. "I mean, I'm basically high, so I'm just really happy."

"What led to it happening this time?" she says.

"Well, Louise was pressuring me to go out to eat," I say. "I was getting frustrated, and I did this move where I clenched up, and it was like something popped in my head. I think I can probably do it at will. Haven't tested that yet, but I think so."

Babinaux rolls her neck.

"She was pressuring you?" she says. "You two are dating, I take it?"

"Yeah. And I hate going out to eat," I say. "She was busting my balls about it pretty good."

Her lips purse into something just shy of bitter beer face.

"You know," she says. "You're supposed to be with somebody that makes you feel good."

"Well," I say. "Yeah. What?"

"Maybe I'm reading into things, but if she's putting all of this pressure on you…" she says.

"Oh. No, I probably did a bad job of describing it," I say. "So how will this work? With the League, I mean. Is there like a clubhouse or something?

"There's a compound," she says.

Wow. This cult is legit.

"I'm just kidding," she says. "We mostly meet at people's houses in small groups. Every week or two there are bigger gatherings at an old church we have on Spring Street. The building is not in the best shape or we'd probably utilize it more frequently."

I am beginning to detect a pattern with this old hospital and old church being in disrepair. They like buying things but not necessarily doing the work required to make them useful. Interesting. I'm not sure if that's a quality I'm looking for in the people I make responsible for protecting me, but I can relate to the path of least resistance ethos.

"Once I make some calls, I'll let you know when and where you'll be making your first appearance," she says. "But if you want some advice? Keep your head down. With all the talk about your dreams, you're going to draw a lot of attention at first, but if you leave well enough alone, all of that will pass and things can be normal."

"Sounds good," I say.

But really what it sounds like is the opposite of what Louise suggested.

CHAPTER 10

None of this seems real.

I pull on the maroon robe. It and the matching pants are both crafted of a shiny fabric that reflects yellow wherever the light catches it. It looks like it would be the perfect material for curtains in a king's bedroom or something. Regal as hell.

I'm the only one left in the little dressing room. Everyone else is out in the nave waiting to get this thing kick started.

According to Babinaux, because of my reputation, the higher ups want to put me on the "fast track." Apparently that means I will go through the "blood ritual" tonight. They only do it every six months, so they wanted to squeeze me in now rather than wait.

I guess for the average member, you wouldn't go through with this bad boy until your mentor feels you're ready, and this usually takes months if not years. Jeff Grobnagger gets the express pass, though.

Boom.

Babinaux said someone would walk me through the details, but this didn't happen. Instead everybody just walked out of the room upon my arrival, so I'm going in blind.

I cinch the belt around my waist, but the chest area keeps coming loose and exposing my dumb nipples. I adjust everything, re-tie the belt and seem to get it under control.

I throw the hood up over my head. It's the oversized style made popular by the grim reaper. I check myself out in the mirror. So long as you can't see my nipples, I actually look pretty intimidating, I think. The hood does a lot of the heavy lifting in that regard.

I walk out toward the main chamber of the church, past a row of arched stained glass windows. I assume they depict churchy things, but I can't tell in the dark. The only light is provided by a shit ton of candles. If I had to guess, I'd say they cleaned out an entire Pottery Barn.

A bunch of hooded heads snap away from me as soon I set foot across the threshold of the door, and then they all freeze in that position, faced away.

I see how it is. I'm the freak show everybody wants to sneak a peek at without getting caught. I take a seat in the back row. There are maybe 30 people in the pews in front of me.

Up in the sanctuary, a guy with a white beard and a medallion hanging from his neck carries a goblet up to an altar and places it there. He kind of looks like Dumbledore, so I assume this is the Goblet of Fire.

He stands facing us, his arms raised above the cup resting between him and all of us. After a silent moment of rapturous facial expression, he speaks.

"We gather here, a League dedicated to answers of the spirit, the light that shines in us all," he says. "We seek not power. We seek not wealth. We seek only an understanding of the light."

He picks up a dagger from the altar and holds it up. It's ornate – both the blade and the hilt are curved. The blade is sort of a wiggly shape, the kind I associate with a cartoon dagger.

"We spend our time, we spend our lives, we spend our blood on this journey. The sacrifice is great, but the light is greater than all in this realm," he says. "Would thou join us on this quest?"

Voices rise from the crowd in unison:

"I shall join you."

He touches the palm of his left hand to the tip of the dagger and then holds it up facing us. I'm too far back to see whether or not he broke the skin, but this is getting a little weird.

"With this blade, spill thine blood," he says.

Uh-oh.

Dumbledore points, and a guy in the first row rises and walks to the altar. He lifts the dagger to his wrist and drags it across his skin, arm suspended over the goblet. I sit forward, squinting. He switches hands and drags it across the other wrist. Then he sets the dagger down and drinks.

I don't think he cut himself, though. I think he pantomimed it. Maybe these guys are half-assed in areas beyond fixing up the real estate they get ahold of.

The man returns to his seat, sneaking an angry glare at me just before he sits. I better watch out. He might pretend to stab me.

The next guy goes up, mimes a wrist slash, drinks some pinot noir and sits down. And then the next, and then the next.

As the procession of fake bleeding moves through the pews from front to back, I get more dirty looks. A red headed lady scowls at me, a guy with a shaved head tries to stare me down but blinks and looks away, the hooded heads in the crowd sway and bob and rubberneck my way. Everybody wants to have a quick stare at ol' Grobnags.

Yeah? Well, if they want a freak show, I'll give them a goddamn freak show. I'll give them something they'll understand.

Sitting in the back of the room, I'm up last. I stride to the altar, my head down. When I reach the sanctuary, I turn to face the crowd. Only a couple of the weirdos dare to make eye contact: a heavyset lady that seems a little oblivious and a guy that looks remarkably like that professional wrestler the Undertaker. He looks at me with contempt. Everyone else makes a more or less hostile expression as well, but they won't look directly at my face.

They don't want none.

I lift the dagger and hold the opposite hand over the goblet. I hesitate, watching all of the hoods lean forward to see me spill imaginary blood.

Instead, I pull the top of my robe open. I bring the knife to my chest and take a breath. The blade etches a line there diagonally just above my sternum, and then carves another diagonal going the other way. The sharpness of it stings at first, but then I only really have the sensation of cutting thick paper in a weird way. As I move the dagger away, I watch the flaps of skin pull apart from each other in slow motion like two sheets of fleshy fabric. I feel opened up, the air touching my insides.

The blood trickles out of every part of the X at once, oozing thick and gummy red. Rivulets leak down from the corners. It moves slowly like the streams of water about to get erased by the windshield wipers.

Before I look up, the silence in the room surrounds me. There are no words. There are no gasps. I'm not even sure anyone is breathing.

And in the quiet, it becomes real. The violence of the act sinks in. The drama of it all strikes me. And it occurs to me suddenly that this is exactly like something I would have done in the alley and never ever done in real life… until just now, anyway.

I look up to see all eyes locked on the crossed lines above my heart. Jaws hang open. Hands clutch at chests and cup lips.

I hold the goblet up to the bloody well springs and let the fluid drain from my torso into the cup for a bit. It's not so much blood, really – maybe a couple of ounces, maybe not even that. I smear my fingers in the red and wipe them across my brow, following that stroke with a perpendicular line down my forehead and onto my nose.

I wait for that Undertaker looking bastard to make eye contact. Nothing moves for a beat as he gazes at my injury like everyone else. Finally, he senses my stare and returns it, but he looks frightened now. Once we lock eyes, I raise the goblet to my lips and drink, long and cool. It's a sloppy swig, the wine running out of both sides of my mouth and down my chin. I can't even taste the blood. It just tastes like Riuniti or some other cheap wine.

I plop the goblet back down on the altar, wipe the drink off of my chin with my sleeve and smile a moment. I wait. I want this image to linger. Then I return to my seat.

Nobody moves for a long time. I return to my seat in the back and watch the backs of their idiot heads.

Eventually, they stand and mill around and shuffle out, guffawed and dismayed and unhappy. I sit with my arms crossed over my wound, and no one dares to look at me.

Isn't this what they all wanted? Now they can get all scared and aroused and believe in magic and shit. They can gather around water coolers with some juicy new story to share. They can lie in bed quivering and wonder about it and dream about it and fear it.

I mean, I'm sure this was pretty intimidating, even if they could see my nipples.

I lie on my back on the couch, awake in the dark again. I tried to call Louise when I got home, but she didn't answer, so I decided to go to bed early.

With the lack of light, I can barely make out the rectangle of white bandage taped to my chest. The dull ache in the trunk of my body isn't what keeps me up, though. It's the one inside my head. Where the pain comes from, I can't even say.

I replay the event time and again. I see my blood flowing. I watch their faces, their sneers. But I don't really feel the same wrath toward them that I did. I'm not so hateful now. I just feel separate from everything.

And as those pictures play, my thoughts descend to that place they haven't been in a while, the endless circles of words that turn everything into nothing - the big nothing. The words spiral themselves into weapons that attack everyone else to get me alone, and once all the others are defeated, they turn on me.

I try to reason my way out of it. I try to fight against the words, but I can't. They know me too well. They know every scab to pick at. They know how to win every argument. They know how to twist me around and make me think whatever they want.

So I clench my jaw, and I squeeze my eyes shut. My fists

ball up, and for a second I feel small and powerless. For one second I am nowhere and nobody, and then the bubble in my head pops, and I feel the juice gush out.

And I watch in the dark as the ceiling fades to white above. And heaven opens in my head, and I disconnect from the bad thoughts in a flash. I wouldn't say they're erased for good, but they are erased for now.

The despair disintegrates. Warm and calm, I fall asleep within 90 seconds.

CHAPTER 11

A horn blasts, and I'm awake. I sit up, confused, my hands balled into fists out of instinct. I look around. The world hasn't quite returned to full color yet. It blares again – a car horn out front.

I rise and peek through the curtains. Babinaux's Lincoln waits in the driveway.

Oh, shit. She was supposed to pick me up to go to some League house meeting and to start talking to some of these people in earnest. I guess I slept in. I scramble to dress myself in yesterday's clothes lying in a pile nearby, the wound on my chest stinging momentarily as I pull on the t-shirt.

I scratch my brow on the way to the door and feel something rough in texture like dried spaghetti residue on a plate. Oh, the dried blood still crusted to my forehead. I guess I forgot about that.

I stick my face under the kitchen faucet for a quick rinse and scrub my fingers at my brow until it feels smooth. I head out to the car.

In an alarming display of her all-knowingness, Babinaux wordlessly hands me a paper cup of coffee as I slide into the backseat. I sip, and it's not just coffee. It's some kind of delicious cinnamon concoction, perhaps a little too sweet, but I'm not looking a gift coffee in the mouth hole. Within a few seconds, I'm already perking up.

"Everyone is talking again. You made quite the first impression last night," she says. I can see her eyes crawling all over my face to try to read me.

"It was a weird time," I say.

She nods and looks out the window.

"I worry about you," she says.

"I'm fine," I say. "I can't really remember why I did it."

"That's not what I meant," she says. "I worry about more than just that."

"Either way," I say. "I'm fine."

"I hope that's true," she says.

She looks at me for a long time, and then reaches into her purse. She pulls out a plastic bottle and tumbles three pills into her palm. She reaches toward me, and I open my hand, receiving another gift.

"What's this?" I say, rubbing the capsules between my fingers. They're full of green.

"It's Kava Kava," she says. "It's an herb that helps with anxiety. Don't worry, it's really mild."

"Thanks," I say. I wash them down with the cinnamon sludge from the bottom of the cup.

We arrive, and I climb out of the car. The house looks like a cartoon villain lives in it. Ivy devours the chimney and sends green tendrils snaking out to cover most of the upstairs windows.

Standing on the doorstep, I take a breath. I'm here to dig up dirt about Farber's murder, I remind myself. Nothing else matters. None of these people matter to me. I don't have to be nervous. I just have to wait for the right time to ask some questions.

A sign on the front door says, "Come on in!"

So I do that.

A glare on the window prevents me from being able to see inside. I expect to hear Cruella Deville cackling from somewhere deep within the bowels of the building, but instead the only thing I hear is the door screeching super loud as I open it. A group of six people huddled around a snack bar near the front door wheel around to face me.

I stop in the doorway, light shining from behind me so my face is partially in shadow.

"Hi," I say.

"Hey Jeff," the guy that looks like Dumbledore says. "My name's Randy. Randy Pittaway. Can I interest you in a pumpkin scone?"

He shoves the pointy end of a scone in my direction in a way that seems a little too aggressive, but I don't know. Maybe he's just passionate about baked goods.

"Sure," I say.

Now, obviously I'd prefer to take one of the scones on the platter in front of him - you know, one of the ones he hasn't smeared his greasy mitts all over – but I take the one from his hand for the sake of politeness. I bite it, and it tastes more like pumpkin than hand, so I guess that's a win.

"Tasty," I say, everyone watching me chew.

"Vegan recipe," he says. "I baked them fresh this morning."

See? I knew this guy was passionate about baked goods.

I try to make an impressed face. He seems pleased, so I guess it worked. An older lady with dyed black hair next to him speaks up.

"We've heard so much about you," she says. "I'm Janice."

We shake hands. At this point, I'm bombarded from all angles with handshakes and introductions. It's kind of overwhelming, so I don't register any of the names after Janice. They are kind to me, though, and it seems genuine enough.

The standout among the group is a guy with glasses and really hairy ears – like a puff of curly hair actually sticking out from each of his ears. Not unlike pubic hair in texture, as a matter of fact. Ear beards, I guess you could call them. I think maybe his name is Will… possibly Todd.

"I have a question for you, Mr. Grobnagger," Dumbledore says. Randy, I mean. Shit. I hope I don't accidentally call him Dumbledore out loud at some point.

"What's that?" I say.

"Do you eat meat?" he says.

"Only at, like, pretty much every meal," I say.

There are a few chuckles from the snack bar, Janice the loudest among them.

"Do you have any pets?" he says.

"Yeah, I have a cat," I say.

"Would you kill it and eat it?" he says.

"Nope," I say.

"What if you were starving?" he says.

"No," I say. "He weighs like 10 pounds, and I figure most of that is bone. It wouldn't make enough of a difference to be worth it."

"Do you think you'd be able to kill a cow if that's what it took to eat a cheeseburger?" he says.

I imagine myself jamming a knife into a cow's throat and

slashing, blood spraying like a fountain. Then I imagine it again, and this time I just pat the cow on the head.

"Nope," I say.

He squints at me and nods and then looks away. They go on talking about animals and spirits and such. I guess that's the topic of the day, though I'm not 100% clear on how all of this works.

Anyway, once the attention is off of me I relax a bit and zone out. Maybe the kava kava kicked in or something, but it's pretty cool in any case. I take a seat in an antique rocking chair in the corner, happy to be off in my own world.

I watch out the window as a bird picks up clumps of dried grass, flies off with them, and then comes back for more. Must be building a nest. It's a finch, I think.

Snippets of the conversation filter through to my consciousness, particularly during the moments when the bird is away:

"It's not about that," Randy says. "It's about blocking out the animal urges that constantly clutter our thoughts, stripping away those shallow wants and desires and trying to truly understand our existence in the moment. Once we do that, we realize that so much of our experience is shared among all of the creatures walking around out there. That the things we think and feel and do are largely universal."

Later the guy with the hairy ears, Will or whatever, says:

"Surely a clam can't have emotions or consciousness. Look, I'm more than willing to stop eating steak and pork chops, but once we work our way down the food chain to clam chowder, I no longer get the point of abstaining. Is anyone seriously suggesting that a clam has complex feelings?"

I thought for sure someone would reply, "I am serious... and don't call me Shirley," but no one did.

Someone passes around the tray of scones, so I indulge. They taste better when you're not thinking about whether or not there's residue from Dumbledore's balls all over them. Damn it! Randy's balls, I mean. Randy's balls! I've got to remember that.

The bird pecks like crazy at the bark at the bottom of an Oak tree. Not sure what he's playing at. And suddenly I realize that the room is silent, and the last thing said was my name a few seconds ago.

"Hm?" I say, rotating my head to face everyone.

The whole group looks at me with these wide eyed expressions that remind me of the face a mom would make at a toddler after their first day of preschool.

"I suppose Jeff wouldn't want to dive right into regaling us with dreams on day one," Randy says. "Let's all give him time to get acclimated to our little group before we start bombarding him with questions, OK?"

OK wait. Maybe the kava kava is slowing me down here, but I start putting the puzzle pieces together. So someone must have asked about my dreams, and my not hearing the question resulted in me not having to answer it.

That.

Is.

Awesome.

I should probably keep that trick up my sleeve for future use. Pretending to not hear what someone said. Genius.

They go back to yakking, and I go back to finch watching. Somewhere along the way, time speeds up, and suddenly the group is standing up and gathering their things. I guess it's over already.

Everyone makes a point of saying bye to me. Janice hugs me – one of those strange hugs where I can distinctly feel her saggy breasts squishing into me.

Will claps me on the shoulder and says:

"Really glad to have you here this week. We all hope you come back."

The crowd thins, and before long, it's just me and Randy. He wipes down the snack bar with a rag. I guess this is my shot.

"It's too bad about Farber, eh?" I say.

I pull out the nonchalant shrug and give that a whirl. I can leave nothing to chance here.

"Yeah," he says. "Too bad, indeed."

He looks up from the partially wiped countertop to meet my eyes. His expression is hard to read. I want to say forlorn here, but I don't remember what that means for sure. I have earned like three college credits in my lifetime, so I know almost nothing.

"Seems like there's something you want to tell me about it," I say.

Total stab in the dark. Randy sighs.

"So you're as perceptive as they all say you are," he says. "I do have thoughts about the murder, but they're just that – thoughts. I don't make a habit of speculating about such things. And I'd rather not start. Not yet, anyway."

I ponder this a moment.

"People say I'm perceptive?" I say. "Like who?"

"Marcy Babinaux talks about you like you're her only son and you're some kind of violin prodigy or something," he says.

"And I guess the others parrot those sentiments."

Her first name is Marcy? Weird.

"I will say that I saw your passion first hand, and it was jarring," he says. "But impressive."

He might as well be speaking Parseltongue.

"What?" I say.

"Taking the dagger to your chest last night," he says. "To perform the blood ritual the ancient way. I knew from the stories that you were fairly adept at most things metaphysical, but I got the impression that you were fairly indifferent toward it. I had no idea you were a true student of the occult with such a fire in your heart for it."

I don't say anything. Randy sweeps the crumbs from the edge of the counter into his cupped hand and tosses them in the trash.

"That alone gives me hope for the future," he says. "Now that you've elected to join us, anyhow."

I continue to not say anything. I look out the window, but the finch is long gone. He probably caught wind of this conversation and flew South to avoid the awkwardness.

After a long moment of silence, I think of a way to change the subject.

"Oh hey," I say. "What can you tell me about Farber's disciples? Are the stories about Seth Cromwell true?"

Randy's eyes go wide.

"I do not speak his name," he says, whispering. "Perhaps that should tell you whether or not I believe the stories to be true."

He clears his throat.

"I've always been much more uneasy around *him* than I

ever was around Farber," he says. "You just sense a violence about him. I've known his type in the past, desperate men. His ilk share a lust for power, but it's a hateful lust that wields its power only in destruction."

He stares off into space a moment.

"We best get going," Randy says, draping the rag over the side of the sink.

I grab a scone for the road.

CHAPTER 12

Randy gives me a ride home in his Prius. Though on the whole the excursion wasn't as nerve wracking as I anticipated, I still feel quite relieved to be done with it – just shy of euphoric. It's like when you've been dreading going to the dentist forever. Once it's finally over, you feel like some kind of champion.

When I walk in the door, Louise is already there waiting for me. She sits on the couch, an afghan draped over her lap.

"How did it go?" she says.

"Not as bad as I figured," I say.

"Did you make any progress?" she says.

"Not really, but Dumbledore knows something," I say, sliding my shoes off. "He said he doesn't want to talk about it, so it might take a while to pry it out of him. Either way, I figure that's better than nothing."

"That's great," she says. "You know, I always figured you'd be pretty good at getting people to talk. You're not a bullshitter. People talk to people they think are being real, and a lot of people, maybe most, never are."

She stands and smiles, and the blanket falls away revealing that only underwear clothe her bottom half. For a second, I am frozen, watching her. Nothing else in the universe exists but her. She walks to the bedroom in slow motion. And as she crosses the threshold, moving out of sight, real time snaps back, and I unfreeze.

I am in there in a flash.

She crawls into the bed, and as I follow she says:

"No pants allowed."

I undress down to my boxers. Without thinking about it, I take off my shirt as well.

I climb under the sheet with her. We kiss a moment, but she pulls away. Her fingers caress the bandage on my chest.

"What happened?" she says.

"Well, I made a spectacle of myself… like you wanted, I guess," I say.

"Let me see," she says.

She pries the corner of the bandage free with great care and peels it open. The scabbed X underneath puckers angry red.

She gasps a little, and her eyelashes flutter. Then she leans forward and kisses it. Her touch is light, so it doesn't sting or anything. In fact, I can barely feel it at all.

She reattaches the bandage over my heart and then leans back and strips off her shirt.

Holy shit. There are boobs… and stuff. I don't know. It's hard to concentrate on words just now.

Kissing. Touching. Her skin brushes against mine, and I feel the goose bumps crawl across her. She is the softest thing I have ever felt.

Time changes. I can't decide if it speeds up or slows down, but it's definitely different. I am here, and I am somewhere else at the same time. I am nowhere and everywhere. I am nothing. I am connected to something bigger than myself.

At some point in there, a sweet make out session becomes a sweet do it session.

She writhes on top of me, and the volume of existence gets turned up. And we are beyond ourselves, beyond human. We are more like animals and more like spiritual beings at the same time somehow.

And part of me can't believe that this is a real living person lying with me. She is alive. She is conscious. Her imagination is an endless well of pictures and dreams and memories just like mine. And we are, in some way, joined for a while.

It is too big to comprehend. I can't quite accept it as real.

It feels tremendous, though. I will give it that.

Later that night, I lie awake in the dark, Louise dozing next to me. I can't sleep, so my mind reaches out into the blackness.

It does that.

I look over, and I can see Louise's face, a white glow in the shadows. I can't make out all of the details, but I can see the half smile of sleep on her lips.

And part of me finds great satisfaction in all of this. Romance and companionship and sex and everything. I mean, I got the girl I want, you know? Being with her is the most exciting thing that has happened to me in a long time.

But another part of me feels only a greater emptiness than ever. That my whole existence in some way revolves around those three seconds bothers me. Not on a rational level, on a feeling level.

As a man, my imagination, my emotions, my thoughts and dreams, in some way boil down to a desire to breed, to spread my seed, to jizz, whatever you want to call it. Most every moment of every day comes back to that. I don't mean that in a "men think of sex all of the time" raunchy way so much as on a subconscious level. Like I got good at poker and made money and had this sense of conquest, but isn't glory seeking just a way to prove yourself a worthy mate? Isn't acquiring wealth the same? Doesn't every guy that picks up a guitar want to meet a girl? Isn't every stand up comic braving the risk of bombing and embarrassing the fuck out of himself for the mere chance to prove their wit and skill to the ladies?

We are driven to make our lasting mark on the species.

Sometimes this instinct gets subverted into more of a general legacy thing. Guys like Donald Trump build huge towers with their name plastered on them in giant letters. But it comes from the same place. He wants his lasting mark to be in the physical world instead of the species, but I think it's just a confused version of the real impulse. I mean, huge towers are on the phallic end of the spectrum, no?

All of our time and efforts and thoughts and skills get poured into this, whether we realize it or not. And if we're lucky, we get there. We get the girl we desire. We prove ourselves worthy.

And so the sex act happens. And all of the feelings build up into something sacred, some sense of being connected not only to a woman but to heavenly bodies above, some belief that everything finally makes sense. All of the pieces of the universe slide into place, and it satisfies beyond comprehension.

For 3 seconds life has meaning.

And once it's over, you realize there's really nothing. That all of your identity, your imagination and thoughts and dreams, that spark of divine madness that makes each of us unique - they are all just functions of a brain serving an animal urge to keep the species going, no different from the urges that an ape has or even an insect. More elaborate, perhaps, but of the same essence.

And if the urge gets its way, you will produce kids that live to serve those same urges and on and on. And maybe that's all we really are, and all else is an illusion.

I don't know. Part of me thinks that, I guess.

I look over at Louise, and I want to believe otherwise. I want to feel something else entirely. I stare up toward the ceiling, but there's no guiding light to be found up there – only the black nothing.

And then I glance over at her again and her eyes are open. She sees my head tilt in her direction and mumbles something.

"What?" I say.

"I said I want a milkshake," she says.

"What? It's the middle of the night," I say.

"I want," she says. "A milkshake."

We sit on the couch, milkshakes in hand. Turns out Louise makes a damn good shake. She even used real vanilla beans, slitting down the side and scraping the insides out. Mind blowing.

I explained the cutting incident to her in greater detail in the kitchen between blender blasts, pantomiming some of the dramatic moments with a spatula playing the role of the dagger. Replaying it got me thinking about something Randy said.

I pull her laptop off of the coffee table and get to Googling. If she ever gets charged with a crime, it'll be hilarious for the police to find all of these searches about blood rituals in her browser history.

"OK check this out," I say. "Aleister Crowley had a technique that involved cutting your chest like I did as part of a blood ritual. It's called the Mass of the Phoenix."

"That's interesting," Louise says, flipping through infomercials on TV.

"It says something about eating a 'Cake of Light,'" I say. "I definitely did not see any refreshments that evening. That's one thing I would remember."

"What the hell is a Cake of Light?" Louise says.

I look it up.

"Says it's a wafer made from meal, honey, olive oil, oil of Abremalin – whatever the hell that is – and blood or other bodily fluids," I say.

My eyebrows go way up, and Louise's mimic the gesture.

"Yikes!" she says.

I search further.

"We have semen!" I say. "Apparently, they eat their own sperm… in cake form. Though, I guess there are probably worse forms. Like I bet sperm burgers aren't that great."

Louise gags on milkshake and laughs super hard. She sounds a little hoarse.

"I wonder if they were at all bashful about that," I say. "Like, 'Listen, guys, let's maybe not tell my mom about the sperm cakes. I was thinking that would just kind of stay between us cult members.'"

Louise topples onto her side, and her face turns all red, tears wetting her cheeks. Silent laughs rattle her ribcage with great force. It sort of looks like the chestburster scene in Alien.

"Why sperm?" she manages to hiss out.

I read on.

"Says here it's for the robust flavor," I say.

"What?" she says.

"Just kidding," I say. "It's a eucharist. The cake symbolizes the union between man and the divine. Eating it confirms the connection between the two and strengthens the bond. Like communion in a way, I guess. Really gross communion."

Louise's laughing slows, and she does some of those gasp sobs. It sounds like when a baby can't stop crying.

"Jesus. It says of the blood options, moon blood is the best. I assume that means menstrual blood?" I say, "So yeah. That cements it. Aleister Crowley – worst pastry chef ever."

The next night, I look up from my book to see the headlights in the driveway again - Babinaux's Lincoln. Maybe I should invite her in for once. I wonder why I never thought of this until just now.

I walk out to the car in the half light of dusk. The moon looks down, shaped like an egg. I open the door to the backseat.

"Hey, you want to come inside?" I say.

A look of mild confusion crinkles her eyebrows. I think this concept had never occurred to her, either.

"Sure," she says.

Inside, she sits on the couch while I pour a couple of Arnold Palmers. After much experimenting with the various brands and varieties Glenn has on hand, I've figured out that I like an Arnold Palmer made with Meijer brand green tea best. It's one of the cheapest teas available, but I prefer it to any other. I call it "Grobnag's Nothin' Fancy Arnold Palmer." I describe all of this to Babinaux in great detail as I prepare the beverage. For some reason, I can't shut up about it.

"So how has everything been?" she says, once my mouth finally pauses for a few seconds.

"Pretty good," I say. "Randy seems like an interesting guy. He makes a killer pumpkin scone. Very passionate about baked goods, that one."

She smiles.

"Have you had any… seizures… or…?" she says.

"No seizures," I say. "It's been a low key time."

I think about how I never told her, or anyone else, about seeing Glenn in the white world, but I don't think there'd be much point now.

"Yeah, aside from carving your chest like a thanksgiving turkey, it's been pretty laid back, huh?" she says.

"OK, that's a good point," I say.

"Things good with your girlfriend?" she says.

I sip my drink before I answer.

"Yeah," I say. "I mean, it doesn't even feel all the way real most of the time."

"What do you mean?" she says.

"I don't know," I say. "It's hard for me to process that a real person is with me, wants to be with me. Does that make sense?"

Her eyes flick to the side, and she does a cautious half tilt of her head.

"Maybe," she says. "Like when? Give me an example."

I think about it.

"A specific example?" I say. "I don't know. It's hard to call one to mind just like that."

"Let me rephrase my question: Do you mean during sex?" she says.

I lean back, my shoulders digging into the couch cushions.

"Sheesh," I say. "I didn't know you were going to leap straight for the jugular."

"I'm sorry. If you're not comfortable talking about that…" she says.

"No, it's fine," I say. "And yeah, I think that's a pretty good example of what I meant. It's not the only time, but yeah. Yeah."

She strokes her cheek in thought, staring off into space.

"I think I understand, then," she says. "I knew someone like you once, a long time ago. He detached like that in intimate moments, sexual or otherwise. It wasn't a conscious effort to escape or anything. It wasn't that he didn't like the people close to him. He just couldn't absorb it – that connection between people. Too intense, I think, for someone that sensitive. It overwhelmed him."

I don't know what to say.

"He was the saddest person I ever knew. Even as a kid," she says.

She shakes her head, and her eyes don't look so far away after.

"It's weird," she says. "I haven't smoked a cigarette in years, but I just got the urge for one. I guess thinking about old times jars your brain and the old habits shake loose."

I have a hard time imagining her smoking. She seems too classy for that.

She brings her hand to her mouth and nudges the side of her index finger into her lips. I don't know if that's because she's thinking about cigarettes or what.

CHAPTER 13

At the next meeting at Randy's there are tasty wafer cookies filled with coconut and lemon cream. Delicious. I grab another from the tray. I want to grab three, but I decide to play it cool and take one at a time.

At first I thought they must not be vegan, but I think the cream is coconut oil based maybe. Randy Pittaway is to dessert what Albus Dumbledore is to magic.

I sit in my rocking chair in the corner and watch the people talk. I don't necessarily listen the whole time, but I do watch. The corner of Janice's mouth twitches. She seems preoccupied.

I can't be sure, but I think Will might have trimmed his ear beards. They're still there, but they have a more manicured look, like the bushes outside of a fancy hotel.

Piecing together bits of the conversation, Randy seems to be attempting to discuss spiritual clarity. I can hardly stand to listen to even one complete sentence of it, though, so I can't be sure. My brain shuts down all aural functions when it hears certain keywords, and Randy is hitting them pretty hard today. I must not be alone in my lack of interest, however, because Janice keeps going off topic.

"I wanted Kim, that's my son's fiancée, to wear my mama's wedding dress like I did, but she insists she will need to pick out her own," Janice says. "Now, I don't want to press it and make a scene, but my goodness! Whatever happened to tradition and family coming first? Is that era of America just flushed down the commode?"

Janice has a slight Southern accent, but I think she might be one of those people that inexplicably employs a twang even though she's never lived in the South. It seems like most of them say po-lice, too. Fun fact.

Everyone is silent.

"I know where you're coming from, Janice," Randy says, tapping his fingers on his mug. "That kind of ties into what I'm talking about, because I think we'd all be more chill if we stopped listening to all the noise outside and set aside quiet time to pay attention to the light inside."

Chill? I immediately vomit lemon and coconut all over the snack bar.

Well… not really, but damn near. Randy seems like a nice guy, but I don't know why he has to get all Dudley Do-Right in these group meetings. I take a bite of a cookie, and the coconut cream squirts into my mouth.

I freeze. Visions of sperm cakes dance in my head. I look at Randy, this saint of dessert-hood before me. Could there be an ulterior motive to his passion for desserts?

I cup a napkin to my mouth and feign a cough, spitting the cream out.

If Randy has done the unthinkable… let's just say that ain't vegan.

After the meeting dies down, and the others stream out into the sunlight, I find a way to ask him about it.

"So these cookies," I say.

"Did you like them?" he says, gathering up stray dishes

from the counter.

"Yeah. They're great, but I have a question," I say.

I pause for a beat.

" These wouldn't be in anyway 'Cakes of Light' or anything like that, right?" I say.

"What?" he says as he places some dirty mugs in the sink.

I say nothing. I let the question hover in the space between us and try to watch his face for micro expressions like a detective in a murder of the week TV show. His face does change, but it's no fleeting micro expression. It lights up with shock – eyes wide, mouth agape.

"Oh!" he says. "Oh, lord no! Wait. You thought… ?"

He busts out laughing, his hands falling to the corner of the counter. After a second, he bends at the waist and rests his head on his hands. Tears fall from his eyes and spatter on his glasses.

He has one of those crazy laughs that sounds louder on the inhale than the exhale. It has a wheezy quality to it.

I don't think I've ever seen an old person laugh like this. He looks like a maniac. I mean, I know laughter is supposed to be the best medicine, but Randy is flirting with an overdose at this point.

I wipe down the counter while I wait for this episode to pass. Randy's wheeze slows and eventually peters out, but he keeps his head down a while longer. I eye the cookies while I wait for his recovery, but I can't bring myself to eat one. Even though I know they've been cleared for consumption, I would just think about sperm while I ate them, so…

Randy finally stands up. He gives me a look and shakes his head. The corners of his mouth flutter, and for a second I think he's going to go relapse back into giggles, but he holds it together.

He slides the leftover cookies off of a tray into a Tupperware container and pops it in the fridge. I figure now is the time to make with the interrogation.

"Heard anything new about the Farber case?" I say.

He stops in his tracks, and his chest heaves once with a deep breath. He holds his eyes closed for a beat before he speaks.

"I have mixed feelings about it, but I'm going to tell you what I know, and what I fear it means," he says. "I think in some way you will play a big role in all of this, Grobnagger, so concealing information from you might be unwise."

I bob my head a single time, and he continues.

"Rumor has it that Farber acquired a book of great power recently," he says. "I believe you're already aware of that. Well, I happen to know a bit about the book. There's a passage – an incantation – regarding the final rituals for achieving divinity on Earth. It involves a final display of faith, see. This particular ritual ends with a trial by fire."

I wait for him to go on, but the words hang in the air. He just looks at me.

"What are you saying?" I say.

"I'm saying Farber lit himself on fire to prove his faith. To become a God on Earth," he says. "He failed it seems, so that's not what worries me about it. What worries me is that his ilk remains out there, likely the Sons of Man, and they will continue to try."

"So the bad guys are burning themselves to death," I say. "I think that's kind of a good thing."

"Sooner or later, one of them will get it right, Grobnagger," he says. "And believe me, we'll all be up shit creek at that point."

We're quiet for a moment. I imagine myself wielding a turd paddle, fighting against the frothy rapids of shit creek.

"What's with the name, anyway?" I say.

"The name?" he says.

"The Sons of Man," I say.

"They're declaring themselves the peers of God," he says. "In other words, they are not the sons of God. They are the sons of man. Does that make sense?"

"Pretty much," I say.

Louise is off gathering information for a divorce case, so I sit around alone and read most of the afternoon, stopping only to feed the cats and myself. The daylight drains from the sky. By the time she gets home, it's late enough that we start getting ready for bed.

After I brush my teeth and rinse my mouth with various blue liquids, I join her in the bed. The light goes out, and the dark surrounds us. I tell her about the info I pumped out of Randy.

"What do you think?" I say.

"I think the old guy is loony," Louise says. "You really think he set himself on fire?"

"I don't know. They wanted that book badly enough to trash this place," I say. "Who knows what they're thinking?"

"Loony or not, Randy makes one good point, though," she says. "We should be following those two disciples of Farber's."

"You think so?" I say.

She nods in a way that reminds me of kindergartner.

"Think about it," she says. "Whether Farber set himself on fire or not, those are the guys most likely to know something. I doubt they'd talk to us, but we could tail them."

"Would we really learn anything just following them around?" I say.

She rolls her eyes.

"Following people around is about 80% of my job," she says. "We can learn plenty."

"Alright," I say. "I guess you're the expert."

"There's not much to it," she says. "Keep your distance. Observe and don't be observed. That's about it."

"Pretty straight forward," I say.

"Still, you're a noob," she says. "I should follow the psycho and you should follow the wimpy one."

"Not a chance," I say.

"You said that everyone is scared to death of Cromwell, yeah? I've heard some of the stories," she says. "Well, what if he spots you? I've been at this a long time, I know he won't see me."

I kind of want to ask her about the stories, since I've yet to actually hear any of the specifics. But I feel that would weaken my position, so I skip it.

"I'm following Cromwell," I say. "I know how to handle these people."

She gives me a long look.

"Fine," she says.

CHAPTER 14

I stand in the foyer of an apartment complex across the street from Cromwell's, watching his place through the window in the front door. So far, there are no signs of him.

This hallway smells like clam chowder, New England style, which reminds me of the Thai soup as well as Will's impassioned speech about his right to eat shellfish a few days ago. It also reminds me of the puffs of kinked hair sprouting from his ears.

Time drips by in slow motion, and Cromwell remains out of sight. Every few minutes, someone comes out of their apartment to get their mail or leave the building. They give me dirty looks as they enter the foyer and spot me, so I glare at them. I find glaring gets people to leave you alone most of the time. I bet if I tried to play it all incognito, someone would have confronted me by now about why I'm standing in their apartment building. By behaving aggressively, I put them on the defensive. They decide the confrontation would be too risky. It's sort of like how they say if you try to rip a shark's eye out during a shark attack, it will leave you alone. It's just looking for food. It doesn't want to risk permanent damage.

Or maybe I'm just really bored, and it's more entertaining to glare. For example, I decided an even better way to get people to leave me alone would be to say hi to them while scratching my dick for an uncomfortably long interval. Only a man bored to the point of despair would conjure an idea like that.

Someone finally exits Cromwell's building, but it's not him. It's a lady with sunglass and a scarf over her hair. She looks like she's from a different era, like a Jackie Onassis type. She walks slowly with her head down. One hand pins the scarf to the crown of her head like the wind might blow it away.

Is this the walk of shame? It could be. It could very well be.

You know what? Now that I think about it again, I want to revise my prior statement. It definitely smells like Manhattan style clam chowder in this hallway. Not sure what I was thinking when I said New England style earlier. Frankly, that couldn't be further from the truth.

After about six years pass (very slight exaggeration), Cromwell finally pushes through the front door of his building. My spine straightens to attention like a dog spotting a squirrel through the window. I almost want to press my face to the glass and bark maniacally at him, but instead I just watch as the target of my stakeout saunters down the avenue.

He's one of those short guys that seem excessively wide without being fat. His hair is black and has a lot of volume to it, particularly for a man. It's a side part with a pompadour-ish puff to it that bounces with every step. Actually, it might be more accurate to say that it flops rather than bounces.

I let him get some distance on me and slip out of the foyer, leaving the chowder smell behind for the smell of the city, which I'm sure will be just as pleasant.

We move through the streets, me trailing by about a half of a block. I track him by the flop of black hair and the bobbing navy blue hoodie. We pass the bums hanging out in front of McDonald's and take a right on Ninth Street. That's the first prominent smell– McDonald's fries. Not so bad after all.

Cromwell stops at a hot dog stand, so I guess this guy is some kind of health freak. After waiting in line, he acquires a meat tube I can't identify from my vantage point, but I'll take a guess and say he went with the bratwurst.

He mills around eating it, so I have to mirror his milling around at a distance. I pretend to tie my shoe for a long time. A lady with a kind face looks like she's about to offer me some help with it, probably assuming I have a number of problems, but I shake my head at her and she lays off. Really thankful I didn't have to resort to the dick scratching thing here, because she seems like a genuinely sweet lady.

Cromwell moves on, and I follow suit. We walk for a long while this time, making a right here and a left there. Block after block of chain stores and restaurants slide by on the sides of the road.

We climb a hill. The view from the top looks down on a swarming mass of humanity. I'm not sure what's going on. It appears to be a park with maybe a couple of rows of booths set up. The crowd undulates around the booths. From this distance it seems more like one entity that moves like choppy water rather than a bunch of individuals.

As I get closer, I pass a man toting a plastic bag full of corn on the cob, and it clicks. It's a farmer's market. I can't help but wonder how many people ate a bratwurst on their way to get a bunch of organic lacinato kale today.

Suddenly, I don't see him. No flop of hair. No navy blue hoodie. I pick up the pace a little, scanning the sidewalk in front of me again and again.

A tall guy wearing a beanie takes a quick right, and the flop of hair swings back into view. No worries. He was just screened from my vision. Still, I close the gap quite a bit. He'll be a lot tougher to stick with in this crowd, so I'll have to take some chances.

We stride onto the walkway that runs past the booths, and now we're completely engulfed by human bodies. Cromwell takes high steps and twists his shoulders and contorts himself to pick his way through the crowd. He looks like a salmon fighting his way upstream.

I lose him for a split second and then find him again, stopped at a fruit vendor. He picks up peaches from a bucket one at a time, pressing each of them with his thumb before putting them back. He gets out his wallet and hands the farmer some money. The vendor dumps a little bucket of peaches into a bag and hands them over.

With that, we're moving again. He stops to look over some eggplant and asparagus but gets going within seconds. He isn't so quick at a booth with a ton of greens – spinach, kale, collards, chard. Cromwell feels up every leaf in the place. I'm waiting for him to start shoving dollar bills down into the little band that holds the bunches of green together.

He purchases a variety of the leafy stuff. After paying, he turns, and he's gone. Just like that, he disappears into the crowd. I stand on my tiptoes to no avail. I dart between people in the direction that seemed to make the most sense as his likely trajectory, but I find no trace of the guy.

Changing gears, I turn around and hustle out of the booth area, thinking that so long as I beat him to the exit, he'll eventually have to come out. If I wait at this bottleneck I should be able to catch him and resume following.

I lean on a lamp post and watch the people file in and out of the market, all walks of life. I hold my phone in my palm in front of me and pretend it's a smart phone I can use to do awesome stuff instead of a 2004 shitty phone I really need to upgrade as soon as possible. I figure from a distance, it's at least a plausible thing for a guy to be doing while leaned up against a lamp post without drawing attention. Onlookers can't see that this is practically a rotary phone I'm holding.

Rows of endless people stream into the market with nothing and exit with produce. I guess, technically, many walk in with empty reusable cloth grocery bags and walk away with said bags filled to the brim with organic fruits and veggies. None of them are the guy I'm looking for, in any case, so it's not of much use.

I wait. I pretend to swipe the touch screen that doesn't exist on my phone. I chuckle at the imaginary text I just received and piston my thumbs in a fake reply.

Cromwell doesn't show. It's like he crawled into a display of potatoes and hunkered down to wait me out. I feel like a fool.

So my first following session was a bust. Louise is going to be disappointed. She always thinks I'm going to be great at everything.

I turn around and Cromwell is standing about three feet from me, sucking a grass green drink through a straw and looking right at me. He looks bored.

"Hey, Grobnagger," he says, easing the drink away from his mouth. "You tried one of these smoothies?"

I hate how everybody knows who I am.

"No," I say.

"Why you following me, bro?" he says.

"Seems like you're the one following me," I say.

"Nah. You followed me for like six blocks," he says. "Watched me eat a bratwurst and everything."

I knew it! I knew he'd go for the bratwurst.

"How was that?" I say.

"The bratwurst?" he says. "It was baller as hell, bro. It was a beer brat. That's the way to go, I think. I ain't down with any of that cheese stuffed crap."

Baller? So he's one of those.

"Yeah, that's cool," I say.

He squints at me, so I squint back at him. I'm not sure why I'm so quick to antagonize people of late, but it's kind of fun.

"You still have them seizures or what?" he says.

"It's been a while," I say.

He laughs a little, the wrinkles around his eyes relaxing.

"I can only imagine the shit you've seen, Grobnagger," he says. "From the way people talked, I kind of figured you'd be all stuck up and what not, but nah. You ain't like that at all."

"From the way people talked, I thought you'd be a lot more psychotic and a lot less drinking a green smoothie right now," I say.

Upon being reminded, he takes a big drink and then points at the cup.

"This shit is bomb, dude," he says. "It keeps me feeling up."

"So now what?" I say.

"What do you mean?" he says.

"Well, I was following you. Now you know about it," I say. "So what do we do now?"

He squints again and sucks down the last of his drink, the straw doing that annoying puttering noise when it runs out of fluid.

"Are you hungry?" he says.

I don't have to think about this long.

"Well, yeah," I say.

CHAPTER 15

As we stride through the doorway of Cromwell's apartment building, part of me wonders if this is a terrible idea. I'm voluntarily walking into the home of the enemy. I guess playing all of that poker, I've learned to trust my read on people, though. This guy doesn't seem like a threat at all. A little dim, maybe? Sure.

Plus, he said, point blank, that he has food. Sounds pretty legit to me.

We walk up two flights of stairs and bank left into a hallway, stopping outside of apartment 336. A piece of wood stands between us and this weirdo's apartment. I'm given one last chance to turn back as he digs out his keys. I search my feelings and find no urge to flee the scene, though.

"I think you're going to like this, Grobnagger," he says as he twists the key and opens the door.

I'm not sure what to make of this statement, but it all comes clear as I cross the threshold into his place. The first thing my eyes are drawn to: a mural on the far wall depicting what looks like a mish mash of tarot imagery. In the dead center and largest of all, a winged, horned demon perches on an altar with his weird bird feet. He's fat and red with a stark white face and a black beard. He holds a flaming torch in his left hand, and a pentagram gleams above his head.

Below him a naked man and woman are shackled in chains that lash them to the beast's altar. Looking closer, though, they are not a normal man and woman after all. Small tails and horns sprout from their bodies as well.

A yellow sun gives off jagged, triangular light in the upper left. Another demon sits on a rock pile below the sun, playing a violin. This demon's skin gleams gray, and he looks more slender than his brethren. Something about his demeanor and facial expression suggests that his fiddle playing style would be best described as "shredding."

Elsewhere in the room, two coffins lean up against the walls as decorative flourishes. Black flags serve as curtains. Macabre carvings and sculptures line the shelves and tabletops.

All together, the interior design looks like something out of the Satanist issue of Martha Stewart Living or possibly the set of an Ozzy Osbourne music video circa 1983. I could see Randy Rhoads standing up on the arm of this couch with his legs about double shoulder width apart, playing a sweet solo with that devil mural behind him.

"What do you think?" Cromwell says after a while.

"It looks awesome," I say. "Good luck getting your security deposit back, though."

He laughs.

"I didn't show you the best part yet," he says.

He leads me over to one of the coffins and opens it. A crushed velvet looking material lines the inside, looks pretty normal. He grabs the velvet and pushes it to the side, though, revealing that this coffin is covering a doorway.

"What?" I say.

He smiles like he's in a Crest commercial and does one of

those hiss laughs through his teeth. The sound sort of reminds me of a cat puking. His face glows, though. I think people have won the Nobel Peace Prize and been less proud than this.

"Go 'head," he says, gesturing to the doorway.

Please don't be a sex dungeon. Please don't be a sex dungeon.

I step through the casket, and my eyes adjust to the dimness in this hidden chamber.

Great.

It's a sex dungeon.

Just kidding.

The wood floor in this room is sparse. A black table cloth drapes a small piece of furniture in the center of the room. Atop its surface, I spot a dagger, a fake skull, a cup and what looks to be a few bundles of herbs and spices.

The rest of the room is pretty barren. A couple of wooden chairs sit near the table, but the rest is exposed wood floors and blank white walls. It's quite sparse compared to the Satanist's wet dream that is the living room.

"This is my altar room," he says.

Not sure what to say, so I say:

"Nice."

"Yeah, I like to keep this a little more low key," he says. "The living room out there is for show, but this?"

He stretches out his arm, gesturing around the room.

"I don't need all of that glitz in here, bro," he says. "Nah. That kind of tinsel would only distract my focus. I figure you know what it's like, though. Shit, I don't need to tell Jeff Grobnagger about all this."

I nod, but I have no idea what he's talking about. And

frankly I'm starting to get a little upset.

I was told there would be food.

When Cromwell invited me over for food, I never would have guessed it'd be spaghetti, but here we are. It has come to this. He plops noodles out of a strainer and into a sauce pan full of simmering red marinara. Then he flips the pasta around with some tongs. He lifts the pan and dishes a serving of spaghetti onto a black plate and places it in front of me.

"I ain't braggin'," he says. "But I make a killer marinara."

Steam rises from the plate, coiling toward my face. It smells pretty good – a tomato aroma that has some foreign notes. He swivels away from me and twists back to grind aged Parmesan cheese onto the noodles.

"There," he says. "Now keep in mind, this is a frozen version of my sauce. Still killer as hell, for sure, but it's massively baller when it's fresh, bro. Massively."

Baller.

Again.

Massively so, for good measure.

I take a bite. It's quite acidic but also a nice balance of sweet and tart. The flavor grows more complex as it unfurls on my palate. It's a pure tomato flavor, not shrouded by spices or anything like that, but seasoned to enhance the actual tomato taste into something unbelievably delicious, somehow bold and subtle at the same time. I realize that if tomatoes tasted like this off of the vine, I would eat them like apples.

"Well?" he says, watching me chew.

"Baller," I say, shaking my head. "Massively, massively baller."

He smiles and nods. Now that the reviews are in, he plates himself a smaller serving and takes a seat across from me.

"Druzba tomatoes," he says. "That's my secret. They don't sell them at the super market or anything, so most people have no clue how delicious they are. They don't pick the produce varieties at the store based on flavor. They pick them based on looks and durability."

We eat.

As I finish up, I realize this might be a good time to ask some questions.

"So all of the League people say you're a crazy freak that wants to drink baby's blood and stuff," I say.

He laughs.

"They're just scared of the League dying off," he says. "The way I see it, the League has run its course. If it ever served a purpose, as a gateway to get people into this kind of stuff or what have you, that is past. It's a dog and pony show now. A club for people with quirky tastes and not much more. Solely superficial in practice – the little meetings and whatever. I've always wanted for our group to split off and be more serious. No baby's blood or nothing stupid like that, but I thought we could just be serious students of the arcane, right?"

I nod.

"Farber never wanted that, though," he says. "He said the League is an institution with some history, some tradition, and those things have power. Why throw that away, when we can bend the organization to our will and utilize its strengths? He was always more political than me, though."

"So what was the deal with Farber, anyway?" I say. "Why'd he kidnap me?"

Cromwell chews, swallows, looks at me.

"He didn't like to divulge the details of his plans. Even to the people closest to him," he says. "But I can tell you this. Everything he did, he did for power. I'm sure he thought you were a way to get power. Beyond that, I don't really know."

He shrugs.

"I don't get it," I say.

"Well, think about it this way," he says. "People believe in you. Your seizures and dreams and all of that? They believe in it. That gives you power right there. To Farber, belief was like a currency. It was energy that he felt could be spent. All of those illusions he did at the diner? Just a way to make people believe."

"So those were just illusions?" I say.

He smiles.

"I think so," he says. "Riston would never tell me how he did any of it, so I was torn. On one hand, if he had that kind of power, he'd probably use it for something bigger. On the other, I always thought he was too lazy to practice enough to get that good at sleight of hand."

He slurps down the last of his pasta.

"I guess anything is possible," he says.

"Do you think he set himself on fire?" I say.

"No," he says. "He was the type of guy to never be out of control. Never got drunk or anything. Never really loosened up, even in private. I can't see him taking a risk like that. He'd find a way to be sure before he pulled the trigger."

"I'm going to level with you. He doesn't exactly sound like a barrel of laughs," I say.

A lone puff of laughter exits Cromwell's nostrils.

"For real," he says. "He could be a total dick. He was an interesting cat, though. He knew how to do so many things, and when you hung out with him, you felt like epic events were always just around the corner."

"So if he didn't torch himself," I say. "Who did it?"

"I couldn't tell you," he says. "I mean, I've thought about that at length, and I've got nothing. No hunches. Not a single guess. It makes no sense to me."

He rises and moves to the sink to rinse our plates.

"Can I ask you something?" he says.

"Sure," I say.

"Were you scared?" he says. "When you had those seizures and went wherever the hell you went, you know? Was it scary?"

"In a way, yeah," I say. "But then I wasn't as scared as it seems like I should have been. It was hard to think straight sometimes."

"I get that," he says. "Man, I wish I could see it for myself."

I walk in the dusk, the sky going ashy around me. Apart from me, the streets are just about void of pedestrians now, nothing like when I followed Cromwell to the farmer's market earlier. The bustle died off, and the city feels lonely again, stark and gray and harsh. That's how I know it best.

It's getting chilly, so I zip my hoodie up all the way. It helps a little.

I'm not sure what to feel at this point. I'm a little confused, I guess. Everybody told me over and over again how scary Cromwell was. I was basically expecting him to be a werewolf wielding a chainsaw, but it was nothing like that. He just seemed like a regular guy with exceptionally bad taste in home decor. I'm starting to think that these cult people are all too imaginative for their own good. They see a monster in every shadow.

I go back over the things he said about Farber. He seemed pretty genuine about all of it, but he sure didn't seem very upset. I've known people that got choked up about a dead dog 15 years later. I'm not saying he needed to squirt out some tears or anything so dramatic. He just seemed unfazed entirely, and something about it felt off.

Whether that means anything important is another debate all together, of course. Maybe he's just not so in touch with his emotions. I find there's a direct correlation between a human being's sensitivity and the frequency of their usage of the word "bro." If you say bro more than 50 times a day, for example, I think you're clinically considered a sociopath. Use over 100 bros? Now you're a psychosexual sadist. Fact.

Either way, maybe Louise's hunch was right. She said there was no way Farber lit himself up, and Cromwell said the same.

I wait at an intersection, and the wind from the cars rushing past saps the warmth from my face until my cheeks sting. For a split second I consider clenching everything up to make the world turn warm and white, but it doesn't seem right somehow.

The light changes, and I cross the street. The cold crawls down my face to spread over the rest of me. I shove my hands deeper in my hoodie pockets, but it doesn't seem to help much.

I wonder where Glenn is right now. Is he OK? What about Amity? Will we ever cross paths again? I hope she's safe, either way.

I see the hot dog vendor pushing his cart on the other side

of the street. I guess he's done for the night. And then the stalking mission flashes through my head in fast speed – watching Cromwell's building from the foyer, following him, and ultimately eating a meal with him.

It occurs to me suddenly that this never would have happened before. Back before all of the alley dreams and the time spent with Glenn and Babinaux and Louise, I never would have gone into someone's house like that and stayed pretty comfortable. I'd have stayed home. Even if I somehow wound up there, I would have been nervous and taken the first opportunity to get away.

All of this has changed not just my circumstances, but all of me. These experiences, they crept into my eyes and seeped into my pores and etched themselves into the wiring of my brain. They became a part of me, and the whole was changed.

I like that.

CHAPTER 16

Babinaux sits in the living room once again. This time we drink vanilla chai with a touch of honey.

The conversation winds its way through the usual recap type stuff, and then we're quiet, sipping tea.

"So hey, whatever happened to your friend?" I say.

"Which one?" she says.

"The one you were telling me about," I say. "You said he was the saddest person you ever met."

She takes a deep breath before she answers.

"When he was 44, he killed himself," she says. "Hanged himself with one of those orange extension cords in his garage."

"Oh," I say. "Wow, I'm sorry."

"It was very sad, but it was a while back," she says. "We weren't very close by that time."

We're quiet for a while. I can't help but feel really weird that this is the guy she compared me to.

"If you were ever feeling that down, you would tell me, wouldn't you?" she says. "Or you'd talk to someone about it, right?"

And this officially just got really uncomfortable.

"Yeah," I say. "I'm doing great, though. So, yeah."

"I know," she says. "I know."

Her words trail off into nothing. No sound. The silence squats on the room. It pins us to our seats and shifts all of its weight onto us, and the pressure builds and builds. We'll surely be crushed any second. Babinaux leaps into action, slaying the quiet with words:

"Listen," she says. "I came over to tell you that Randy wants you to do the water ritual tomorrow."

"OK," I say. "What's that? Like a baptism or something?"

"Kind of, yeah," she says. "It's not a big deal. You meditate in water for a bit."

"I can do that," I say. "Will there be a bunch of us like last time?"

"No," she says. "It's pretty rare. Only people that have shown an aptitude for this kind of thing do it."

"What do you mean by that?" I say.

"Things such as your dreams. It's an ancient rite of passage for potential shamans. It's supposed to clarify your spiritual thoughts and show you your path," she says. "Only a handful of our people have ever been deemed worthy, and it's been a while."

"Really?" I say. "How long?"

"Four years ago," she says. "Riston Farber did it."

"Oh," I say.

When I arrive at the old church, there's no sign that anyone is there. No lights in the windows. No cars in the lot. It's one of those small churches that probably had a congregation of about 40 at its absolute peak in 1956 or something. I look around the grounds for a minute, taking in the overgrown bushes lining the perimeter of the building and the pair of dead trees raising their rotten branches over the yard out back.

I walk back toward the front of the church. Weeds poke their way through the beds of gravel on each side of the doors, and the blades of tall grass sway in the breeze and hiss as they brush against each other.

Whenever the wind dies down, it's quiet enough that I can hear the lights over the parking lot buzzing above me. I stand in the stillness just outside the door a moment longer, and a car engine growls somewhere in the distance.

I turn the knob, half expecting it to be locked, but the door swings free. It's dark inside, and it smells like old people, like all of the carpet and upholstery sucked up the elderly smell like a sponge for all of those years, and now it wafts the odor around whenever it gets someone alone in here. I feel around for a light switch and find one a few paces into the foyer. I flip it. Nothing happens. My fingers find another switch next to the first and try that. Still nothing.

The door slams behind me, and I jump at the sound, wheeling around in the blackness to brace myself for the attack from whoever slammed it. Panic grabs me by the throat. A quiver travels up my spine, my shoulders convulse, and my hands flail at the dark in front of me.

There's just enough light from the parking lot to see now that my eyes have adjusted a bit, though, and there's nothing there.

It was probably the wind or something.

I am dumb.

I take a deep breath, and as I exhale, a clatter arises somewhere in the building. It sounds muffled.

"Hello?" I say.

Nothing.

I shuffle a few steps further in, my arms stretched out in front of me, my fingers bouncing around like feelers on some creature from the bottom of the sea. Would this be a really weird time to start laughing? Because I feel the craziest smile on my face. It's making my cheeks ache.

My foot connects with something solid, and I totter forward. Now my arms shoot out to the sides to help me catch my balance. My torso lurches back and forth a couple times, but I remain upright.

Another clang and rattle. This time I can tell that it's coming from my left. I start moving that way, my feelers finding the smooth cinder block wall to the right to guide me. It's quite cool to the touch.

A few strides later, a glimmer of light becomes visible to my right. I look at it for a long time, trying to make sense of it. It's not enough to help me see much. The wedge of illumination comes from near the floor somehow, which I can't wrap my mind around. I tap my hands in that direction and find a doorway leading toward the glow, and a step beyond that, I feel some kind of handle or rail.

And with the shape of that metal railing, the answer pops into my head – a basement. It seems so obvious now, but it's a crazy feeling to look at something for a long time in the dark, unable to comprehend it.

I feel around some more, but I find no light switch in the vicinity. With quite a grip on the railing, I descend. I let my feet feel their way down, toeing up to the edge of every step and easing onto the next. It's slow going, yeah, but it beats death by staircase. They say that's one of the worst ways to go. OK, no one has ever said that, but still…

As I near the bottom of the steps, I peer deeper into the cellar, my eyes scanning the area for the source of light. There. It shines through a crack along the bottom of a door on the other side of the basement.

"Hello?" I say again, pausing on the steps.

Still nothing.

I press forward. My feet touch down on the basement floor, and I work my way toward the light, weaving around tiny chairs and a table that I assume are relics from some long forgotten Sunday school operation.

When I reach the door, I realize that I'm unsure how to proceed. Do I knock? Do I just barge in? I listen for a moment while I ponder my options. A series of squeaks and clicks emit from the other side of the door. I don't know why, but they sound harmless to me.

I twist the knob and push open the door, and the light spills onto me. Squinting, I see Randy fiddling with what looks like a giant washer or dryer partially set in the basement floor. The hatch on the front looks like it's made out of parts scavenged from an antique submarine or something ridiculous like that.

Randy throws open the door on the front of the tank. I expect to see a huge load of whites in there, but instead I see light dancing on the top of the tank, reflecting off of water. He pulls out a string with a pool thermometer on the end. Water drips off of it as he brings the thermometer to his nose and squints at it. It occurs to me that the dryer looking thing is about the length of a coffin, and for the first time in a while, I think I know where this is going.

I take a few steps into the room, and Randy senses my

presence, looks up and pops an ear bud out of his ear.

"You're late," he says, tossing the thermometer back into the water.

CHAPTER 17

As I climb into the tank, it occurs to me that this would be a great prank to pull on someone else. I'm climbing into a tank that looks like a big dryer, completely naked, with a person I don't know that well manning the lid from the outside. And oh yeah, the handle on the inside? Broken.

Seems legit.

I bet I could kick my way out if I needed to, though.

I scoot into the tank, doing something like a crab walk until I'm all the way in and then stretching my legs out and leaning back on my elbows in a position somewhere between sitting and lying down. The water covers my legs and laps against my torso, one rivulet rushing over my chest. It's just warmer than lukewarm, sort of like bath water a couple minutes before you'd want to get out.

"Here," Randy says. "You don't want to get salt water in your ears. Trust me."

I turn, and he hands me some earplugs.

"So what do I do?" I say.

"You put them in your ears, genius," he says.

"No, I mean what do I do in here?" I say.

"Just lie back and relax," he says. He slaps the tank. "This thing will do the heavy lifting. After a time your brain flips over to theta brain waves. It puts you in a different state of mind, like meditating. It kind of opens the valve to your subconscious."

"That's it?" I say.

"Look, let's just say that anything that happens beyond that won't involve you trying," he says. "Just let yourself relax. It takes time to realize that you can trust the water. You won't sink."

I pinch the tips of the ear plugs and push them inside of my head. At first, it almost seems louder than before from the sound of the foam expanding to fill my ear canal. Right away there's a crackling noise that reminds me of adding milk to Rice Krispies, but as that is muffled, it sounds more like listening to the ocean in a shell.

I look back to give Randy a thumbs up or something, but he's already closing the door. The rectangle of light compresses into a tiny sliver, hesitating as he fumbles to latch the door, and then disappears all together.

The dark closes in on me, and the air seems to get thicker. I can't decide if that's my imagination or if the humidity in the tank actually causes that. Maybe it's a little of both. It's not exactly hard to breathe, but it's a little unpleasant.

I ease back into the water, letting myself float, though it's hard to do that all the way. I fight it a little. The water reacts to my motion, and I bob along with it. A little wave hits just right and a splash of warm salt water gets into the corner of my mouth.

Yum.

My neck is all tight. I try repositioning my limbs. It seems to help if I keep my feet shoulder width apart and my arms straight out to the sides. I hold still like that a while.

I try to let my mind wander away from the physical experience a bit, but it's hard to not consider all of the sensory information. My penis is significantly more buoyant than my sack, for example. Good to know.

Once the water settles and my bobbing ceases, I feel like I float a little higher on the water. With less of a risk of swallowing the water, I can really start to relax. I don't force it. I just let the muscles in my neck go first, and it spreads from there a little at a time. My calves and then thighs release their tension. Then it feels like the fiber in my biceps and triceps and deltoids uncoil.

I don't fight anymore. I just float. I lie awake in the dark, my eyes wide open. I realize that in a way this is nothing new for me. I spend a lot of time awake in the dark it seems, in bed at night looking at the warped reflections rippling in my imagination.

I have no idea if it's been five minutes or 30. I haven't moved in a long time, though, and I feel a calm building in me. It reminds me of a bubble expanding somehow. There's an element of anticipation to it, a sense of something forming and growing. Even so, it is without anxiety.

I'm so calm. It's like I'm floating inside and outside at the same time. The salt water forms a sea around me that helps me understand the sea within.

Pink shapes swirl in the air, stretching out to fill my field of vision. They kind of look like a multiplied version of what happens if you stare at a bare light bulb for too long except they seem to move with more purpose. I think they've been there a while, actually, and I didn't really notice them at first.

Now the pink swirls writhe around each other, somehow

more solid than before, like claymation tendrils braiding and coiling everywhere. It's not like I'm dreaming them. They exist physically, there in front of me, occupying space.

And then my arms and legs tingle, pin pricks advancing across my flesh, going wherever they like, and within seconds the tingle blossoms into an itch. This isn't like the pleasant itch in the white world. It packs some intensity. One part of me is tempted to scratch, but the majority says nay. It would break up the trance, so I'll have to ride it out.

Tangible objects begin to form among the pink tendrils now, but the tentacles cover them over so fast it's hard to see what's what. Watching it pries my mind away from the itching some, anyway.

And then I see the acoustic guitar I saved all of my paper route money for when I was 12. It's close enough to touch for a moment. But the fleshy pink cords wrap around it quickly, and for a second all I can see is the sound hole and the pick guard, and then it's erased entirely.

Next I see body parts tangle over each other. At first they look like mannequin arms and legs entwined and wriggling, but they're flesh. The wrists flick. The fingers twitch. But the tentacles usher them away as well.

And then I'm floating up and up and up, though I'm not really sure which way up is anymore. My body ascends, though. I can feel that. It just keeps going. Or maybe drift is the better word for it. It's slow, like the way a cloud moves.

Nothing is real anymore, not where I am. I'm just a shell in empty space, rising endlessly.

And I see my face in the tendrils, eyes closed, a warped version of myself like it's reflecting from the surface of swirling water. The eyelids flutter. The skin quivers. The tentacles surge and undulate about the face but do not touch it. It's me, but it's hollow. It's empty.

And I'm nauseous, and as I look upon the face the calm seeps away from me like the tide pulling away. And hatred and panic well inside of me. All the bad feelings that only find their way out in nightmares come out now. Shame opens in my mind. Guilt flowers. Doubt blooms. The dark touches the places that wither on contact, the places that I can't regulate or protect or understand, the injuries that need to be stitched up.

And the bubble bursts in my head, the insides gushing out like flood water overtaking a bridge.

And everything goes white.

CHAPTER 18

Everything is bled white again, but I'm somewhere else. I lie on a stripe of dirt etched into the grass – a path running through a sparsely wooded area. The wind blows, and the leaves whisper and hiss. So I can hear. I probe my ears with my pinky fingers and find no earplugs. Interesting.

I'm still naked, though.

So that's good.

For a moment I lie still on the ground, watching the branches sway in the breeze. If I try hard enough I can kind of see through the wood. Everything is partially translucent, myself included, which I realize as I hold my hand in front of my face and look through it to watch the flit and flicker of the leaves.

My hand falls to my chest, and I let the bliss wash over me. No more hatred. No more panic. No more hollow face in the tendrils. The white makes it all go away, and nothing can hurt me. I feel whole – a universe all of my own that the outside world cannot touch.

I stand. This patch of nature looks familiar, but I don't know why. I don't think I've ever been here.

I stretch and feel a spiral of pleasure in the space between every pair of vertebrae. I roll my neck, and the comfort touches there as well. I take a deep breath, and my chest heaves.

There's little else to do, so I walk along the path. I don't get the sense that it leads to anything, but I follow it anyway. I don't really need to know where I'm going, I guess. I'm already here.

The trees reach gnarled limbs out over the walkway. In a couple of spots, I see branches from the opposite sides of the path crisscrossing each other in the air above me, and it looks like they're sword fighting. Or touching tips. Or both.

I walk for some time, though I have little sense of it in terms of minutes or hours. Step after step stretches back in my memory so far that it's hard to remember what came before the first one.

The ground about me seems to grow sandier as I move forward, and the trees grow smaller and more sparse. When the wind gusts little clouds of dust billow up like tiny smoke signals for no one. The sand squishes between my toes, all gritty and warm.

The sun heats the back of my neck. It's pleasant enough, though, and I note that I'm not sweating. I don't think I need any SPF here somehow.

The path leads me up a hill, my feet now sinking partially into sand with each step. I climb. As it gets steeper, I use my hands to help scale the peak, fingers clawing at the earth. There's little to grip, but I keep at it, fighting, ripping, scratching the ground. I earn every inch of progress.

I reach the summit, out of breath, little lines swirling at the corners of my field of vision. I feel the vein in the center my forehead throbbing, its meter erratic. When I picture it, it looks like a pulsing garden hose with skin draped over it. The throb evens out and then recedes, though. I pick the grains of sand out from under my fingernails while I regain my wind.

From the top of the hill, I can see a long way. The diminishing woods give way to desert before long, dunes rolling away into the distance. There's a fork in the trail up ahead, but the two paths seem to run in parallel, at least as far as I can see.

I jog down the hill. It's more like falling and catching myself over and over again than running. I'll give gravity the credit for the assist on this one. By the time I'm at the bottom of the hill, my knees are a little sore from the repeated shock absorption, but it's a sore that feels good - in the white world, at least - sort of like the itching. I sit for a moment and massage my knees just to focus on the ache. It feels so good, my eyelids half close and flutter, and my mouth waters.

And then I wake myself with the drool draining onto my leg from my nodded out head. I'm not sure how long I was out, but the sun sits higher in the sky. I wipe the saliva from my chin with the heel of my hand, and my fingertips brush the tip of my nose which is as cold as a bomb pop. It's weird because the rest of me is really warm.

I rise, ready to move forward, and so I do. The sand stings now as I trudge through it, crawling hot and dry up onto my feet with each step and reaching up for my ankles. I power through it.

I reach the split in the path and stop to think my options over, hands on my hips. The terrain to the right and left look about the same to me, just as they did from afar. I have no coin to flip, either. No reason to belabor the decision, though, I guess. For no particular reason, I choose the right handed path and get going again.

The sand sprawls to the horizon in front of me. One tiny sliver of me thinks walking into the desert nude is a terrible idea. The rest is down to do whatever.

I have to pick up my feet higher now because walking in the sand is so awkward. I feel like I'm marching, patrolling the dust, the decay. The stand stomp slows me down quite a bit, but I'm not that concerned. There's nowhere I'm really going anyway, right?

As I mount the first big dune, I feel the needle of fatigue in my legs for the first time. The soreness in my knee was one thing, this is another. The muscles clench up too hard, and I can feel it bite at every little fiber.

And for the first time I think about where the hell I really am. Suffering fatigue - something so human and ordinary and not at all of the white world I know - shakes my confidence a little. The white always soothes me, gives me faith that everything will be fine or already is, but this is no heaven. I'm walking into the desert – the place where the sun chars all, the place where the heat cooks the life out of everything.

And as if on cue, a black blur rises above the sand on the horizon. It bounces up and down and appears to shimmer in the heat haze vibrating off of the ground. A person, a human being dressed in black, walks on the other trail – the left handed path. I can't tell if they're walking toward me or away.

And then the blur descends, sinking out of my view. From my vantage point it looks like the person walked down a flight of stairs into a doorway in the sand, but they must be walking into a valley between dunes. The way they disappeared makes me think they're headed my way, but it's hard to be sure of anything out here with the heat distortion in all directions.

I speed up, trying to walk on the sides of my feet so I don't sink quite as deep. With urgency in my step for the first time, I cover a lot of territory in a hurry. The ground works at my flesh like an infinite supply of exfoliating beads, grinding away the outermost layer of skin.

I try to keep calm, to stay patient. But I can't. I can't.

And I'm running, sprinting, somehow willing my tired legs to push through the ache. I glide over the sand by sheer force of will.

The black shape rises from the horizon again, closer. Much closer. I see the face take shape as it pokes out from behind the dune, a familiar face.

It's Amity, plodding toward me, her face angled at the ground.

I freeze on the spot, going from full sprint to dead stop in 0.2 seconds.

And I want to yell and jump up and down and wave my arms, but I can't. I can't move. I have to concentrate to even make myself breathe.

And then her head pops up, and it tilts in my direction. She stops walking.

Does she recognize me?

"Hey," I manage to say.

Unfortunately I say it in a normal speaking volume that she couldn't possibly hear. Still, it's some progress.

She shields her eyes from the sun by cupping her hand at her brow. Her head juts out a bit. She's definitely looking right at me.

And then she turns and runs.

"Wait!" I yell.

And I'm sprinting again, sand flying out from under me.

"Amity!" I say.

Why is she running from me? Did she recognize me?

And then I remember that the last time we met I kind of killed her. Plus, I'm naked. I look down to see a whole lot of shakin' goin' on. It really could be either of those things that set her on the path away from me, I guess.

So now I'm a naked guy chasing and yelling at a girl.

Pretty sweet.

I cross the sand between the paths on a diagonal, taking this trajectory to try to best erase the distance between us. I'm gaining on her.

Amity looks back over her shoulder at me, and her eyes get wide. I want to say something to her, something that might calm her. Instead I get the strangest feeling in my throat. I cough and a gush of water fills my mouth.

I stop running and cough again, and I feel the water enter my throat and the shock and revulsion as it touches the parts it's never supposed to touch. For a split second I can feel the burn of the sand on my feet, and the completely different burn in my wind pipe.

And then the desert vanishes, and I'm plunged into darkness.

Confused. Black nothing surrounds me. My eyes burn. I can't breathe. My limbs don't want to respond to my commands. I grit my teeth and will myself to not panic, and time goes into slow motion.

Think about what this could be. There must be some piece of information that can help me. I might only have a few seconds.

Salt.

I taste salt.

The saltwater.

I'm back in the tank, and I'm floating face down.

I try to reach out and push myself off of the bottom of the chamber, but my arm doesn't jolt into action so much as twitch a little, if even that. I twist my head to the right instead, pushing, pushing , rotating my shoulders to try to put as much of my weight as I can muster into it, and the momentum causes me to capsize.

I'm on my back again, head above water, but when I try to inhale, it doesn't work, like my chest is stuck. I turn my head, and my abdomen spasms. My diaphragm clenches so hard that my body arcs, and the liquid spurts out my mouth like it's spraying out of the jet on a hot tub. It pours out of me for what seems like so long, though perhaps the slow motion warps my perception, and then it pauses and starts again. After three bursts, the air gasps back into my lungs, all gurgle-y.

My lungs scald, and it feels like my mouth and nose are full of salty snot, but I can breathe. I listen to the repeating rhythm of the inhale and exhale, thankful to hear it.

Within a few minutes, my motor skills fade back in, a little dull but functional. I bang on what I guess to be the door to the tank.

I believe I'm done here.

CHAPTER 19

I sit in a lawn chair, looking out at the courtyard bled white behind the church. A blanket drapes my shoulders, much of it dangling behind me like a cape. Randy set me up out here. He said it takes a while to reacclimate yourself to time and space after a long deprivation session, and it's common to sit somewhere peaceful a while and let it all come back to you.

My feelings vacillate between excitement and exhaustion, awe and fear. I crane my neck to stretch it, trying to get the balled up muscle to loosen its grip a bit.

I remember the events and images I just experienced in bits and pieces, like I can't have access to the whole all at once. Much of it is clouded around the edges, and I struggle to put the pieces in order. It's like trying to piece together the fragments of a dream. With every glimpse I do get, my belly twinges with equal parts butterflies and a fist clench of dread.

I see things when I close my eyes, pink tentacles and piles of sand stretching out into infinity, my warped face wavering as if on the surface of the sea. And Amity running from a naked man, of course. I picture myself – sprinting, red faced, yelling, dong flopping like crazy.

It seems funny in a way now, of course. More than anything, I'm glad to know she's still out there. That what happened back in the alley wasn't for keeps. It gives me hope that Glenn and I can find her at some point.

Where the hell is Glenn, anyway? I consider the notion that if I go back there, I may be able to find him as well. Maybe next time I can even wear some pants.

The wind blows in the courtyard, and the dead trees moan and creak. The door next to me swings open, and Randy leans out.

"You alright?" he says.

"Yeah," I say. "I think I'm ready to go."

He squints at me.

"How long do you think you've been out here?" he says.

"I don't know," I say. "Five minutes."

"Try 40 minutes," he says. "You should sit a while longer and let your brain get back to the Earth's physics."

"OK," I say.

He heads back inside. According to him I was only in the tank for 25 minutes before I started pounding on the door. He said typically people take about 40 minutes to reach a meditation like state and achieve the switch to theta brain waves – opening the valve to the subconscious as he called it. It makes me wonder how long I was actually having that experience. If it took me 20 minutes to get there, did everything else happen in five minutes? It seems impossible. It feels like I walked miles on that trail.

Of course, I'm certain that I saw Amity in the white world for real. Could it be a hallucination? Maybe it's possible, but I don't think so. It triggered the white world, which is still transpiring for me. It made it stronger while I was in the tank, though. I wasn't just looking through the white world. I was there.

Maybe it's just the eternal bliss affecting my brain, but I feel lucky to have seen and felt all of this tonight. If this exact stuff happens to anybody else, it's maybe a handful of people on the entire planet. Everybody else's imagination craves images and emotions like these so much, they line up around the block to go to the movies. I just close my eyes, and it's all there in front of me, lurching and swaying and writhing. Back on the beach, Duncan said there are others like me, but maybe their version is different from mine.

And I remember that there's one person I want to share it all with. I pull my phone out of my pocket and press the appropriate buttons. It goes to voice mail immediately, and I hear her voice encouraging me to leave a message. I never leave messages, though.

Oh well.

I hang up and shove my phone back into my pocket. I adjust in my seat, and the lawn chair squeaks under me.

All of my senses are heightened from my time isolated. The sounds and the smells out here take on such nuance, such richness of detail, that I feel like one of those wine tasters sensing every fruity and zingy and earthy note. I smell the way the grass scent mixes with the wet wood chips nearby. I hear with great clarity the scrape of dead leaves moving over the pavement on the other side of the lot.

These details calm me somehow. They make the part of me that's perpetually on the verge of despair from sheer boredom shut the hell up for once.

I know I won't be able to sleep tonight, though. I can feel the electricity flickering behind my eyeballs, a level of stimulation cranked well beyond the state of mind where sleep is possible. I can already picture myself, rolling around on the couch like a coked up werewolf, growling, snarling, grunting out weird phlegmy throat noises.

The door swings open again, and Randy leans out, thrusting something blue at me.

"Almost forgot about this," he says. "You need to stay hydrated."

It's a blue Gatorade. I take it.

"Thanks," I say.

I pop the top, and when I look back to say something to Randy, he's gone already. I wonder what he's doing in there. Maybe there's a kitchen, and he's baking some kind of strudel or something. Wait. Strudel or streusel? I can't remember.

I sip the blue drink. It detonates on my pallet – a bright, acidic punch laced with sweet and salt. The world about me jitters and fizzles around the edges. I feel my eyes drawn inward, crossing, and then the dizziness spirals into my head with such force that I grip the arms of the chair so it won't hurl me to the ground. I hold still, eyes narrowed to slits, knuckles gone whiter than white.

In time, the dizziness lets up, and the fizzle dulls away.

So yeah, I forgot about all of that. You really have to tread lightly with beverages in the white world. Sheesh.

I screw the cap back on the Gatorade and set it down on the grass next to the leg of the chair. I need to get stickers that say "high octane" or something to slap on all of my drinks from now on.

I pull the phone out and try again. Straight to voicemail. Louise's voice rings in my ear, but it's not real. It's empty. I hang up and cut it off.

It brings me down somehow, as down as you can be in the white world, anyway. I guess even bliss becomes meaningless if you're left alone. I take a deep breath and let it out slow.

No more of this.

I will myself to stop thinking, to let the swirl of words circle down the drain and be gone. I don't wonder. I don't ponder. I don't reason or reflect. I just sit.

I stare out at the dead trees, blank as hell.

When I get home, there's a note on the fridge that says:

"Sorry I've been so busy. Let's have lunch tomorrow.

-Louise"

And I feel a little dumb for getting so upset.

CHAPTER 20

We sit at a picnic table, rotten wood coated with green lichen. Louise unzips a lunch satchel and pulls out a couple of sandwiches, peanut butter and jelly. Her hand sinks into the bag a second time, this time yanking free a sandwich baggie full of potato chips. She looks distracted, her eyes darting away from the food over and over.

I told her about most of the stuff that happened in the tank and the white world last night on the way over, but she didn't say much. I guess she's pretty obsessive about her work. Plus, she's remained pretty skeptical about what is happening to me. I get the impression that she thinks it's cute that I think any of it is real. I don't blame her, though. I probably wouldn't believe it either, if I were someone else.

I unwrap my sandwich and take a bite, following her gaze across the park to a man and woman sitting on a bench. This must be the perp and his mistress, up to no good. He's probably 60 with puffy white hair, sporting a damn turtleneck. It seems weird that someone is even willing to pay to document whatever infidelities this guy might be getting up to. Seriously, I struggle to fathom that someone's happiness hinges on Turtleneck's behavior.

Louise jots something in her notebook. She also has her camera at the ready, the gigantic lens partially shielded from sight by the lunch bag.

The first triangular half of my sandwich is gone, but she has yet to touch hers. I'm tearing into the chips pretty good, too. If she doesn't hurry, she may regret it. Then again, maybe she's not hungry. There's no evidence to suggest she is.

"I might need to go back at some point," I say. "To find Amity or Glenn. Or both."

Her eyes remain fixed on the bench beyond me. Without looking away she reaches for the camera, her hands moving with a steadiness I assume is to avoid drawing the notice a jerky motion might arise. She brings the camera to her eye, the off eyelid clinched tight. Her finger hovers over the button, ready to pull the trigger. After a long moment, she pulls it down and tucks it behind the bag again.

"False alarm," she says. "I thought that was going to be the money shot."

"Yeah," I say.

We're quiet for a moment. She finally takes a bite of the sandwich.

"Weren't you saying something?" she says.

"Yeah," I say. "I said I might need to go back to find Glenn and Amity."

"Back where?" she says.

"Back into the tank," I say.

"Dickhead!" she says. "You ate all of the chips."

"Yeah, sorry," I say. "I didn't think you were hungry, I guess."

Her eyes snap back to the bench, and the camera is in her hands in a flash. She adjusts the focus and snaps a few shots. I don't care to look, but I like to think that the lady pulled down the collar of the Turtleneck to give him a hickey.

"He put his arm around her," she says, snapping the lens cap back on. "Better than nothing."

I watch her eat a couple more bites of sandwich. Mine is long gone.

"I'm sorry," she says. "What were you saying, again?"

"I might need to go back in that tank," I say.

"What for?" she says.

I can't quite hide the agitation in my voice.

"To find Glenn and Amity," I say.

"Oh, right," she says. "Yeah, you should do that."

"It's kind of scary in a way," I say, but she's already locked onto the bench again, so I don't bother going on.

The Passat rolls down Park Street, whisking us in the general direction of home. Flecks of water flit against the windshield, so apparently our lunch in the park endeavor ended just in time. The rain taps out a steady rhythm on the windshield, and the sound calms me a bit, I think.

I try to tell myself that Louise is just busy. She carted me along while she worked so we could spend some time together since she's so swamped with cases right now. She's got a lot on her mind and all that.

But I can't help but feel rejected anyway. I get that when people don't listen to me, I guess. I don't know. Someone told me once that I have a habit of looking for rejection in all things.

Her phone buzzes from within her purse, and she digs it out and hands it to me.

"A text," she says. "Will you check it?"

I'm confused for a split second, but I guess it's because she's driving. I hate using other people's phones. Most of the time, I somehow press like 50 buttons on the touch screen accidentally as soon as the phone hits my hands, and then I'm panicking because the phone is calling someone saved in the contact list as "Mo-Mo," and I'm in no mood to explain all of this to Mo-Mo just now.

Anyway, that doesn't happen this time. I press a thingy and read the text.

"It's Dennis," I say. "He says, 'You gotta meet me ASAP. It's about your burn vic.'"

After a quick back and forth with Dennis, we change routes to meet him in the parking lot of a Marathon on West Street. I use the term quick loosely here, though. I had to type on the tiny keyboard, thumbs all atwitter. The worst.

We pull into the lot and park next to the police cruiser behind the building. Dennis gets out and strides over to the Passat. He wears a pair of wrap around Oakley's that remind me of Glenn and Mark McGwire.

"This is some crazy shit," he says en route.

He leans into the driver's side window of the Passat. He looks across the car and sees me. His face looks blank for a second, and then something registers.

"What up, Grobnagger?" he says, reaching through the vehicle to shake my hand.

"Hey," I say.

I never know if it's better to answer any variation of "What's up?" as though the person is literally asking what I'm up to or take it more as a general greeting and say hi. I feel dumb either way, so I guess there's no way to win this game. Whatever.

"So check this out. That burn vic, Farber?" he says "His body – POOF - vanished. It ain't at the morgue. It ain't nowhere."

"For real?" Louise says.

He smirks. I feel like Dennis is perpetually pleased with himself.

"How long do they keep bodies at the morgue?" I say.

"Someone's been watching some CSI. So the thing is, we hadn't officially identified him yet," he says. "Louise says word among the culties is that it's Farber, but officially, without cooperation from any of the League people, he's John Doe. He'd be at the morgue until we made a positive ID."

He spits on the ground.

"Anyhow, they want to keep that hushed up, so you didn't hear it from me," he says, moving back toward his car.

He stands in the open door for a second, one elbow leaned on the roof.

"Thing is, they keep that shit locked up, and that part of the building is under 24 hour supervision. Everybody through there has to sign in and out. So it's like some Houdini shit to get a stiff out of there," he says.

A drone of chatter blares from his walkie talkie. He presses the button and mumbles into it, rolling his eyes. Then he holsters the walkie talkie and turns back to us.

"I gotta go," he says.

He's in, slams the door, and the car is moving almost immediately. The cruiser rips out of the parking lot, Dennis gunning it to take the turn onto the street at top speed. He honks an obnoxious two note goodbye.

Dread bloats in my belly as we roll out of the Marathon parking lot. The absence of Farber's body bothers me, maybe even scares me a little.

Silence envelops the Passat's interior on the ride home. The tires slosh over the wet asphalt, but that's outside. Inside? Only quiet. Our thoughts tangle around us and keep our tongues still, I suppose, though I suspect the two of us are thinking about completely different things.

Louise probably wonders who, what, when and how someone got the body out of the morgue undetected, and where she can get said info to give to her client for an agreed upon sum. I'm wondering whether or not Riston Farber has risen from the dead. If so, is he stomping around all burned up? Like a burnt chicken skin version of the crypt keeper or something? I can't really imagine that frail piece of extra crispy walking the Earth.

The prospect scares me, nonetheless. I picture the fear in Randy's eyes when he talked about the notion of someone using the book to come back, the power it would bestow upon them. I believe he said that if it happened, we'd be up shit creek. And immediately the image resurfaces of me brandishing a turd paddle, fighting my way upstream.

Louise puts on the turn signal, and the click clack breaks the spell of the silence, erasing all turds from my mind. We both seem able to move again, and we look at each other.

"We need a plan," Louise says.

"I know," I say.

I bet Glenn would have a kickass plan at the ready. And probably a thermos of chamomile tea, too, to calm our nerves.

"You should talk to Cromwell again, and I'll talk to Stan,"

she says. "Don't tip off that you know about the body, at least not right away."

"Yeah, I get it," I say.

She thinks I might be able to tease something out of him or trip him up if I play it right. Let's get real, though. In a best case scenario, I might tease out a free meal.

Not that I'm knocking that. I mean, I could eat.

CHAPTER 21

I stand on the doorstep of Cromwell's building, my fingertip still lingering on the button next to the scrawl of his name. A buzz sounds from somewhere inside, and the door pops open. I grab it and pry it wide, finding it surprisingly heavy.

I climb the steps, passing a lady with crazy eyes on the way up. She smiles at me, but with her eyes open that wide, it looks more like an animal baring its teeth as a warning.

When I get to apartment 336, the door is opened a crack. I assume Cromwell left it open as an invitation for me to come in, but I hesitate anyway. What if burned up zombie Farber is in there, hovering spoons to force throw at my face?

I move through the doorway, passing through the entry hallway into the living room. No charred zombies here. Cromwell sits on the couch with a bag of pretzels in his lap. His eyes are so glued to the TV that he doesn't notice my presence. There's something funny about a person snacking and watching TV in front of that devil mural. I picture his mom fixing him a snack, "Now, who wants demon pretzels and bug juice?"

"Hell yeah!" he says, raising a fist full of pretzels in the air.

I glance at the screen. Football.

"Oh, hey Grobnagger," he says. "What up?"

"Hey," I say.

He looks at me for a second.

"So what's up?" he says, and there's an edge to his voice this time.

Goddamn it! I guess he meant the question literally and not as a greeting, and now he's annoyed that I didn't answer it. See? You cannot win this game.

"Nothing much," I say. "I was just in the neighborhood."

He squints and tosses a couple of pretzels in his mouth.

"That's cool," he says, between crunches. "I'm just watching the game."

He raises a hand clutching pretzels, which I guess is a gesture to the TV.

"I see that," I say.

"Well, have a seat," he says.

I do this, plopping onto the loveseat perpendicular to the couch.

"You watch sports?" he says.

"A little," I say.

He chews with his mouth open.

"Seems like most people either watch a lot or none," he says.

"Well, I watch a little," I say. "I guess it puts me in the minority, but I can get some entertainment out of it without painting my face and starting a blog."

He chuckles, but the laugh dies in his throat, and he's yelling at the TV, flecks of food spraying from his mouth. I look up to see players scrambling for a loose ball on TV.

"Unreal," he says, leaning back. "Second turnover already, and it ain't even halftime."

He watches with such rapt fervor, I don't feel there's a good opening to ask him anything Farber related. I decide to table it until the game reaches the half.

We watch for a while. The announcers spout clichés and mock outrage and feigned excitement. One guy implores the audience to "hold on to your hat" four times in a 10 minute segment. Meanwhile, Cromwell strings together obscenities and hurls them at the screen. Many of the combinations make little sense, which makes them more interesting.

During the next commercial break, he points the open end of the bag of pretzels at me and gives it a shake. I take a few. Not bad, but I could really use that bug juice to wash them down.

Seriously, pretzels without a beverage? Lunacy.

Cromwell must sense my ire. He runs out of the room during a booth review and comes back with a pair of beers. He uses a lighter from the coffee table to pop the lids off and hands me one without even looking at me.

"His left foot was out of bounds," he says, pointing at the screen. There's a sense of pleading in his tone.

I examine the bottle in my hand. It's Sam Adams. I take a sip. It's been a long time since I drank a beer, so I can feel my lips pull down a touch at the corners due to the bitterness. It's not bad, though. Out of the mass marketed beers, I think this is among the best. There's almost a spiced flavor in there somewhere.

To Cromwell's disappointment, the play stands as called. The game gets back underway. In the distraction, my old habits kick in, I guess, and a couple slugs later, I've chugged the beer down. I set the empty bottle on the table.

"Damn, Grobnagger," he says.

"I was thirsty," I say.

"If I knew you were going to pound 'em down like that, I would have brought you more than one," he says.

He runs to the kitchen to grab a couple more and sets both of them by me. This time he remembers a bottle opener, too. I didn't know I was signing on for this. I consider nursing the next one, but then I figure screw it. It's almost halftime now. Maybe the beers will lubricate my brain and help me come up with an angle of approach in my interrogation.

Alcohol slows other people down, but it doesn't seem to do that for me. It just relaxes me, makes it easier to talk to people, dulls the outside world a bit. My mind stays sharp, at least until I drink enough that I can't walk.

I pour 24 ounces of Sam Adams down the old drain between the two minute warning and halftime. Cromwell seems impressed by this.

"I didn't know you partied like this, man," he says.

"Can I ask you something?" I say. "Did you ever think Farber would figure out how to do it?"

"Do what?" he says.

"Come back from the dead," I say. "I mean, you talk about being a serious student of the arcane, but you also talk about Farber like he's a con man, more or less. I was just wondering if you believed in him or not."

"That's a good question," he says. "It's hard to say, bro. I mean, faith is a choice, right? I choose to believe that there's more going on in the universe than the physical realm that we perceive. It makes some sense to me intuitively, and I want to believe that. I look for ways to connect to it or experience it or verify it or whatever the shit you want to call it, and I do that both internally and externally. But it's not like I believe it entirely on a conscious level. Like say you ask me that question about Farber resurrecting, and part of me thinks 'Of course not. It's ridiculous.' But the part of me that wants to believe and pursue all of this occult stuff still believes it to be possible. That's why I put my time into it. To me, that's what faith is. It's the choice. It has nothing to do with believing all of it absolutely. Like the beliefs people inherit from their parents without putting any thought into it? That's not faith to me."

OK.

What the hell?

That was well put. This guy might be singlehandedly disproving my theory about the correlation between the usage of the term "bro" and IQ or sensitivity or whatever. Or perhaps he's the exception that proves the rule.

"Well said," I say.

I think for a second.

"So did he talk about resurrection a lot?" I say.

"It came up," he says. "He talked about a lot of shit, though. If I had to sum up his point of view, I'd say he often brought things back to the realm of control. He was always talking about using the things he learned and acquired to gain power, to use them to achieve something in the physical world. I was probably always more philosophical and shit in my approach. I just want to connect to something outside of myself, you know? He didn't seem as interested in that part of things. That was his flaw, I think, and maybe it's what did him in."

He slaps the wall behind him.

"That mural?" he says. "That's what it means. People think

it represents pure evil or some nonsense. In the tarot, the devil is the symbol for obsession with the physical realm. His chains shackle the two people here, right? When they throw away their spiritual desires in favor of dedicating their passions and thoughts and hearts to money and sex and their careers and so on, they do as the devil pleases, they chain themselves to his altar. I wanted it up there to remind me of what I really care about and what I don't."

He scratches his chin.

"Oh, shit. You already finished both of those?" he says, pointing at the empties on the coffee table.

"Yeah, I'm probably good, though," I say.

"Nah," he says. "Game's only half over."

He hustles out of the room and returns with more beer. This time it's tall boys that are blends of Bud Light and Clamato called Chelada.

"What the hell is this?" I say.

"Just try it," he says. "It's delicious."

I open the can. It smells like tomato juice with a little bit of beer. I taste it. It tastes like tomato juice with a little bit of beer. There is also a salty punch, a clam flavor and a hint of something like lime.

"Well?" he says.

"Not bad," I say. "If I'm ever in the mood for beer mixed with tomato juice mixed with clam juice mixed with lime, I'll know what my go to beverage is, that's for sure."

He chuckles.

"So let's say a burned up Farber zombie walked through that door right now," I say. "What would you do?"

His eyes tilt toward the ceiling as he imagines this scenario.

"I'd chop its head off with that katana blade leaned up against the coffin over there," he says. "And then I'd probably go change my pants."

I laugh.

"Well, he's bound to turn up somewhere," I say.

His face looks blank, and then his brow crinkles.

"What do you mean?" he says.

"You know," I say. "About the body."

He doesn't move. He just stares at me.

"I think I don't," he says.

"Oh," I say. "Farber's corpse? It went missing from the morgue. I figured you already knew."

"No way!" he says, sitting forward.

On TV, a running back breaks off an 86 yard run for a touchdown, but Cromwell barely notices. His eyes don't waver from me.

"Yep," I say.

"Unbelievable," he says. "Do the cops know what happened?"

"I think they know something," I say.

I pause here under the guise of taking a drink, but really I just want to watch his reaction.

"But they're playing it close to the vest for now," I say.

"That's… Wow," he says. "Wow."

He sits back in his seat and takes a long slurp from his can.

With the sun gone, the city chills down to the point that I can see my breath hover in the air. I'm thankful for those beers after all. The drunk keeps me warm on the walk home from Cromwell's. Even without a jacket, the heat radiates out from my torso like my insides are a cranked up furnace.

I feel reasonably confident that Cromwell had nothing to do with the disappearance of Farber's corpse. Unless he's an Oscar caliber actor, which I doubt, that's the story his words and demeanor tell me. Anything is possible, yes, but I trust my instincts. I trust my feelings.

I step over a pothole filled with sludgy water as I cross the street, and it reminds me of the alley. It seems like all of that happened years ago now. It's weird how time winds you on a path away from every event in your life until it feels cold and distant.

I replay some of Cromwell's answers in my imagination as I shuffle down the sidewalk. When I said the police knew something, he showed no signs of alarm. He looked pretty much ecstatic from the moment I mentioned the disappearance, in fact. I also felt like he was a little dismissive of Farber's motives and ideas in a way that suggested little chance of collusion. His comments also didn't seem like the kind of remarks you'd make about someone you recently killed.

That seems to rule out most of the angles I could see for him being involved.

Then again, maybe I should have been more direct. Perhaps I should have asked him point blank about the morgue toward the end there. I don't know. I'm not some interrogation expert.

As the blocks pass by, the cold crawls up my arms and legs to do battle with the furnace in my abdomen. I'm not far from home now, though. Soon, I'll be with Louise, and we'll be warm, and none of this will matter for a little while.

CHAPTER 22

I dig through Glenn's fridge. I've put a pretty big dent on the local food supply, so all that's left is a six pack of beer, condiments, a jar of homemade pickles, a package of frozen dinner rolls along with a bunch of random stuff in Tupperware containers in the freezer. It appears to be tomato based liquids for the most part - like soup or sauce, most likely. Hard to tell for sure in a solid state.

At some point I'm going to need to go buy groceries, I guess, which I dread. He kept the place stocked pretty well, but I've eaten like a king for a few weeks now.

Sitting at the snack bar, I wrench open the pickle jar, scissor a pickle spear between two fingers and take a bite. It crunches nicely. The vinegar is bright, the garlic robust, and the jalapeno bites at the back of my throat. In other words, it's effing delicious.

I try to call Louise again, and it goes to voicemail immediately. Yep. I fight the urge to throw the phone through the wall. When that swell of rage passes, I get the impulse to shatter the pickle jar, which I meet halfway by savagely eating another pickle from it, tearing, gnawing, grinding it into mush.

Pretty convenient that she stops answering my calls now that she gets what she wants, isn't it? I join the League and start following all of her orders, and she vanishes into a puff of smoke more and more frequently.

I pull the rolls I found in the freezer out of the oven and slather peanut butter all over them, scraping it out of the bottom of the jar. Open faced sandwiches. A goddamn delight.

Even as good as the food tastes, eating is supposed to be satisfying, and I find no contentment in this meal. I just grow angrier and angrier. It'd be nice to talk to someone about the stuff that's going on, namely the person I know that supposedly cares about the shit I do. Instead I'm sitting alone eating goddamn pickles.

Let's just run through the list of recent events: a capital x slashed into my chest, regular visits to cult group meetings, which may serve exceptional baked goods but also weird me out, spending quality time with Seth Cromwell, the man everybody fears like he's the damn Night Stalker, and oh yeah, running around naked in the white world after a weird isolation tank session.

Shouldn't I have someone to talk to about this for Christ's sake? Why am I doing this alone? It doesn't make sense anymore. There is no point.

I hold still a moment, and I can hear the clock on the kitchen wall ticking.

I'm all alone.

Doesn't anyone actually want to be with me? Did she ever really care? Why did I start believing in all of this kind of crap again?

I take a deep breath.

The peanut butter is long gone, so I get the pickles back out to cap the meal with a final spear. It doesn't cleanse my pallet so much as scorch the hell out of that shit.

One thing Glenn does have is a shit ton of coffee. I dump some extra dark beans in the grinder and jam the button down a few times. The bag boasts of this blend's cocoa nib after taste, which I'm anxious to try. It kind of smells like tobacco, though.

I catch my reflection in the window as I move to the coffee machine. And that first blink is one of those weird moments where my own face surprises me. I see myself when I'm not at all expecting it, and I don't just see what I expect to see. I see myself as foreign for that first fraction of a second. I see myself the way a stranger must see me. An imperfection in the glass warps my face so one cheek bone looks bigger than the other.

And the fact that I am here alone gorging myself with pickles and coffee becomes more real.

And I'm not even mad anymore. I'm not.

Just please, please come here now. Call me. Anything. Don't leave me here alone.

I put the pickles away, and I sit in the quiet. The clock ticks.

Please.

I close my eyes. I try to will my mind to go blank, but I can't do it. It just keeps circling back to this despair, this neediness that I don't even recognize in myself. This desire to plead, to beg, that I want to erase and can't.

I stand up and go to the living room like I can walk away from the feeling somehow. Now the kitchen clock is the tiniest pulse in the distance. My thoughts still spiral through the same progression in this new room, of course. I can't shut it off.

I turn off the light and sit in the dark, shoulders leaned back into the couch cushions and chin angled up toward the ceiling. There are no stars above, though. There is only the dark. I guess this is where I always end up.

Awake in the dark. Alone.

Please.

Please.

Please.

I feel like I should be able to float away from this. I should be able to drift off to some other plane because this one is too painful for me to exist in. Because no one should have to feel this way. I know other people must, but I think they can just forget it or something. It always sticks with me, though. It marks me up good.

Or maybe they don't let themselves feel it all the way. Their subconscious does some sleight of hand to keep them safe from themselves. I don't have that ability somehow. I feel all of it.

And the purr of a car engine outside interrupts the silence. I sit upright to listen. A car door slams. After a pause, the key slips into the lock on the front door with the clink and grind of metal on metal, and the deadbolt retracts with a snap.

I watch the door swing into the room, and Louise steps into the opening. She hovers there in the threshold a moment, kicking off her shoes before she closes the door.

She strides into the dark of the living room, her head angled toward the floor. Even after she flips on the lamp, she seems so lost in thought that she doesn't realize I'm sitting there for a full second.

"Oh, hey. I didn't think you were home," she says. "Why are you sitting out here in the dark?"

"Yeah, hey," I say. "I don't know."

"Well, you could have said 'hi,'" she says. "I mean, you must have watched me walk in."

"Yeah, sorry," I say. "I was thinking, I guess."

She walks out toward the kitchen as she goes on.

"Well, Woods knows nothing," she says. "He got all excited once I got around to mentioning Farber's disappearing corpse act."

"Same with Cromwell," I say.

I hear the fridge open and shut about two seconds later.

"Yikes," she says. "We need to go to the grocery store at some point."

"I know," I say.

The ascending melody of running water filling a glass echoes off of the walls. She walks back into the living room and sits next to me.

"Are you all right?" she says.

"Yeah," I say.

She stares at me.

"You just seem quiet is all," she says.

"Sorry," I say.

She hugs herself against my shoulder.

"I missed you," she says.

But it's not real. It's not real. I can't take it. I want to pull away. I want to float away. Instead I say:

"Me too."

"It's not so late," she says, her head leaning on me. "We could still go do something fun tonight, if you feel like it."

I don't feel like it. I feel like disappearing. All of these words are wind. All of these feelings are lies. I'd be better off erased, really, my existence wiped away like I was never even here at all.

"I guess a bunch of people are going to Up and Under tonight," she says.

Here we go. An invitation to a sports bar that a bunch of college kids hang out at. Maybe it will be like an episode of Cheers. Taking a break from all of my troubles sure would help a lot, right? We can drink Jägerbombs with frat guys and shit. Play some darts.

It's too much. It's too much. Take me out of this place. I want to go away.

I clench my teeth and my fists and my brain, and the familiar tidal wave arrives with a crash as the white world opens in my head.

CHAPTER 23

I lead the way into the lawn care section, Louise pushing the cart behind me. The floor is made of egg again, a three to four inch layer of hardboiled egg white flooring, I'd say. I bounce on the balls of my feet for a second just to feel the squish.

"You looking into a weed whacker purchase?" she says.

"Hell yeah," I say.

I rip one down from its display and brandish it with my maggot hands, mock whacking the bags of grass seed below, complete with awesome sound effects. I get a little carried away, though, and knock over several bottles of some kind of fertilizer.

"Calm down," Louise says. She takes the weed whacker from me and puts it back.

"Calmer than you are," I say.

"What's gotten into you?" she says.

"The holy spirit," I say.

She just stares at me.

"What? I'm just in a good mood," I say.

We move past a bunch of lawn mowers and rakes. There's even a little display of snow shovels for the impending winter.

Something about the lighting in here is so weird, manipulated. I remember reading that they light these stores a really particular way to make it as comfortable as possible to encourage sales. They lower the lighting in the lingerie section, for example, to help people relax around a bunch of panties and all. Fruits and vegetables look better in natural light. Meat looks tired in natural light, though, and fares better under bright white light. And so on. Every store and department has their own illumination strategy for separating you from as much of your money as they can.

"Didn't we come here to get groceries?" Louise says, interrupting my thoughts.

"We're browsing," I say.

"Come on. Are you actually considering buying those tiki torches?" she says.

It's not until she says this that I realize I'm holding two tiki torches, one in each hand. I don't say anything. I just put the torches back all smooth and do the nonchalant shrug.

We walk past the electronics, but it's not that interesting to me. I want to pick stuff up, concrete items I can touch and consider. Everything cool in the electronics section is locked behind glass or wrapped in plastic.

As we move into the hardware section, my limbs seem to get heavier and heavier, like they're filling with sand with every step I take. I lift my arm to test it, and it shakes a little, so I drop it back down before Louise can see this. I lean up against a shelf in the aisle where all of the wrenches and hammers hang.

"Now what?" Louise says.

"Hang on," I say. "I feel sick."

After I say it, I realize that I do feel pretty sick. My hand clutches my gut. I lean forward a little, expecting gallons of fluid to come cascading out of my mouth like a waterfall.

Instead, nothing happens.

"Let's go," Louise says. "The groceries are this way."

She leads us past a bunch of pillows and a shelf of beach towels with Justin Bieber's face on them. My legs don't feel heavy at all now, at least. I lift my arms, and they're all light now. Weird how these things seem to come and go.

We stop momentarily when I grab a Panini press and shove it in the cart. Louise puts it back. We're in an aisle of junk appliances such as – an electric ice shaver, a quesadilla maker, an electric can opener, and my favorite, the breakfast sandwich maker. The two outer chambers toast the English muffin and melt the cheese. The middle chamber fries an egg. Then you remove the plate under the egg, and bam, your sandwich is made.

"I already have a breakfast sandwich maker," I say. "It's called a frying pan."

We enter the grocery area near the cookie aisle. The lighting here is different than the hardware and Panini press aisle. More natural, I think.

On sight, I throw some Oreos in the cart, Double Stufs, the way Glenn would've wanted it. If it were possible to pour a little out of a 40 ounce of liquid Oreo right here in the store in honor of my missing friend, I would do that.

The next thing I know, we're stalking down the foreign foods aisle, and let's just say I'm handling a lot of the merchandise. I discover about 17 Asian sauces I want to try, some weird Mexican drink mix that's made of chocolate and cinnamon, two flavors of ramen noodles I was previously unfamiliar with and a jar of Mario Batali vodka sauce that runs about six times what the other jars of marinara cost. All of this gets twisted about in my hands and then tossed in the cart. When I turn around, though, Louise has put most of it back.

"Stop messing around," she says. "You need to get stuff for meals, not just sauces."

She seems to be finding it all at least somewhat humorous, though. She thinks I'm joking. What she doesn't realize is that I never joke around about Asian cuisine.

Ever.

Seriously, though, it seems a bit insane that she has no sense of my state, but maybe it's for the best. Maybe.

And for a second, reality bleeds through, and I see the real color of things. I feel lost, adrift, surrounded by people that I can't connect with and can't connect with me.

Then I spot the ice cream and practically sprint to the freezer door with all of the Ben and Jerry's behind it. My maggoty hands press on the glass, and my nose hovers a few inches shy of touching it as well.

I decide to limit myself to three flavors for the sake of propriety. Cherry Garcia goes without saying as flavor number one. Right now I'm thinking Chubby Hubby for number two, but I'm wavering a little on that one. I like the peanut butter swirl a lot, but the chocolate covered pretzel bits are a little on the massive side and not that tasty. For number three, I'll have to take a dive into the ice cream abyss and get something I've never tried before.

I realize Louise has been talking for a while, and I totally missed it, lost in ice cream land.

"I think I'm going with Milk and Cookies," she says.

Genius. She is a genius.

She reaches into the freezer and pulls free the pint,

smudging finger marks into the frost running around the side of the carton. Now it's my turn to brave the cold. I open the freezer door and lean in.

"Maybe you should just pick one," she says, just as I get the third pint tucked inside my elbow. "We can always get more next time."

True. True.

I put back the Chubby Hubby and, to my surprise, the Cherry Garcia. I'm going off the beaten path this eve. I'm going with Karamel Sutra. Half caramel ice cream, half chocolate ice cream with chocolate chunks and a core of molten caramel. Ok, it's not molten, but still…

We walk the aisles a while longer. I kind of wish this would never end.

I lie in bed, awake in the dark like always. The white is fading a bit, but I still feel pleasant enough. Louise sleeps next to me.

I try to replay the evening in my mind, but I can't quite get my head back to that place I was right before I went to the white world. I can only replay the shininess of Wal-Mart.

I know I hurt before that, but I can't remember exactly what it was like. I can't remember the feel of it.

I suppose it doesn't matter much. I can always get away, right? I can always make it OK, so what is there to worry about?

CHAPTER 24

The next morning I'm awakened by my phone beeping – a text from Babinaux. Apparently she's stopping by in about 20 minutes, and it's important. I want to lie back and let the blankets hug me longer, and I consider doing so. Instead, I rise from the bed anyway and stumble toward the shower. I don't recall choosing this action, but I lean my head forward and go with the momentum.

En route, I kick a crushed Ben and Jerry's carton. Wow, so somebody was partying pretty hard last night. I guess I really got after that Karamel Sutra. It's just a foggy memory now. Maybe it means I've finally built up a tolerance for eating and drinking while in the white world.

I turn on the water, adjusting the temp. I guess I'm pretty used to this beastly water pressure by now. Just don't let it make direct contact with the genitals, and you're fine. I should make a sign that says that to hang in here.

As I towel off, I get a single flash of that feeling I had just before the world went white last evening, a pang of vulnerability and panic and nausea climbing my throat.

But now I'm numb again, the colors of the world muted ever so faintly.

I dress, and by the time I get out to the living room, Babinaux is already there, sitting on the couch. Guess I left the door unlocked, too. Between that and pounding down the ice cream, I'm really turning into a bad boy type like Charlie Sheen or something.

Babinaux looks up from her phone as I enter the room. She smiles and points to the paper cup of coffee on the table as she says:

"Good morning."

"Morning," I say, scooping up the beverage. "And thank you."

I take a sip. Another crazy concoction, though I think it's caramel instead of cinnamon this time. Now this might be because I ate about 1600 calories of caramel ice cream last night, but I think the cinnamon was better.

"Are you feeling ok?" she says.

"Yeah," I say. "I'm great."

She frowns.

"You don't look so great," she says.

She squints and leans forward to get a better look.

"Thanks," I say. "What do you mean?"

"Your eyes look all puffed up," she says.

I press my index and middle finger to each of my eyes. My right eyelid is actually a little tender, swollen and painful to the touch. I guess I was too tired to get much of a look in the mirror.

"Must be some kind allergy thing," I say.

"Well, if you're feeling up to it," she says, leaning back. "Randy wants you to do the third initiation tonight."

"And what will that entail?" I say.

"First there is a feast," she says.

"I can get behind that," I say. "What else?"

She hesitates.

"I probably shouldn't tell you the exact details," she says. "But there's a ritual reenacting your spiritual rebirth."

"Like a baptism?" I say.

"Sort of," she says.

I try to read into her expression, but she is stoic as always.

"Well, many of us will be there for the meal, myself included, and he said there will be four of you doing the actual ritual this time," she says. "It's not as rare as the water ritual."

"Well, whatever," I say. "I guess I may as well do it."

She had me at "feast."

"How are things with you and Louise?" she says.

"Good, I think," I say. "Maybe. I don't know."

"What's wrong?" she says.

I plan to say little, but the words pour out of me like water rushing out of the mouth of a downspout during a storm.

"It's my fault. I feel like I can never shut my brain off and just be," I say. "So say, for example, she doesn't get back to me right away when I call, I start freaking out. At first I'm all mad, but then after a while I'm just pining for her affection. Feeling lonely and abandoned and stranded. It's really pathetic. By the time she actually comes around, I've twisted myself around so much that I'm actually resentful toward her for finally showing."

I tap at my pant leg.

"I guess it feels like she put me through all of that, even though I know that's not the truth," I say. "And then another part of me just doesn't believe her anymore. Like I pine after her affection and then reject it when it comes. I see it as not real, all phony like she's pretending or maybe fooling herself.

Does that make sense?"

She tilts her head.

"Well, it makes sense in that I understand what you mean," she says. "It doesn't make much sense, though, as far as a way for a person to behave. I mean, it's pretty irrational, no?"

"Well, yeah," I say. "I get what you mean."

"Have you tried talking to her about it?" she says.

"No," I say. "I guess I should do that."

"I would say so," Babinaux says.

"Sometimes it's hard to talk," I say.

"I understand," she says. "But a lack of communication is like cancer for a relationship. It grows and grows until it kills its host. If you don't talk to her about all of the stuff bouncing around in your head, it will only grow. It will only isolate you from her more and more."

We're quiet for a moment.

"He could never accept love," she says. "My friend I told you about, I mean. He never learned how to accept love. I don't want that to happen to you."

CHAPTER 25

I get to the church early, and judging from the lack of cars in the lot, no one else is here yet. I stroll around the grounds for a bit, circling the dead trees tinted green with lichen. With a little more daylight than the last time I was out here, I notice that the grass is coming up on ankle deep. I wonder who mows this. Does the League pay somebody to come out here and mow around a building they barely use?

I meander toward the door as I contemplate these maintenance matters. It's unlocked, which doesn't shock me. I wasn't planning on going in until someone else arrived, but I guess I will.

It's an eerie feeling to walk around in an empty church. Padding across the blood red carpet so many have walked on before, I get a sense of the building's history. There's an energy here, a past that vibrates in the air, that you can feel in your chest. This room meant a lot to people for decades before I was even born. It was sacred to them. It was a pillar that held up their community. And now it's being used for some pretty weird shit as it crumbles. But that's better than not being used at all, I think. I guess I can't speak to how they might feel about it.

I work my way past the pews and poke around the sanctuary. Under a bench, I spot a box of ancient microphones.

Ribbon and dynamic mics with the grills beat to hell. I bet some are valuable, even with the scuffs and dents. People love vintage audio equipment.

There's a stack of old hymnals in the corner. I pick one up to find that it's falling apart, the spine of the book disintegrating, so big chunks of pages pull away from each other. Gold lettering on the cover says it was published in 1898. I flip through the pages the best I can and read the song titles. I feel like the word "majesty" was a lot more popular back then.

"You in the mood to sing for us?" a voice says from the back of the room.

I look up. It's Randy.

"Not really," I say. "Unless you're offering to tickle those ivories over there."

I point at the piano and wiggle my fingers on the imaginary keyboard in front of me. Randy does not seem amused, so I guess it wasn't that funny. I bet if you're old you've heard "tickle the ivories" throughout your life, so it's not an obscure reference or anything like that. I really need to better tailor my material to the elderly for events like this.

"At least you're on time," he says.

What the hell? I swear it wasn't long ago that Randy clearly thought I was awesome. He praised my passion and so forth. Well, I guess that honeymoon is over, because now he's belittling me left and right.

"I heard there will be a feast," I say.

"You heard right," he says.

He walks out of the room and heads downstairs, ending our conversation without telling me a single culinary detail. I'm pretty sure that in some parts of the world, confirming a feast without elaborating on the menu is considered treason. I will let it slide – I'm a merciful Grobnagger - but still…

I think about going downstairs to check out whatever might already be set up food-wise, but I decide I'd rather not be around Randy. That level of grumpiness is infectious. I'm trying to keep a positive frame of mind, get my food, and get out of here.

I sit on one of the folding chairs in the sanctuary. There are two rows of seven of them, which I'm guessing were used for a choir at some point. Facing the pews, I watch the front door. People trickle through, many of them toting casserole dishes and crock pots heavy with food. The mix of smells is interesting – I detect at least a couple varieties of baked beans and some form of fried chicken, but some of the other spices and combinations are hard to place, which makes them all the more enticing. My mouth lubes itself up pretty good during all of this smelling.

I recognize a few of the people entering from the blood ceremony, and I spot Janice from the meetings at Randy's, but others I've never seen before. It's an older crowd on the whole, and a smiley crowd on top of that. These ladies carting in the food, in particular, beam at me like I'm Ryan Seacrest or some other guy that older ladies like a lot. My point is that I'm pretty sure me and Seacrest could have our way with many of these women, but we are both gentlemen.

After a while, the stream of people entering slows to a stop, and I hear a growing rumble roll up from the basement - the tangled mess of conversations piled on top of each other. I ease myself off of the chair and get a good stretch in. I like to get limbered up before a feast like this. The last thing you want to do is pull something before you're able to complete the meal.

I move down the stairs, and I feel like a kid walking into an adult party by himself. There are a few rows of tables in the middle of the room for sitting, and then a line of tables running around half of the perimeter of the room sporting quite an impressive spread of homemade dishes and desserts.

It looks like people are starting to get around to fix plates of food for themselves as I step foot on the basement floor. They are forming a line along the food tables, so no one seems to notice me. This is good. Lids get pulled off of dishes in rapid succession like this is the reveal stage at the end of all of the magic tricks at once. Little clouds of steam puff everywhere, and the multitude of vapors intertwine in the air to create an intense smell that I want to call mystical.

I slip into the line unnoticed and try to keep my head down. I grab a plate once I'm close enough, and it's straight out of a school cafeteria – plastic with five rectangular segments, a big one for the entrée and four smaller ones for sides. I do like that it has more total real estate than your average pot luck plate, which might be disposable plastic or paper. Whoever is calling these kinds of shots for the League, that person gets it. This is how you build something special with your cult.

That said, I still only have five segments for my first run through. I'll need to be selective.

My first choice is a pasta salad with chunks of feta in it. I figure anybody taking the time to crumble some feta in there is not fucking around. Next up, I get some biscuits that look insane, fluffy as hell. An old lady with a wig the shade of cherry shoe polish nods at me as I take one, so I take two and she closes her eyes and nods even more emphatically.

For the protein, I opt to keep it simple with some fried chicken. I guess I have to get a vegetable now, so I go for some green beans that seem popular. And last but not least? Mashed potatoes with gravy. Duh.

I turn toward the seating area, and I see a few people gawking, but they look more intrigued than anything. Then I spot Babinaux waving at me from her seat in the corner, so I head that way.

She eyes my plate as I approach.

"Lotta starch, Jeffrey," she says.

"What?" I say. "Oh."

I look down at my plate. Looks tasty enough to me, starch or no.

"You know, they have this new thing called salad," she says. "Rumored to be good for you."

She takes a bite of something green and leafy.

"Oh, this is only the beginning," I say. "This is phase one. Maybe I'll feel like something light like a salad when I go back for thirds or fourths."

I tear into the food like a dog tearing into some food. I don't know. I'm not always that great with similes. In any case, I eat in a way that not only makes me feel guilty but likely brings shame to the rest of my family as well. If you can curse your family through sheer expression of gluttony, I fear I have done so today. So that's something I'll have to live with.

After my dessert plate – peach pie, blueberry pie bars, chocolate cheesecake and homemade oatmeal cream pies – I go in for a coffee. Now I'm not actually in the mood for coffee, and as you can imagine, I'm quite full. I've come up with a plan, though. I feel like dumping a mug or two of black coffee onto that pile of calories in my gut might kick start the process of breaking the food down and give me the upper hand in the impending intestinal battle ahead of me.

It's risky, but it just might work.

I sit down with great care to avoid bursting at the seams – not the seams of my clothes, the seams of my body. Once I'm down, I plan to stay that way for a good hour as motion of any kind would only incite discord in my digestive tract.

Some of the older people go about cleaning up, and looking over the others, I start to get a sense of who will be going through this "symbolic spiritual rebirth" with me. There are a couple of girls near my age that appear to be sisters that I suspect will be rebirthing pretty hard in a bit here. They look like they're not of this era. I don't mean that as a slight or anything – they're not ugly. They just look like young versions of someone's grandma somehow or maybe more like a picture in an old photo album. It's not the way they dress, though, it's how they handle themselves and their facial features.

On the other side of the room, there's a guy with thick stubble that sticks out as well. His face wears a blank expression and does not waver from it. I'd say he's probably 30 to 35.

Randy starts working his way around the room, flitting from table to table to tap someone on the shoulder here or whisper something in someone else's ear there. Those tapped rise and move with purpose. He moves to the stubble guy and talks to him, so that pretty much confirms my suspicion. We're about to do this, I believe.

This isn't perfect. I hoped we'd have another half an hour of a post meal breather. I know my belly will put up a fight.

Randy moves toward me, and I try to send mind bullets at

him – not to kill him or even injure him seriously – just to graze a leg and slow him down or something. The mind bullets go wide of the target, however. I've yet to actually hit anything with them.

He leans over when he reaches me, and his breath smells exactly like Boston baked beans with extra onions on top.

"It's time," he says. "Meet me and the others by my car."

I stand the way I imagine an early model android will stand – very stiff in the waist and hips. Stuff gurgles in my gut right away, something large shifts deep in the bowels, and the shame and guilt well inside of me again.

I eyeball the stainless steel coffee dispenser and contemplate dumping another cup of black down in there to try to take a proactive approach, but another part of me sees it more like pouring gas on a fire, so I do nothing. Sometimes there's no quick fix. You've got to take responsibility for what you've done and accept the consequences.

I walk with a gait that I believe minimizes the chances of anal leakage, though I don't have a lot of experience in this area. Squirting may not be a strong possibility at this juncture, but those that don't prepare themselves always get hit the hardest. It's like I always say: Hope for the best, prepare for the anal leakage.

Passing through the basement seems easy enough. My shuffling trot keeps me feeling secure and seems to go unnoticed from what I can tell. As I near the edge of the room, though, it occurs to me that the stairs are going to be a problem – possibly a big brown one.

I try to take the first step sort of sideways as I feel like that will involve less hip and thigh movement. It's harder to step sideways with much of your body clenched up tighter than a clam shell, however. My foot clubs around the step without ever getting high enough to mount it.

Then it dawns on me that because of all of the old people often at church, there are two hand rails here-one on each side. I can lift myself up a step at a time with my arms. It's genius.

I lift and step and lift and step until I make it to the top. My instinct is to laugh at top volume while I do this. I feel like if I draw a lot of attention to my odd behavior people are more likely to interpret it as goofing around. I get some weird looks, but it could have been worse.

I trudge through the nave and out the door toward Randy's car, my middle churning liquid like my intestines have been tasked with fermenting some kind of prison hooch. I see the girls from a different era in the parking lot, but they're standing by someone else's car. Not sure what to make of that.

Stubble walks up to Randy's car as silent as a ninja, so I don't see him approaching. He just appears there next to me. And then I figure it out. We're riding separately. Me and Stubs will ride with Randy, while the ladies are taking a ladymobile.

I say hi to him, and he grunts. Somehow I don't think Stubs is much of a conversationalist.

Before I even know Randy is in the vicinity, Stubs calls shotgun, and I wheel around to see the old man just stepping though the doorway. So I guess this guy gets real chatty when it counts.

Randy hugs his arms around a big cardboard box, but I can't tell what's in it. Looks heavy. He rotates his wrist to point his keys at the car and pop the trunk. He strides toward it, presumably to load the box in.

"Get in," he says.

Upon settling in the backseat, the tectonic plates in my lower abdomen shift, and the churning slows down. I think I've navigated past the danger zone, and it should be smooth gut sailing from here on in. This comes with a feeling of accomplishment. The sea was awfully angry today.

Randy says little when he gets into the car. He just starts it up and drives.

With no talk and no radio, it's pretty quiet in here, the kind of quiet that harbors a nervous energy. It's a Prius, so there's barely even any engine noise. I want to ask a few questions, but the atmosphere in the vehicle is stifling, so I hold off. Air sucking through the sliver of an opening in Randy's window creates the soundtrack, which is fitting since this pretty much sucks.

We ride out past woods and field after field of corn and soy beans and brush. It's interesting how far you can see looking over a field, especially as you rise up on a small hill. The plants stretch on and on until somewhere out there the dusk swallows them up.

The car slows as we take a left onto a dirt road, and I realize it's been quite a while since I've seen a building of any type. There was a rotting barn back there somewhere, but that was a while ago. Now that I think about it, I don't see the ladymobile behind us. I guess maybe Randy is a bit of speed demon.

But then I remember that scene in Casino where Joe Pesci gets driven out into some rural cornfield area, and his voice over internal monologue is interrupted midsentence by the sound of one of the guys cracking him with an aluminum baseball bat. He never sees it coming.

Though I don't know Stubs all that well, I can't see Randy beating me to death with a baseball bat. It's like I always say, though: Hope for the best, prepare to be pummeled to death.

Yeah, I probably shouldn't recycle my material so frequently.

Anyway, Randy takes it real slow on the dirt road. Rocks kick up in all directions and clang out steel drum noises when they hit the undercarriage. Not much of a melody, but with the radio off, it's almost good enough to pass for music.

We inch down the slit of dirt bisecting a field of overgrown weeds gone to seed. The beige blades of grass sway in the breeze in clusters that collectively form odd shapes and patterns. It looks like people at a stadium doing the wave but more chaotic.

And then we're climbing a small hill, the lack of speed adding a sense of suspense. I think I know what will be at the top, though: more grass. We ascend and ascend for quite some time, mimicking a sloth climbing a tree.

At the top, I see that I was right: more grass, indeed. Sorry to spoil that for you.

No, wait. There's something poking out from the top of the plant life. Something gray and roundish, but I can't see much of it. It almost looks like a trash can with a wooden frame above it from here.

We draw closer, and there's just enough sunlight left to discern that it's stone. Then it clicks – a well.

I'd think that we'd blow right past such an ordinary field item at the speed of a tortoise, but I can see now the road leads right to it and ends.

Interesting. I thought I already did the water ritual.

The Prius saunters up near the well and parks. Again, Randy doesn't say anything, he just gets out and pops the trunk. Stubs doesn't move, but I decide to get out and stretch my legs.

As I rise, there's one last gurgle of prison hooch sloshing about inside of me like a rogue wave, and then things settle once more. I take a few paces out of the car, my feet grinding pebbles into the dirt road. I raise my arms out to the sides and rotate my neck back and forth to try to loosen everything from the shoulder blades up a little.

Then I turn to get a look at what Randy has in the trunk. It's on the edge of getting dark out, so at first I only see the red of a couple of gas cans. Then Randy pulls a shadowy garment out of the box. I glean that it's a robe as he slips it on over his clothes.

I'm guessing we'll get dressed up in our robes, draw a little water out of the old well, splash it on our foreheads, say some sacred words and be done with it. So I mosey over to the well to take a gander. The first thing that strikes me? It's huge. I'm no well expert, but this one is a good 8 or 10 feet across. Seems big to me. I find a large wooden crate instead of a bucket. It dangles just below the lip of the wall up against the side closest to me. The rope suspending it runs up to a pulley attached to the wooden frame over the well. It looks very sturdy, the crate, and there are gaps between the boards, so it would suck ass at hauling up any water.

Well, that doesn't make sense. Randy must have another trick up that robe sleeve of his.

The second thing that catches my attention is the odor. I get a whiff of something chemical. I want to say it smells like witch hazel, but I barely even remember what that smells like.

Going back over to the car, I hear the two of them mumbling. They both sport their robes. I go to grab mine from the box, but before I get there, Randy closes the trunk.

"You forgetting something?" I say.

"Get undressed," he says.

"What? Don't I need a robe?" I say.

Randy doesn't look straight at me.

"You need to be undressed," he says. "It's part of the ritual."

"What about this guy?" I say, pointing at Stubs.

"You're going first," he says. "He'll go second."

I try to find a good angle to argue this. I could refuse, but with all of this new stuff about the missing body, I probably need my League contacts more than ever. I could run, just live out here off of corn and soybeans until the pesticide kills me.

"Alright," I say.

I go behind the well and strip down. Really, Randy has seen me naked almost as much as my girlfriend at this point, which I did not foresee back when we first met. Back then, he was just a guy that looked like Dumbledore. It was a simpler time.

When I turn around, Randy and Stubs approach with lanterns aflame at their sides. Their hoods are up so I can't see their faces. I cup my dick and balls in my hand and sort of waddle in their direction, stopping a few feet short because, you know, I'm naked.

Randy waves me over the rest of the way, though I can only tell it's him by the white hair on his knuckles. He directs me to stand between the two of them, and the three of us face the well. They set the lanterns down in unison.

When Randy speaks, his voice takes on a quality I haven't

heard from him before – a vocal projection so loud and thick, it's almost hoarse sounding. I hate to mix wizards here, but it kind of sounds like when Gandalf yells at the Balrog.

"We are born into this world naked, innocent," he says. "And so shall ye be reborn."

I would probably say "Check," here as a joke, but the Gandalf voice is too intense to mess with. I don't want him to yell at me like I'm a fool of a Took.

"We are born into this world blind, unaware," he says. "And so shall ye be reborn."

He pulls out a strip of fabric, but it's not until he's fastening it to my head that I realize it's a blindfold.

So that's good.

"We are born into this world from the dark to the light," he says. "And so shall ye be reborn."

We're cutting it a little close on this one, considering it's getting dark now. Of course, behind the blindfold, I can no longer confirm this with my eyes.

A hand on each side of me takes my hand. Randy's is cold and dry, Stubs' is all clammy. They pull me along a few paces, and now we're at the well.

"We've got you," Randy says. "On 3, take a step up."

There's a pause. I probably should have gone with that running plan a while ago.

"One."

I suddenly have to piss.

"Two."

Really bad.

"Three."

I step up onto the edge of the well, totter for a second, but they help me get my balance.

"Now step down into the well," Randy says. "On 3."

"What?" I say.

"You're stepping into the crate," he says. "You'll step with one foot until you feel the crate under you, then step with the other. We'll have you the whole time."

"Maybe I should take the blindfold off first," I say. "Might help."

Nobody speaks, but I think I hear Stubs snicker.

"It's a leap to faith," Randy says.

I don't know whether to correct him for saying "to" rather than "of" or "leap" when I'm stepping. I mean, I'm stepping or plunging, there will be no leaps, I can tell you that.

"One."

Oh yeah, pee feeling again. Almost forgot.

"Two."

My bladder is about to burst.

"Three."

I step down, feel the wood plank under my foot.

"You've got it," Randy says. "Now grab the rope and step with the other foot."

He lets go. And I'm tipping forward. I reach out for the rope, but it finds me instead, my chest and torso ramming into it, flinging the crate crashing into the wall. My other hand wrenches free of Stubs' grip as I fall. And the crate doesn't feel solid under me. I know I'm about to fall the rest of the way when my hands find the rope and grip it. Everything totters a bit and then stabilizes under me. I'm squatting in the crate, choking the rope the best I can.

"What the fuck?" I say.

"You're fine," Randy says.

I rip the blindfold off just as the crate begins its descent. The pulley groans as the rope scrapes over it, and the circle of dusk gets smaller and smaller above. And I realize that chemical smell is stronger now. Much stronger. It's not witch hazel, I think now. It's familiar, but something is off about it. Maybe it's just so unexpected here that I can't place it.

The crate touches down on the bottom. So it's a dry well after all. The smell is overpowering. Could it be-

Voices above interrupt my thoughts. They sound so tiny now. Are they talking to me?

"What?" I say.

"Get out of the crate," Randy says. His voice echoes in a way that makes the volume swell later in the delivery, making the last word the loudest. It's strange.

Wait. Did he say get out of the crate?

"What?" I say.

"It's a simple display of faith, Jeffrey," he says. "Now step out."

After the letting go incident, I have little trust in Randy. I hesitate.

"Look, you step off," he says. "We yank it back up here and in a half an hour we pull you out. It's that simple."

I hate to do it, but I step out of the crate. As I watch it ascend to the tiny circle of half light up there, I think over and over again that this was a huge mistake. At last, it's gone. No more squeaking pulley. No more crate up there. Nothing.

The chemical smell is pretty unbelievable, and I feel light headed. I sit down in the dark and concentrate to keep my eyes from drifting closed. I can hear my heartbeat in my ears.

And then a few drops hit me, wetness. I figure rain, but it stings, and it stinks. And then it's more than droplets, it's gushing down.

I yell. It's wordless and powerless and small. Scrambling back to get away, I bump into a bucket and knock it over. Liquid gushes everywhere, and I feel around, and there are more of buckets all around the perimeter of the well. And I know now that the stuff raining down, and the stuff down here making that smell are one and the same.

It's not water. It's gasoline, possibly mixed with some other flammable fluid so I couldn't quite place the smell.

And then the pouring stops, and I look up. I can't quite see straight, I guess from the fumes.

But I spot a light fluttering down toward me, all slowed down. It looks like a firefly coasting down to check things out. But as it gets closer, the image comes clear – a wooden match tumbling end over end.

In the split second before it hits, I picture the burned body in the vacant lot. I see the eye socket where the melted skin re-congealed. I see the permanent smile framed by blackened lips. I see the shriveled man reduced from flesh to ash.

And the match hits, and the fire flashes so bright it almost looks white, and it's everywhere, and it's on me, crawling hot up onto my chest, my face, heat searing all of me. Every nerve ending wails as loud as it can, all shrill.

I feel my skin drying and cracking on my arms first, flesh gone black. My entire body flails, and the back of my head cracks into something solid - the wall, I guess. I flop onto the ground, and I try to roll a little, but it's no use. Everything is covered in a blaze of gas. I can see only fire in all directions, flames billowing up and up, and that shimmer of heat distortion like I'm watching it all through imperfect glass.

It sounds like wind roaring with periodic crackles and pops of things being broken down by heat, of me being broken down and sizzling.

And I smell it. I smell my hair first, like something rotten consumed by flames, and then the stench of my charred and melting flesh hits my nostrils. It smells like pork chops blackening on a too hot grill, the outside charring immediately with the inside left raw. The image pops into my head for a split second - juicy fat dripping out of a rack of ribs, tumbling between the bars to the flames below.

And I go to scream, but when I open my mouth and inhale the flaming vapor sucks between my lips and enters my throat and lungs in a flash. And the fire steals my breath, and the scorch fills my chest. And I choke, and I feel my throat collapse into wet flaps of melt, and I want to cough, but I can't. I can't. It's caught. It's stuck in what used to be my throat and what used to be my lungs.

And then everything fades to white.

CHAPTER 26

The white shines everywhere. It is everything, and it is perfect, and I am nothing.

But I am here. I am thinking. I am conscious. I can't be nothing.

I am small, though. I am one tiny piece of everything, then, one ray of light shining with all of the rest.

I don't know. Maybe something like that.

Maybe what I used to be is nothing. That might make more sense.

I was something but now I am everything, one piece of it, anyway.

And it's not so bad when you look at it that way.

CHAPTER 27

I wake in a grass field, the world gone white around me. I wriggle my maggot fingers in front of me and laugh. How to even describe it, I feel so complete, and I feel no pain. I throb with pleasure. It hugs me. It holds me. Everything makes sense. The universe makes sense, and I am everywhere and nowhere, and it is perfect.

I rise from the ground, and it strikes me that I'm not naked anymore. My normal clothes adorn my body – t-shirt, jeans, hoodie, hat, sunglasses.

I like it. I like to feel covered up. My feet are bare, though, which seems a little weird.

Looking around, it's just grass as far as I can see with one huge tree standing way in the distance. The grass stands about knee high, but it's not all scraggly and whatever. It's even and symmetrical and seems to shift in the air in unison, like the whole field is inhaling and exhaling. And I realize that it's green. Even though the world has been bled white, this grass shines bright green. It seems so natural somehow that I didn't even consider it at first.

And so I stride through it, thousands of blades reaching out to brush the legs of my pants. It swishes around me, and it chills the skin on my feet where it makes contact, brisk but refreshing. I'm thankful to be barefoot to feel this, to experience the frosty touch of these plants.

I walk toward the tree. There's nothing else to go for, I guess. It's far, though. The clear air and flat land mean I can see a long way, of course, but the tree branches reach up into the heavens. I can't see the top. It's difficult to express the scale of this. The trunk girth seems impossible, but I'll withhold judgment until I get a little closer. Interestingly, from here, at least, I only see wood. I don't see any leaves.

The air moves here. It's not like wind, exactly, or at least it's not like any wind I've ever felt before. It pulses too evenly, and it doesn't build and recede like wind. It's just on full blast and then off with no in between.

The air gusts in, cool and heavy. It has some wet to it, but it's not sticky like a humid day in the summer. It's a little too cool for that, I guess. It feels more like walking into a basement, the way the air takes on some substance, some texture.

I jog for a bit to try to gain on the tree, but it's hard to tell if I'm getting any closer, so I go back to walking. Probably best to save my energy, even if jogging didn't seem to tire me so much.

Just like that, I come upon a dirt trail, well worn, running perpendicular to my path to the tree. Never saw it coming until I stepped onto it. I stop and stand on it a moment. The sand is warm underfoot, as though the sun shines down upon it, but when I look up I find no sun in the sky, just white everywhere.

Looking both ways, I see nothing but trail and grass stretching on and on. I have no real desire to follow it. The tree seems much more intriguing.

I move on, entering the field on the opposite side of the trail. The grass feels different here, almost like it's trying to stick to my feet. Not in a slimy or gooey way so much as the way a grasshopper's leg kind of attaches itself to your skin. It's almost like Velcro somehow. It presses itself onto me and latches on with its little ridges, and with each step I just pry away from it and move forward. It's not the worst feeling, but it is not pleasant. I feel a sense of it being gluttonous, and that sort of grosses me out.

And for some reason it pops into my head that people in caskets are barefoot. They put that blanket over their feet, so you never really think about it, but they don't wear shoes and socks when they're buried.

I stop. The tiniest pin prick of fear penetrates my brain, entering just above the brain stem. I try to remember where I was just before this. I close my eyes, and I let my mind reach out for it. It delves into whatever ether memories are stored in. But all it comes back with is the image of fried chicken and biscuits and green beans and mashed potatoes smothered in gravy. Pretty sure I ate all of that just before this, and that chases the fear off.

Frightening? No.

Frighteningly delicious? Absolutely.

I jog a while again, the fact that I crossed that trail renewing my confidence some that I'm making progress. I think part of me feared I was just running in place or something, that I would somehow never get there.

And at some point the sound of distant thunder arises about me. The noise fades in. I'd say that's the most accurate way to put it. It doesn't crash all violently or anything. It's just a constant rumble somewhere far away, swelling and shrinking and turning over onto itself. In some way, the rhythm reminds me of the ocean.

Maybe it's that sound that draws my attention, or maybe it's just running a long way in such a peaceful place, but my mind wanders. My thoughts turn further and further inward until I'm no longer all that conscious of the world outside. My consciousness sucks up into my head, almost all of it.

I try to fit the puzzle pieces of my life together based not on reason but on feeling. It's hard to describe since it comes to me in emotions that are more like colors than words, and maybe it can only make sense inside and not outside.

I think of the white world, and I feel a sense of incomplete things made whole, imperfect beings made perfect. It's almost overwhelming, the feeling it gives me, and somewhere in my belly erupts a twinge of nausea at the sheer intensity of it.

That fades as I think of Glenn, and I feel the sun shining down, the light guiding me, warming me. I see the pink glistening on his Explorer's bumper in my imagination and feel the sense of clarity I felt when we were back in those cells and he gave that long speech about fear and love. And then I see him open the wall and walk through, the light washing over his being to the point of total obscurity.

Those feelings morph when I think of Babinaux, and I feel the Earth itself, the way the soil nurtures the plants, the life it gives, the nourishment. I picture her touching my arm, the way she was moved to the verge of tears by the care she feels for me even though I'm a little shit mouth to her about half of the time. I feel her hugging me, and I feel love. Not romantic love, you know. That is something else all together, much more complicated. What I feel now is the most basic and perhaps most pure love a human being can feel for another, even if they don't know each other all that well. The big love that weaves us all together. The thing that makes someone brave getting hit by a train to pull a stranger off of the tracks. The love that heals us and saves and us and comforts us and makes us want to stick around a while, even with all the pain and death all around us.

I think of Louise, and I feel bliss and fulfillment peppered with pangs of frustration and doubt. It's all mixed up, with strong feelings on both sides. I see her twisting her hair while she reads a book, and then that flashes to that warped reflection of myself I saw in the deprivation tank. This puzzle piece doesn't seem to fit with the others as well somehow. There's a murkiness surrounding it. Trying to make sense of it is like trying to look through clouded water.

And the wet snaps me out of it. My consciousness wakes up to my physical surroundings. The grass smears wet on my feet with every step now, droplets of frigid water that confuse me. I bring my hand to my face to brush at my brow and realize that it's wet as well. In fact, I'm soaked from head to toe.

I stop. I try to remember how this could have happened. How could I get this wet without realizing it? It's definitely not raining.

Wait.

I paw at the air with my hand and tendrils of mist undulate in response and then resettle into motionlessness. Nearly microscopic drops of fluid hang in the air, and when they're not moving, they're almost invisible. They don't fall or flutter or even float. They are completely motionless until I touch them, stuck in midair.

I wait for a second, curious to see if the mist shifts when the air moves, but it never happens. I guess the air doesn't gust on this side of the trail, or maybe that changed at some point while

I was lost in thought.

Looking up, I realize that I'm much closer to the tree now as well. Its immensity grows more impressive as I draw near. It looks like a skyscraper with branches coming out of it. Chunks of root breach the Earth around me to form hills of gnarled tree not far ahead of me.

I run.

Soon, I'm among the root hills, surrounded by them. I change trajectories to avoid some, bobbing and weaving and running faster than ever.

And I stop. The overwhelming feeling of being watched crawls over my flesh, pricking it into goose bumps. I hold my breath. My neck cranes in slow motion, my eyes scanning the horizon.

There.

A haggard figure sits atop one of the chunks of root about 150 feet from me, stick thin with a salt and pepper beard that even at this distance reminds me of a lawn hedge in bad need of a trim. I see that he's looking right at me. We regard each other a moment, and he leans back and slides a navy blue baseball cap on his head.

"Took you long enough, Grobnagger," he calls out.

There's a familiar rasp to the voice that immediately conjures memories of Funyuns and wheat grass and vomiting cats: Glenn.

CHAPTER 28

I run over and watch Glenn clamber down from the root, finding footholds and spots to grip as though he has built up some experience at this. He smiles the whole way down, but his body language betrays his facial expression. His hands and feet know where to go, but when he shifts his weight, I sense hesitation and pain in his demeanor.

Indeed. Upon touching down, he grimaces, the corners of his mouth turning down to expose his clenched teeth.

"Are you OK?" I say.

"It's fine," he says. His eyes glance in the general direction of his feet for a moment, and I note that he's wearing shoes rather than his usual sandals. "I'll explain it all later. Come here."

He hugs me. He smells a bit like a barn, but I'm glad to see him. He's so thin now, he feels almost frail. Coils of beard hair graze my cheek as we part, scraping at me like steel wool.

"I found Amity here," I say. "I didn't get a chance to tell you about it, but we've met up a couple of times in the… wherever we are."

"She told me," he says. He smiles. "Yeah, as soon as she said a naked guy chased her through the desert with a crazy look on his face and his genitals flopping around like a puppy on a trampoline, I was like 'sounds just like Jeff Grobnagger.'"

We chuckle, but my mind abandons the humor and races to the next question.

"So you found her?" I say. "Where is she?"

His smile fades.

"We got separated," he says. "Or, well… I got captured, and she managed to get away, I should say."

"Captured? By who?" I say.

"Look, there's really not time to go into all of the details," he says. "Let's get out of here while we can."

After saying this, however, he stops and stares at me, tilting his head back and forth like he's sizing something up.

"Are you high?" he says.

"No," I say. "Well, I mean, in a way, yeah. Aren't you?"

"Not at all," he says.

"Whenever I arrive here, I'm sort of high, and everything looks all white," I say. "I thought it must be like that for everyone."

"That's interesting," he says. "I guess it must be a little different for each of us."

He leads the way toward the tree, but he limps along at a much slower pace than I'm used to. His breathing gets all heavy, and flecks of spit froth between his teeth. I want to ask questions, but his intensity puts me off of it. We walk in the thunder and the hissing and wheezing without a word between us.

The mist sops and soaks and chills me down, especially since we've slowed to this mosey. It saps my body heat away from me one tiny droplet at a time.

The grass grows sparse and gives way to bare dirt as we get even closer to the tree, and the mist seems to cut off as well. My bare feet leave footprints in the soil, which is gray and sandy.

Glenn bends over and puts his hands on his knees. He fights for breath.

"What's wrong?" I say.

"It's nothing," he says. "I'm old. Just give me a minute."

As he leans over, I notice a charm dangling from a chain around his neck. It sort of looks like a hand, palm open, fingers pointed down.

"What's with the necklace?" I say.

"It's for protection," he says, tucking it back into his shirt. "Not that it has done me much good."

I want to ask protection from what, but he launches into a coughing fit. His face turns all red and veins bulge every which way from his forehead and throat. He spits a few times.

I don't think he has a cold or anything like that. I think old people just hack up crazy gobs of stuff periodically. Like my grandfather? He used to just spit phlegm into the garbage all the time. All day, every day. Insane. No particular cause. His old body just produced mucus at a very high rate, especially when he was active. It's like everybody turns into a weird troll when they get old or something. So I will fit right in.

"Let's go," he says all gravelly.

He wipes his chin with the heel of his hand. He looks miserable.

We stride on, kicking up dust in all directions. I look over and see Glenn's eyes narrow to slits. Again, his grimace reveals clenched teeth. I guess he must be in a lot of pain.

I wonder what the hell happened, but I can't bug him now. He can barely breathe, let alone speak.

We walk a long time without saying anything, and the tree

seems to sneak up on me. I look up, and we're there. We're less than 100 feet from it. The girth is inconceivable.

"We need to tread lightly up here," Glenn says through gritted teeth. "Just remember to take it slow and think everything through before we act."

Upon getting this out, he gasps in pain. Again, I have follow up questions that will have to wait.

Up close, I realize there's the faintest red hue to the bark near the base of the trunk. Moving in, divots and crevices pock the outside of the tree, running jagged indentations that form a mess of crooked lines. It's a thick bark with a lot of texture.

We take a few more paces, and Glenn suddenly leans forward and vomits on the ground. And for some reason, for a split second I think maybe the tree is making him sick, being this close to it. But nah, it wouldn't make much sense. I think whatever is paining him is effing him up pretty good.

He holds a hand up to me, I guess preventing me from asking after his condition.

"I'm OK," he says, head still tilted toward the ground.

After a long stretch of heavy breathing, he pulls himself to his feet, and we walk the last few feet to stand by the tree.

So this is it. It strikes me for the first time that there's not really anything to do upon arriving at such a huge tree. If it were a normal tree, we could entertain the possibility of climbing it, though we wouldn't since it'd be pointless. This way, we don't even get the option of considering climbing it before we shut the idea down. We just crane our necks to look up at the monstrous thing.

Pretty big.

"Look," Glenn says.

He points to the ground where I see a shape etched into the sand, and then as we circle the tree, it becomes apparent that there are three such shapes forming a triangle around the base of the trunk. The first shape appears to be a snake like shape forming a sideways figure 8. Next, there's the waves of the ocean, and the last image depicts a flag billowing in the wind.

"What do you see?" he says.

I explain it to him.

"I figured it would be something like that," he says. "We all see something different here. It's showing us something. I think it's like when you chose the cup, remember? I see the sun, a lion and a lightning bolt."

I think about this.

"Do you mean the tree is showing us?" I say.

He doesn't answer. He seems lost in thought, staring into the sand. I kind of think it's not the tree, though.

Still, it's an interesting piece of timber even if it's not communicating with us through sand symbols. I move closer and see little clusters of moss clinging to the bark that make it look like the tree sprouts green five o'clock shadow.

"They're symbols," Glenn says, his voice so hushed I'm not sure if he's talking to me or himself.

"It's a lemniscate," he says.

"What?" I say.

"The shape you described," he says. "It's not a snake forming a sideways figure 8. It's a lemniscate, the infinity symbol. It represents the way that energy cannot be created or destroyed. It stays in motion forever, the way the line of an 8 wraps around and around itself endlessly."

"Oh," I say, but I'm not paying that close of attention. I'm too drawn in by the crazy texture of the tree.

"And the ocean represents mystery and vastness and the infinite possibilities all around us," he says. "It's the force so massive and deep we almost can't understand it. It is something bigger and stronger than us."

I step around the ocean to avoid mussing up the drawing and reach my fingers out to feel the bark.

Glenn gasps, and the last thing I hear before I put my hand on the tree is his voice yelling:

"Grobnagger, wait!"

CHAPTER 29

Before I open my eyes, they come to me, flashes of fire, of blackened skin cracked and peeling, of my body shriveled down to gristle and bone. But it doesn't scare me. It feels like a memory of something that happened a long time ago, immobile and nonthreatening images, like old pictures glued to the pages of a photo album.

I feel no fear. I feel renewed.

I open my eyes and look up through a long stone tube to a circle of illumination above. Something in the nature of the light fills me with certainty that it's morning, I'd guess around 8:30, though maybe my perspective is skewed since I'm trying to judge this from the bottom of a well. Still, even if the precise time is wrong, I believe it to be morning.

I prop myself up on my elbows and examine my body in the paltry light. I'm fine from what I can see, no signs of burns. I run my hands over my skin, calloused fingers scouring abdominals and pectorals and so on. Everything feels normal, smooth, the nerve endings all coo and murmur when I touch them like newborn kittens with their eyes still closed.

I am alive.

I am awake.

I lie back down. The light dims a bit as a cloud passes over the sun, and then, after a beat, the world brightens again. In my mind, I replay my entry into the well. I remember almost falling as I stepped onto the crate, the feel of the rope pressed into my chest, and the lurch and sway of the box teetering under my feet. I smell the chemical stench, the gasoline, all around as I reach the bottom. I see the match tumbling end over end, fluttering down like a toy soldier with a plastic bag parachute dropped down the steps.

But wait. I go back earlier. I picture the meal – the fried chicken, the green beans, the blueberry pie bars. I see the old woman nodding at me, reinforcing my choice of the biscuits, though she wasn't eating any herself. And I try to remember whether or not anyone else was eating them.

Could they have been drugged as part of the ritual? Even if it wasn't the biscuits, was it something else?

I feel around for the buckets. They're still here, and they're empty. They're steel, so it's hard to say whether or not they could have withstood a real fire anyway.

If they drugged me, the fire could have been a hallucination, with Randy like a puppeteer controlling the images in my drugged up brain with the power of suggestion.

I remember reading once that getting someone naked is one of the first steps to effectively brainwashing them. Like when you join the army, the first thing they do is get you naked, give you a physical in a brusque manner and shave your head and stuff, because that rewires your brain in terms of boundaries on the most basic level. The message in that case is that your body belongs to the army now, and it will do what it likes with you. The old order, the personal space you thought you had a right to, is thrown out, and just like that, they've already taken one step toward convincing you that their authority is absolute, and you should be willing to die rather than to disobey an order.

The same is true for many cults, though. They have rituals that involve getting people naked and vulnerable early on. If you rewire somebody on that most basic level, it opens everything else up. It sets a suggestible tone. Their mind becomes a malleable thing that can be bent to the master's will. Even Charles Manson progressed from drugs and orgies to murder.

I try to recall whether or not Stubs or the old timey sisters ate any biscuits. I remember seeing Stubs chewing, but I don't remember what he was eating.

Damn it.

Well, either way, Randy left me down here all night. That has to be significant. He said it'd only be a half an hour. Of course, he also neglected to mention the drugs and fire.

And for the first time, the idea that they aren't coming back seeps into my head. No matter how accurate or not my speculation about drugged food might be, it's at least plausible that they just left me here, right?

Jesus. What if I'm stuck down here?

I stand up, my fingers tracing lines along the mortared creases between the stones. I test my grip on the wall, but there's no chance of that. Climbing can't happen.

I look up into the circle of light. Judging by the way the rope trails off to the side, they left the crate on the ground beside the wall. That removes any possibility of me throwing buckets at the crate to try to shake it down somehow. As ridiculous as that sounds, at least it'd be something to try.

So it'd be pretty ironic to die of thirst inside of a well,

wouldn't it?

Don't panic. Don't panic. We'll have plenty of time to panic later if it gets all the way dark again.

Staring up at the light makes my eyes ache, so I look down to give them a break.

I hear something crash somewhere up there. It's quiet, but it's there. I look up again.

"Hello?" I say.

I wait.

Nothing.

"Help!" I say. "Is someone there?"

Still nothing.

My eyes water from staring into the sunlight, so I rub at them. There's no use yelling, I know. The sound wouldn't carry very far.

But then there's a new sound. The crate crashes into the wall and wobbles, and soon after the rope begins to rotate the pulley. The wooden box descends upon me.

So Randy did come back. I bet I was right about the biscuits.

The crate touches down next to me, and I step in and grip the rope.

"Ready for lift off," I say, projecting my voice up toward the opening.

The rope goes to work again, but the crate jerks and quakes its way up, much slower than my last ride. I suppose lifting me would be quite a bit more difficult than lowering me. It's hardly a concern vs. the prospect of being trapped down here, in any case.

I ascend in that herky jerky fashion, cupping my junk in my

hands, though it would be a lot funnier to shout "Surprise!" and gyrate in a manner to best flop my genitals around when I get pulled into view. I'm a gentleman, however, not unlike Ryan Seacrest, so I cover myself.

As my crate elevator climbs out of the darkness, more and more light surrounds me. Near the top, a bar of actual sunlight slants across my face, and I close my eyes. I feel its warm touch on that thin skin on my eyelids and across the bridge of my nose, and in a way I do feel reborn after all. It's weird how the simplest things bring the greatest perspective. The sun shining on my face makes me feel so lucky to exist at all, to be conscious of the world and spend my days in awe of the wonders all around me.

The crate stops near the top of the well, but it's a touch too low for me to see out there. There's no welcoming party, but I'm not waiting for anyone's permission before I get the hell out of here. I reach up and grab the lip of the wall, pulling myself up. Now, I'm half expecting Randy and Stubs to rush to my aid any second. They do not.

I yank myself up so my chest rests on the corner of the wall, and then I adjust my grip, placing my hands on the opposite corner. As I do this, I realize this is the most vulnerable moment, so I move with great care, pulling myself forward and swiveling the weight of my legs up at the proper second to swing myself over the wall and onto the dry land.

I land on my side. The open air all around me seems to stretch on forever. I roll over onto my back, looking up into a blue sky. The wind blows and goose bumps ripple across the skin on my arms.

Still no one converges on me or says anything, so I sit up. A man lies on the ground near the other side of the well, his face turned away from me. I'm alarmed for a second, until I take note of the beard hair jutting up from the side of the obscured face and the suede sandals adorning his feet.

"Glenn?" I say.

"Yep," he says, turning toward me. It strikes me that his clothes are different than they were in the white world a bit ago. I suppose mine are, too, though.

"You're back," I say. "Back in the real world, I mean."

"In the flesh," he says. "Most of it, anyway."

He sits up, and I follow his gaze to his left foot. It takes a second to process what I'm seeing. The sandal appears to be empty, but no, it's half empty. No toes occupy their proper place. Instead a cauterized stump ends his foot in the middle of the arch.

I gasp.

"What?" he says. "Oh."

He ruffles his mustache with his thumb and index finger.

"It looks worse than it is," he says.

"Really?" I say. "Cause it looks like about half of your foot is gone."

"Well, yeah," he says. "I guess you're right. It looks about as bad as it is."

"How did this happen?" I say.

"We'll discuss it later," he says. "It's too… I don't want to talk about it."

He stands and dusts himself off, careful to put little weight on his left.

"Come on," he says. "We better find you some pants."

CHAPTER 30

We walk through a cornfield, the stalks all papery and knocked over. Glenn seems to have a good sense of where we are, so I follow his lead. He's slow, but considering the foot thing, I can't blame him. We mount a little bump in the field, not a true hill but something like that. Glenn stops to look around.

"Damn," he says.

"What?" I say.

"See that farmhouse up there?" he says.

I look to the house in the distance and nod.

"I was hoping there'd be some clothes on the line," he says.

I see what he means. The rope bounces in the wind, just as naked as I am.

We press forward, trudging over the soil and the busted up corn plants.

I explain everything that's been happening while we walk – about Farber's burned body and the rituals and the stuff with Louise. Glenn listens, but he doesn't say much.

With every step, we inch closer and closer to town. This is good and bad. The only thing I want is to get home, but it's going to be tricky to get around in civilization while straight freeballing like this. Glenn said people would get the wrong idea about us.

We veer off to the right where the field ends, and within a few paces we're in a cul de sac. Leaving the cover of the corn and soy beans behind, I feel quite exposed. The roads and houses nearby only make it worse.

"We had to head right into this subdivision, huh?" I say.

"I'm just keeping us off of the main roads," he says. "I think we can cut through a few yards and get to a wooded area, keep making progress. But at some point we'll need to cross some streets. Some busy ones."

My balls get butterflies in their stomachs at this prospect. We sneak behind houses as we leave the subdivision and get closer to a real street, weaving around swing sets and flower gardens as we stay in a run of backyards to avoid the traffic. This stretches on for a couple of blocks, and we have to hop one fence along the way. It's almost hard to believe that we haven't run into anyone yet.

We round another corner, and I see the woods Glenn spoke of ahead. We have another block to go, but it looks pretty treacherous.

We hustle through the first yard, which, although it's void of humanity, does feature a grill with smoke spilling out of the sides. I picture someone running out to fling hot dogs and hamburgers at us while yelling a lot.

This does not happen.

The second and third yards prove to be free from obstacles, but the fourth yard is the one I meant when I said treacherous. A chain link fence stands between us and the next yard. By itself, this is no problem, of course. It's just that the chain link fence contains a dog. Some kind of pit bull mix that growls deep and long now that we're close.

To go around, we'd have to go out by the street in either direction, which would mean exposing my nudity to the lunch hour rush. But then, none of those people driving by will stop to bite my genitals or face, so I guess I choose that option.

"Let's go around," I say.

"You sure?" Glenn says.

The dog snaps his jaw in the general direction of my nads.

"Yep," I say.

We hustle out around the front of the house, doing a quick yet quiet walking thing that makes me feel like a naked ninja. Judging by the sound, the traffic hit a lull at just the right moment. Almost no cars go by.

Just as we careen around the corner of the house, inches from moving into the clear, the single WOOP of a police siren chirps behind me. I freeze.

"Run!" Glenn says.

I can't run, though.

Because I'm frozen.

Glenn fast walks a few paces, but he can't really run with his half foot, so he gives up.

"Grobnagger?" a voice calls out from behind me.

It's Dennis. Perfect. I turn and get a look at him, sitting in the front seat of his cruiser. His eyebrows are crinkled up, but he's sort of laughing at the same time. Well, at least he'll have a good story to tell for a couple of days.

"Get in," he says.

I call shotgun, but Glenn rides in the front seat anyway since Dennis says it wouldn't look right for an officer of the law to drive around with a naked dude in the front seat. I guess I can respect that.

"Got a call about a naked white male with orange pubic hair running around in the subdivision over here," he says. "I never would have dreamed it'd turn out to be Jeff Grobnagger. Guess I should have, though."

I look down at my pelvic region.

"You think my pubes are orange?" I say.

"Yeah, bro," Dennis says.

"Big time," Glenn says.

Since he was gone for so long, I sort of forgot how everything is "big time" with Glenn. I wonder where he picked that turn of phrase up. Because he should probably consider putting it back as soon as possible.

"I'm gonna go out on a limb here and guess that this.... situation... has something to do with the League of Light," Dennis says. "Would that be accurate?"

"Yep," I say.

I almost expect Glenn to chime in with another big time, but he fails to. I look over, and his hands are cupped over his eyes. After a second he retracts them. He looks pretty exhausted.

Dennis chatters on the CB for a while. And I realize how tired I am as well, once the prospect of this being over soon finally enters my mind. My nudity induced hyperawareness fades a little, and I slink down in my seat. All of the sore in my back wakes up, that faint ache that accompanies relief once you can finally relax. I stretch and rotate my neck back and forth all slow. Every muscle fiber seems to let go a little bit, and my eyes close.

And as I fall into a deeper and deeper relaxation, I realize that I don't care much about any of this cult stuff. I don't care about who killed Farber or stole his body from the morgue. I don't care about Randy's rituals. I barely even care about what is happening to me and why, at least on the most basic level of my being. See, I really only care about one thing, and I need to talk to Louise as soon as I can. Wait. I need to get dressed as soon as I can, and then talk to Louise. Would be difficult to have a serious conversation with my dingus flapping in the breeze.

For a while I stay in that floaty place that comes just before sleep. I hover there, just being, my brain shut off for once. I drift along.

And then a little pang of something builds and builds just outside my conscious thoughts. Some part of my brain sends the rest an urgent message about the outside world that arrives in slow motion, like I can see it coming, I can feel it, but it's not quite there yet, still not there, and then BAM! I'm awake, I'm looking around, mildly panicked.

Oh. We're home.

The car stopping in the driveway somehow woke my brain back up. I guess the disruption of the ride's movement maybe shook me out of my lull.

"Thanks for the ride," I say.

"Not a problem, Magic Mike," Dennis says. "If I hear word about any bachelorette parties coming up, I'll be sure to hand out your card. I'll tell 'em Grobnagger's the best dancer in the biz. He goes full nude, so you will get a little something dangled in your face, and his pubes are the color of fire and Cheetohs."

I don't know what to say, so I say:

"Thanks."

We walk into the house, and Glenn moves straight for the

cupboard. He pulls out the unopened package of Double Stufs, gives me a look.

"I made sure to keep Oreos on hand," I say. "Cause I knew you'd be back eventually."

"Jeff Grobnagger, you are a gentleman," he says, ripping open the package.

See? Remember all of that stuff about me and Seacrest being gentlemen? Confirmed.

CHAPTER 31

Home at last. I shower and get dressed. It feels great to cover my balls with multiple layers of fabric. I think Glenn went straight to bed, and I can understand that, but I'm a little too keyed up to sleep. When your life becomes a non-stop series of symbolic adventures transpiring on other planes of reality, it can sometimes be hard to unwind and get some shut eye. It's almost like I'm so happy to be home that I can't stop reveling in my happiness enough to relax all the way. It will come in time, though. It always does.

I lean back on the couch, my back gone all floppy, my chin aimed at the ceiling. I watch the blades of the ceiling fan go round and round. This isn't so bad, anyway – to feel the tension drain out of my back like I pulled some kind of cork near the bottom.

All this time, I imagined myself calling Louise as soon as I stepped out of the shower onto the heated tiles, but for some reason, now that I'm able, I am hesitant to actually do it. I keep touching my phone in my pocket, running my finger back and forth along the jagged edges of the volume button and the jack where the charger plugs in. Something makes me wait.

The ceiling fan clicks with every rotation of the blades. It reminds me of the clocks in high school. I feel like I spent the bulk of my school days watching the clock, waiting for the time to trickle by. When you're a kid, you have nothing but time. It goes all slow. You just want to throw chunks of it away to be done with the boring bits. The older you get, the more precious it becomes, and the harder it gets to wrangle it. Time picks up speed until it's a blurry object blasting by, and you chase after it and reach out for it over and over, but you can never quite wrap your hands around it. You can never quite catch up. And it only goes faster and faster and faster.

I let my head loll to the right side, and the wind from the fan brushes the side of my face with cool. My eyes droop closed. Everything goes really still, and I realize that I no longer hear the click of the fan. Am I sleeping?

There's a sound, a door opening, footsteps. Is this real or a dream? The click fades back in. It's real.

I jerk myself into an upright position. Louise stands just inside the doorway.

"You're alright!" she says.

She rushes over to me and hugs me, and I feel her warmth against me. She smells clean. I can't think of anything to say right away, so I say nothing.

I lean my head and shoulders back to get a look at her, and to my surprise, she looks pretty sad.

"What's wrong?" I say.

"It's nothing," she says. "Just…"

She trails off into silence. The only thing I can figure is that she was so worried about me that she's still sort of upset. Something like that? I don't know. Trying to figure out how a girl feels is like trying to solve a Rubik's cube in the dark.

"Look, I've been thinking about a lot of stuff that I wanted to talk to you about," I say. "I have this problem accepting affection. My fears get so big, I think that it clouds everything else up, and I can't believe in the good things anymore. And I think I am bad to you and to me sometimes because of it. I injure myself, and it effects how I treat you."

She doesn't say anything. She just looks really sad.

"But it's ok," I say. "Cause I can learn. I can do better. I can be better to you and to myself."

Still nothing.

"What are you thinking about?" I say.

She takes a breath.

"Jeff, I think we want different things," she says.

"What do you mean?" I say.

"Just that you seem quite a bit more serious about all of this than me. About us," she says. "I'm not looking for any kind of commitment or anything like that. I just want to have fun. But you are so sincere and sweet and serious. I just don't think it's right to carry on with you getting the wrong idea."

Her words wash over me in waves. I can only process little bits of it at once, so each wave carries a little more information over the wall of shock and into my brain.

"Oh, yeah," I say. "I get it."

I do the nonchalant shrug.

An awkward pause follows.

"I should go," she says.

"Right," I say.

She walks to the door, slides her shoes on. She yanks open the door.

"It might be weird for a while, but we should stay friends, OK?" she says, standing in the open door.

"Right," I say.

She walks through the doorway into the sunlight and steps away from the building, the door clicking shut behind her.

After she's gone, I do the nonchalant shrug again, like it might convince me it's not so bad.

It doesn't.

So take me away from this place, please, as far as I can go. Elevate me to some other plane, and just erase me from this one. Because I could never figure this one out.

I sit, and I clench my teeth and my fists and my mind. I squeeze and squeeze, and my lips curl and veins pop out of everywhere.

But nothing happens.

I try it again, squeezing, arms shaking, torso quivering.

Please.

Nothing, nothing, nothing.

So the white world left me, too.

I flop my head back onto the back of the couch again and watch the blades of the fan chop at the air. I stare straight at the ceiling, but I can barely sit still. It's here again. There's a violence in me now with no place to go.

I go to the fridge and dig out the six pack of Sam Adams nestled in the back. I carry the half dozen beers and the bottle opener with me back to the couch and pop the first. There's more than one way to disconnect your brain.

CHAPTER 32

After the beer is gone, I poke around the kitchen until I find a half gallon bottle of Jameson Irish whiskey under the sink that's about two thirds full. Not a huge whiskey fan traditionally, but it will do.

Drink up, drink up.

I unscrew the cap and tilt the bottle toward my face, which is harder than it sounds because it's large and heavy. Once my mouth connects to the opening, I dump and chug, long and deep. It burns all the way down, but it feels right somehow. It has to burn like that to change you, to take you away from yourself for a while. It has to sting a little so you know it's in there.

I stop and take a deep breath and wipe the moisture from my lips with the back of my hand. My breath feels all heavy with booze fumes and warm. Water fills my eyes, saliva juices up my mouth, and the burn keeps running up and down my throat.

It's not bad, though. Not bad at all. Maybe I could like whiskey after all. Jameson knows what's up.

See, the big nothing has wormed its way inside my brain again, but if I drink enough, I can keep it at bay. I can stave off the emptiness and the loneliness and the hurt and the boredom and the death all around me. I can forget all of that for a while.

If you drink enough, the part of your brain that records memory stops functioning. For a while in there, you're running around, talking to people, doing whatever, but the part of your brain that is supposed to remember it all is passed out in the corner. The next morning you wake up with no memories of the prior evening. Chunks of your time are lost forever. It feels like they're erased, but they're not really because they were never there in the first place. People call it blacking out, but I like to think of it as traveling in time. I drink, and the next thing I know, it's 14 hours later, and I'm somewhere else.

Not that I think that will happen to me right now. I mean, I guess it could, but I was just thinking about it.

I take another long guzzle, and I look out the window at the sun shining on the trees and the sidewalk and the street, and it feels weird that it's the middle of the day somehow. I should be looking out there at a blackened sky. It should be the night time, so late that I'm the only one left awake.

And my phone gurgles. It's a text from Babinaux. It's just a question mark.

"Hi," I write.

"Where are you?" she writes.

"At Glenn's," I say.

"I'll be there in twenty," she says.

It's weird. Knowing that someone will be here soon only makes me want to drink more. I take another toot off the big bottle, but I don't go balls out this time. I need to pace myself.

By the time Babinaux arrives, the whiskey has kicked in. I'm pretty effed up. It's too bad, too, because I'm really in the mood to operate some heavy machinery for the first time in a long while.

She knocks at the door. I'm a little too wobbly to answer it, so I just yell:

"Come in!"

Pretty classy.

She enters and crosses the room, her eyes squinted and brow furrowed as she regards me.

"Are you drunk?" she says.

"Yep," I say.

"It's three in the afternoon," she says.

"It feels like the night, though," I say.

When I close my eyes, I can even see the moon hanging low in a sky gone black.

"Is there some occasion that led to this?" she says, pointing at the whiskey bottle on the coffee table.

"Well, no," I say. "I mean, Glenn is back, and Louise dumped me. So it's a sad-abration."

The sympathetic look she sometimes gets crosses her eyes, and now I feel bad that she feels bad.

"Are you OK?"she says.

"Yeah, I guess so," I say.

"What happened?" she says.

"I tried to tell her about that stuff we talked about," I say. "About how I bottle things up and let the negativity get to me. And then she said that I'm too serious and she just wants to have fun. Well, I mean, that was a terrible summary of it, but I guess it's something like that, yeah."

She leans forward and puts her hand on my shoulder.

"I'm sorry," she says.

And I get this weird feeling. Because she didn't try to tell me it doesn't really matter. She didn't try to tell me I'm better off. She didn't try to tell me that what I feel doesn't really matter and I should forget it. Isn't that what people usually do? Try to rationalize some reason that you should just stop being sad. "There are other fish in the sea." "I never really liked her that much, anyway." So on. So forth. What they're really saying is "how you feel doesn't matter, because (insert reason here)."

But something about that pure empathy overwhelms me, and I feel all shaky and tingly around the sternum. And I get up, and I go to the bathroom. And I think I'm about to cry and possibly vomit at the same time. But I don't. And I think that's for the better. Because grown men aren't supposed to cry. Crying after you drink whiskey is punishable by law in Texas, I think. You hand in your man card and are asked kindly to leave the state.

And when I walk out, she's standing in the hall, and shc hugs me. And I feel love, like a mother's love, and it's OK. And I think that even if things are all screwed up for me, some of them broken so bad maybe they'll never be right, there are people that care about me, and I am lucky.

We sit in the living room again after that, and I can hear Glenn snoring in the distance.

"So where were you?" she says. "I tried to call a bunch of times."

"I did the ritual in the well, and we got back here this morning," I say. "I left my phone here, and it died, so I didn't know you tried to call."

"Jeff, that was three days ago," she says.

"What?" I say.

"The ritual?" she says. "That was three nights ago."

My brain is too slow to keep up with all of these damn revelations, so the concept of what she's saying washes over me in those slow waves again. I run over every word a few times before I can make the whole idea stick to my cerebral cortex.

"Randy said you took off or something after," she says. "Everybody was kind of freaked out."

I'm speechless. I drool a little bit on myself. Not sure if I can chalk that up to the shock or the whiskey.

Babinaux's phone rings in her purse.

"Here's Randy now," she says.

She takes the call, and I want to listen to her side of the conversation, but I can't. I can only think about the idea that three days have gone by. I guess Glenn said time works differently in the white world. Could that explain it?

"We have to go," she says, interrupting my thoughts. She stands, still looking at the phone like it might change its mind. "Randy called a meeting at the church. He said he knows what happened to Farber's body."

Interesting.

We burst into motion, and everything seems a little hectic. I catch my reflection in the mirror, my hair all smashed weird in some places and poking up in others. I find a dark green winter hat in a basket by the door and pull it on. Maybe it'll even help me avoid some of the freak show type stares I sometimes get around these cult people.

As Babinaux freshens up in the bathroom, I look in on a sleeping Glenn, laid out on his back, snoring like a hibernating bear. I decide not to wake him, and we head off without him.

CHAPTER 33

The church crawls with people. Watching the human figures cluster and march back and forth between each other reminds me of ants swarming and separating in an ant farm, carrying bits of cricket back to the queen. All of this stands in glaring contrast to the emptiness I've encountered upon arriving here the last couple of times. Bodies jitter and pace and fidget and generally struggle to keep still all around me.

Nervous energy permeates the air. Even in my drunken state, I can feel the anxiety like smoke getting in my eyes.

Babinaux and I file in, picking our way through the crowd to take a seat in the second to last row of pews. The hat seems to serve its secondary function well. No one notices me, from what I can see. I suppose the general level of stimulation in the room helps my cause, of course.

The chatter builds. It sounds like a school cafeteria, the drone of a few hundred voices melding into one noise.

A hush spreads among us as Randy steps into the room, sliding open this weird plastic curtain that sets off the side chamber that I believe I heard someone refer to as the study room. Right away it strikes me as odd that he's sporting a baseball cap. I guess maybe he got so caught up in all of this fervor, he forgot he's wearing it, but it seems quite out of place. He slides the divider shut behind him and strides to the pulpit.

"A new dawn rises," Randy says, his voice reaching yet again for those Gandalf tones. "A new era is upon us."

He pauses, and the silence is shocking after the chatter held sway over the room for so long.

"To live and die is the gift we're given, to walk the Earth for a while, and then to pass on," he says. "For some of us, the living lasts a long time, for others, just a short while. Whatever the circumstances, it is a noble thing, to live and to die."

Another pause. An old lady clears her throat somewhere to my left.

"But to live and die and live again?" he says. "That would be beyond human. That would be divine. But search your feelings. Does not some part of you already believe in this? Does not some part of you wonder that your dead loved ones might return? That your dead pets might come home one day? Isn't some part of you just waiting to hear that death isn't certain, isn't necessary? Hasn't it always been waiting for that?"

And then gasps erupt all around, and I'm confused. My eyes dart from side to side, and then I find it. Riston Farber walks through the opened curtain. He's not some shriveled zombie. He's not scarred and blackened. He's not burned at all. He does look very thin, though, and his posture looks worse than when I last saw him.

Following behind him, 10 or so of his minions stream out of the study room. The tops of their heads are shaved like Friars.

The crowd stands. I don't think anybody consciously does this. We just stand in spontaneous awe. It almost doesn't seem real, but another part of me reacts just the way Randy suggested – that I knew this was possible all along. Like the wild part of my brain that believes in magic wants to lord it over the rest of me, it told me so from the start.

As Farber arrives at the front of the room, Randy takes off his hat to reveal that he too has the top of his head shaved. Just then, I lock eyes with Randy, and he looks terrified for two seconds before he composes himself. He does not look at me again.

Farber stands before the crowd, soaking up the adulation. It reminds me of the spoon hurling back in the diner. He coughs then, hacking, dry coughs that sound to rattle from deep within. Several people crowd around to aid him, and I realize he's quite a bit more frail than I realized. His cheeks are all sunken, and the skin around his eyes looks almost purple.

A motion catches the corner of my eye, and I see that Cromwell stands off behind Farber. His hand waves until he sees that he has my attention. He points at me, then he scrapes his finger across his neck in a throat slash motion and points his eyes and thumb at the door.

I'm not the best at charades, but I'm able follow this.

"Gotta go," I say to Babinaux.

I shuffle out with my head down. One head snaps around as I pass, and I think someone spotted me and is about to yell and point, but then the guy sneezes, and I realize that explains the jerky motion.

As I walk through the doorway into the clear, images flash in my head. The flames in the well, the fear on Randy's face a moment ago and Babinaux telling me I'd be gone for three days.

And I think maybe I accidentally resurrected.

TIM MCBAIN & LT VARGUS

RED ON THE INSIDE

SMARMY PRESS

RED ON THE INSIDE

BOOK 3

CHAPTER 1

Houses sway around me on the sides of the street. I'm pretty sure I'm on the way back to Glenn's, but it's hard to tell. All of the houses out here look about the same, and the street signs are a little blurry at the moment. They should really consider color coding these things for the sake of excessively drunk pedestrians. I mean, it's hard enough to navigate with the lawns undulating on either side of me like this. Reading is out of the question.

So I might be lost, but I know this much: I'm moving away from the church, away from Farber and his minions with the tops of their heads shaved bald, away from the crowd rendered breathless in the presence of resurrection.

I walk. All of the booze makes the world want to spin around me, but if I keep walking in a straight line, it's more like the world tilts than spins. So, like I said, I walk.

I lean into it.

My head feels heavy, like there's a bowling ball sitting on my neck that wants to veer whatever direction the world is sloping at the moment. I have to concentrate to keep on the trajectory I want. It's sort of like steering a ship in an angry sea. It's OK, though, because I've done it all before. Once you get the hang of it, you never forget how to walk into a spin.

I realize that this whiskey has continued to make me

drunker and drunker, even though I stopped drinking some time ago. It's been so long since I drank liquor that I forgot how it worked a little bit. You chug and then wait. It's like it's on a time release.

To me, alcohol is like going underwater in a way. You're putting something dense between you and the rest of the world, some fluid that insulates you from everything else. It's like you get so isolated from everyone, you don't have to be scared or worry anymore, though. Nothing can touch you.

I guess I shouldn't be thinking about that so much. I should be pondering the intricacies of my possible resurrection after being burned alive. I mean, that's a pretty big deal, right? Getting torched at the bottom of a well? You don't run into that scenario every day.

I don't know. It either happened or it didn't. I'm too drunk for all of that critical thinking just now.

I reach the corner of a busy intersection, cars buzzing past. I lock my eyes on the gleaming orange hand telling me not to walk. I wait for the white glow of the walking person to flip on below. Well, I guess I lock my eyes on it a little too hard because the next thing I know I'm seeing double. It somehow makes the world stop spinning, at least, so that's good.

And then I realize that I'm not seeing double at all. I'm seeing the other world blurred over the top of this one. I say "other world" instead of "white world" because it's not white this time. It's a full color version of that translucent overlay like when I talked to Glenn in the mirror at that Mexican restaurant.

The other world sharpens into focus, and rolling hills of green grass take shape in front of me along with a couple of trees with buds on the tips of the branches. For a split second, I can feel the wind from this place whip across my face. It hisses through the blades of grass, and then the sound abruptly cuts out. And the wind feeling is gone as well, but the branches still wag, and the grass still lies down and pops up. It's like watching a silent movie.

The orange hand fades to black, and the white walker lights up. I set out to cross the street and also wade through the grass. I am in two places at once, and I'm very, very drunk in both of them.

To my surprise, the grass tangles around my feet and ankles when I take a step, and I almost trip. I didn't anticipate being able to feel it, but here we are. It's dense enough to constrict my range of motion, so I lift my feet high to better trudge through it. I realize that I probably look absurd as I traverse the crosswalk, doing a weird, kicky leg march. I'm not embarrassed so much as I kind of wish I could see it from afar.

I walk down a sidewalk past a few vacant buildings in the real world and climb a grassy knoll in the other world. It's kind of confusing to be going up and flat at the same time. My legs can feel the hill, and I step accordingly, but somehow I'm also walking on flat concrete.

And then I think about where Amity might be. Maybe I'll climb this hill and she'll be on the other side, and she won't even run since I'm not dangling any meat in her face this time.

I reach the top and let my eyes scan the hills.

No Amity. Nothing but grass.

But at least I can see it. The white world closed itself off from me, yes, but it seems I can drink my way to a glimpse. It's better than nothing.

And then a fist clenches in my gut, and the whiskey catches all the way up in a flash. It's usually not so sudden that the sickness comes over me, but today? Very much so.

I lean forward and vomit, and the foamy brown sick sprays into both worlds somehow, which is actually pretty awesome. It spatters about the grass in the other world, and splats the lip of a storm drain in the real world. I'm almost glad to be ill just to see this.

I give it a thumbs up without thinking about it, and then I imagine what this looks like to the cars passing by. Some guy hunching over the gutter, all giddy, with his thumb in the air like he's rating movies with Ebert, except instead of giving his take on A Few Good Men, barf cascades from his mouth like a waterfall of beer and booze and saliva and stomach juice.

Good times.

CHAPTER 2

As I get closer to home, the layer of semi-transparent grass running along the sidewalk fades, and then the other world flickers out all together. Interesting. So there's not necessarily a huge window there, but it's something.

Arriving at Glenn's, I let myself in. I figure he's still zonked, so I ease the door shut behind me and slide my shoes off all quiet like. I move toward the couch, but a sizzling noise stops me mid-stride. Then the smell hits me.

Oh man, someone's making breakfast. I smell eggs and some kind of breakfast meat and possibly a touch of cayenne pepper.

I change directions, passing by the dining room where I note the two halves of the puzzle sphere resting on the table like a clam shell, and head for the kitchen.

"Hey Grobnagger," Glenn says, unfazed by my ninja-like approach. "Jesus, is that puke on your face?"

"What?" I say.

I wipe around my mouth with my sleeve and examine the smear of brown foam it leaves.

"Oh yeah," I say. "Definitely puke."

My glance shifts from my sleeve to Glenn in time to see him close his eyes all disgusted.

"You know, we have napkins here on the premises," he

says. "And if you use the bathroom later, you'll even find toilet paper within arm's reach. Not sure if you've been using your sleeve in there this whole time, but I find the toilet paper gets the job done."

I tilt my head.

"Well, it sounds crazy, but I'm willing to try anything once," I say.

Glenn shudders, his shoulders shimmying. I don't know if he's picturing the nugget of puke foam on my face again or contemplating the logistics of sleeve wiping in the bathroom.

He serves up two plates of breakfast, and I tell him about Farber's return while we eat. He looks mildly concerned, but he doesn't say much. Then I talk about the drunkenness and how it opens a door to the other world. I leave out the part about vomiting every which way since we are eating. I finish my story, and we dine on in silence.

"Well, what do you think?" I say after a while.

"I think I'm taking two days to myself, maybe three," he says. "That's what I think. You know what I'm going to do? I'm going to go to Outback. I'm going to order a bloomin' onion. I'm not going to worry about all of this for a couple of days. And then I'll get back to you about what I really think."

For a guy that crafts such delicious food, Glenn has the worst taste in restaurants. I'd think he'd be into fine dining or weird little ethnic places no one has heard of, but instead he's all about riblets from Applebee's and stuff like that.

I take a bite of omelet with a lot of cayenne involved. The spice catches my throat just right and makes my eyes water.

"It's been too long since I've had a bloomin' onion," he says.

His eyes look all far away like his brain is playing a bloomin' onion memory montage. My only memories of Outback involve a commercial with John Madden back when he was in about 50% of all commercials. I don't remember for sure, but I think he probably said "Boom!" in there somewhere.

"So here's my question," I say. "Did I die and resurrect or what? I mean, did that tree bring me back somehow?"

Glenn answers all sassy like I'm being an idiot:

"Well, yeah, the tree brought you back," he says. "That's what it does."

"How was I supposed to know that?" I say.

"Well, if you weren't always rushing into trouble like a kid sticking his face into the blades of a fan, I was about to tell you before you touched it," he says.

"Oh," I say.

"Let me take a step back, though," he says. "The tree brought you back here. I can't say whether or not you resurrected. I'd assume not, but who knows?"

"Can't get a straight answer around here," I say, half under my breath.

I think about the blindfold. Damn. That'd be the perfect evidence, but I didn't look for it. If it was burned up at the bottom of the well, the fire was real. If not, it wasn't. I can't imagine going back to try to verify it, though. I'm not in a huge rush to get back down into that well, believe it or not.

"So here's another question," I say. "You said someone captured you, and lopped off the end of your foot, right? Who was it?"

He sighs.

"It's not like physical people caught me necessarily," he

says. "It's like a force in the air there or something. Like when you got strung up in the alley, right? Who knows who did that?"

He waves a chunk of omelet on his fork while he talks, sort of like a maestro.

"It's like how people talk about mother nature sometimes as though it is a sentient being asserting its will. I can't actually say it's sentient, though. I don't know. Sometimes I think it is, but other times I think it's more like a reflection of my imagination or my energy or something."

He finally eats the bite of omelet and loads another as he goes on.

"Whatever it is, it speaks in symbols, like it's trying to teach us things, yeah? But it wants us to earn it, not just to give it to us. Like your thing with the cup."

I think about this.

"Is it, like, God?" I say.

"No," he says. "I don't know. Truth is, you could call it that, maybe, but I don't think of it that way. I think of it as like the big consciousness, like how Carl Jung talked about the collective unconscious. If you look at the way he described it, he always worded it carefully. You could interpret the term as just meaning that the stuff in our right brain, our subconscious, contains all of these inherited instincts and archetypal understandings of things that have been passed down through the species, but he left the idea open that the term could refer to some communication between us, some divine connection. To me, it's all of us together, connected, but none of us at the same time. It's the place we connect to when we're dreaming. It's like a collective memory bank."

He shovels in another egg bite, chews for a second.

"They did this experiment in England with crossword puzzles," he says. "They had subjects do the puzzles when they were brand new and no one else had done them, and then they had the people do crossword puzzles that were a few days old and people all over London had done them. When the subjects did the older puzzles, their results improved by five percent."

I guzzle down the last of my coffee and pour a refill.

"Or another phenomenon is that IQ test scores keep going up," he says. "There's no other indicator that intelligence is increasing rapidly, but as more people take the tests, the average score goes up. As more people experience something – in this case particular tests – future people attempting it seem to inexplicably have an easier time at it. Maybe they can tap into this shared memory slash dream place, right?"

His eyes drift up and trace along the seam where the wall and ceiling meet.

"That's just one interpretation of it, though. That's what my gut tells me," he says. "I'm not saying it's right on some absolute level, or even that the conscious part of me believes it all the time."

"Wait a minute," I say. "I watched you rip open a door in a concrete wall and walk through it, into blindingly white light, and you still don't believe all the way?"

He laughs.

"All I'm saying is that I don't understand it or know what the hell it means," he says. "I mean, yeah, I can do a couple of things, but I'm like a guy that can play a couple of songs really well on the piano. People that don't know how to play the piano are impressed, but I'm no Beethoven. Knowing how to do that stuff doesn't mean I have any goddamn idea what it is, what it wants, why we're here or any of that. My guess is no better than anyone else's."

He takes our plates to the sink and rinses them.

"Anyhow, we're not supposed to be talking about this," he says. "We're supposed to be talking about ribs and chicken on the barbie."

Great. More Outback stuff, I guess.

"OK, wait," I say. "Let's at least talk about the symbols around the tree before we move on to Aussie-tizers."

Glenn closes his eyes and sighs.

"Fine," he says. "I think the fact that you touched the side of the tree nearest the ocean is significant, so let's talk about that. The top of the ocean lurches in the form of sunlit waves. That's the water we typically know – for swimming, fishing and traveling over. Underneath, though, lies the darkness, the depths that would freeze us to death or crush us with inconceivable water pressure, the place where nightmares come alive in the form of creatures too weird to live in the light.

"In a way it represents the conscious and subconscious mind. The sun shines on the surface, but we know that there's so much more below we can't see. It can also be the depth of human emotions, the things down in your psyche that drive you to behaviors that you don't quite understand. But in a broader way it merely represents mysteries, deep and dark."

He sips his coffee.

"Sounds familiar, though, doesn't it?" he says. "Obsessing about the dark places."

"I guess so," I say.

"You're married to the sea, Grobnagger," he says. "In the

old days, the sailors that went out exploring didn't learn how to swim. They said that if they fell in or if their ship went down, their body should belong to the waves. There was a superstitious element, of course. Learning to swim was considered tempting fate."

"I'm not married to the sea," I say.

CHAPTER 3

Once we wrap up our symbol talk, things seem to simmer down into something more normal. We watch some cooking show where a guy makes a cabbage, sour cream, and bacon dish with the cabbage cut into strips to serve a pasta like role. Intriguing. Glenn writes down the recipe. He has a special notebook for writing down recipes like this. Unreal.

I nap my drunk off, sleeping into the afternoon, and Glenn wakes me in the evening for the much anticipated trip to the Outback. We head out to the car.

For once, the prospect of going to a restaurant doesn't bother me so much. Not that I'm looking forward to it, it's more that I don't care. I don't know if some kind of depression is settling over me or what, but I feel like the world burns dim about me, just the faintest glow like an oil lantern turned all the way down. After all of the excitement the past few weeks, it's not unpleasant, at least not in a painful way.

I feel nothing. Or close to that, anyway.

As we park, it occurs to me that I didn't even get nervous on the ride there. It barely even seems like it really happened. It feels like we got into the Explorer and transported to a primo parking spot by the front door.

Anyway, this is it, the Outback Steakhouse. As Glenn pulls open the door, the red glow of the neon light shines on his neck and lights up his beard from below. Something about the way the scarlet glimmer illuminates him makes me really look at him for the first time in a while. No navy blue cap tonight. His hair has grown out so I can see the border line where his blond highlights give way to all dark roots. I never knew he was dying his hair. I guess he wore the hat so much, I didn't get a great look. To trump this, he wears a pair of Elvis style sunglasses on the back of his head. Chrome. So I may as well be going out to eat with Guy Fieri. While I observe all of this, a hostess with bleached teeth and too much lip gloss asks us how many and tells us to follow her.

The chain restaurant sounds drone all around. Forks scrape plates. Dishes clink and chime against each other in the bus boy's tray. Ice cubes grind out wet sounds as they swirl in seas of cola. The small talk bleeds together into one wavering tone. All of the quiet nothings add up into a louder nothing, a static in the air, a buzz that leads nowhere.

I scan the room, but I find few signs of intelligent life.

I kid.

The people slurp and chomp and gnaw and smile. They all look the same. Up at the bar, they chug and take slugs and a fat lady has big jugs.

Sorry. Every once in a while I can't stop rhyming for some reason.

Sometimes I realize that I've been watching too much TV when I look around at the people in a restaurant or some other public venue and am astounded by how ugly they are. Now, ugly may be a strong word for what I mean here, but it fits in a way. They're just normal, but after so long looking at warped versions of humanity through the filter of the photogenic people cast for reality shows, things start to get weird. Even the people on TV that aren't very good looking often have striking features. I remember watching an episode of the Bachelorette once, where this guy with all close together eyes and a too huge smile had the Bachelorette girl visiting his family, right? And it astounded me how normal the family looked. The guy wasn't really handsome at all, but he looked like a TV person somehow. He had a remarkable face that sort of reminded me of a weird bird. By comparison, his family looked hollow and plain. Not especially ugly, but somehow not fit for TV. Not worthy.

And the girls on these shows are even stranger – primped to the point of creepiness, caked in makeup, surgically altered faces. They look all phony and inhuman with personalities to match more often than not, but then you see them around their families who look totally mundane, and it's like normal people are so much less stimulating that the level of plain seems dull. Dreary. Ugly.

Looking around the Outback, I see a lot of this. People buzzing around, standing, smiling, lost in conversations and thoughts and realities that I'll never know. Bodies that pull clothing taut in the wrong places. Faces you forget before you even look away. Not one of them looks worthy of the Bachelorette or the Amazing Race. They're hideously plain. And I know I'm one of them.

The waitress comes and goes in fast forward, bearing menus, then drinks, then food. I get a steak covered in a weird spice rub that I guess makes it more Australian. Not that great, but I bet John Madden would love every morsel of it.

The meal progresses quite rapidly. I almost feel like a sloth moving in slow motion while the world rushes around me at a pace I can't comprehend. And it occurs to me that the world isn't burning dimmer around me. I'm the one burning dimmer.

My mind drifts as we finish up our food, circling back to Louise over and over, which feels about like an ice pick to the heart. With my senses dulled and slowed, however, even a heart stab feels less painful than it should. I guess I'm thankful for that, but I don't know.

I feel like part of me should be angry, resentful. Part of me should harbor that little bit of hate that tells me I'm better off without her. I'll find someone better and so on. But even that part feels no hatred, no aggression. It just wants to crawl out into the cold sea and let the tide pull me away.

But it's fine. It's fine.

"Wouldn't it be great if life were this simple?" Glenn says, tearing off a deep fried onion chunk and dipping it in that weird orange goo. "If we could just find the things we enjoy and partake in them with no worries about the future or meaning or any of that?"

I think about it.

"Would it?" I say.

I must convey my snark a little too openly as he just glares at me. I guess I'm supposed to pretend that life would be great if we could just eat at Outback for eternity, like John Madden's vision of heaven.

"Do you ever stop and enjoy anything the world has to offer?" he says. "Or are you too busy living up in your head to appreciate what's going on around you?"

This from a guy with frosted tips and sunglasses on the back of his head.

I look around the restaurant. All the people swarm and flit about and churn their jaws endlessly like grasshoppers. I don't see why they bother. I don't see what drives them to it or what they get out of it. I could understand it, maybe, if I felt the people were seeing their own lives clearly, if they were seeing their own dreams clearly. But I don't think they are. I think they rush into marriages and families and careers that seem like what they want, but they have little interest in them once they're real. They're more interested in chasing some comfort at a restaurant, checking their phone every two seconds, hoping for something novel to happen. From moment to moment, they spend their lives seeking stimulation and little else.

Doesn't there have to be some illusion dangling in the distance for any of this to make sense? They prop up this dream of love and happiness. They gaze on it from afar as some goal they're vaguely pointed toward, but they don't really spend the days connecting with the people they care about on a genuine level. They spend the days concerned with comfort, with stimulation. They grind away their time working some job they care little about so long as that empty dream sits on the horizon in front of them.

And realizing that this is how the world operates around me makes most every encounter hollow. It renders most every experience impossible to enjoy. How can I connect to people who are perpetually distracted on purpose?

"Everything is all around you," Glenn says.

But it all means nothing to me.

CHAPTER 4

With his belly full of faux Australian cuisine, Glenn prepares to retire for the evening a little early. He steps into the hallway while brushing his teeth, and I get another quick glance at his stumped foot. The texture of the scar makes me shudder. The flesh puckers like maybe it was cauterized. I guess we got sidetracked before he could explain what the hell happened there. He said it was like an energy that captured him, right? Like a wave in the air. In my experience, air rarely exerts the force necessary to lop a foot off, but who knows?

Once he's down for the count, I'm left to my own devices. I flip through channel after channel, but nothing catches my interest.

I turn the TV off and sit, and the world gets so still. Nothing moves.

I know it's her before the headlights even twirl into the driveway. I walk out to the Lincoln, climb into the backseat. She's wearing a pirate blouse with puffy sleeves and a collar that winds up around her neck. She smiles when she sees me, but something about it looks timid.

"How have you been?" she says.

"Not bad," I say. "I don't know. Everything feels a little funny since, you know, I got set on fire and all of that. What's your take on that, by the way?"

"My take?" she says, eyelashes fluttering.

"Yeah," I say. "Do you think I resurrected or what?"

"Well…" she says. "After all that's transpired, I take it at face value, so yes. I think Randy burned you and you came back. And I think Farber set it all up. We all thought you were just going through rituals at an accelerated rate because of your dreams, but Farber wanted this for some reason. That's my take."

Oh yeah, I sort of forgot about that in a way. The guy that came back from the dead and probably wants to kill me. Just sort of slipped my mind. I suppose it would make sense for him to have a hand in these events. Interesting, though. I didn't expect her to buy in all the way.

"So Farber wants me to be, like, divine?" I say. "How does that help him?"

"It's hard to say," she says.

She chews her lip as both of us get lost in thought for a moment.

"Oh," I say. "I never asked how you've been, though."

She smiles, and I think I see a little tension drain from her shoulders.

"A little stressed," she says. "This Farber thing is hard to get a read on, but thankfully, the news isn't all bad."

I picture Farber standing at the lectern in the church, coughs racking his torso, purple veins bulging around his eyes.

"He seemed pretty sick," I say.

"Yes, he's quite weak. He's mostly slept since his… return," she says. "So the bad news is that he has formally declared you a false idol."

Now, I never really considered myself any kind of idol in

the first place, but what the hell? Pretty sure we both came back from the dead, jerk-off. Or maybe we didn't. I don't know.

"The good news?" she says. "He said he wants no harm to come to you. He said we're best to turn the other cheek and ignore the lost souls that know no better than to attempt to deceive us. He said, with great emphasis, we should leave you be."

"You know what? I can respect that," I say.

"Still," she says. "I could never trust him after what happened before. If it means you're OK for now, so be it, but I'm concerned."

"I'm not that worried, really," I say. "What's Farber going to do? Cough on me?"

She grimaces.

"That would be pretty gross," she says.

"Plus, I figure you've got those guys out in the car watching me at all times, right?" I say. "Those guys have large firearms on their persons, correct?"

"They're armed," she says.

"See? If Farber comes at me, we'll get to see a new magic trick," I say. "One of your men will hover a bullet into his skull with a simple squeeze of the trigger."

The silence hangs in the air moment, the conversation pausing on that awkward note.

"You seem a little down lately," she says.

"Yeah, I don't know," I say. "I've been tired."

I remember the numb that came over me at the Outback, but what's the use in describing it?

"That's all it is?" she says.

"Yeah," I say.

I smile. She looks like she doesn't quite buy it, but she doesn't say anything. I can live with that. It's not worth explaining these things anymore. Words are wind. They fly out into the air and float away into nothing.

"So what's up with the League these days?" I say. "Everyone has real weird haircuts now, eh?"

"I'm afraid I'm out of the loop some as of today," she says. "The haircut people won't talk to me. I thought about taking an electric razor to my head, but it wouldn't help. Everyone knows I'm your friend."

I pick at the door handle with my fingernails.

"Yeah, you're getting blackballed. You finally know what it's like to be a Grobnagger," I say. "Do you think it's unsafe for you to keep hanging around there?"

She rolls her eyes.

"Oh, I'll be fine," she says.

"I never really thought about it," I say. "But this all kind of means the Sons of Man took over, right? They used Farber's resurrection story to charm everyone, and now the whole league is along for the ride."

"It would seem so," she says.

She looks far away.

I lie on the couch in the dark, drifting to that half asleep state almost immediately. I feel empty inside, like one of those crispy locust husks stuck to the side of a tree, all hollow and shit.

The sheet goes from cool to warm to hot against my skin, and the blanket grips me in a way that almost feels like a hug. It's a knit blanket. I'm not sure what the material is, but it has some weight to it.

As sleep takes me, I think maybe this is the best life actually gets. Warm and secure and floating away from reality.

CHAPTER 5

When the morning comes, the light glares in and disturbs the peace. It's not even glints of sunlight that might provide some biologically wired reward. This light is gray and cold. Do not pass go. Do not collect the burst of endorphins.

From what I can tell, no part of me wants to get up. My joints are all stiff. My muscles ache. My mind only wants to lie in the dark forever where the light will never wake me.

But I get up anyway.

I look out the window. Dead leaves litter the front lawn, the world muted to shades of brown and yellow. It's weird how fall sneaks up and chokes the green out of everything all sly like. And for a split second the grass field from the other world flashes in my memory. Still green over there, I suppose.

"Mornin' Grobs," Glenn says as I step across the threshold to stand in the kitchen doorway.

Talking seems like too much effort, so I nod a return greeting. He holds court in his kitchen just like the good old days, oven-mitted hands pawing at a tray of baked goods, setting it on the counter. At first I think he's made a homemade version of those pecan pinwheel things, but no. Cinnamon rolls.

He pipes frosting out of a legit pastry bag. Or maybe it's icing. I don't know the difference.

I sit at the snack bar, and we eat.

We don't talk much, and the things that we do say aren't all that interesting.

I chug coffee between bites, and it wakes me up, but not all the way somehow. It's like my eyes are wide open, and I feel all the physical feelings of being alert, but my brain is still a little bit dead.

It's enough that I have a hard time staying tuned into this disjointed conversation we're having that is punctuated with long pauses, loud chewing, and coffee slurps, but this is the second day of Glenn's culinary walkabout, so we make plans to go to Chili's.

Wait.

You know what? He makes plans to go to Chili's. I have no say in these matters. I am just along for the ride.

The cinnamon rolls are pretty good, though.

After a morning spent watching awful daytime TV, we sit around in silence much of the afternoon. I read part of the introduction to a Kierkegaard book, but even the translator's intro is a little hard to follow. Probably doesn't bode well for ol' Grobnags' chances of digesting the actual text, but whatever.

Glenn reads some book about war. For real. I can almost remember the title, but wait, that's right. I died of boredom before I could finish reading the cover.

On the plus side, he does not bust into the baby back ribs jingle at any point during our reading session. This is a major victory for good taste and decency, though I admit that a certain part of me is a little disappointed. I could have chimed in with that baritone "barbecue sauce" at just the right moment, and now I may never get that opportunity.

A few times while reading the mind numbing words of Kierkegaard's translator, I get the urge to ask Glenn more questions to clarify whatever happened to him in the other world, but… Well, I know he doesn't want to talk about any of it for at least another day, but I kind of don't care anyway. Even when I think of the questions, it feels more like I'm pretending to care.

Makes no sense, right? Right.

I mean, a lot of shit hangs in the balance: My life. Amity's life. Other stuff, I think.

So I should care, but it all seems like too much of a hassle just now. And I have this feeling that it won't lead to anything anyway. Not really.

I read some more. Now Kierkegaard has his own introduction to the writing. I don't know. Getting pretty frustrated with the endless introductions. Without thinking, I speak:

"You think Farber wants to kill both of us?" I say.

Glenn looks up from the war book and just stares at me through the glasses perched on the tip of his nose while this question processes… or doesn't.

"What?" he says.

"Do you think Farber wants to kill both of us? Or just me?"

He turns back to the book.

"I don't concern myself greatly with what Riston Farber wants," he says.

"He must have been the one that wanted Randy to set me on fire, though, right?"

"It seems likely."

"Did he want me dead, though, or did he want me to resurrect?"

"Look, I told you I'm not getting into this today, but I'll set something straight for you right now. Riston Farber is a phony. He's a con-man. I'm not worried about him or anything he might have planned."

Sheesh. Bite my head off.

The pieces don't fit together in a way that makes sense, though. If they just wanted to kill me, why go about it in a way that semi-fit the resurrection rituals Randy alluded to? But why would they want me to come back from the dead? Was it just a test? That wouldn't make much sense either considering Farber had seemingly been burned up some weeks before.

As these thoughts circle toward the drain in my head, Glenn squints my way and gives me the nod. You know, the, "We're going to Chili's now," nod.

I stand and stretch. It occurs to me that I don't even get that twinge of nervousness that I usually get just before an excursion such as this anymore. But am I growing used to all of this additional stimulus, or am I giving up?

At least I'm not to the point of wearing sweat pants in public yet. There's still hope.

We file out to the damn Explorer, which Glenn starts with a thunderous muffler free rumble. I lean back in my seat, and the leather is just cold enough to chill my skin through my t-shirt and give me goose bumps. I don't mind, though, somehow.

I close my eyes and drift right down to the almost sleep state again. The volume of the exhaust gets turned down until it sounds really far away. I guess I'm still awake but just barely.

It's weird to go down so quickly. It's like my anxiety is

turned off. I don't feel like myself much. I don't like it in some ways, but it does numb everything out. Maybe that's why I don't mind the cold. It fits the numb.

Time goes faster somehow, and then we're parked at Chili's, and then we're shuffling inside, and it all feels like something I'm observing, like it's not quite real.

I don't feel it at all.

And we're seated. And there are drinks and mozzarella sticks.

Glenn orders the baby back ribs. Duh.

I don't know what to get. I'm not even hungry, really. I wind up going for chicken fingers. I almost feel like I should apologize for this choice, but I don't know. It seems like they'd be easy to eat. Slather those things in some kind of sauce so they slide right down, I figure.

I put my head down while we wait for the food.

"You all right?" Glenn says.

"Tired," I say.

If I let myself, I could fall asleep right here with my forehead adhered to the table. Don't I know I should be readying steak knives or finding a swordfish or something to plunge into a potential attacker's throat? Especially now that I've been set on fire and zombie Farber came back from the dead to say bad things about me.

Whatever, though.

I let myself drift, and the black grows blacker, and the Chili's sounds fade out into nothing.

I float in empty space. It is warmer than the real world, and I can let go all the way. Maybe that's all I've really wanted all along.

"Dude," Glenn says. "Food's coming."

The black dissolves to light. I sit up and hear myself slurp saliva from the corner of my mouth. The waitress smiles at me and sets my plate of chicken fingers onto the little puddle of drool in front of me. I think I forgot to smile back. I hate when I realize that too late.

I dunk the chicken into sauce the color of the Dalai Lama's robe. It doesn't taste like much, but I chew and swallow all the same.

Glenn's eyes take on a demonic look as he regards the meat in front of him, and his lips look all juicy. This kind of freaks me out. He mutters to himself as he tears into the ribs, gnawing hunks of meat and gristle from the bones.

"Oh yeah, babe," he says just above his breath.

Barbecue sauce smears about the perimeter of his maw like maroon lipstick applied on a roller coaster. His mustache looks like a loaded paintbrush. I think about telling him about this, but hey:

His mustache. His problem.

Still, I have no choice but to stop and watch him eat for a while. It's a ferocious act. It's like watching a lion rip apart a gazelle on the Discovery Channel.

"Pretty good, huh?" I say.

His eyes do not leave his plate.

"Off the chain," he says. "Big time."

Glenn watches Top Chef in the evening, but I can't stay focused. I keep involuntarily leaning over onto the arm of the couch and then snapping back upright to try to pay attention.

A chef wearing a cabbie hat is making sea bass tacos, if I'm understanding this correctly – a ballsy move in my opinion. I think he is overcooking the sea bass, but then the tiredness hits again, and I'm staring at the floor, tipping until my shoulder meets the arm of the couch, and then – BAM – my eyes are closed.

This is getting weird. I'm all slowed down, and I can't keep up with something as mindless as a TV cooking competition. I was kind of wondering how those sea bass tacos would come out, too.

Once again I hover in that place just short of unconsciousness. My body grows warm where it touches the couch, though the tip of my nose is freezing. My thoughts get clear and calm.

And I realize that depression – like the kind I'm feeling now – is the only peace I've found in this life. When my serotonin levels decrease, and the light inside dims to the faintest glow, I can finally keep my thoughts still for a while. The sad takes me to a tranquil place. It shuts off the endless levels of self consciousness, that bottomless well of inwardness that keeps me awake in the dark.

Maybe it's better to not fight it. Maybe it's better to stay down.

Because I feel cold inside and useless and worthless, but it's also a form of peace. And when it's like this, I know it will be okay in a way. Even if I float face down to the end, and there's no one to help me.

It will be a relief.

CHAPTER 6

I dream of the woods.

Green surrounds me so thick that I can't see more than a few feet in any direction. I bend branches out of the way and step forward. Somehow I already know it's a dream, so I kind of think it doesn't matter which way I go.

Maybe.

The trees get thicker, and the green thins out a bit, at least on the ground. The leaves above form a canopy that blocks out the light, so I walk in the endless shade. I realize that these things mean I'm getting deeper into the forest.

Even with the growth on the ground a little less full than it was a moment ago, I still can't see much. There's enough brush to block my vision, even if I can pick my way through a little easier than before.

Leaves hiss as they brush against my shorts.

Wait.

Shorts?

I look down at my legs.

OK, I'm wearing cargo shorts. No idea.

And as I gaze upon khaki shorts that I don't recognize at all, it occurs to me that I have this nagging feeling buried somewhere in my thoughts, a feeling like I've forgotten something important. The sensation has fluttered there beneath the surface this whole time, though I just now drew it into the light. It almost feels like an itch.

I move through an area cluttered with a bunch of tiny trees about the girth of a pool cue, some of which have those red cone shaped clusters of something on them.

I feel lost, like I'm just meandering. I mean, I'm trying to walk in one direction, but the undergrowth seems to push me where it wants me to go, which might be in circles. I'm not sure.

Can you be lost if you have no destination? Or are you always lost in that case? I can't decide.

Branches and leafy bits reach out for me and try to prod at me as I walk, so I slap them away. Look, I'm usually not so violent with plant life, but what the hell? Leave me alone.

Wait.

I stop.

I listen.

Did I just hear…

The wind picks up, and the leaves above rustle against each other. It's a scrape and swish that sounds like when you first put the needle on a record. Anyway, there are no other sounds.

Maybe it was nothing, the wind and shit.

I walk on, kicking through stems and stalks and seed pods and other plant body parts.

The light seems to dim a little more around me, and I stop again. The hair on the back of my neck stands up. A tickle crawls across my skin like fingertips creeping over all of me. I don't know why.

And then that forgetful feeling perks up again, but I realize that it's not exactly forgetful after all. It's more like I'm missing something. Something is happening in these woods, or maybe something is being transmitted to me from elsewhere, and I'm missing it. It's like there's a wave in the air intended for me, but I can't quite tune the radio right. It can only muster an unpleasant sensation in my frontal lobe.

I bring my hands to my forehead. My head hurts, and something about all of this makes me feel physically nauseous. My stomach tightens up like it wants to blow, and I get these queasy little muscle shimmies in my obliques, so I guess they want to chip in and do their part in the heaving process. The combination is overwhelming.

But instead of a vomity spray, laughter spews forth from my lips.

Now, none of this is funny, of course. Just the opposite, really. Feeling lost and sick in a darkening forest with an overwhelming sense that I'm missing something of vital importance? It's all so serious that it feels inappropriate to laugh.

Well, I guess the cargo shorts are a little funny, at least.

Anyway, I feel like a crazy person, hunched over in the middle of the woods, laughing like a fool. I can see the rounded tops of my cheeks tinted the hue of pink lemonade at the bottom of my field of vision. My eyes are opened too wide, and they have this sting to them like I can almost feel an electric current flowing through there. The laughter keeps spilling out of me oblivious to all of these unpleasant feelings, and the dread in my gut just grows and grows.

See, I want to stop laughing, but I can't. Any notion of self control careens away from me with the rest of my thoughts, jumbling themselves up into blasts of word salad that fire every time I try to collect my wits.

Am I hallucinating?

Wait.

I stop laughing.

I definitely heard something this time.

A voice.

I wonder if this is what it's like when you start hearing voices?

I suck in a breath all loud like a baby that finally stopped crying, and I can hear my heartbeat thrumming in my ears.

I realize that I'm in a karate stance, which is weird because I don't know any martial arts stuff at all. I guess I watched The Karate Kid, Part II a lot at the babysitter's house when I was a kid. I might have picked up some shit.

Trying to think of any signature moves in there that I could unleash if necessary… I remember there were definitely bonsai trees which seemed pretty temperamental. You had to take care of them just right or Mr. Miyagi would go apeshit. I guess I don't know if that knowledge will be very helpful here.

The voice comes in more clearly, but I can only make out every fourth word or so. The rest sounds all smeared and watery like when you can sort of hear the TV while you sleep on the couch.

"apologize… making… like this… didn't… work… hear me?... Hello?"

It's a girl's voice. It doesn't sound familiar.

I ease out of my karate stance and squint my eyes. My brain starts tumbling all of the pieces of information around. I get that feeling like I got back in high school, when my brain would switch over to autopilot while I did 25 algebra problems in a row for homework. I think maybe I'm about to realize something.

The voice drones on, mostly sounding like Charlie Brown's teacher, and I swivel my head to look at the woods around me. It's all so green. Almost too green, like the saturation is turned up a little. It reminds me of the grass field I vomited in the other day.

Oh yeah. That's it. This isn't a normal dream. I'm there. I'm in the other world.

This raises more questions, of course… How did I get here? I've never come through via sleep. Only seizures, drunkenness, and whatever happened to me in the bottom of the well. (Death, I think, though I haven't ruled out drugs.)

Also, if this is the other world, then the voice is really happening. It's not just something I'm dreaming. So who it is becomes relevant. Plus, where the hell is it coming from?

It definitely sounds weirdly detached and distorted, almost like it's being broadcast over a PA. I try to decide if it's literally in the air around me or in my head. It's hard to say for sure, but I think the latter seems more right. So what the hell does that mean?

"there?... hear me?"

"I can hear you," I say. "Kind of."

There's a pause.

"… s'good… think…. work."

"I can't understand," I say. "Who are you?"

The voice gurgles 3 syllables of gibberish and stops.

"What?" I say.

"Amity."

It takes a long, slow motion moment to sink in. I rub my

eyes like that could help clear things up. I've seen her. I've read her words. In many ways I feel like I know her, but I've never heard her voice.

Until now, I guess.

"How?" I say.

"brought... here... concentrating... focusing."

She sounds stronger than I imagined, like a girl that wouldn't hesitate to get right in someone's face if she felt it necessary. Not bitchy, though. Just strong. When I was a kid, that was the kind of girlfriend I wanted. A fearless girl. A violent one.

"Where are you?" I say.

"Out... forest... you?"

"I'm in the woods, too," I say.

I try to think of a way I can find her. I run forward, doing swim moves with my arms to help me move between branches. Once I've made it a hundred feet or two, I stop and try to decide if the droning voice sounds any closer or farther, but I can't tell. I don't know if it'd make sense. It's like it's being broadcast somehow, so I don't think it'd get louder as I got closer, maybe.

Shit.

Here we are again. Another opportunity to figure some of this stuff out that's maddeningly close and still out of reach entirely.

"I don't know what to do," I say.

She babbles more words I can't understand. I realize that this isn't that much different than many of the conversations I have with people in a certain way. We can't actually communicate. I can transmit my ideas, but I get nothing back but meaningless noise. Or at least that's how it feels.

I sit down, and ferns reach over to tickle my calves. Stupid cargo shorts.

I don't know what to do. I wipe my fingers across my brow, and my hands feel all rough.

Shit.

Someone tell me what's going on. Someone tell me what to do.

Amity gibbers out more and more nothing. Or maybe it's something, but I can't understand it.

The sky blushes around me, going red like the sun is setting. As I remember that there's no sun out here that I've seen, the red glow washes out all of the green and overtakes me. I watch it all disappear.

CHAPTER 7

When I wake the next morning, my eyes still have that hallucinogenic sting, and I feel a similar, almost sizzling, sensation in my skull about three inches back from the center of my forehead. I sit up, and the ache of tiredness unfolds in the lines on my face and the curve in my upper back where my shoulders stoop. It doesn't feel like I got much rest.

Then again, the woods, the voice – it all feels so far away now. Argh. Is it possible it was just a dream? I guess. I mean, I guess it's possible.

Damn it. Constantly trying to decide what's real and what's not? Starting to get old. Sure, it's a barrel of laughs at first, but…

I stand and pull my shoulders back to stretch, and some tendon or cartilage or something seems to give just under my sternum. My torso quakes, and then there's sharp pain.

The words "ruptured it" pop into my head. Goddamn it! Hopefully I didn't actually rupture anything, but one of those little crab forks stabs me in the chest every time I take a breath now. So that's good.

I shuffle into the bathroom and make eye contact with my grimacing reflection for a split second before I rip open the medicine cabinet. (Note to self: Don't grimace. Ever. You look like Scut Farcus when you do it, and nobody thinks you're cool.

I'm sorry.)

I dig through Glenn's pill bottles. There are a lot, and let's be honest. Probably at least some of these pills have something to do with pissing constantly. From what I understand based on watching the commercials during Jeopardy, all old people turn into weird, leaky piss machines that need some combination of medication and/or diapers just to make it through the day. So there's something else to look forward to.

I finally find the ibuprofen, pop open the bottle, and wash a couple down with a handful of water from the sink. For some reason ibuprofen is the medicine that works for me. I know other people that like all that Aleve and shit, but not me. Ibuprofen gets rid of headaches and sore muscles and even heartburn pain for me. I think if a doctor told me I had ebola, I'd try two ibuprofen. Just in case.

I hunch as I walk out to the kitchen. It seems to hurt less if I keep my chest a little concave, though I probably look like Igor about to go off about Abby Normal's brain.

"Morning," Glenn says.

He sticks his lips out as he takes in my Quasimodo gait, and it looks like his mustache is reaching out to touch his nostrils.

"What's with the silly walk?"

"Well, I ruptured it," I say.

He wiggles his nose and lips and for a split second his mustache is in his nose. I imagine it feels like sticking a Brillo pad into your snout.

"What?" he says.

"I don't know," I say. "I stretched this morning and something popped in there or something."

I rotate my hand over the ruptured sternum area.

"Felt like a rubber band snapping or something."

For a second I picture my insides like the engine of a car: belts coiling around wheels, pistons pumping, spark plugs sparking.

Glenn seems distracted, though. He peels open a foil sleeve and puts some Pop Tarts into the toaster oven.

Wait. Pop Tarts? Aren't we supposed to have some gourmet breakfast? Something isn't right here.

When he goes to microwave two mugs of leftover coffee from last night, I put my foot down.

"What the hell?" I say, and then the crab fork pierces my heart pretty good, so I hunch more.

"What?" he says.

"Are you feeling OK?" I say.

He pauses with the microwave door open, the wedge of light from within illuminating the, "I heart fishing," coffee cup in his hand.

"Oh. Yeah, I don't know. Weird dream, I guess," he says.

A dream.

A weird dream.

And the world goes into slow motion. A crowd bolts upright into a standing ovation, the applause crashing everywhere. Fireworks burst in a night sky. All of the dogs for blocks yip and howl at each other like there's a full moon.

I want to throw back my head in ridiculous, Amadeus style laughter, but the crab fork would make me pay dearly, so I let out a single, "Ha!"

Glenn glares at me. I realize he was privy to neither the fireworks nor the ovation since they were imaginary. Fair enough.

"Let me guess," I say. "You dreamed of the woods."

He just looks at me, his mouth partially agape, and then the microwave beeps.

"Amity," he says. "Did you… Could you hear her?"

I nod.

"I couldn't make out most of what she was saying."

"Me neither."

The toaster oven ring-a-dings, and Glenn plops the Pop Tarts on a plate, which he holds toward me. I take one and bite it. Hard to tell if it's cherry or strawberry.

I never thought about how British the name Pop Tart sounds until just now. As a breakfast item, it's not too bad, but the edge parts are weirdly dry. It takes some conscious effort to power the crusty bits down my gullet so I can talk, and they scrape on the way down.

"So if it happened to both of us," I say, my voice a touch hoarse. "It was really her, right? She was really talking to us."

Glenn chews, swallows, thinks it over.

"I'd think so," he says.

He sets his Pop Tart on the plate and gets the coffee out of the microwave, placing one in front of himself and sliding the other my direction. I take a sip. It's pretty good for being a day old. I think it makes the Pop Tart seem better, too.

"Thinking back, she seemed to be asking if it worked at first," he says. "And asking if I was there."

"Yeah," I say. "That might be what she said to me, too."

He nibbles at the dry crust and washes it down with coffee.

"Makes me think she did it on purpose," he says. "I mean, that she somehow pulled us there."

"Could be," I say.

"She's been out there a long time. I guess she could have learned more than a few tricks by now."

"You spent some time with her, right?" I say. "What is she doing out there?"

"What do you mean?"

"I mean, why doesn't she go to the tree or something like that to get out of there?" I say. "She's been in the other world for like eight months or something in our time."

"Well, there could be a lot of reasons," Glenn says. "You've been there. It gets weird. You're not necessarily thinking clearly the whole time, and it's not intuitive to find your way around."

His eyes look all shifty for a second. He takes a slug of coffee before he finishes his thought.

"Anyway, I'm not sure that she wants to come back."

I run this sentence back and forth a few times in my head to try to make sense of it.

"You're not sure?" I say. "What does that mean?"

"Well, she said she doesn't want to come back. She told me that."

What the shit! Ever since the seizures started, nothing has made any sense. And yet I am somehow not surprised. Why shouldn't our mission be rooted in nonsense like every other goddamn thing?

I try to picture Amity wandering around, crossing deserts and trekking through woods. It's an odd choice to stay out there. In a way I can understand it, but…

"So all of this effort is to save someone that doesn't want to be saved?" I say.

Glenn curls his fingers into his mustache like he's thinking about trying to claw it off, but instead he releases his mustache claw grip and slams the heel of his hand on the countertop.

"She can't just stay out there, Grobnagger," he says. "That's no life."

I think this over. I think maybe it's all no life – no matter what you do – at least if you think about it hard enough, but I don't tell Glenn this.

"I guess if she was trying to contact us, there's still a reason to find her," I say. "Even if she doesn't want to leave."

"Yeah," Glenn says. "Yeah, there you go. See? I knew you'd get it."

I eat the last of my Pop Tart and wash down the grainy bits with lukewarm coffee.

"So we're going to find a way to go back and get Amity, yeah?" I say. "Maybe now would be a good time for you to tell me what happened to you before. With your foot and everything."

He takes a deep breath.

"You're probably right," he says.

He rinses out his coffee cup, hesitates a moment as if deciding whether or not to refill it, and takes a seat at the snack bar.

CHAPTER 8

"When I try to remember it," he says, and then he stops himself to gather his thoughts. "You ever watch a movie you know you've seen before, but you somehow can't remember how it ends? You might remember a few key moments, but you can't quite pin down where it's going even though you've already seen the damn thing? And that somehow makes you more enthralled to keep watching to find out? Like it's almost more perplexing to have seen it and forgotten?"

"Yeah, I think so," I say.

"Well, thinking back on what happened there is kind of like that," he says. "I remember a lot of it, maybe most of it, I think, but I can't quite put the sequences together in an order that makes sense."

He stands, refills his mug and shoves it in the microwave.

"I can't stop thinking about it, trying to make it all fit together," he says. "You want more coffee?"

"Well, yeah," I say. I push the mug across the counter toward him.

"I remember finding Amity in a cornfield," he says.

"OK, so who do you think is planting corn over there?"

"How should I know?" he says. "Anyway, thinking about it now, I feel like I was trying to get away from something, but I'm not sure. I was running through this field, crashing through row after row of corn, and I saw something out of the corner of my eye. I stopped dead on the spot and looked, and there she was, just sitting Indian style in the middle of a field."

I picture her sitting in the field, and in my imagination she is meditating.

"I just realized that sitting Indian style means like Hindu meditation type sitting," I say. "For some reason I always thought of Native American style 'Indians' before. Didn't really get it."

Glenn looks at me for a long time.

"First of all, you're racist," he says.

"What? How is that racist?" I say. "I'm not racist!"

He grunts, thinks it over.

"Fine. Whatever," he says. "I guess you're not necessarily racist."

He sips his coffee before he goes on:

"But you are like a regular Sherlock Holmes when you wield those powers of deduction like that."

"Sorry for not understanding the origin of an idiom that was probably imprinted into my vocabulary when I was three years old."

"Can I finish my story now, or are you going to defend your idiocy at some length?"

"Finish it."

"Perfect," he says, a puff of breath exiting his nostrils just after that reminds me of a pouting Boston Terrier. "Like I said, I found Amity. She was a little non-responsive at first, just staring off into space. I probably said seven or eight different sentences to her and tried to squat and hug her, but she didn't move. It wasn't until I pulled her wrists to help her stand up that she kind of came around."

"Do you think she really was meditating?" I say. "Like in a trance or something?"

"It's possible," he says, tilting his head. His eyes flick back and forth a few times. "She was definitely hiding things from me during our time together."

"What do you mean?"

"I don't know," he says. "More than once, I got the sense that she knew things. Her own version of my few parlor tricks, right? But she never wanted to talk about what all she had seen or done there. And she often wandered off on her own. I'd find her sitting by herself. And then later, after she told me she didn't want to leave, she wouldn't explain herself. She reverted to blank stare mode."

His index finger grinds at the corner of his mouth like there might be some Pop Tart stuck there.

"She didn't quite seem like herself, at least not all the way," he says. "But she was so peaceful that I didn't think much of it, you know?"

"How long were you together?" I say.

He buries his forehead in his palms.

"I have no idea. Time is fucked there, Grobnagger. You know that. There's no day and night there, so it becomes impossible to keep track of time. I mean, there are places where it's night, but..."

He trails off, and we sit in the quiet for a while.

"We walked a long way," he says. "Walked across a stretch of flat land for what must have been days, grass plains mostly. But eventually that gave way to a more arid climate. Still flat, but all dried-out red Earth with cracks etched everywhere into it, yeah? Looked like the surface of Mars or some goddamn thing."

"Where were you going?" I say.

"Hell if I know. Thing is, I felt like I was headed for something. I felt like a purpose drove my actions. I just don't know what that purpose was. I can't even say if I knew what it was at the time and don't remember or if I never knew. That make any sense?"

"Yeah," I say. "I guess I felt kind of like that when I was there."

"So the terrain got hillier and rockier with a few taller trees here and there. Pines or maybe firs, I guess. And then it got dark. Like I was saying earlier, there are places there where it's always night with the only light coming from the moon. The night seemed awesome in a way. Having gone so long without it, I really wanted to get a night's sleep out there. You don't really get tired there. I think you take breaks and sit down solely out of habit, you know? Out of a fondness for it, or the nostalgia factor of doing it or something like that."

"Yeah," I say.

"We didn't have much to set up a camp with, but we started a fire."

"You started a fire? Rub two sticks together or what?"

"Nah, Amity had a lighter."

"A lighter? Did she take that over there, or find it or something?"

"Don't know. You really get hung up on the minutiae, Grobnags."

"Sorry. I just don't understand it."

Glenn shrugs.

"Anyway, we slept by the fire, yeah? There were no stars in the sky, but the moon hung up there so huge. Not quite full, but it seemed close. It was a weird sleep, for me at least. It was like as soon as I closed my eyes I was dreaming crazy stuff. I was lost. My brain coughed out gibberish over and over, and all of the scenery about me kept morphing so I was repeatedly shifted into new locations. Like I was moving from set to set on some studio lot. So I was lost in the woods, then lost in the frozen tundra, then lost in the desert, then lost in the jungle. Just nonsense, you know? But aggressive nonsense, somehow. Like my mind was yelling it at me the whole time."

He scrapes his thumbnail on the handle of his mug, and it shrieks a little.

"When I woke up, Amity was gone. I really didn't think much of it at first. Like I told you, she'd wandered off before. I always found her sitting nearby, gazing out into the distance."

He turned to look out the window over the sink. I don't know if he was pantomiming Amity staring out into nothing or doing so himself.

"I kicked sand over where we set up the fire and called out for her a few times, started looking around for her. But she was gone. I knew almost as soon as I started looking that I wasn't going to find her."

"I thought you said you got trapped," I say. "No wait. 'Captured.' That's what you said."

"Will you let me finish?" he says.

"Yeah, sorry."

"I walked in the dark a while. I was in a valley with rock walls on either side of me, so I just followed the path dictated by the terrain. Soon I could hear the faint rumble of thunder, which seemed to be getting closer and closer as I advanced.

"Somehow I wasn't too upset about being separated from Amity. I mean, I missed her already, but out there it just feels like everything that happens makes sense. You feel like it's all for a reason. Or I do, anyway.

"The sky turned gray a little, like that half light before dawn. Now the thunder was really rumbling all over. I came around a bend, and I saw a tower on the cliff to my left. I could really only see the silhouette of it. Looked like a spire off of a castle or something but on its own.

"And just as I stopped walking to gaze up at it, lightning flashed. Everything lit up for a fragment of time, and the bolt of light split the sky and struck the tower. The thunder hit immediately and shook the Earth.

"The rumble rolled down the canyon, and the ground vibrated beneath my feet, and hunks of rock rattled and scraped against each other all around me. And as the flash of light died out, I saw fire in its place. Flames licked out from the roof, and it was like a delayed reaction, like watching a tree get chopped down when the top of the tower crumbled away a moment later.

"Blocks of stone separated from the wall and fell in all directions. The roof spire tilted out of place and slid off of the structure, capsizing like a ship as it hit the open air and plummeted. And the fire was everywhere now, raining down with the falling pieces, streaks of orange snaking across the sky.

"And that's when I saw the bodies. Two of them. They looked like rag dolls twisting in the air, but I knew they weren't. I knew they were people. I could mostly see them in silhouette, but I could tell that one wore a dress and one wore pants, so I figured it to be a man and woman. With everything moving at once, I didn't see where they fell from exactly – the tower, I guess - but it seemed like they were in the air forever. I guess time got slow on me just then. I don't know.

"I got that feeling, that acid taste you get in the back of your throat, when you realize that you are in the middle of this profound moment, yeah? Then after it happens, everything can be divided into before and after this moment. Forever. But right now you're in it. And you're powerless to affect it at all.

"And then the bodies descended out of view. The sky throbbed with light when the lightning struck again. I realized that I'd been holding my breath for some time, and when I inhaled, my chest spasmed a couple of times.

"I ran to where it seemed like the bodies fell, scrabbling up a part of the cliff face that wasn't as steep. As I got close I could hear the fire crackling. I could smell the burned smell all around me. I assumed it was coming from the top of the tower, but then I saw that there was another fire on the ground. It looked like it was contained – like someone had a bonfire going unrelated to all of this stuff going on.

"Anyway, I stepped up onto the plateau where the tower stood, and the girl's body was on the ground maybe 30 feet in front of me. I knew it couldn't be Amity, but that's all I could think as I got closer. Her face was turned away so I couldn't see much.

"And then something heavy thumped me on the back of the skull, and I was out."

He looks at me, and I realize I haven't moved in a long time. I've been sucked into this story, the images dancing in my head. I figure he's about to go on, but he just keeps on looking at me. I don't know what to do, so I clear my throat even though it's not necessary at all.

He exhales through his nostrils in a way that reminds me of a dog again, but a more aggressive breed this time. Not sure why he's staring me down like this. Glenn is an intense dude sometimes.

"When I woke, I was standing. My arms were bound, and I was blindfolded. I could still smell the ash in the air, so I knew the tower was near. I leaned a little to my right and felt something metal and sharp there against my leg. I had this sense that I was in a trap of some kind.

"I took a deep breath and waited. I listened. I couldn't hear much, though, except for fire crackling somewhere in the distance. I tried to reason out who would have done this to me or what the hell was going on, but I knew there was no way to make sense of it. This negativity just welled up in me - this total belief that I was trapped. Powerless.

"It's weird how if you believe you're defeated, you are. I was so certain that I had no control that it became real. And the only option I could see was flinging my body into the walls around me. Not even a real attempt at an escape, you know? Just an expression of despair."

He paws at his jaw a moment as he continues.

"So after that long moment of hesitation I hurled myself toward the trap, thrashing and kicking into that sharpness I felt to my right. Well, I fell over immediately. I guess it wasn't much of a trap after all. With my arms roped to my sides, I couldn't catch myself and just flopped teeth first onto the ground.

"Landing pulled the blindfold loose enough for me to see

some. First, I saw the tower not far off. Looking back, I'd been standing in a row of swords. There was nothing in front of me or behind me that whole time – just blades jammed into the ground to my left and right - but I threw myself directly into the swords like a goddamn fool. When I looked down at my arms, I saw how loose the bonds were. I pulled free with almost no effort."

He winces.

"I almost laughed at how ridiculous it all was. And then I felt this little prick of pain in my foot. My gaze swung over just in time to see the blood start gushing out. I guess one of the blades got me pretty good cause the front half of my foot was dangling. I think I was in shock or something cause it didn't hurt as bad as it should. I crawled to the bonfire and jammed my foot in to cauterize the wound. "

We're silent for a moment.

"Can you bleed to death there?" I say. "I mean, when that hooded man killed me I just came back here. No damage."

"I think it's different when you do what I did," he says. "I crossed over by walking into the light. Physically crossed over, you know? It's not the same as what happened to you. I mean, hell, just look at my foot. Seems pretty permanent to me."

"Yeah. Jesus. Good point, dude."

I can't help but look at his foot, and though it's covered by a slipper, I can see that stump in my mind.

"So wait," I say. "What about that belly wound? You were gut shot and healed yourself."

He squints.

"It's not exactly…"

His words trail off into a smile.

"Ah. But that would be telling," he says. "Anyhow, I'm more concerned with how we'll get back there to find Amity. Like we just talked about, taking the physical route has its risks."

We're quiet for a moment.

"I know what we can do," I say.

CHAPTER 9

The brown fluid glugs out of the bottle and splashes into the tumbler. For some reason the words "hair of the dog" pop into my head, though they don't apply here in any way. It's like the sight and smell and taste of alcohol conjure a bunch of booze jargon whether it applies or not.

Done pouring, Glenn sets the bottle down on the counter. With his hand out of the way, I get a better look at the red wax coating the neck of the bottle. A few streaks lay frozen in place where they ran down onto the body. They look like red rain on a windshield, like the wipers will come along any second to erase them. I take my glass as Glenn chugs from his.

The words "Kentucky Bourbon" play in my mind as I drink. I guess I read them on the bottle. It tastes exactly like every other bourbon I've ever had. I don't really understand the displays of state pride in these matters, but whatever.

To me, it tastes like something a doctor would give me in some dire situation. He'd grit his teeth and say, "This is our last hope," and hand me a glass of this.

I'm not sick, but I drink the medicine anyway. Of course, I would've been just as happy to mix this with a delicious cola or something, but Glenn kept going on and on about how smooth this bourbon is. He's a boastful man when it comes to his drinks, a beverage braggart. So the longer he goes on, the harder it gets to say, "It all tastes like fermented garbage water to me, dude. Let's mix it with some barrel aged Sam's Choice Cola for its robust flavor, premium carbonation, and syrupy mouth feel."

I drink again. My field of vision narrows to the tunnel leading to the bottom of the cup. I watch the ice cubes slosh around and clink into each other as the fluid ripples. Pretty sure Glenn said, "on the rocks," three times while he was getting the glasses around. Three times! Unreal.

"So what if this works for you and not for me?" he says.

I pull myself out of the tunnel, look at him, and blink. I give my brain a beat to try to catch the meaning, but I still don't get it.

"What?" I say.

"Well, I've had a few drinks plenty of times and never… crossed over or whatever," he says. "What if this is just happening to you?"

"Oh," I say. "Yeah, I don't know."

Glenn huffs. I drink. When I come up for air, he's still glaring at me.

"What do you want from me? I'm neither an expert on the rules of going to that place nor a drink-ologist," I say.

"Seems like you've got me on another of your goose chases," he says.

"Another? When did we chase geese before at my behest?"

He grumbles, but no discernible words come out before he cuts himself off with a slug of whiskey. I swear, Glenn is getting weirder by the day.

We drink a while, and we don't say much. The glasses rise and fall and clang on the counter. The ice cubes swirl and bash against the glass barriers encasing them. My fingers chill from holding the cup, but warmth rolls up and down the rest of me.

The liquor gurgles as it hits the back of my throat and falls into my stomach in a way that seems rough. Undignified. Glenn seems to be able to pull this off with more composure, but I at least match him drink for drink. It's not a total loss.

I can sort of sense the effects of the booze coming upon me. Weirdly, though it's a depressant, it seems to energize me. My eyes open a little wider, and I feel awake. My thoughts come out of the clouds and sharpen into focus. They start to wander.

And somehow the dilemma before me grows clear. If I've learned anything in my recent travels, it's that I don't think the physical realm can fulfill me… or maybe anyone. And yet I don't necessarily believe in anything beyond what's here and now. Even if I've had what felt like glimpses of something else, I don't know what they mean or what they really are.

So I'm left with a choice: I can try to accept that all that truly exists is the physical world and try to cope with the anxiety and dread that piles upon my existence since I know it can't satisfy me. Or I can choose to try to believe something unbelievable, which would be a lifelong effort and perhaps equally anxiety inducing.

I don't know. There may only be one thing I am sure of. Whichever path I choose, I will be disappointed.

Glenn clears his throat, and my mind snaps once more to my immediate surroundings. I'm drunk now. My face is warm.

Glenn's cheeks are flushed all red, and he looks a bit shiny, so I believe he's drunk as well. He keeps licking his lips.

"Well," he says.

That's it. He doesn't go on. He stares out at nothing.

My eyes trace down the tendrils of stem dangling from the plant hung over the sink. They seem so motionless. Even though we're inside, it feels like a breeze should pick up and swing them around or something.

I figure Glenn will eventually expound upon his aborted thought. Nope. He drinks. I hate to feel left out, so I follow suit.

We sit in the quiet. It's not unpleasant. It's tired in a way, but everything holds still better than usual. The world fails to overwhelm me the way it sometimes does. It doesn't squirm and twist around me anymore. It just lies there, barely breathing, perhaps asleep.

Apart from the hum of the fluorescent bulb above, it might be peaceful, even. I'm not quite sure.

That burst of alcohol fueled energy erodes with a quickness, and the depressant qualities begin to take hold. I can feel it in my eyelids first. It's not a heaviness so much as a tightness - the sense that the corners of my eyes can't open all the way, even if I stretch them.

And then sounds feel a little farther away. I can still hear everything, but the noises transpire way outside of me now, somehow dampened. It doesn't get to me the same way. It's like someone turned up the plate reverb and now everything is sitting further back in the mix, all wet and smooth. Except for my thoughts, that is. They're dry and bright and right up front.

Even so, the calm cranks up. It's that sad calm that I've been feeling a lot lately, the kind that saps the energy out of everything, but now it's intensified.

And I'm stuck inside myself, and I can feel the wind suck in and out of me and my chest puff up and collapse, and the air scrapes over the back of my throat, and the dry forms cracks in my lips, and my tongue is all coarse like it belongs in some lizard's mouth. The distance between me and everything else just grows and grows.

But I don't mind, really. I guess that's the benefit of falling into this particular hole. It seems like it's all just as well. What's the difference, yeah?

Yeah.

Yeah.

So what?

I blink a few times like that might change all of this somehow. It doesn't. It just reinforces how odd my eyelids feel and how dry my eyes are. I picture the whites webbed with the red of blood vessels.

I drink some more. And some more again.

And it occurs to me that before long I'll be too fucked to move, which is also just as well. There's nowhere to go anyway. There's nothing to tell you. There's no one to tell.

There's nothing.

Nothing but the minutes and hours and days getting sucked down the drain.

Glenn jerks forward in his chair, forcing me to remember that he's still there. I realize he put on aviator sunglasses at some point, and they make him look a lot like a mustached John Goodman. He gasps, and his feet snap to shoulder width. It's somewhat of a defensive position, as though he's bracing to lose his balance, which generally is difficult to do while sitting in a chair but not impossible.

"It's happening," he says.

CHAPTER 10

"It's happening," Glenn says again.

His voice is quiet with some grit to it, so it sounds pretty important. Even so, I try to think of what he must be referring to and can't. I look around the room. The only thing happening is nothing.

"Oh, shit," he says and brings his fist to his mouth. "You were right."

My lips purse to ask what the hell he is talking about, but I scan the room one more time first in case I somehow missed something. Everything looks to be conveying the same motionlessness as before. However, my eyes cross or something as they move over the far wall. There's a blur in that area that even squinting won't erase. I rub at my eyelids a second, but it's still there.

Wait.

It's not a blur. It's the other world, a smudged version of it, anyway.

"Do you see it?" he says, batting at my shoulder.

"Yeah. I see it," I say.

"Well, good," he says. "Good."

We sit and look at the blur for a moment, though whether or not we're seeing the same thing, I couldn't say.

I can't really tell what I'm looking at. It's all out of focus, but I think I see some trees.

"So what do we do now?" he says.

Good question. Damn. This guy is good.

"I don't know," I say.

I think about it a moment before I go on, and I rub the back of my fingers over my chapped lips.

"Maybe if we drank more we'd cross over all the way?" I say.

Glenn's eyebrows go up, and even through the aviators, I can see his eyes open up real wide for a second like he just saw Jacob Marley shaking some chains in his face. He turns toward me.

"Grobnagger," he says, his voice half gasping. "Yes! It's freaking brilliant, man. We will drink our way there."

I can't remember him saying the word "freaking" before, but it makes me laugh for some reason. When I look over, Glenn is laughing, too, and that makes me laugh harder, I guess in part because I doubt we're even laughing at the same thing.

Mid chuckle, he tips the bottle and more whiskey gurgles into our glasses. He doesn't stop pouring in time, and the overflow spills all over the counter. We both stop laughing as the flood of booze washes onto a pile of mail.

Glenn wheezes like a man that has just been shot.

"Oopsie," he says.

We laugh more. His mouth looks all juicy again, like a weird, wet John Goodman maw. This freaks me out, and I can't take my eyes off of the laughing hole in his face.

It's weird how gross it is to be alive in a way. Saliva and snot and mucus coming out every which way. The jagged bones in every mouth going ever darker yellow unless the owners pay people to smear bleach around in there. Breath wafting the stink from inside until the whole world smells like dried spit.

I don't know. Maybe I'm just drunk.

I drink again. I realize that it doesn't taste like anything anymore. It's just a stinging tingle draining down the tube to my stomach. This whole drinking process seems tedious at this point. It seems like there'd be a better way to ingest this, but then I guess that's probably what those high school kids were thinking a few towns over when they injected Jack Daniels into their veins and died.

I refocus on the wall across the room, and the blur is a touch less smudged looking. Translucent trees stand before me on a sparsely wooded hill. These images sort of look like they're being displayed on the wall by a projector with a bulb that's about to die, but it's at least a little brighter than it was before.

And the air I breathe feels and smells and tastes differently now. It's fresh and a little humid. The odors of outside and plant life and dirt enter my nostrils.

Glenn giggles, and looking his way, I see that he's slipped his sandals off to put his feet into the scraggle of grass and dead leaves that are becoming visible above the tiled floor. Even when it's half see-through like it is, the green is striking. Watching his toes wiggle, I remember how cold it felt to trudge through this stuff back when I moved through the mist toward the tree. I feel a weird tingle in my shoulder like I'm about to shiver, but I don't.

I lick my lips, but they're too dry to help at this point. It's like licking the Grand Canyon. Glenn keeps making noises I guess I would call cooing. He sounds like a cross-eyed baby that's trying to wrap his fat fingers around a block.

I drink a little and watch this fool swish his feet around in the grass. His mouth hangs ajar in a smile like one of those slack-jawed weirdos that can only grin with their uvula on full display. You'd think that quality would have been bred out of humanity by now.

Nope.

More like survival of the dimmest.

And as I watch the man dip his toes into the green, the fundamental difference between me and Glenn occurs to me by way of metaphor. Glenn lives his life like everything is music, and I live my life like everything is words.

Music is immediate. It never stops to think about itself. It lives in a moment, and for all it knows, each moment is infinite. It doesn't worry about whether or not this particular song will end. It doesn't examine itself or its existence. It doesn't reflect. It just is.

Words are always one step removed from the moment, though. They detach and describe the moment to themselves. They can only reflect.

So Glenn looks out at the world for what it is, but I look inside to try to make sense of the outside with words. He simply is, while I am reflections of reflections of reflections. I am layer upon layer of self awareness that never ends. I never stop thinking about myself. I am never immediate, never purely in the moment.

Always partially detached.

Always partially withdrawn.

I go back into my cup for a second, and when I come up for air, something is different. I stare at Glenn for a long moment before it hits me. He is now translucent as well. He's like a ghost kicking his feet in some grass. Something about his posture and jerky motions make me think of a toddler thrashing his legs in a kiddie pool, except it'd be a see-through, ghost toddler, I guess. Sounds like a terrible horror movie.

"Holy shit," I say.

Glenn does a double take. He rips off the aviators to look around.

"Cripes," he says.

Again, the word "cripes" seems funny just now. I laugh. I don't know. Perhaps it's this intoxication thing.

My eyes close as I chuckle, and out of the blue, Louise pops into my head. I remember sitting on the couch with her legs draped over my lap, watching TV. The heat emanated off of her. She was one of those perpetually warm people, like a broken radiator that you can never turn down. I'm the opposite. I'm always cold with icy fingers that make everyone recoil, but she made it go away. She warmed everything up.

And I remember that. I remember feeling safe and warm.

But I open my eyes, and now my nose is all cold, and I'm drunk as hell, and I'm laughing at nothing.

"Shit. I'm crossed over now," Glenn says. "So drink up, Grobs. We got shit to take care of."

I take the bottle straight to my face and guzzle the rest down. At least I'm good at one thing.

CHAPTER 11

The booze gurgles about in my gut and attacks my liver and works its way up to kill some more brain cells. It's all for a good cause, though. A damn good cause.

I watch a hazy Glenn tromp around the woods while I await my turn at the weirdness. His mouth hangs open still, a dumb smile gaping out at the other world as he moves around there. He walks through the kitchen wall during this process and makes his way up the hill, which is not as weird to watch as it probably sounds. I've seen it all before and shit.

Meanwhile, the alcohol seeps into my bloodstream and continues its creep up toward my head. I can't feel these particular bodily functions transpire. I merely feel the slow and steady escalation of my drunkenness. I'm getting to that point where I keep getting dumber and slower and sadder. Alcohol is a depressant after all. It's depressing itself on my brain bits and squeezing the serotonin and stuff out so all that's left is the sad juice.

But it's all good, yeah? Soon I'll be in another place, checking out some mystical woods and shit, staggering around with Glenn, possibly even hanging out with Amity. She seems cool as hell, too. I mean, who else would go out into that crazy place and try to live there? Who else would throw the whole world away to try to understand a place that can't be understood? I think that's pretty awesome somehow.

I mean, is it desperate? Of course it is. But we're all going to die, you know? We only have so long to try to do anything that means something to us. I think it's cool that she just goes for it. It's desperate, but the honest kind of desperate that makes sense. Some amount of urgency is a good thing, I say.

My eyes focus on Glenn in the distance as he leans against a tree at the top of the hill. After watching him a second, it occurs to me that he looks solid again. And so does the tree. I look around. The woods about me look opaque. It's the kitchen wall that I can see through now.

I stand and wobble a second, and there's a faint tingle in the backs of my knees. Taking a step forward, I realize how drunk I really am. My feet are dumb. My legs are dumber. My top half wants to flop about like a rag doll. My neck seems to lack interest in holding my head up. It goes through the motions, but you can tell its heart's not in it, so my skull lolls around as I walk.

My body is the worst.

"All right, Grobs," Glenn says. "Welcome over."

He removes his shoulder from the tree and stands with his arms folded across his chest. His legs are well past shoulder width apart, so he looks like he's standing like a super hero or something. I laugh. He laughs, too. Apparently, he doesn't really need a reason for laughter at this point. I guess the laughs come cheaply once you kill a significant enough portion of your mind. Good to know.

I follow a path beaten into the grass that leads up to where Glenn stands on the hilltop. As I ascend, I note that this hill is steeper than it looks from afar. With my motor skills diminished, it's a struggle to mount the damn thing. My head flops indifferently on my wet noodle neck. Glenn laughs more.

What fun, what fun. What a goddamn delight life is.

I kick and scratch and paw at the path to work my way up, but my eyes stay locked on Glenn's dumb head, bobbling atop his body in a fit of laughter. What a jolly motherfucker he turned out to be this afternoon, shaking like a bowlful of jelly and everything.

"Laugh it up," I say.

After I say it, I realize that I didn't speak the words so much as yell them as loud as my vocal cords could muster, my voice breaking up into that rasped out half yell, half scream thing. That vocal delivery always reminds me of some jungle predator about to kill something in a documentary.

"Whoa," Glenn says, dabbing his fingertips at his brow. "Chill, Grobnagger."

Chill?

Chill.

Unbelievable. He stopped laughing, which is something. Maybe I should be thankful that he didn't tell me to take a chill pill.

"I'll chill," I say.

Again, I don't realize the bitter sarcasm I'm employing until I hear the words coming out of my mouth. I feel like I never realize how angry I am until it's vomiting every which way.

Glenn doesn't say anything. He just looks at the ground.

I get to the top of the hill and return to a semi-upright posture, and Glenn turns so that we're standing just about shoulder to shoulder looking out over the other side of the hill. The trees seem to grow thicker from here until they turn to fully fledged woods a little ways on.

Up on high, the air seems brighter somehow. I don't know what that means exactly, but that's how it feels. Deal with it. I have a feeling that won't be the case up ahead. It seems darker up there somehow. I don't know. I might just be shitfaced.

"Now what?" I say.

Glenn scratches under his eye.

"I kind of figured we'd just follow this path," he says.

My eyes trace along the lines where the grass gives way to the dirt walkway under my feet.

"Makes sense," I say.

"Then let's roll," he says.

I follow him downhill. The slope on this side is more gradual, which is nice. The words "leisurely stroll" spring to mind. A little embarrassing, but I will try to remember to not tell anyone that this thought happened, so it should be fine.

I take in Glenn's sloppy gait, however, and I realize that there's nothing leisurely about this after all. He stumbles and bumbles, his legs seemingly drunker than the rest of him, and I guess I must be doing something similar. I look down at my legs, watch them jerk and buckle and sway over the terrain.

Yep.

What a pair of idiots we are.

We move into the woods before long, and tree roots pock the path with their gnarled bits poking up from the Earth. It's a matter of time before one of us trips, I'm certain.

Also, I was totally right. The air doesn't feel as bright down here. It's like a dark wind right in my face. Total bullshit.

"Air is dark," I say, not necessarily meaning to say this out loud.

"What?" Glenn says.

I repeat it all pissed off like he's an idiot.

"THE AIR," I say. "IS DARK."

He doesn't say anything, but I can see the faintest smile curl the corners of his lips, and yet again I can't tear my eyes away from that juicy, disgusting hole in his face he calls a mouth. Yeah, smile away, you dumb son of a bitch. Smile for miles and miles at what a delight it all is, you pussy motherfucker.

OK.

OK.

Wow. Calm down, Grobs.

I make a concerted effort to unclench my jaw, and I feel all the muscles all around my temples let go in unison. I take a deep breath. The pressure in my head dies down a little further.

Red heat pulses in my cheeks. I don't know anything about blood pressure numbers, but I bet right now the gauge would read, "1,000," over "Holy Shit!"

I close my eyes and take another deep breath. My toe kicks at a root, but it doesn't hit squarely enough to trip me. See? Not everything is awful.

Just almost everything.

Glenn steps on a stick, and the crunch and snap pulls me out of my head a little. I remember where we are and what we're doing. We're here to find Amity. She doesn't want to leave here probably, but we're going to talk to her anyhow if we can find her before the alcohol wears off.

Like I said before, it's a damn good cause.

Amity. She's an interesting girl, yeah? I remember reading her journal, and though I can't call most of the specifics to mind just now, I remember she was scared of a man. She was scared that he knew things. She was scared to even write down his name. That seems important, right?

"You think it was Farber?" I say.

I watch Glenn's eyes return from dazed to alert.

"What?" he says.

"I said 'Do you think it was Farber?'" I say.

"Huh?" he says. "What are you talking about?"

"Riston Farber," I say. "Stands about yay high. Shaved head. Hovers spoons like a goddamn champion. Possible murderer and returner from the dead."

"I know who Farber is," he says. "I don't know what the hell you're talking about."

Hm… Did I forget to explain something?

"Um…" I say. "Farber. Something about Farber. Oh, do you think he was the guy Amity was scared of? In her journal, I mean?"

Glenn scoffs.

"Amity would have no reason to be scared of Riston Farber," he says. "Trust me on that."

His soggy lips curl up again. He's such a smug bastard sometimes.

"You sound awfully sure, but you've been wrong about shit before. Seems to me that the guy came back from the dead," I say. "And he tried to assassinate me, for shit's sake. I wouldn't be so quick to take him all lightly."

"Thing is, he did neither of those things," he says. "He's all smoke and mirrors, Grobnagger. He ain't nothing to be scared of."

"That's bold talk for a guy with half of a foot," I say. "You know so much you got your toes lopped off. You were wrong then, and you're wrong now. Just think about that. Farber tried to kill me. I heard the glass break and saw the bullet holes in the door. How is that smoke and mirrors?"

It occurs to me that Glenn is no longer walking. I stop and turn back to him to find his face the color of hatred itself, which it turns out is a deep shade of red with just a hint of a purple hue in certain areas. His jowls quiver. His demon eyes lock onto mine, and I can feel them looking through me.

The aviators are gone. They cannot help me now.

"Farber didn't do that," he says, through gritted teeth. "He's a phony."

"How do you know? You act like you know it all, but you don't make any sense," I say. "I mean, if Farber didn't try to kill me, who did?"

His lip curls.

"I did it," he says. "It was a trick, just like one of Farber's bullshit illusions. I had to do it. I had to get you on board for finding Amity, so I made it look like…"

But I don't hear any more of the words coming out of that cock holster he calls a mouth. I just watch those dumbass lips flap in total fucking silence for another millisecond, and then I'm on him.

As my fists loop in a flurry of overhand rights and hooks that connect with his face and neck, some detached part of me is concerned. See, I don't remember deciding to do this. It is just happening. I'm just pummeling his face in without consciously saying, "Yeah, let's do that."

I guess for once I'm in the moment.

He's either too drunk or too dumb to get his hands up to block my combinations. To his credit, however, he does backpedal, bob and lean away from the punches enough to make some of the blows glance off. Probably some instinct leftover from his boxing days. Anyway, I'm throwing pretty wildly, so most swings don't connect with full force. Some are close enough, though.

I finally land a clean shot right on his mouth. The sound is part crack, part slap, part thud, and weirdly wet. He totters backward, leaning further and further back like a tree getting chopped down, but before I see him land, I'm down, too, in a flash.

Straight down. Flat on my face.

Did he somehow get me, and I never saw it coming? My mind races to replay the last few seconds.

No. He didn't hit me.

I tripped on a root.

The moment of confusion snaps me out of my murderous rage somewhat, anyway, and we both stay put, a good 7 or 10 feet apart from each other, breathing all heavy through open mouths like dogs in the summer.

After a while, I get my wind back and sit up. I swivel myself so my shoulders are pointed away from him, but I can still keep an eye on him out of the corner of my eye. I don't want to kill his face anymore, but I'd rather not look at him much just yet.

I am drunk. It is hard to think right. But apparently Glenn tricked me. He made me think someone was trying to kill me. He lied to me this whole time.

Shit. I don't know. This guy was supposed to be my friend, right? Maybe my only friend.

And by now the rage is long gone. Numb takes its place. It feels like someone pulled out the cork or something and all of my feelings are leaking out, like all of my nerves are severed now, like all the pieces are shattered.

"Why?" I say.

At first he remains quiet. I shoot a glance his way. His face is angled away from me, but I can see some bruises on his cheek starting to show. A thoughtful look occupies his features. He clears his throat and speaks:

"The human brain is a funny piece of work, Grobnagger," he says. "It fools itself time and again. It sees what it expects to see. It's sort of like how detectives get tunnel vision for one suspect or one story to explain a crime, and then they start seeing all the evidence in whatever way necessary to support their story, even if it's wrong. They see all the data from the angle of what they expected to see, and they ignore the pieces that don't seem to fit."

He bats a hand at his chest, I guess to brush some dust off.

"So if I plant the suggestion properly, you'll see the reality I want you to see, because subconsciously you already expect it."

I feel the air suck into my lungs and realize that I've held my breath during his speech.

I should say something. Right? It feels like I should definitely say something.

"So you hypnotized me or something?" I say.

"Something like that," he says. "Another of my parlor tricks. I can't make people do things they don't want to do or anything like that, but I can kind of flash them into a suggestible state for a few seconds, influence how they'll see certain things. When you were in a suggestible state, I told you you'd hear broken glass and see bullet holes. All I had to do was bust up the door pretty good and throw a rock through the window, and your brain saw what it expected to see."

"Dude. That seems like a dick move," I say.

No regard at all for my security deposit, but I guess that should surprise me least of all.

And still I feel nothing. Am I in shock? How has the anger abandoned me so rapidly? It seems like I should be more pissed than this. I turn it over a few times, feeling around my various brain parts to see if I'm pissed deep down somewhere, but I think I'm not. It's just a dead sensation inside. Nothing else.

It's weird.

Glenn plucks a tall piece of grass gone to seed from the ground and rubs the stem back and forth between his fingers, so it spins super fast. His eyes don't leave the twirling plant as he speaks.

"Do you actually regret getting involved, though?" he says. "Would you rather you sat alone in your cell all this time instead of helping me find my girl?"

For a second I think he means I'd somehow still be stuck in the cell in the basement of the League's empty hospital, but then I realize he means I'd be home alone in my apartment. I guess it was my cell in a lot of ways.

I was a single-celled creature.

I'm not anymore.

"I guess not," I say.

He turns his head so his eyes face toward the sky. I see now that his right eye is swollen just about shut. I guess I got him better than I thought. After he stares out there for what seems like a long time, he nods.

"I figured as much," he says.

We sit still a while. It's quiet.

And the air out here feels dark as hell.

CHAPTER 12

In time we gather ourselves and walk some more. Deeper in the woods, the shade grows a touch thicker, but there's little else of note to report.

No Amity. No nothing. Just a bullshit waste of time like every other damn thing.

We walk a little further on the path, and Glenn grunts something I can't understand. I realize quickly, however, that he didn't say any words. It was the sound of him heaving. I am able to deduce this when he leans over to puke all over some ferns.

I stand aside when the man "upchucks" as he would say. The real world is beginning to fade back in some for me. It's blurry and see-through, but I remember how it all faded out with great quickness last time.

Glenn rights himself, and I rejoin him.

"We might need to bring some booze with us or something next time," I say. "I mean, if we're going to make this work, we'll need to stay drunk longer."

Glenn smirks and vomits some more as if to point out what a bad idea that would be. I can't say that he puked on cue like that to make a point, but it sure worked out that way.

A well-timed barf is worth a thousand words.

So this plan kind of sucked as it turns out. The only things we accomplished were a one sided fist fight and a lot of idiocy. I guess I also learned that everything everyone says is a stupid lie.

Yay.

I realize too late that I'm standing a touch close to Glenn's spray this time. Some of his vomit spatters onto my shoes, and that's enough for me. I retch.

And what seems like gallons of regurgitated bourbon flows through the grass on this heavenly plane.

It is brown. Pretty foamy.

I lie on my bed, my own bed in my not so dangerous apartment. It seems darker here. The street lights shined into Glenn's living room so it felt like the world never really went all the way to sleep. My bedroom blocks out everything. The world might as well be dead outside of this room for all I can tell. Tonight I will sleep under cover of the black nothing for the first time in several weeks.

The drunk wore off some time ago, but I still feel dead on the inside. Ever since the fight, I've felt nothing. Maybe there's some sense of disappointment in there, but it's pretty faint, I think.

After the vomiting session, we gave up. We sat down in the brush and let the real world fade back in around us. Nobody said much. We came back around on someone's patio a couple blocks from Glenn's house.

It wasn't until we made our way back to Glenn's that I realized that I could just go home now. I could sleep in my own bed. Glenn didn't object. He didn't say anything. So I packed up my cat, and here we are. Mardy is asleep at the foot of the bed. I can't see him, but I can feel him there near my feet.

Apparently the maintenance man fixed the door and window and cleaned up all of the glass at some point. Will I get a bill for that? I'm not sure how this works.

Anyway, I am back to where I started. Alone in my cell. Will I find a good reason to leave this time or nah?

The alcohol made me feel much worse, at least. The lining of my stomach burns, and liquid keeps sloshing around in my gut, so that'll need to rocket out of my ass in a violent spray eventually. Good times.

Even with the physical ailments, on some level it feels pretty great to be back. It's better than I thought it'd be. Being apart from everyone fills me with such relief. I remember now why I always liked it so much. It smells like home. It feels like home. My body uncoils like all of my muscles can unclench for once, and I can let all of my weight rest on the bed, as limp as a wet towel. Never underestimate the pleasure of letting yourself be dead weight for a while. Being completely idle is underrated, I'd say.

And it occurs to me that maybe I haven't changed a bit despite all that's happened. Maybe I do prefer my cell to whatever the hell kind of freedom exists out there in the real world. Maybe I just want to be left alone, like I said all along.

Maybe.

Is this it? Is this what life is? Does no one ever really change or grow? Do we just spin in place for the duration of our lives and fool ourselves into believing that we're becoming something new every so often?

I roll over, and pull the blanket up over my shoulders so the edge rests on my top lip. My eyes open for a moment. I can see nothing in the dark, but I can feel the sting of the tired in them whenever my eyelids move.

It will feel so good just to turn everything all the way off for a while.

I'm in the woods again in my dreams. I'm on the move, too, moving away from the path. I don't know why, but this seems the way to go. I bend a branch of thorns out of my way and press forward into the foliage.

The green mess of plant life surrounds me. Leaves shake. Vines dangle, twisted around tree branches. The light spills out of the sky in the ever shifting gaps in the canopy of leaves above, the spots of illumination seeming to constantly slide across the ground as the air moves branches all about.

And I realize that Amity has been talking to me this whole time. I hear her voice, but I can't make sense of her words. It's different from before, though. I can hear everything she says. It just doesn't make sense. I can't even hold on to fragments of it in my mind long enough to repeat them. Her words just drift past like the wind.

I can tell she is talking to me. Just me. And she is not scared. I can read that much in her tone.

She is an interesting creature. Even though I can't understand what she's saying, I feel like I know her a little bit just hearing her voice. She is smart and quiet and focused in an unusual way. She talks slowly, seeming to choose her words carefully, though they mean nothing to me.

She seems like the kind of person that you'd lean toward whenever she started talking so you wouldn't miss anything. She seems like the kind of person that has no sense of how entertaining she is.

But I know more than her sound, I guess. I know she is out here by choice.

And I know she wants something more. More than McDonald's and sitcoms and video games and movies and money and sex and all of it, all of the things the physical world has to offer. She wants more than that.

And I like that.

CHAPTER 13

The sidewalk stretches out into the distance, and I stomp my way toward the horizon. Cars rumble past on the street, all of the engine sounds combining into a drone that makes it seem quiet to me somehow, quieter than actual silence. It's weird how that works. Constant noise always has a weird privacy to it, too, like no one could possibly notice me among all of this loudness.

My head throbs with that morning after headache. I took some ibuprofen, but so far the headache remains. It's not too bad, at least.

I cut through the grass as I round off the last corner, and there's Glenn's house up ahead. The red door stands out even from a distance. I smear my palms against my pant legs.

I've made this trek enough times now that it feels a little like going home in a lot of ways. So why am I nervous?

I hesitate at the door. I swallow in dry throat, and I can distinctly feel that lump shift, my Adam's apple or whatever. I knock.

I hear something thumping on the other side of the door, and then it opens. Glenn squints at me from the shade inside of the house. After a beat, I realize it's only one eye that's squinting. Is that weird? Seems like a weird face to make, right? Is that aggressive, or…? When he leans into the light, the purple shade of his bruises refreshes my memory.

That's right. I sort of bashed his face in a little bit. Perhaps that's why I was nervous on the way here. So he wasn't squinting at me. His eye is swollen into a perpetual squint for the time being.

"So you're knocking now?" he says.

I look at the concrete step underfoot.

"Well, yeah I guess so," I say.

"You don't have to do that, Grobnagger," he says. "We've traversed the astral plane together, buddy. That's a lasting bond. My casa is your casa. My Oreos are your Oreos. Apart from the Double Stufs, at least. Those are mine."

He steps out of the doorway, but I'm still hesitant to step through. I consider apologizing for the face pummeling, but I decide against it.

"Come on in," he says.

I pass through the doorway and stand in the foyer. It takes a second for my eyes to adjust to being out of direct sunlight. Glenn closes the door behind me.

"You hungry?" he says.

That's one of the things I like about Glenn. He always knows exactly what to say.

We sit at the snack bar, shoveling food into our mouth parts. It's a typical day at Glenn's house, really, except the sun seems extra bright. It slants in through the window, lighting a rectangle that stretches across the countertop and onto the wall. Somehow the light isn't harsh, though. It's pleasant.

Glenn takes a big bite of waffle and then talks with his mouth full.

"Thing is, drinking our way there is just as dangerous as going the direct route," he says. "In terms of the injuries being permanent, anyway. Just take a look at my face if you want an exhibit A on that assertion."

Awkward.

I start to reply:

"Yeah. Listen, I'm sorry about the-"

But Glenn interrupts:

"Forget it," he says. "It's nothing. We were drunk. Drunk folks resort to fisticuffs with some regularity as a rule. Way I see it, it could have been worse. I'm glad one of us didn't snap an ankle on a tree root or some goddamn thing. I say we're lucky. This won't cause us any problems. It will heal."

I consider suggesting he heal his face the way he healed that gut shot, but I don't want to push it. He's not pissed about me using his face as a piñata? Great. I'm not about to mess that up.

He opens the waffle iron and pops out a fresh waffle that's all golden brown. My mouth gets all wet just looking at a well caramelized piece of breakfast confection like that.

"You want another one?" he says.

I think about this for about one millionth of a second.

"Well, yeah," I say.

He smiles, and the skin around his puffy eye wrinkles all weird. His face looks like a half-finished special effects makeup from a boxing movie. I should remember to not tell him that, though.

He plops the waffle onto my plate and hands it back.

"You tried that birch syrup yet?" he says, pointing an elbow vaguely in the direction of the assortment of syrup bottles off to one side of the counter.

"Not yet," I say.

"It's kind of interesting," he says. "I mean, I wouldn't want it all the time, but it's a unique flavor. I'm glad I got it."

"I'll give it a go," I say.

The birch syrup looks pretty well indistinguishable from the various maple varieties here. I pop the top open and take a smell. It's somewhat subtle, but the aroma reminds me of caramel with just a touch of spice.

I'm intrigued.

I pour a decent amount into my syrup cup. (Glenn insists that you use less syrup and achieve superior flavor if you use a small syrup container and dip each bite rather than pouring the syrup directly onto the waffle or pancake or French toast ahead of time where much of it gets soaked up. As usual when it comes to matters of cuisine, he couldn't be more right. The man is a hero to me. I honestly can't stress that enough. He is a hero.)

I dip and taste. Perhaps interesting was the right word for it after all. It's like syrup with a faint chemical flavor mixed in. I don't know. It's pretty complex. Maybe I'd like it more if I had it a few times. Right now my palate is somewhat befuddled.

We eat some more, and the talking dies down for a time. The sunlight continues to shine with an abnormal brightness, so I watch Glenn's shadow stuff its face with shadow waffle on the wall. This is entertaining somehow.

It's weird how much something like the sun can affect us, though. It feels nice in here, even with a dull headache and hangover. Like here in the bright sunlight, it's just exciting to be alive. Maybe it's partially the endorphins from eating delicious food, but I'm thankful to be here.

"So what are we going to do?" Glenn says. "I mean, the drinking thing is out, obviously. You got any other ideas?"

"I've been thinking about that," I say. "You have any dreams last night?"

His eyes rotate toward the ceiling as he thinks about it.

"No," he says. "I had a hard time getting to sleep. Last time I looked at the clock it was after 4 am. I don't remember any dreams, though."

"Well, I had a dream," I say. "I was back in the woods, and I could hear Amity again."

Glenn gets all quiet. He licks his lips.

"She seemed safe," I say. "She wasn't scared."

"What did she say?" he says.

"I don't know," I say. "I couldn't make sense of it. I don't know if she was talking nonsense or my sleep brain couldn't concentrate on it properly, but I didn't understand her."

His lips press into each other and wiggle a few times, which kind of makes him look like a rodent, I think. I guess he's thinking about this.

"Well," he says. "I don't see how it helps us any more than it did last time."

With his eyes closed, he presses his index finger into his good eyelid and rubs at it.

"Do you?" he says.

"Maybe. I think she is pulling us over there," I say. "She can connect to us when we're sleeping somehow."

"That probably makes sense, but how do we use it?" he says.

"Well, when we're asleep, we can connect to her, but we're not in the right frame of mind to do anything with it, yeah?" I say. "What if it's like I said, and it has something to do with our brains being sort of asleep?"

"Could be," he says.

"Maybe there's a way to fight that," I say. "Like if you could drink a bunch of coffee and then fall asleep maybe. I mean, I know you don't want to mix an upper and a downer together necessarily. That messes with your heart, but maybe there's some way to do something like that safely, a way to fall asleep while our minds are fully alert."

Glenn stares out into the distance, his shoulders tilted away from me. He mumbles something half under his breath, so quiet I almost miss it entirely.

"What?" I say.

"Hypnosis," he says. "Sort of."

CHAPTER 14

The coffee machine gurgles, slurps, drips, suddenly wet with life. I watch the first few droplets develop into a trickle and then a full on stream of caffeinated dream juice. I'm still not totally clear on how we're going to drink this and then sleep. Either way, it smells tremendous.

Glenn dries his hands on a towel draped through a cabinet handle above the sink. He turns toward me, his eyes fixed on the pair of cardboard boxes on the countertop between us. He looks at them for a split second before he rips open one of the boxes and pulls the instruction leaflet out.

I already forget what these things are called, but they're some kind of sleep aid machines or something, whatever that might entail. I just followed Glenn around the sketchiest aisles at Meijer to find the damn things. I still don't know what they have to do with hypnosis either. I asked. Glenn just grunted unintelligible responses. He was in no mood to talk, I guess. His eyes looked all manic.

I rotate the open box so I can read the front. Apparently it's a "Nightwave Sleep Assistant Nw-102." Peeking inside, the device itself looks to be a black plastic box a little wider than a deck of cards. There's a decal on the front depicting a starry night and some kind of rolling hills or something. An LED bulb sits in a hole punched into the middle of the front of the box.

The bulb looks blue.

"How does this thing work?" I say, turning the box over in my hands.

Glenn holds up a finger at me, his nose hovers about two inches away from the instructions. His eyes flick from side to side like they're in fast forward as he reads.

"It's a pulsing light," he says, his voice all far away and distracted. "You lie in the dark with your eyes open and adjust your breathing to the time of the light. It slows down, and the light fading to dark fools your brain into thinking it's your eyelids drooping closed."

I think this over.

"That sounds pretty weird, dude," I say.

There's a pause before he answers, his eyeballs still flicking away.

"It's basically to help anxious people get to sleep without their swirl of thoughts and worries getting in the way," he says. "They just focus on the light and sort of trick their body into thinking they're already going into the physiological steps of sleep. I think there's a hypnotic quality to the process. I've always wanted to test them out, but I've never had a problem getting to sleep. Now we have the perfect reason to give them a shot."

"I guess that makes sense," I say. "So they actually work?"

"Not for everyone," he says. "It doesn't click for certain people. But for most people, it works great."

I nod even though I know he's not looking at me. I watch him read a while.

The coffee machine chokes out that stuttering, throaty sound as the brewing process comes to its end. I saw that Glenn opened a new bag. Some kind of extra dark roast. Based on the smell filling the room, it's going to be delicious. The smell is kind of earthy, and it reminds me of chocolate, too, somehow.

I look down at the little black box in my hand, spin it around a couple more times and hold it up.

"How did you even hear about these things?" I say.

He looks up at me for the first time in this conversation. For a full a second his eyes stare into mine with about as much blankness in them as a human expression can muster. Then he blinks a couple of times, and I can sort of see my question register.

"Oh, I saw Dr. Oz recommend them on TV," he says.

The blanket tumbles down onto my face, filling my field of vision with navy blue and white stripes.

"Hang on," I say.

I flop the edge of it around until I regain my grip, lifting the blanket back over my head once I do. I press it flat against the trim above the window while Glenn stretches duct tape along its edge and adheres the bedcover there. The roll of tape screeches as he pulls out a second layer of gummy gray stuff, tears it off, and swipes it into place with his fingertips, then presses the heel of his hand all along it to seal it up good.

I can't help but wonder what any passersby would think if they saw two grown men duct taping blankets over the guest bedroom windows in the middle of the day. Meth lab? Grow room for marijuana? Nope. Nothing weird like that. We're just astral projecting, dude. That's all.

"So the curtains wouldn't be enough, huh?" I say, stepping out of the way.

Glenn shakes his head as he tapes the left side of the blanket down in similar fashion. No need to double up on the tape here, though.

"Nah," he says. "It's too damn sunny today. We need it as dark as possible in here for these lights to work right. We need absolute blackness, if possible."

He turns to the other side and slaps some tape up there as well, and then we repeat the process on the other window with a tattered bedspread.

Even with the door open into the sunlit hallway, it's already pretty dim in here. I feel around until my fingers find my coffee mug sitting on the nightstand and take a sip.

This is coffee number three. The dark roast is delicious - everything I'd hoped it'd be, sure - but drinking three of these babies in rapid succession makes my throat feel all scorched and raw and gross somehow. And I know as I drink a couple more, the lining of my stomach is up next on the list of things to feel like they're on fire.

This is a small price to pay, however, for a chance to find Amity. I don't mean to complain. Glenn said we should try to finish two pots before we make our way toward the dream world, and I'm down to do my best toward achieving that goal.

I follow Glenn out into the hallway, the sudden snap to brightness overwhelming my pupils for a moment. We move toward the other end of the house.

"I kind of figured we'd each set up our own rooms," he says. "I thought about pulling my recliner into the guest room and using that – thing's like a damn nap machine – but after giving it some thought, I figure isolation to be best. No chance of distracting each other. No chance of my lights interfering with your lights or our breathing being in different rhythms and messing each other up or anything like that, you know?"

"Makes sense," I say.

He tosses me a quilted bedspread with pink and blue rectangles all over it, and we go to work taping blankets over the windows in Glenn's room as well. The process mostly resembles what we did in the guest room, but the windows in the master bedroom are quite a bit wider. On the first window, the tape holding the top left corner keeps pulling free before we can get the top right corner. It's kind of a bitch.

We anchor the tops of both blankets in time, though, and I chug a coffee while Glenn secures the sides.

Yep. I was right.

A small grease fire smolders in the center of my abdomen where my stomach used to be.

CHAPTER 15

I lie in the dark for a few seconds, my thumb tickling around the edges of the button on the plastic box clenched in my hand. For some reason, though I'm a little excited to see what Dr. Oz's sleep box is all about, I'm reluctant to actually press this thing. I don't know why.

The sheets warm against my body, going from cool to lukewarm to toasty as my thumb toys with the button. My heart beats too fast, though that's probably the caffeine. Shit. I'm trying to keep a positive attitude about all of this, but I'm pretty wired. This little box better pack some big time sleep magic or this isn't going to work.

To Glenn's credit, we did achieve total blackness in here. I pressed a rolled up towel along the crack at the bottom of the door as per his instructions, and that blocked out the last sliver of light from the hall. So that part, at least, works in my favor.

Maybe I need to get comfortable. Maybe that's the cause for hesitation.

I adjust in the bed, pulling the blanket down off of my shoulders so it only comes up to my sternum or so. Then I fix the sheet so it's still covering up to my neck. I wiggle my shoulder blades a little as though it might help me feel more settled in. When that doesn't change anything, I kick my feet a few times, like maybe I can work some of the restlessness out of my system that way. Kicking makes my legs feel warm, and the tingle of static electricity grips every leg hair and pulls it toward the sheet. That combination of warm and tingling is kind of pleasant somehow.

No excuses left, I depress the button.

The blue LED bulb lights up, vanquishing the dark. Blue light reflects off of the walls and reminds me that there are blankets duct taped over the windows, which I guess I already sort of forgot about in the dark.

I set the box on the nightstand, so the light will shine onto the ceiling above me. I lie back, already oddly conscious of my breathing patterns. After a few seconds, the blue pulsing begins. The light dims slowly down to nothing and brightens. Something about it does seem just like eyelids drooping closed, though mine are open. I adjust my breathing to match its rhythm – in as the light swells to full brightness, out as it fades to black.

So here I am, awake in the dark once more, doing weird breathing exercises. In retrospect, I'm really glad Glenn isn't in here breathing up the place from the comfort of his la-z-boy. It'd be too weird.

I focus on my breathing. The light shines and recedes and shines and recedes. A peace comes over me, a stillness. Just as my mind clears of all other thoughts but the light and the breathing, a rapid fire montage of Louise plays in my head – she hugs me in the doorway, she laughs with her mouth full of milkshake, she walks down the hall with no pants on, she smiles in the moonlight in the backseat of the Explorer - and I'm alert again.

Wide awake in the dark. My mind scatters like it often does, one memory leading to another and another. I sigh, and that knocks my breathing out of rhythm.

Damn it.

I blink a few times and stare into the blue light on the ceiling. I can't let frustration or anxiety derail this. Too much depends on our success. I focus again on my respiration. Slow inhale. Slow exhale.

I lie still and think of nothing. Time passes. I'm not sure how much. The machine has options for a 7 minute cycle or a 25 minute cycle. I went for the longer one, so I know it's been less than 25 minutes, I guess.

I am just vaguely aware of the heat crawling into my face, that sleepy anesthetic warmth that comes over you in slumber, but I don't let my mind dwell on the sensation.

I watch the blue illumination extinguished repeatedly. It is the only thing. I almost feel like I'm not even physically here. I am like part of the light.

I feel my eyelids sag a little, and I almost jerk to alertness to wake myself up out of habit, like when you realize that you're falling asleep in class, but I don't do it. I stay zoned out, somehow not all the way conscious of my physical being. My eyes drift into a half closed position, but it feels far away.

I let myself forget about them. I let my body go a little more, and it's like my consciousness moves out into the ever slowing pulse of light. It hovers there, a couple of feet above my chest.

I am weightless. I am all energy, only energy. And the things that have worried me and hurt me suddenly don't seem to matter, the things of the Earth suddenly seem insignificant. It's all so small. The meaning we put into Earthly things, be they objects or even flesh itself - it isn't real. It's all in our heads.

Energy.

Energy is all that is real.

I think of Earthly goods – sports cars and big screen TVs and ipads and such – and as they flash through my consciousness, I can feel them try to pull me back down, but they can't. They can't stick in my mind. I float on, and they all fall away.

And the light fades out and does not return, and I am in the black stillness, and all is quiet. I am calm. It feels like something is missing, something important, but I am not alarmed.

I move forward into the blackness. I lean into it and direct myself that way. It almost feels like something pulls me, but I think it's more like the energy flows the way I want.

I make steady progress for what feels like a long time. I wouldn't call the pace slow, but it's relaxed. I guess when you're moving in darkness, it's harder to gauge the speed anyway. It's more like just the sense of motion.

It gets weird, after a while, to just drift in empty space like this. I keep my calm, but there's an uneasiness out on the edge of things trying to creep into my energy. Maybe it's a coldness.

I stop.

A light. A tiny pin prick of light emerges before me, a dot of bluish white illumination disrupting the black nothing all around. It looks to be far, far in the distance. And somehow it is a relief to see it, though I didn't feel anxious before. I am happy to look upon it. I guess I like lights.

I walk toward it.

Huh?

Yes. I am not directing energy anymore, not flowing. I am walking now. In the dark, I can't see my feet kicking forward one after the other to take steps, but I can feel it.

If I'm walking, there must be something under my feet, too. It all feels a little far away, a little numb like I'm asleep, but I think I'm barefoot. And the floor feels smooth and cool, like painted concrete in a basement or garage.

I take a deep breath, and the air feels cool in my throat. Ah. I'm breathing now, too. I can't remember if I was before. I think not, but maybe I just wasn't conscious of it.

I walk toward the light for a long while, inching ever closer to the end of this black tunnel.

Wait.

How did I get here? How did I make my way to this tunnel? I try to think back. It feels like I can almost remember it somehow, but I can't. The best I can conjure is a flash and dim of blue light. It's not much to go on.

This lack of memory doesn't concern me greatly, though. It's a familiar feeling, to not remember how I arrived at a location. I think I probably have experienced this before.

I walk and walk, and the dot of light grows. It's hard to believe that it's not a ping-pong-ball-sized source of illumination as it appears. It's the hole far at the end of this dark tunnel. At least, that's what I think.

Now, it's not expanding to fill the horizon as quickly as I'd like, but it is getting bigger. I'm not complaining. Don't look a gift hole in the hole and what not.

As I walk, I feel the cold creep into my feet. They seem to be getting more sensitive. I can't say the same for the rest of me, but my feet feel more awake.

The scuff and patter of my footsteps echoes all around me, and for the first time it occurs to me how massive this tunnel is. I sense by the reverberations that the walls are nowhere near me. They exist somewhere out in this expanse of darkness. I think just the idea of this helps that chill begin to spread from my feet to the rest of me.

And I wonder, were the sounds of my footsteps always there? Or did they just fade in now?

I can't say for sure.

But I don't let any kind of anxiety take root in my head; an unease maybe, but nothing approaching panic.

I walk. I focus on the movement, on the new depths of sensation traveling up and down my calves like surging currents of electricity. The muscle balls and releases with each step. I can't see it, so I picture the muscle flexing.

And as I key in on my lower legs, it occurs to me that I can feel fabric tug against my knees as they bend. I'm not nude.

So that's good.

I guess I was a little worried about getting out into the light to find my scrotum staring back at me. Instead I look forward to seeing some relaxed fit denim by the feel of it. Would be weird if I was wearing sweatpants or something, right?

OK, wait again.

What am I doing? Do I have an objective here?

I can't think of one. Did I forget it? Did I ever have one?

My mind goes blank as I reach out for these memories, and the sound of my feet padding over the concrete comes back to the forefront of my consciousness.

The dark tunnel stretches on and on. The light looks to be just bigger than a baseball now. It seems to be growing faster, whether that makes any sense or not.

My fingers feel the cold now, the chill spreading from the tips down to the place where knuckle meets palm. It stings. I rub my hands together, but it's sort of like rubbing frozen fish sticks against each other and hoping they'll thaw.

"Friction cannot help you here," a voice says, and I jump, startled.

The surge of adrenalin that shoots up and down my limbs feels colder still. My torso jerks. My hands squeeze into fists.

After a second I realize it was my voice.

I am dumb.

In retrospect, the words seemed to come from outside of me somehow, though, and that seems familiar, too. Yeah. Yeah, I have heard a voice before in a situation like this, haven't I? A girl's voice, I think.

Think, Grobnagger, think.

Amity.

Yes!

Her I remember.

I see her in my head. I see her in the photo album at Glenn's, sad in every shot. I see her running away from me over the dunes, my johnson swaying back and forth like an elephant's trunk. I even see her meditating in a cornfield, though I wasn't there to witness that firsthand. That image is encoded in my brain the way I imagined it, I guess. It pops up like a dream just like the others.

She is interesting to me. Sometimes I think she might be like me. Is that why I remember her? Hard to say, but it brings back a lot.

We're going to the other world to help her. That's my

objective. I need to find Amity. This tunnel must be the way, right?

And then I remember covering the windows with blankets and the blue light and the coffee and all of it. It all makes sense. I think knowing what the hell is going on helps me walk a little faster, so that's good.

CHAPTER 16

By the time I near the mouth of the tunnel, I realize how huge it is. I feel tiny, like an ant walking through the Grand Canyon.

Shit. I probably should've compared it to a really huge mouth instead since I called it the mouth of the tunnel. Like an ant walking out of a whale's mouth or something like that. Too late. I totally blew it. I'm sorry.

In some detail I can see the forest on the other side of this threshold. The green of the leaves stands out against the gray of the sky. Somehow it's not real yet, though. It won't be real until the light touches my skin, I think.

I can see my arms and feet in the shade now, at least, and if I strain I can make out my legs, though they look darker as they're clad in jeans. It's good to see these limbs again, like being united with old friends. Plus, I'm wearing pants this time. Bonus.

I hear something squeak and crackle out, and it occurs to me that the sound isn't echoing around in the tunnel at all. Not sure what that means. I think about stopping to listen for whatever it was to make more noise, but at this point I want to get out of this place as soon as possible. I press forward.

The cold has a pretty good hold on me now, from head to feet. My fingers and toes ache with that painful level of chilliness. I want to run the last few hundred yards out of here, but it would hurt my feet too much. I walk, as ever, but I picture myself cutting open a small animal and warming my hands and feet in there. I mean, I wouldn't actually mutilate an animal like that, but damn would it feel good, right?

I squint as the light gets brighter and brighter. Even with all of this time to adjust, my pupils seem unable to cope with the changes. I rub at my eyes, and it feels so good, like I can erase all of the sleep and tired and the sting of the light if I just keep pressing my fingers on them, so I do that.

The sound around me changes – it kind of opens up - and when I pull my hands away from my face, I'm outside of the tunnel. I look back at the hole I've just walked out of and find it carved into red rock that seems to go straight up as far as I can see.

The forested terrain out here doesn't look right to be situated so close to a mountain – it's too vibrant and green to be growing out of rock, you know? And the cliff wall itself is somehow too uniform in its 90 degree angle of ascent. It doesn't necessarily look man made. Crevices and serrated edges and other imperfections etch their lines into the stone. Still, something is off about it.

I scratch the back of my neck and move on. I make it about six paces farther when her voice intervenes.

"Are you there?"

I stop.

"Yeah," I say.

"Good," she says. "You don't have to talk out loud, though. We are connected for now. "

"Oh," I say out loud.

Damn. I always get real smooth as soon as I'm talking to a girl.

"Oh," I say again in my head.

She laughs. Her laugh consists of a rapid series of inhaled breaths, that repetition of squeaks as the air rushes in. It reminds me of the laugh of a nerdy girl in a sitcom. Maybe a little cuter, though.

"I brought you here," she says. "That's why we're connected. I'm glad you can understand me this time."

"Yeah," I say. "Well, we drank a shitload of coffee to try to keep our minds sharp. Seems like it worked. Did you bring Glenn, too?"

"I'm working on it. He might not be deep enough asleep yet. I think it happens between sleep cycles. If I'm calling on you right as you shift into the deepest sleep, the connection opens up. I'm not certain, though."

"Where are you?"

"I'll tell you, but I don't think it'll be of much use: I'm in the woods. You?"

"Woods. Just walked out of a big ass tunnel."

"I see."

"So is there some way I can find you? Some set of landmarks or something?"

"Mm... Not really. Bunch of trees, mainly. Branches. Leaves. Stuff like that."

"Damn it," I say. I think about this a moment. "You ever see a huge red cliff type deal? Real gargantuan cave leading into it?"

"Not that I recall," she says.

"Yeah, you'd probably remember this thing," I say, pointing

at the cliff wall even though I know she can't see my gesture. "Real big cave."

I feel weird hanging out by the cave, so I start picking my way through the foliage as I think to her. It sounds like she yawns before she goes on.

"It gets weird out here. Things have a way of changing on you. I can't decide if the landscape itself changes, or if something out here wears holes into your memory so it only feels like everything around you morphs and melts into new shapes that surprise you because you don't remember them. Either way, though, that's how it feels: perpetual surprise and confusion, like living in a dream."

"Yeah, I see what you mean," I say.

My strides chop and stutter in dinky little steps, all careful as hell. I guess I'm scared of stepping on something weird with bare feet. The ground feels cool and soft underfoot for the most part. Out here I'm walking on a layer of mulch comprised mostly of dead leaves.

"So hey, are you in trouble or something?" I say.

"What?" she says. "No. I'm just sitting in the woods."

"Oh," I say. "Well, we thought you might be in trouble or something. I mean, I guess we thought that's why you were trying to contact us."

I bend at the waist to pass under a crisscross of low hanging branches. Leaves tickle all of the places where my skin is exposed.

"No," she says, and I think I hear the faintest edge of incredulity creep into her voice. "You two are the ones that are in trouble."

I stop in my tracks, still folded in half with leaves brushing at the back of my neck.

"How do you mean?" I say.

"Farber," she says. "He walks among us, Grobnagger. I've seen him out here, though only from a distance. He means you harm."

"Harm?" I say. "How do you know that if you've only seen him from a distance?"

She is quiet.

I shuffle forward to a place where I can stand up and stretch out my back and neck. The trees grow a little sparser here, a thick tangle of brush taking their place.

"I can't remember how I know," she says. "But I know that I know. Does that make sense?"

"Yeah," I say. "I know exactly what you mean."

CHAPTER 17

This brain to brain conversation feels so much like being on the phone. I keep wanting to put my hand by my ear out of habit. Instead I trudge deeper into the brush, green coming up to my knees. My feet pad on firmer soil now, though I'm tramping down a layer of various grasses as well.

"So why are you doing this?" I say.

"Doing what?" she says.

"Why are you staying out here?" I say. "Why don't you want to come back to the real world or whatever?"

She clucks her tongue against the roof of her mouth a few times like she's doing some kind of mental math. When I remember that she is doing this in her head rather than out loud, it seems funny somehow.

"I don't know," she says.

That's it. She doesn't go on. The silence hangs in the air a moment, but then some grass swishes against my pant legs as I step through a particularly thick patch.

"You don't know?" I say. "What the hell kind of an answer is that?"

She makes a throaty noise that reminds me of an elf dying in a role playing game.

"It's boring there," she says. "I mean, sure, there are potentially interesting things there, but I mostly understand the way things work pretty well. I can see the range of possibilities in the paths before me there. Out here, anything is possible. I don't understand it much at all, and it's great."

"So you like it because you don't understand it?" I say. "You might be even weirder than I thought."

"When you think about it," she says. "Aren't the possibilities in life always better than the realities? When you dream of how things might be, that's when you're at your happiest. That's when you're most excited, most captivated. Once your dream becomes a reality, even if things go as well as you could possibly hope, it can never quite live up to the excitement in that original possibility, can it? Nothing can ever fill us up the way we think it might, can it?"

I let my fingers stroke the divots and craters pocking the tree bark as I pass an oak.

"I don't know," I say. "I guess not."

"Not much to say now, eh? You must know I'm right," she says. "Based on what I've heard about you, this is probably all stuff you already know. I mean, you're not exactly an outgoing guy with a can do spirit, right? Don't you not have any friends or family?"

I kind of wonder what all she's heard about me, but I push the conversation in a different direction.

"You do, though. So what about your family?" I say. "I mean, your Dad worries about you. I'm sure your Mom does, too. Do you feel bad about that? And don't you get lonely out here, anyhow? Don't you miss people?"

Her imaginary tongue clucks again but just once this time.

"Way I see it, we all walk our own paths based on what we think is right," she says. "I can't fix things for other people. I can't be responsible for that. I have to do my own thing, because this is the only chance I have to do it. There's no do over for good behavior if you waste your life trying to please other people. You don't get another crack at it for being a good Samaritan. Every second you waste is gone forever. You never get it back."

I crunch through some dried-out stalks that look like a cross between corn and cat tails.

"So you don't feel guilty. I can understand that, but you have to get lonely sometimes, right?" I say.

"Fuck that," she says. "To me, lonely is being surrounded by people and never feeling connected to any of them. Staying there, fighting in vain against that inevitability would be a lifetime of loneliness. Maybe my way will, too, but I'm doing what makes sense to me. I'm trying."

The tinge of anger in her voice surprises me, but I can't disagree with her, at least not enough to argue. She goes on:

"Maybe what happens out here is just as pointless as what happens there, but I feel like if I buy into the emptiness all around me there – the worship of technology and pharmaceuticals and sports and sit-coms playing in HD on big screen TVs – I feel like if I accept that materialistic worldview as the order of the universe, I am putting my faith in nothing. Out here, maybe I don't exactly know what I'm putting my faith into, but it's something or at least it might be. I'd rather put my faith in something, you know? Something is better than nothing. Anything is."

As she talks, my feet plant themselves in the ground. I move no longer. I stand and listen. When she seems finished, I remain motionless. The air feels so still just now.

"Don't you think it's just energy, though?" I say. "See, Glenn thinks it's energy that connects us all. It kind of reflects pieces of all of us and in that way seems to have a personality, but in the end it's just energy."

"It could be," she says. "There's no easy answer here. Even if it's something like that, though, isn't that more worthy of exploring than the material world?"

I look up at the sky, the billowing blanket of gray and white fluff above me.

"Maybe," I say.

"Don't you get the feeling this place likes you?" she says. "And I mean you personally, Grobnagger. Seems to me it likes you in particular."

"Is that why it had the hooded man... Is that why it had you strangle me over and over?" I say.

She laughs.

"It was trying to teach you something," she says. "That's what I think. "

After a pause she continues:

"I didn't know what was going on during that, by the way," she says. "I just had the overwhelming urge to, you know, kill you."

"Yeah, it seems like I inspire that a lot in people these days," I say. "They mean me harm and all."

She laughs again, harder this time. It kind of sounds like a seal's bark, but an especially cute seal, I'd say. Not one of the ones with the tusks and the crazy mustaches or whatever. Are those walruses?

Wait. What's a sea lion? It could be either a walrus or a sea lion I'm thinking of, but yeah. You know what? I'm going to go ahead and say she doesn't sound like either one. So there.

A real cute seal is what I'm getting at here.

"What?" she says.

Fuck. Did I think that out loud to her?

She laughs harder still, so I guess I did. I try not to picture baby seals clapping for fish at Sea World. I don't know if I can transmit pictures to her or just dialog, but I would rather not risk it.

CHAPTER 18

I've been trying to walk in more or less a straight line, but I frequently have to go off course to get around various barriers. Just now it's a giant patch of thorny looking bushes.

"So what's with all these tricks you guys have figured out?" I say. "I can't do any cool shit."

"Like what tricks?" she says.

"Well, you figured out how to pull me here and talk to me through your mind, right?" I say. "And your Dad healed himself and cut a doorway to this place. I want to do kick ass stuff like that."

"I can show you one right now. An easy one," she says. "Lie down."

I look down at the ground. The sand and scraggly weeds don't look that inviting.

"Well, what is it?" I say. "I should know what I'm getting into before I commit to it."

"Just lie down on your back if you want to learn something," she says. "It's interesting. I promise."

I ease myself down to a seated position and lie back. Plants tickle my neck. The sand grits itself into the backs of my arms, and the heat works its way through my t-shirt to press its warmth into the flesh on my back.

"All right. I'm down," I say. "Now what?"

"OK. Close your eyes and feel your consciousness rising up through your eyebrows," she says. "Don't think about it too hard. Just let it happen. Feel it happening."

I try this. The muscles in my forehead contort a few different directions. I open my eyelids a slit to confirm that nothing awesome is transpiring.

"I don't think anything happened," I say. "Actually, I think I just raised my eyebrows, so I probably look pretty surprised, at least."

She laughs.

"No, not toward the top of your head," she says. "Toward the sky. Feel it flowing like water from just above that spot where your nose meets your forehead. Feel yourself disconnect."

I try to let myself feel these things she says. I imagine the sensation of the place where my thoughts transpire ascending through a spot in the center of my skull. I feel it trickle upward, squeezed a bit to fit through the skull spot and then expanding once it's free, floating more than flowing now, drifting up like a buoy popping up from below the surface and bobbing about, turning over a few times. But it all feels far away, too. A passing feeling that is forgotten as soon as you're done experiencing it.

"Did it work?" she says.

I peel open my eyes to find myself floating just above the tree line. It feels like a dream. And then I rotate, and I see myself – my body, I guess – lying on the sandy patch below. I floated out of myself.

This scares me. From this height, all I can think about is falling, so I float back down some. It's a slow process.

"Hello? Did it work?" she says.

Oh. I forgot to answer.

"Yeah," I say, looking down on my body. I look peaceful enough. "Am I going to be able to... like, get back in there?"

She laughs again, the rapid gasping inhalations.

"Of course. You'll be fine," she says. "Pretty cool, though, right?"

"Yeah," I say. "Just... I'm going to get back in there."

I push myself back into that place just above the spot between my eyes. All goes dark, and I feel constricted for a second. Then I open my eyes. I am myself again.

"You're a bit of a nervous pervis aren't you?" she says.

"What?" I say. "No. I mean, I just wanted to make sure."

"It's OK," she says. "I just thought you'd be more excited to try it out."

I pat at the ground, the dirt coarse against my fingertips. Satisfied that the land remains solid, I stand and dust myself off.

"So hey," I say. "Why do you think that's possible? I mean, my real body is back in bed asleep, right? I'm already disconnected from it. Why would I do that again here? It's like a dream within a dream or something."

"Well, I'm not 100% sure, but I think of it like this: We have avatars on this plane that look like our physical selves because it's what we understand. It makes us comfortable," she says. "But we can sort of disconnect from it into pure energy."

I scrape my toe into the ground.

"That makes sense," I say.

I trek over a patch of barren earth, sandy soil slithering up between my toes. The dirt is the exact shade of the coat of a

Prussian blue cat, gray with just the faintest blue tint.

"So what do you even do out here?" I say. "Apart from no one to talk to, there's no TV to watch, no internet, nothing to read."

"Aw, don't worry about me. There's a lot of terrain to wander over. A lot of thoughts to think. I manage to make my own fun," she says.

"What does that entail, though?" I say. "From a practical standpoint, I mean."

"A little bit of everything, I guess," she says. "When you read or watch TV, what are you really doing? You're triggering things in your imagination, right? It's not the words on the page that entertain you or teach you or change you, it's what they evoke in your imagination. Would you agree with that?"

"Yeah, I guess so," I say.

"Well, out here your imagination gets going on its own," she says. "You don't need external stimulus to elicit the good stuff. It just pours out pictures and ideas day and night, and you realize that your imagination is a world within a world, maybe even a universe within a universe, yeah? Who needs the outside world when you came equipped with your own? You've got your own universe sitting idle in your brain pan. I mean, if you bother learning how to use it, anyhow."

I find a spot where the ground is warm and stop and wiggle my toes in the sand. I don't really know what to say, but I talk anyway.

"I don't know. It doesn't seem right somehow," I say.

"What doesn't?" she says.

"Spending a lifetime alone voluntarily," I say, and the irony of my words isn't lost on me, considering my prior position on the matter. "It seems like an empty existence to me."

She is quiet for a time. I don't know why this particular spot in the sand is so warm, but patches of skin on my feet now feel on the verge of blistering, in a good way if that makes sense. Like right now, it feels good like a hot bath at the perfect temp, but if it were 5 degrees hotter, my flesh would be crisping up like fried chicken.

I'm almost ready to check if she's still there, but she answers me.

"Where do you think philosophers look for answers?" she says. "Sure, they're educated, well read, all of that. But when they go to create or lay down some new tract, they sit down by themselves and write, don't they? They look inside. Not outside. I'm not a philosopher, but that's what it's about for me. Don't confuse it. It's not about loneliness for the sake of loneliness at all. I mean, I brought you here, didn't I?"

"Well, yeah," I say.

"And we're talking now, and I'm enjoying it," she says. "I'm not here to be alone. I'm here to look inside. It just so happens that I'm probably going to spend a lot of this time alone in the process, and I'm OK with that."

That makes sense in a way. I go to tell her so, but my words catch in my throat and come out wrong:

"I'm some, I'm some, I'm some, I'm some kind, I'm some kind, I'm some kind of, I'm some kind of a, I'm some kind of a memory."

I don't know what I'm saying. These don't seem like the words I meant to speak, but I can't remember for sure. I feel like I'm falling.

"A memory, a memory, a memory."

I finally stop talking. I can feel the heat in my face, can just make out my cheeks going red at the edge of my vision, and I'm embarrassed. Something crazy is happening to me, I can't talk or move or breathe, I'm fucking dying for all I know, and even still I'm really embarrassed. That's the overwhelming emotional response here. I feel dumb.

"Ah. I hope I talk to you again soon," she says.

She doesn't seem alarmed, but I don't know how she might be experiencing this. To her it's just some gibberish, I guess.

I collapse on the line where the sand ends, my torso sprawling among thigh high grass while my feet and legs still touch the warm of the sand. Spindles of plant life whisk stems and stalks across my face as I descend. The icy green fingers plead with my face to cool down, but it's no use. The heat just bloats in my cheeks and swells further.

Air bursts from my lungs in fits both choppy and involuntary. My throat chokes out nonsense words like, "Snarf!" over and over. I sound like a Miniature Pinscher coughing up chunks of rawhide.

And the light seems to dim about me. And I gag and hack and wriggle the best I can, arms knocking over grass, toenails scraping in the sand, though my motor skills seem inarticulate. And my neck arches back to look at the gray sky going darker still. And my shoulders shimmy without my telling them to, like a weird palsy vibrating my upper body.

It's no use, I know now.

So I try to be calm. And I try to be still. And I try to wait for the black to overtake me.

Darkness surrounds me. Warmth envelops me. I bring a

hand to my face. My fingers feel a little rough. The flesh along my jaw and cheek bones is toasty, oddly slack somehow, a little numb. It's not unpleasant. This verifies my suspicion. The other world, the grass, that surge of fever heat invading my face – they're all gone.

This new warmth strikes me as familiar, though. I go to sit up, but something prevents my knees from bending all the way. Huh? My hands pat around. Fabric pulls taut over my body. I know this, don't I? Oh yeah. A blanket.

That triggers it. The memories wash back over me, and the corresponding images flicker through my frontal lobe: Two pots of coffee, multiple layers of duct tape stretched over the edges of bedspreads to block out the windows, the little black box shining its blue light onto the ceiling.

My sense of my setting restored, I lie back, my head sinking into the pillow. A deep breath expands my rib cage, and it shrinks back to normal as the wind escapes me all slow.

I open my eyes and look into the blackness, blink a few times, see nothing.

Now that I'm over freaking out about a blanket pinning my legs down, the relief fades away and a sense of excitement tinged with melancholy settles over me.

I remember all of the things that Amity said. Sure, she said Farber meant me harm, but I kind of figured that for a strong possibility already. It was all the things she said about looking inside that I can't stop thinking about.

On one hand, I find great excitement in talking to someone so full of passion for things close to my own heart. On the other, her outlook has such a fatalism to it, it just makes me sad. I think she is wrong about being alone, just as I was wrong about being alone. I don't think pushing everyone away is a path to any kind of happiness, not anymore.

Life is like a choose your own adventure book, and she keeps taking the gloomiest route. But if you choose gloom, you get gloom. That's how it goes.

Like me? I sometimes think I just preferred being sad in a way. I constructed a narrative to make it make sense. I held my head sideways to see my life as I wanted to see it, to see a black and white explanation for how I felt as though it's an unchangeable thing. But we're all responsible for how we feel, too, at least in part.

I am not perfect, but I can try. I can try to do better. I can try to be happy. There's nothing wrong with that.

And just as these words cross through my head, I hear the floorboards squeak on the other side of the room.

My respiration cuts off mid breath. My diaphragm clenches, and my ribcage quakes.

Someone is in the room with me.

CHAPTER 19

Adrenalin gushes into my head, and I feel the pangs of chemical excitement race up and down my frame. The dark around me seems much darker all of the sudden.

I don't breathe. I don't move.

I listen.

I hear nothing.

Based on the total lack of light, I know that the bedroom door remains shut with the rolled up towel still blocking out the crack at the bottom. Did someone come in here, close the door and put the towel back? And if so, what for? And also why did they just wait in the dark for however long I've been lying here thinking?

What a creep.

My brain races through the possibilities. None of them make much sense. I know a cat wasn't in here when I closed the room up. I know there's no reason for Glenn to do this. Could it be the night stalker? I'm not even sure it's the night, actually, but could it be a home invasion?

I sit up with care, making sure to remain soundless. I keep my legs straight out, too scared the friction of leg moving against sheet will be audible. I gaze into the abyss in front of me as though I'll suddenly be able to see in the dark now that I'm upright.

I try to stop myself from thinking it, but it's too late. A replay of Amity's voice plays in my head, emphasizing that Farber walks among us, that he means us harm.

Is that possible? Could he be here now?

Could this be why Glenn never arrived in the other world as planned?

Considering that prospect leads to more adrenalin. The electrical chill surges all through me again. Sweat oozes out of my forehead and slicks up the back of my neck. For a second I picture the beads of perspiration there, my neck skin rippling with goosebumps as the cold feeling comes over me once more.

I scoot the blanket off of my legs a few inches and wait. Then I slide it down a little more. Wait. All holds still and black and silent around me.

With two more bedspread scoots, my legs are free. I'm hesitant to actually move them, though. Can't make a sound now.

My breath goes shallow, quiet. The air enters and retreats almost at the same time, scraping back and forth over the dried-out pink flesh of my throat. I try to not focus on it. I try to think of anything but my respiration as I'm worried about psyching myself out and hyperventilating. Frozen here in this seated position, though, I have nothing else to think about.

What if I just imagined the sound? It's not impossible. I don't think I would've panicked like this, though. My right brain, my animal instincts would know the difference. Some creeping little doubt would have prevented me from freaking out all the way.

The floorboard moans again, a mournful, high pitched creak that sounds like it should have a question mark at the end of it.

Well, shit.

The ensuing panic spurs me to action. Moving like a silent movie, I bring my knees up and crab walk toward the side of the bed that seems to be the opposite of where the sound came from. My hands reach off the bed, down into black nothing. The floor seems a long way off, farther down than it has any right to be, but I find it.

I ease myself onto the floor back first like that - my hands plant on the cool of the hardwood, walk my torso out a little, and then my legs swing down after. All motion remains controlled, careful, silent, bordering on slow motion. I almost feel like a gymnast doing some awful moves on that horse thing or something. A terrible, terrible bedroom gymnast.

I hover there, ass suspended a few inches off of the floor, legs sticking straight out, all of my body weight on my hands. I listen. Nothing. Even so, I freeze. I wait.

In time, my wrists sting, and my forearms quiver a tad.

After what seems like a few minutes, I release my body weight, letting myself rest on the floor butt first, then feet. After another moment spent motionless, I lean forward so my face almost touches my knees. I want to be sure my ears stay above the bed line, so no sounds are muffled.

Something moves. Fabric, I think. I listen again.

There's a scuffing noise, and the floor croaks, a deeper sound this time. A second later it squeaks again, another question. I feel the wood planks vibrate and sag ever so faintly beneath my palms as the weight on the floor shifts. Definitely footsteps. The sounds seem to be getting closer to the bed but approaching from the other side of where I'm seated.

I sprawl into push-up position and crawl forward, rounding the corner of the bed. I don't know. I guess my instinct is to go right at this guy but from an angle that will surprise him. I'm flanking him. Or her. Probably him.

I remember reading that you're statistically better off to be the aggressor if someone breaks into your house. That I shall do. Be it the night stalker, Farber or whomever, he must go down, and he must go down hard.

I move like a sloth, poking one arm out, waiting, bringing a leg forward, waiting. I hesitate at the bottom of the bed, hugging against the foot of the mattress to avoid getting stepped on or kicked. I want to get a better idea of exactly where he stands before I go around the next corner. Believe me, the last thing I want to do is crawl right into him.

That would make a funny story some day, I guess, if I did crawl into him. For him, I mean. He'd have a hilarious burglary story about the time the guy crawled right into his legs, and he snapped the poor bastard's neck before he could even get to his feet.

I listen to the silence, the blank nothing emptiness. My ears try to hear something in it. My eyes try to see something in it.

I wait and sweat and wait and sweat some more. Perspiration battles the heat crawling from my torso up onto face, but it's no use. I'm all warm. I bet rosy patches blotch my cheeks.

He clears his throat. It's not a full on throat clear but more of a faint throat noise. A grumble of mucus and soft flesh.

So it's real. This is really happening. A person violates this room. They invade. They infest. They trespass. A real live human being stands less than 10 feet from where I crouch. And based on the deep bass of the grunt, that human being is an adult male.

I snake forward into the open, leaving the safety of my spot right along the bed. I now have a good feel for where this guy idles.

And I mean him harm.

CHAPTER 20

The room wears its darkness like a black blanket. I can't see anything. It muffles the sound, too, so I can't hear anything, either.

Not the best of conditions in terms of picking a moment to run full speed at someone, but you work with what you have.

I square my shoulders toward where I'm pretty sure he is standing. Still crouching, I get on my feet. My arms lift at my sides and go into a wide curl, as though I'm about to hug him.

I'm not.

This arm move is premature in any case, I know. More of precaution than a preparation. It goes hit then wrap, not the the other way around. I'll be too busy torpedoing my shoulders at him to have my arms preemptively in hug position.

My heart beats so hard that my ribcage convulses in rhythm. Feels like an alien wants to spurt out of my chest cavity. I wouldn't even mind that if the critter would help me fight this guy.

I angle my torso forward to get more of my weight in front of my feet so I can push off better, winding up in a position a couple of notches shy of a sprinter's stance. Acceleration will be key, and there's not much room to get going in here.

So much adrenalin now that my arms tremor and the rest of me spasms off and on. My thoughts flutter. Nausea throbs in my gut.

This is it.

Life or death in 3.

2.

1.

I blitz him, rushing forward at top speed, though the world plays in slow motion in my head. My feet churn in perfect unison, pushing off and sliding forth. I get off and going with a nice burst.

A few paces later, I hurl myself at what I deem the proper spot. My body goes horizontal. My arms go wide.

I collide with him. This is good. But it's a glancing blow. My right shoulder slides off what I think is his chest, only managing to knock him back a half of a step or so.

My arms grapple at him like spider legs, and I hook him pretty good. As my momentum carries me forward rapidly, I get my feet back under me just in time to use it to catapult him into the wall even harder than I hit it.

The bang of my shoulder hitting drywall is loud, but his wall slam sounds much more violent. I can hear the hole being ripped into Glenn's wall, hopefully with this guy's face.

It sounds like multiple concussions.

I go to stand, but our limbs are tangled. It takes a moment of scrambling and grabbing to figure out what is what. We squirm in the dark. I wind up partially upright, leaning on one knee. My fingers graze over emaciated cheek bones and eyelids and grip on the stubble on the shaved head, all prickly like the sharp side of Velcro. And the details of the cranium against my hands confirms what I knew deep down all along.

It's Farber. I don't know how, but it's him.

He wriggles his head free from my grip, and my claws scrabble until they find purchase on his torso. I feel ribs through his shirt, and when I make contact with his skin, he's all sinewy and clammy and weird to the touch. I can't help but picture his flesh all slimy like those two little tentacle antennas protruding from a slug's head.

I lose my balance, tumbling, crashing onto the floor, but I keep my grip and pull him down with me.

Rising to my knees, I jerk him up by the torso and slam him back down. Hard. He's so gaunt. It's more like tossing around a slimy mannequin than a man.

He gasps for breath, his throat struggling for wind, the sounds coming out of him all shrill and dry like a dying bird. I think maybe I knocked the wind out of him.

Either way, the noises are like a bullseye for my fists. I descend on him, straddling his rib cage and letting endless punches rain down.

I pummel his stupid face in.

The heat creeps all the way into my head now. A fevered glow radiates from my face, and I don't hear anything anymore. I break open his face so the red pours out. I don't see it. I feel it. I feel my fists pounding flesh against bone like two meat tenderizers flattening a steak. I feel the cartilage in his nose break into smaller and smaller pieces. I feel the warm blood pour from my knuckles. I see the black around me take on a red tint.

And when the light cuts a wedge-shaped swath of gray into the darkness, it almost doesn't register at first. I keep punching, keep feeling the fire burning in my head like nothing else is real, but part of me gets that feeling like I'm about to realize something important.

"Grobnagger," a voice behind me says.

My fists slow and then stop. It's a weird feeling. It's like I had committed to punching this face forever, backing out now feels like a loss.

"Stand up, son," the voice says. "Are you all right?"

I don't say anything. I look at the face, but it still lies shrouded in darkness. All I can make out is wetness moving in the black.

I stand, consenting finally to the demand made of me.

I turn to see Glenn flipping the light switch a few times. It doesn't work.

"What..." he says. "What happened in here?"

I still don't say anything, so he steps into the room to get a better look at the body.

"Holy shit," he says.

His voice trembles a little. It's the first time I've heard Glenn sound this scared, but there's nothing to be scared of. I handled it. I follow the path of his eyes to the figure on the floor.

The triangle of light leaning through the doorway paints a picture in the muted tones of half light. Farber's legs sprawl into the path of what's visible, black dickies leading down to boots with a waffle pattern on the bottoms. His black shirted torso stretches into the darkness, the details of his face obscured by the shadows.

I stride over to the body and look down on it, my feet almost touching the leg. I consider giving a little kick as a test, but I decide not to. I don't think there's much of a point.

"Is he..." Glenn says. "Is he dead?"

I say nothing. My mouth hangs open, panting like a dog's. I realize this has been the case for a long while now.

And then a sound creaks out of the dead man, out of his mouth. At first I think this is some kind of death rattle or post death nervous twitch.

No.

He's laughing.

Glenn backpedals a few paces to the doorway.

I don't know if it's Glenn's cowardice that triggers it, but the next thing I know, I'm back on the body. My knees pin his arms to the ground. My hands close around the throat.

"Oh, no!" Farber says in a mock tone, still chuckling. "Don't do that. You'll smother me!"

I squeeze. I crush. I clamp his throat closed for good.

His clammy skin seems to go firm now. The scrawny physique goes rigid, suddenly seeming more lean and hard and wiry than floppy and weak. He bucks a few times. It's not enough to free his arms, but he keeps me from securing my grip fully.

He also shifts us enough to shake his face out into the gray light. I see the destruction I've done, the smashed parts, and purpled bits, and his red insides, the wet life juice spilling out into the world. But I can still tell it's him. Even through all of the swelling and bruising, I can see it.

The struggle goes on for what must be a few seconds but seems like a long time, and my sense of control over the situation only grows. His torso quakes. His hips twist. I'm too strong for him, and he knows it. He keeps fighting, but I can feel the defeat in him. His moves don't have the same life in them. His flesh seems to sag once more. He's just going through the motions now. It's a matter of time.

My hands press and flex and squash his neck down to nothing.

I see a jerky motion out of the corner of my eye, and I look up in time to see Glenn's hand cup his mouth, trying to hold back vomit and failing. A gush of brown sprays between his fingers, opaque and lumpy. He buckles at the waist, letting the barf slap on the wood floor and spatter against the wall.

We make eye contact as he heaves again. I see shame in Glenn's expression. I don't think it's because of the puke, but maybe that's part of it.

I almost forget what I'm doing, but the cramping in my hands serves as a reminder. I look back at Farber. The chest holds still, the eyes stare off at nothing like those glass eyes in creepy, old dolls.

He is gone.

I release his neck, his slimy flesh showing a ring of dark where my hands were. The cramped muscles in my fingers refuse to stop curling themselves up, so I press them flat on the floor to stretch them. I close my eyes and feel that stretch fight against the fatigue, feel the cool combat the heat of the hatred still coursing all through me.

"I'll check the circuit breaker," Glenn says from behind me.

His voice sounds all small. He's not himself. I don't open my eyes, but I nod. I hear his footsteps trail away, slow and light. He even seems to walk with hesitation now.

I know I must be in shock at this point. I guess I don't feel much just yet. If anything, I feel pleasure. I feel powerful. Someone meant me harm, snuck into my home, and I eliminated the risk. My brain gives me the huge reward that goes with that. The one people get a miniature version of when the football team they root for wins. I just got the real thing, the life or death version.

But I just killed a man, a human being. Shouldn't I feel... something else, too?

That part doesn't seem real. Not yet anyway. I guess that's what shock is. When the real things aren't real.

I lift my hands from the floor and open and close them a few times. The acute cramp pain retreats for good as I do this, leaving only the dull ache that always trails wild physical exertion like this. My fingers feel almost wrong back in the air again. They miss the cool of the floor.

Something about the floor seems so refreshing, in fact, that I can't resist. I lean over, lying down so my cheek touches the wood. It hurts for a second as I make contact – maybe he got me in the face at some point – but after that initial pain that faint numbness from the cool kicks in.

I close my eyes again. I don't think about the corpse lying near my feet. I don't think about the pool of puke congealing in the doorway. I think only of the cool pressing itself into my face, and I wish it was colder, and I wish I felt it all over.

Time passes without a sound. I don't think I could sleep just now, but a calm overtakes me. I grow ever more still inside. My thoughts go from racing to jogging to walking. My breathing slows down, my heart slows down. Eventually I drift away from reality in slow motion to some place far away from here. I feel like a balloon floating up and away from it all. The real world gets smaller and smaller.

I picture Farber hovering a spoon, force pushing it across the diner like a cutlery shot put. I remember the energy around him, the excitement in the air, the way the crowd wanted to love him and did.

Then I picture his return, his physique gone frail, coughs racking his torso. Again, the crowd responded to him on a mystical level. I could feel the despair in the room, the force that drove them to believe in him like they wanted to so badly.

Finally, I picture his face as it lies now, broken by my hands. The red draining out of him. The dead doll eyes. It hardly seems like a fitting end for such a man, even if he's more or less a total dick. It's not right, I think.

The sound of Glenn's feet trotting over the floor brings me back to reality a bit, though I leave my eyes closed for now. I hear a click and place it as him flipping the light switch.

"There we go," he says, sounding a little more like himself.

Then he gasps.

"Uh..." he says. "What did you do with him?"

I tumble the question over a few times.

"What?" I say, an odd rasp in my voice.

"You know. The, uh, dead guy," he says.

My eyes snap open. I lift my head. I hesitate for a split second before I turn. And when I do, I see exactly what I expect to see.

Farber is gone.

CHAPTER 21

With the lights on, I see the bowling ball sized hole gouged in the wall. I see the nightstand toppled, two of the legs snapped. I see a bunch of chunks in the puddle of puke that look like slices of onion.

Gross.

I look at the empty spot on the floor and picture Farber as he rested there, the broken, bleeding body. He was pretty dead at the end there as I recollect.

So... I didn't just imagine all of this, right?

"You saw him, didn't you?" I say, getting to my feet. "All of that really happened."

Glenn blinks a few times like a drunk trying to see straight. He looks like he doesn't want to be here. Seeing him shaken like this kind of weirds me out. He was always so brazen up until now. This blinking sad sack hardly seems like the guy elbowing his way through the crowd at the airport. He's all fragile now.

Soft.

"Yeah," he says. "I mean... yeah."

"And it was definitely Farber, right?" I say.

"Yeah," he says, scratching the back of his neck. "I think so."

A hard edge creeps into my voice. I can't help it.

"You think so?" I say. "What the fuck does that mean?"

"Look... it was him," he says. "It's just... This is a lot to take in, man. Just chill out."

I turn away from him to stare at the wall, like that might be enough to quell my homicidal rage. I close my eyes and try to count backwards from 10. I only make it to 8.

"I just bludgeoned and then murdered an intruder who subsequently vanished into a puff of steam," I say. "And you want me to chill out?"

Glenn blinks again.

"How about instead you stop being such a huge pussy?" I say. "Because, believe me, that would be tremendous."

I exhale all loudly through my nostrils a few times like Tony Soprano. Glenn's gaze falls to the floor. He's not even going to say anything back. I guess it's probably for the best to drop it, but...

"So Riston Farber is merely a conman, huh?" I say. "This was all just some kind of illusion, of course. Another parlor trick from that huge phony that is no threat to us, yeah?"

Glenn looks far away. I can't stop verbally abusing him. Maybe murdering someone puts you in a bad mood, especially if it somehow comes undone in a mysterious manner.

"Nothing to say?" I say. "Cause you were pretty wrong. He's obviously not a phony. He probably never was."

"No," Glenn says without looking up.

"Look, he somehow got into this room," I say. "And he somehow got out of this room. I'm going to go ahead and guess that the death I dealt upon him didn't take. So he's probably immortal or some shit at this point, too."

We fall silent a moment.

"No matter how you want to look at it," I say. "I don't think there's any way to explain any of this aside from admitting the guy has some kind of power. And admitting that you were wrong. It's not a trick."

Glenn turns and leaves the room abruptly, the wood floor groaning beneath him. Part of me wants to stay on the offensive, wants to keep after him until he admits he was wrong about this. But that part is smaller than it was. I let him go.

I sit down on the bed, my eyes still tracing outlines on the floor where the body should be. It's a weird feeling to have committed murder and then have it wiped out, at least so far as I can tell. The back and forth alleviates any feeling of guilt or whatever I might have been on the verge of feeling and replaces it with frustration at never knowing what the hell is going on.

It's nothing new, though. I never know what is happening to me.

I lie back, my head resting on a piled up section of blanket. The sheet is cool under my back, and for the first time I realize that I did all of this in nothing but boxers. Weird to kill a guy in that state of undress, but I guess I probably didn't really kill him, so it's all the same.

I look at the ceiling. Out of habit I want to go back over what played out here in my memory, run through the sequence of events, establish a timeline and assign the proper meaning to it all. My brain, however, refuses to comply. I just lie here and think of nothing. I guess it'd be hard to even sequence any of the events since it almost all happened in the dark.

Shit. I wish I hadn't been so mean to Glenn. I guess I was still full of adrenalin and hatred. I couldn't stop it from pouring out.

On cue, Glenn returns with a plastic shopping bag and a roll of paper towels. He kneels, scooping his vomit into the bag as best as he can. After ripping off three rectangles of paper towel, he dabs and swipes at the floor, throwing the dirty wad into the barf bag. He spins the roll and rips off three more paper towels.

I crane my neck to watch it all. Glenn speaks, neither of our eyes ever wavering from the vomit smear.

"We need to make sure," he says.

CHAPTER 22

The Explorer rolls by the church all slow. I wish I could say we move in silence, but this piece of shit has no muffler, so it is the opposite of silence. We gaze out the window. I guess we're hoping to catch a glimpse of Farber to confirm he's not dead. In my gut I already know he's fine. Probably not a scratch on the guy.

A few people mill around on the front steps. A guy in a red polo shirt has a stack of leaflets in his hand. The others look to be empty handed. They don't seem to take notice of our vehicle passing by at the volume of a jumbo jet, so that's good.

"So what is this?" I say.

"It's a church," Glenn says.

"I know that, dickhead," I say. "I mean, is this some kind of special event or something?"

"Yeah," he says. "Real special. I guess it's some kind of crazy cult meeting."

He has the aviators on again, so I shouldn't be surprised that he's rediscovered his smart mouth. In a way I'm glad. Anything is better than seeing Glenn turned all soft and scared. I don't like it when he becomes the vulnerable one.

"Ah," I say. "Well, that's good to know. You know, I thought you might actually have some insight into what is going on here. I mean, they don't meet in this building that frequently. It must be happening for some specific reason."

Glenn pulls the Explorer into the lot and finds a spot where we can keep an eye on the front door.

We watch a while. A trickle of people stream toward the front door where the guys on the steps greet them and red shirt hands them leaflets.

"Seriously, though," I say. "How did you find out about this?"

"I have sources," he says. "And I'm also on the League of Light email list. Got an email about it last night."

"Oh," I say. "So what are we talking here, like an ice cream social or something?"

Glenn leans this way and that way, his neck contorting in an attempt to get a better angle of the church door. I can tell he's not listening to me.

"I can't see anything," he says. "Should we go in?"

"We can't go in there," I say. "I just fought the guy to the death like an hour ago. You might remember this. It inspired regurgitation to spray out of you. Made a real mess. Dude, do you honestly not remember that?"

You want to give me mock answers to my questions, Glenn? You have no idea what I'm capable of, do you?

Glenn puffs air out of his nostrils in a way that reminds me of a bull about to impale a rodeo clown ass first on a horn. It looks like he's going to say something, but then I realize he's gritting his teeth.

I look away, avoiding eye contact as though I'm dealing with an aggressive dog instead of a man. More people file into the building. More leaflets get handed about. Nothing interesting.

The parking lot continues to collect cars as well. The spaces around us fill up, which isn't so bad as I feel like it makes us less noticeable, just one of many, you know?

When I glance back at Glenn, he stills looks more or less livid. Again, in a way I'd rather deal with enraged Glenn, his face gleaming red with blood, his mustache atwitter with a case of the shimmy shakes. It's not ideal, but it's less pathetic than scaredy-cat Glenn.

It's not until I see one of the people adjust his hat on the way in that I realize most of them are sporting head wear. He lifts his Atlanta Braves cap up and plops it back on his skull. It takes a second to register that he's not bald, or at least it wasn't male pattern baldness I saw under there. It was the weird monk haircut again. Based on the number of hats, most of these weirdos have it. Even some ladies.

"What do you think is up with the haircuts?" I say.

"I assume it's to do with the original friar reason," Glenn says. "Some kind of mystic status symbol, a sign of their commitment, of their renunciation of the ways of the world."

Weird.

I'm about to ask follow up questions when a black van creeps into the entry way of the lot. It moves slowly, with care. I guess this sticks out to both of us. We both watch it in our respective rearview mirrors as it settles into a spot in the back of the lot, away from the other vehicles. Upon parking, the van is still. No one gets out. I can't make out anything through the tinted windshield.

"Do you think?" I say.

"Maybe," Glenn says.

We wait. I can still hear some anger in the exhalations

emitting from Glenn's nostrils.

A man emerges from the driver's seat wearing a button-up blue shirt and one of those cabbie hats. Are those Scottish? I can't remember. He moves to the back of the van and slides open the door.

Well, well, well... look who's walking upright in a manner that I would call, "especially not dead."

Yep.

Riston Farber.

"You called it," Glenn says. "No bruises or anything."

Indeed. Farber's complexion looks unmarked. His neck lacks the purple ring of death I put there. His nose remains more pointy than flat.

He sports his usual black attire. He takes a few steps out of the van and stretches, his back arching and his arm coming up behind his head.

And then his head snaps our way. Glenn gasps as Farber squints at us and smiles. I feel that cool surge of adrenalin enter my bloodstream again, my heart beating hard like a giant kick drum. I undo my seatbelt, certain we're about to kick off Round 2 of our death match.

Then Farber snaps his head the other way and rolls his neck. The nature of these movements suggests that he was never looking at us, that he was just stretching his neck.

I'm not sure.

Either way, we can't move. Even after he goes inside the church and they close the front doors, Glenn and I sit for a long time, keeping still in the silence.

CHAPTER 23

We sit on canvas chairs on Glenn's deck. It's an unseasonably warm day, and the sun shines down like everything is normal rather than weirder than ever. When I look out at the yard and watch the light change when the clouds move, I can almost believe the lie.

I guess cleaning up all of that puke whet Glenn's appetite. As soon as we got back from the church, he made some crazy Mi Goreng flavored ramen that is probably the greatest thing I've ever tasted. The sauce coating the noodles was all spicy and acidic. Hard to describe. We didn't speak during the meal, but I think getting something to eat lifted both of our spirits.

Now we sit on the deck sipping iced tea out of a pair of mason jars. Though it's warm for a day in the late fall, the cold tea is a bit much. I'm chilly. I believe Glenn to be one of those people that wears shorts year round, however, so I'm sure he doesn't care.

I realize there's something I never told Glenn, something that got lost in the shuffle of murder undone and resurrections verified.

"I talked to her," I say.

Glenn looks confused for a fraction of a second, and then I see alertness snap into his expression.

"It worked? You saw her?" he says.

"Yes and no. I didn't see her," I say. "But I talked to her. Kind of. She was like a voice in my head I could think to."

He sips at the tea as he processes my clarification.

"What'd she say?" he says.

"She said Farber means us harm. That's why she's been trying to communicate with us," I say. "And she elaborated on why she wants to stay out there at some length."

"So she's OK?" he says.

"Yeah, she seems to like it there."

He looks away from me and nods all slow.

"Wonder why it didn't work for me," he says.

"She said it was something to do with changing sleep patterns. And she said something else, too," I say. "She said that Farber walks among us, meaning in the other world. She has seen him there and avoided him."

Glenn closes his eyes for a long moment. He slits them open, and I can see the wet in them.

"I was wrong, OK?" he says, his voice all low. "I was wrong about him. We have to get her out of there."

I don't say anything. Again, I don't know if rescuing someone that doesn't want to be rescued is our best course of action. Her reasons for staying seem well thought out enough.

Glenn clutches my arm. Our eyes lock, his expression pained. Maybe he knows what I'm thinking.

"He wants to harm us, right? Well, hurting her is the best way to harm me," he says. "He surely knows that much."

Glenn heads inside, and I sit on the deck a while by myself. It's cold, and my fingers are icy from the tip to the second knuckle from handling the jar of tea. For some reason I don't want to go inside, though. The wind blows and leaves tumble around.

Damn. I suppose Glenn is right, isn't he? It makes sense. But I wonder...

I pull my cell phone out of my pocket and press a couple of buttons.

"Hello?" Babinaux says. I hear the chatter of a crowd in the background.

"Hey, listen," I say. "This is going to sound weird, but I was wondering if you've heard anything about Farber recently. I know there was some kind of get together today, and he seemed fine, but I don't know. Anything weird going on that you know about?"

"Well, no," she says. "I'm at the church now, actually, and he's here. Like I said, I'm well out of the informed circle at this point, but I haven't detected anything out of the ordinary. Why? What happened?"

"Oh, it was nothing," I say. "He kind of appeared in my room. We struggled. I killed him with my bare hands, at which point he vanished. We checked up on him at the church a bit ago and he seemed upright and animated and full of life juice. And, you know, not dead."

"I have to go," she says, her voice hushed.

"What's wrong?" I say.

"He's staring at me," she says.

The crowd noise cuts out, and then there's silence.

I lie in the dark. Awake. I didn't bother to take the blankets off the windows, so it's a full-on dark. I guess the crack under the door lets in a sliver of light. Not enough to matter.

I decided to stay at Glenn's so we can get started early tomorrow. He insisted I should stay. Would I be able to sleep in this room if the murder stuck? Probably not. It didn't, though, so now this room is just fine. More like a room a heated wrestling match occurred in than a killing.

I pull the lip of the blanket up over my chin and the movement wafts some of the warm under-blanket air across my face. Feels awesome. Feels like sleep.

Even so, I kind of think I won't be able to find slumber since I just went on a dream tour of the woods this afternoon. Sucks, too, cause I'm exhausted in some ways and wide awake in others. Maybe I'll break out that little black box soon. Some blue light would really hit the spot about now.

I feel dumb somehow. Embarrassed.

Embarrassed that Farber tricked us, that he's just openly taunting us, if not also trying to kill us or whatever. That guy is a dick.

I'm going to level with you. I can hardly wait to kill him again.

The murderous feeling rises from my gut, and I try to push it back down.

So here we are. I guess rage and a hateful lust for violence have replaced the level of depression that got me so down I could barely stay awake before. Not sure which is better, really. I mean, I don't feel useless like I did, but if my only use is satisfying some animal urge to eliminate a threat, I'm hardly on a fulfilling path.

Anyway.

Tomorrow we're going back. We will cut a hole in the wall and walk there.

The old fashioned way.

The dangerous way.

Glenn wants to be sure we both get there in a timely manner and together this time. He says he will take Amity by force if he must. I don't necessarily agree with this course of action, but I don't know. What if I didn't help him and Amity somehow got hurt? I'd feel like a huge jerk. It's not my place to decide these things.

I don't know if I have a place at all, really.

CHAPTER 24

I wake to the sound of the coffee grinder, that violent whir as the blade reduces beans to powder, like the noise of someone gargling gravel. I open my eyes, but with the windows covered, it's still dark as hell in here. I don't mind this. I close them, and I drift back below the surface, the surge of warmth welcoming me right back.

I hover there a while, somewhere between half and all the way asleep. Some minutes later I wake again, bobbing back up to consciousness. The coffee smell is everywhere. I'm no smellologist, but I believe this to be a dark roast, and I want some.

I rise, my feet padding over cold wood. I open the door a crack to have a little light to dress by. I know turning on the lights would only hurt after being in the dark so long.

I hear kitchen-y noises and know some special meal is being prepped. Based on what happened to Glenn last time, we might be out in the other world for months in Earth time. You don't march into that kind of shit with an empty belly.

Lord no.

Squinting in the light, I take my seat at the snack bar.

"Morning, Grobnagger," Glenn says, his back to me.

He moves food and dishes around, I think. I can't see through him, but that's an educated guess.

"Good morning," I say.

"Did you call Babinaux?" he says.

"Yep," I say.

She has been tasked with feeding Mardy while I'm away. His life is in her hands. I repeated that a few times. She didn't think it was funny.

I rest my forearms on the corner of the counter and adjust on my stool. As I do so, I feel the part of my brain that records click on like it does in those most dramatic life moments. Like when you visit a dying relative in the hospital or find a dead pet or kiss a girl for the first time.

So right now my camera films the image of the counter my face is tilted toward with my arms pressed on it. I look up to see Glenn swivel with plates. He places mine before me, dead center of the frame. His eye still looks swollen from our fight, but it looks better than it did yesterday.

The recording continues as we pile together our food stuffs and put them in our face holes. We eat a breakfast of champions, and I'm not talking about Wheaties. I speak of huevos rancheros, a Mexican dish comprised of fried eggs served on corn tortillas with tomato chili sauce, refried beans, avocado chunks and rice. Words to capture its deliciousness elude me. Let's just say it's a pretty legitimate reason to keep living.

The meal feels significant beyond that, though. I watch Glenn eat, lifting overfilled tortillas to his face, chili sauce in his mustache, chunks of egg tumbling to the plate and splatting. It all feels important. My brain records everything in high definition. Until the day I die, I will be able to call forward that image of Glenn's sauce mouth with crystal clear accuracy.

Many moments in life come and go like they never happened, but I will keep this one. A quiet breakfast.

Is this how things always feel right before a dramatic moment? A heightened awareness of your surroundings and your companions. It feels like we're going into battle or something.

I don't know why.

We're only going to walk through the wall to some other dimension. No big whoop.

CHAPTER 25

Glenn comes back from the garage with a stone bowl of black powder. Examining the bowl, I realize it's a mortar, and he probably just took a pestle to the black stuff in there. His shoes clatter on the ceramic tiles in the kitchen, and the noise changes abruptly as he moves onto the hardwood, the emphasis shifting from the slap of his feet connecting with the floor to the shifting of his weight and its ever altering strain on the planks.

"So what is this stuff?" I say, rising to follow him down the hall.

"The powder? Oh, it's just a little concoction I came up with," he says.

At this point I don't even expect him to expound. I know what this guy is playing at.

"And what are the ingredients to your concoction?" I say.

"Oh, nothing too fancy. A little chalk," he says. "And a whole bunch of don't worry about it."

Why?

Why do I even ask?

A noise startles me, a sibilant sizzle. It reminds me of an insect or maybe a small threatened animal.

Oh.

It's laughter.

He laughs at his own joke. Hard. It's one of those hissing laughs where you hear spit and air whistling between clenched teeth. Kind of gross.

"So I guess you're in pretty good spirits," I say. "I'm just glad you were able to put that embarrassing vomit episode behind you so quickly. A lot of people wouldn't be able to live something like that down for a long time, but you're not uncomfortable with being the guy that puked on the floor during a tense moment. I think that's great."

As I say it, I realize this comes off a little meaner than the light-hearted sarcasm I had intended. The pulse of his laugh slows down, but it doesn't quite stop. I guess I'm glad for that.

We enter the guest bedroom – my old sleeping grounds as I call it. My eyes can't help but check the spot on the floor for Farber's corpse even though I've seen him up and walking around. There's no body, so that's a relief, I think. It would only complicate things at this point.

Glenn sets the bowl down on the floor. He kneels next to it and pinches some of the black dust between his finger and thumb and rubs back and forth so it spills back into the bowl a little at a time. Once his fingers are empty, he does it again.

His eyes fasten on his work and twitch back and forth over it. I see great inquisitiveness in his features. Something about his expression reminds me of that curious look a bird gets as it's about to rip a nightcrawler out of the ground.

"So how does this work?" I say.

He doesn't break his eye contact with the powder between his fingers.

"Well," he says. "I do my thing, and you kind of keep quiet."

He smiles again, pleased with himself.

Why does the man delight in effing with me so? No one can say.

He reaches behind his back and pulls something out of the rear pocket of his jeans. When his hand returns to my field of vision, I see that it's a flat head screwdriver.

He pokes the tip of the tool into the black powder, taking a few stabs at the middle of the substance before he moves on to grinding the head of the screwdriver against the edge of the bowl.

Was this something like the scraping I heard back in the dark in the jail cell just before Glenn cracked open the wall? I could ask, but I'm not in the mood for a bunch of additional smart ass remarks.

The grinding sound evens out, settling into a droning loop of metal scraping against stone. You can hear the circular quality of his screwdriver stroke somehow, the rise and fall as it loops over and over.

The white noise helps me zone out from my physical surroundings. My consciousness sucks up into my head more fully, and again, I become aware that my brain is on high alert, recording the proceedings for safe keeping in my memory bank.

In fairness, something about the image is striking. A grown man kneeling before a bowl, poking a screwdriver at it? That alone doesn't inspire intrigue, maybe. It's something about the man himself.

The creases at the corners of his mouth show determination. The lines around his eyes convey the faintest squint, communicating some wordless sense of intelligence and vulnerability. His posture gives off a sense of pride beaten down a little, like some fierce animal that's been tamed and forced to jump through too many rings of fire to count. He looks so specific just now. Out of all of the people in the history of the world, there has only been one Glenn Floyd. He's a ridiculous man but an interesting and kind one, too. And I can see all of that in this moment in a way that borders on overwhelming.

Plus, his mustache is perfect.

When Glenn rises and moves to the wall, it takes my brain a second to wake from my daydream of fiery rings. He begins to scrape the screwdriver on the wall, running it up and down to chip out a line of wallpaper in the rough shape of a door. It's another vaguely familiar sound, taking me back to my time in the cell. That was a concrete wall of course, so the scrape was more rough and shrill. Grating. Still, the scraping pattern calls it to mind.

Once there's a clear doorway outlined on the wall, Glenn pulls something from his left front pocket. I can't get a good look at it as he adjusts it in his fingers, so it's small enough to be mostly obscured by hand, I guess. Significantly smaller than a breadbox. He presses it to the wall, and from what I can see, it almost looks like a silver crayon. It smears along the outline, leaving a trail of something neither slimy nor colored at all. Being close enough to see the consistency of the layer of clear smear on the wall, my best guess is that it's a piece of wax or some similar substance.

He steps back and looks over his work, leaning this way and that to get better angles. I guess maybe the wax is easier to see if you get the light to reflect off of it just so.

Just as my mind remains in record mode for all of this time, I get the sense that Glenn operates in an odd state of mind as well. He looks lost in his work, his reality filtered down to just this bowl of black sand and the rectangle etched into the wallpaper. He is no longer aware that I'm still in the room. He looks to be not entirely here himself.

He scoops up the bowl and cradles it in his left arm, hugging it to his ribs. He then sticks his right index finger in his mouth and appears to swab it on the inside of his cheek like detectives using that weird q-tip to collect DNA in every TV cop drama.

He extracts the wet finger from his maw, and I take a step back – perhaps some instinctive fear of wet willies leftover from childhood. The index finger doesn't swipe at my ear, however. It swipes at the bowl, pulling free with a bunch of black powder stuck to it. I can now see that the powder is finer than granulated sugar.

Something about all of this is pretty disgusting. I don't know. I'm no fan of fingers in mouths or saliva used as an adhesive like that. Just not my thing.

Glenn brings the finger up to his face so close that he goes cross-eyed gazing upon it. It's quite a sight, a 50-some-year-old man with a dirty finger about two centimeters rom the tip of his nose. And there's such a sense of reverence in the silence around us now, all anticipation and wonder and just a glimmer of amazement.

The words blurt out of me:

"Checkin' the ol' dipstick, eh?"

I'm not even sure what I'm saying until I'm done talking. In the silence, I run it back in my memory.

And then I laugh. The kind of laugh that brings tears to your eyes within seconds. The kind of laugh that shakes your ribcage so hard, it makes it damn near impossible to breathe. The kind of laugh that stretches out in front of you like it could never possibly end. The kind of laugh that makes you feel like a different person.

I'm not sure why this level of laugh has come upon me. I mean, I don't know if it's that funny. It must be something about this moment, this tension settling over the room.

Glenn looks at me for those first few seconds, and then he laughs, too. Almost as hard as me.

I watch the world through the blur of teared up eyelashes opened just enough to see through. We laugh a long time, I think. Glenn laughs harder when I laugh harder, and I have this crazy disconnected feeling like we aren't even laughing at the same thing that somehow makes it that much funnier.

This goes on for a while. First, I bend at the waist, and then I kneel on the floor. A flash of heat comes over my face.

I start punctuating my laughing jags with deep breaths, trying to get back under control.

Each time I gather the poise necessary to slow the flood of laughter, my eyes dart to that black powder finger just sitting there on its own, pointing at the ceiling, and that image somehow makes the whole thing seem funny again.

The dipstick itself.

Glenn sets the bowl down on the bed and pulls up the collar of his t-shirt to wipe his eyes. He takes a few deep breaths and seems to gather himself.

This self control must be infectious to some degree. My laughter keeps rolling, but it has lost some of its intensity.

Gathering the bowl once more, Glenn moves to the wall. He smears his black powder finger along the wax line. I watch, laughter still twitching up from my gut in little fits.

And I hear something, the tiniest sound. It almost sounds like the rubber seal peeling away as a fridge door opens. What the hell was that?

I sit forward, no longer laughing, ass scooted to the very edge of the mattress.

He keeps working, really rubbing his finger into the wall. I begin to see the first area he coated with black soot, except it's not just coated with black soot. The spot recesses into the wall. Not a lot. Maybe a quarter of an inch.

The fridge sound emits from the crack again as he dips his finger back into the bowl. Will he have to lick it again? Will he have to use a different finger? Neither. He curls the index finger and spoons up some powder, half flinging to the wall before he goes to grinding at it. Clouds of black billow to the ground. Sloppy as hell, this fool.

Looking back at the wall, I see that more of the line has blackened and recessed. I guess that process must produce the opening fridge door noise.

He works faster now, and it seems like the black wants to stick to the line. Some of it spills to the floor, sure, but the bulk of it seems to leap from his finger and adhere itself to the wall. And then it settles for a bit and does that lip popping fridge thingy.

Weird shit.

Glenn squats to finish the very bottom of each side, which he makes short shrift of, and then stands. He almost brushes his finger against his shirt but thinks better of it.

"I'm going to get cleaned up," he says. "Are you ready to go?"

I consider this for a moment.

"I think I'm ready," I say.

CHAPTER 26

Just like in the jail cell, Glenn wedges his fingers into the recessed area and wiggles the door out a little at a time. I see the white light shine through the crack as he finagles the section of wall. He gives me a nasty look, so I go to help him.

Behind the facade of wallpaper, the door looks like smooth stone about four inches deep. I get my fingers around it and we pull. It's sort of like moving a smaller version of one of those blocks at Stone Henge. For some reason all I can think about is how it'd be that much more of a bitch on carpeted floor. I don't even know if that's true, but it seems like it. I picture the corner catching on the fibers over and over.

We grunt and heave and lift with our backs, and soon it's open a decent amount. I move to do more pushing than pulling now that there's a little room to do so. I turn to get a better look behind the door as I take my new position, just glancing at it out of the corner of my eye as the push continues. The light spills into the room through the eight inch opening, bright and white and eyeball scorching. It dapples over my arms as they strain against the block.

"Don't look directly into it," Glenn says.

Immediately, I look directly into it.

I don't really see anything, though. Just some whiteness and what not. Illumination and all. It burns pink spots onto my retinas that seem to flutter about my field of vision.

"Let's focus on getting this open," he says. "You'll have time to look into the light when we're done."

He sounds so much like a dad reasoning with a toddler that I feel bad. I turn back, and we toil some more and exert ourselves and the doorway lurches forward an inch or so at a time.

I notice that the corner of the block is gouging a pretty good scratch into the wood floor. I wonder if this will disappear or something when we walk through. I'd ask Glenn, but I don't want him to blow a damn gasket when he sees how fucked his floor is. I imagine he feels the same way about the floors as he does about the leather in the Explorer, if not touchier still.

"That's good," he says, and we stop inching the door open.

We stand a moment, hands on hips, chests both huffing and puffing. I look at the light for as long as I can stand it. Pretty bright. I grab my hoodie and pull it on.

"Well," I say. "Let's go."

Glenn nods, and he steps forward toward the door, then stops.

"Oh my dear God," he says, mumbling.

"What?"

He clutches at his chest as though he's having a heart attack.

"Just look what we've done to the floor."

CHAPTER 27

We walk into the light.

"Just keep moving forward," Glenn says. "I'll be right behind you."

I step through the doorway, eyes squinted to slits. The light surrounds me, shocking in its intensity. It gets at my eyes and stings a little, but I'll be OK.

By the time I've taken two more steps, I can see nothing but the brightest light. I turn back to get a look into the guest bedroom from this vantage point out of curiosity, but I guess I was too slow. There's only light in all directions now. No door. No Glenn. Just light.

"Keep moving forward," I say to myself, echoing Glenn's advice.

Yep. I do that. Forward, I move.

I see now that there's a blue tint to the light. It looks white from afar, maybe out of sheer brightness, but there's a blue undertone when you're inside of it. Weird.

I realize that I have no feel for how far I've gone now or how fast I'm moving. The light drowns out my sense of these things.

And suddenly squinting is not enough. The light attacks me, forces itself onto me. The sting swells into a sharp pain, stabbing ice picks of blazing glow into my head. I go to close my eyes and shield them with my hands, but it makes no difference.

I run. I plaster my hands over my eyes and run, but it's no use. The light pushes its pointy fingers into my skull, jabs them into my brain.

I want to scream, but I can't muster it. The stabby feelings in my head make all of my facial and neck muscles tense up and writhe in a way that makes vocalizing impossible. I can't even open my mouth. I can sort of hum, if I push from the diaphragm.

So I do that. I hum the sounds of anguish the best I can. I hum the hum of the stabby brained. Let's just say it's not the most beautiful of melodies.

I stumble on my own feet and belly smack the ground. I go to hop up right away, but I freeze. The pain is too much to concentrate on other things now. I slink back down. All I can do is picture blood gushing out of my eye sockets, the red streaming down in two rivers.

And then something gives. Some unexplained shift happens, and I'm OK. The brightness fails to dim even the slightest bit, but it doesn't matter now. It doesn't hurt me anymore.

I rise, and I press forward like Glenn would want.

As I walk deeper and deeper into the light, my thoughts seem to simplify: I am warm. I like the warm. It is bright here. That is OK, too. Sometimes the warm and the bright seem to go together, like the sun. I like the sun. It is warm.

I like blankets. They are soft. They get warm if you wait.

I keep shaking my head, and that seems to reset my brain back to dim as opposed to extremely dim.

And I walk, and the light dissolves around me, and it's like I'm walking through fog. Or like maybe Amity set up a kickass smoke machine to make our entrance more dramatic. That'd be pretty sweet. Like any second now a voice will say, "Ya'll ready for this?" and the beat will drop. Glenn and I will rush onto the scene and do some kind of awesome high five move, probably one of those elaborate high fives with a bunch of steps involved, in fact.

Yep.

Any second now...

Tendrils of mist coil and reach out toward me, and I feel a chill creep into the air. Even through my hoodie, goosebumps wriggle across my arms. At first I think it's that rush of cool that runs through you when things are exciting, such as when the beat is about to drop. But no. It's cold as hell here. Dead of winter cold.

The fog sinks frosted teeth into my skin where it makes direct contact, and my skin feels all dry like it's cracking from the cold.

Maybe Amity opted for a shitload of dry ice instead of a smoke machine, 'cause what the hell? It's chilly.

Starting to miss the bright and warm feeling of walking in the light earlier, even if it tried to burn out my eyeballs for a while there.

I keep expecting the fog to clear and the green woods to appear any second now. I bet it's much warmer there. The woods are always nice and warm. Not too hot. No. Just a real nice temp.

Not like this. This is like walking around in a deep freezer.

I pull my arms in from the sleeves of my hoodie and hug

them against me. Thankfully I'm wearing a t-shirt underneath, as I briefly make the mistake of touching the ball of my thumb to my neck. Frigid.

I try to pick up the pace, but it's hard. The cold makes me want to quit. Every step turns into a battle, but I keep going, keep putting one foot in front of the other, keep kicking into the fog.

Even so, the cold only advances. It edges up my legs and lurks around the perimeter of my torso, waiting for the opportunity to stab icicles all through my core.

Is the fog a touch brighter now? It's hard to tell. It seems like I can see some brighter white gleaming through.

The muscles in the trunk of my body spasm and shudder, and now I'm shivering. The violent shakes only slow me down, though. I can't help but get mad each time my body jerks without my say so. I just want to walk until this is over, and my body is fighting me.

My teeth begin to chatter, so I hold my mouth a little open so they won't bang into each other. My jaw can just wiggle away and make its own fun.

So yeah.

It's cold.

I watch my feet disappear into the fog over and over as I walk. I try to think of nothing but that: the next step and the next, but tears drip from my nose. My body spews water from my tear ducts into my nasal cavity to try to fight the dryness, but it only makes the cold sting worse.

And then my foot doesn't vanish into the clouds. It meets a touch of resistance as it descends, and there's a familiar crunch as it continues landing.

Snow.

I look up to see an utter lack of fog. In its place I find not the green woods I was expecting, but a frozen landscape. Sparsely wooded fields of snow sprawl in all directions, with flatlands to my right and hills to my left. Maybe it's just in contrast to the snow, but the trees all look black. They're probably just leafless for the winter, but it's hard to imagine they're not dead. Crunchy stalks of grass gone beige poke up from the white in patches. They seem like the only thing around that's not a shade of black or white.

No Glenn? I sort of thought we'd come out of there right together? Wait. Maybe he's not through yet. I was a few paces ahead of him after all, and I'm generally a pretty fast walker.

I don't know. Should I wait around or something?

I pace back and forth a little, moving to try to keep warm as I mull it over. With my arms crossed over my chest inside my hoodie, I rub my hands on my upper arms. Friction seems like a good idea, but everything is numb enough now that I can't really tell the difference.

This snow doesn't fluff or billow as I march through it. It's too crisp for all of that. My shoes break it time and again. It sort of sounds like someone eating cereal all slow.

Ah. There we go.

Footprints form a path trailing up over the biggest hill to my left. It looks like one set of prints, so I'll assume it's Glenn. Admittedly the snow is torn up to the degree that it's plausible these could be the footprints of more than one person walking single file. Let's not forget that Glenn is on the heavyset side, though. He could really tear up some snow if he put his mind to it.

I trudge along the path. Weirdly, it may be tougher going in this loosened snow than it was on the crisp stuff. Hm... That's dumb.

Wait. I guess I could just walk next to the path.

Yep. It's genius. I feel like Albert Einstein and myself are men of similar ilk.

I tread along next to the path. It's still difficult to make my way up the hill – the incline is on the steep side - but at least I can get a little traction in the crunchiness.

I climb a while. It's so still out here. No sounds but those of my shoes collapsing snow bits. It always seems quieter when there's snow, I guess. I think it dampens the sound.

I step on an icy patch and slip, landing on one knee.

Shit.

I stand and shimmy an arm back into its sleeve to brush the snow off of my pants. Most of it comes off, but there's a decent sized wet spot.

So that's good.

My hand stings worse than before from touching the wet. I wiggle it back under the hoodie blanket and go back to the friction efforts which may or may not be working. Thinking back, I'm lucky I didn't fall flat on my face with my arms tucked in like this.

I resume the climb, really digging to make the final few steps.

There.

As soon as I top the hill, I make eye contact with Glenn. He stands in front of a pine tree, his hands folded neatly in front of him. Well, well, well... That was a little easier than I thought it might be. I pictured myself trekking a long way as I usually do out here.

But then I notice that he doesn't look happy to see me. He closes his eyes and shakes his head, disappointed. And I realize that his hands aren't folded in front of him. They're bound.

Movement to his left catches my eye. Ah, now I see that he's not alone. Three men stand just behind him, black cowls shrouding their heads. Between the hoods and the fact that they're partially obscured by pine boughs, I can't get a great look at them.

I squint to study them, waiting for the faces to come into the clear. It seems they haven't spotted me yet. I'll just get a better look really quick and then hide.

But I don't make it past the first face. My mouth drops open. My brain shuts down.

Riston Farber.

CHAPTER 28

Snowy hills stretch out before us. Black trees jut from the white here and there, holding their arms up like someone might see them and come pluck them from the cold. Part of me thinks this might be worth a shot, but a piece of rope binds my hands together now. I feel like you need to get those arms out wide if you really want someone to save you, and my ability to do so is hindered.

I mean, who's going to rescue some guy that's making a letter I with his body rather than a Y? I'm sorry, but that's just not how this works.

Glenn and I walk ahead of the others, I guess so they can keep an eye on us. Farber, Cromwell and Woods comprise our captors – the three amigos, as no one calls them. So far Farber has yet to speak. Woods does most of the talking. I've tried to search Cromwell's face for signs of sympathy or friendship, but he won't look at me for more than a second. When he does, his expression conveys no feelings, good or bad. I'm not sure what to make of that.

On the other hand, Farber stared holes through me when they first came upon me. He paced a semi-circular path in front of me while my hands were bound, his eyes never leaving my face. I expected to see some glee there, some gloating smile in his eyes at having caught us, but I saw no sadistic pleasure. I saw a hard expression, a permanent crinkle between his eyebrows. Instead of demonic joy, I found intensity, coldness, perhaps a hint of mild disappointment conveyed in his features.

"Veer left about 45 degrees," Woods says, cupping a hand to his mouth. "We'll cut right between those two trees."

He points, and Glenn and I follow the trajectory of his finger, blazing a trail in the snow. Woods is a small man with fat cheeks. He appears to be older than the other two. There's a tired look about him, a droop to his eyes and a sag to his cheeks. He seems like someone's dad that just wants to be left alone so he can put on his slippers, kick back in his recliner, and watch sports on TV 365 nights a year without speaking a word to anyone. Instead he's out here directing foot traffic on some astral plane, probably missing the big game as we speak.

I submitted to my capture peacefully. I was ready to run for it, but Glenn said I should just do what they say. I see now that Woods wears a scabbard with a handle sticking out of it. I'm going to go way out on a limb here and suggest that perhaps there's a blade connected to that hilt. Anything is possible. I'm guessing Glenn's insistence that I give in had to do with not wanting me to get stabbed, an impulse I can appreciate and endorse wholeheartedly.

Reading between the lines of the conversation as they apprehended me, apparently Glenn had told them he was traveling alone, and they believed him. They were surprised to see me. Pleased, too. If I had just hidden a moment sooner instead of standing there like a fool...

We walk for a long time, passing through the gap between the pair of trees Woods mentioned. The snow grows deeper as we advance, tougher to trudge through, and it slows us down.

It occurs to me that the wintry landscape surrounding us is likely permanent rather than seasonal, or at least that would make sense. I remember Glenn talking about how time seemingly doesn't pass in these places. It's daylight forever in this part, nighttime forever in that part. So maybe this is the forever winter part? I think that's probably right. Not a great place to call home. Not that great to visit either, really.

The march continues, our footsteps crunching out a pulsing rhythm like a sleepy drum beat where the snare always hits a touch late. I don't know if it's the sound or the cold that lulls me into that far away feeling. Maybe it's a little of both.

In any case, my thoughts begin to percolate. As the shock of all of this fades away, an interesting mix of anticipation and dread ripple all through me. I feel like something important is about to happen, and yet I'm not as scared as I probably should be considering my last encounter with Farber as well as Amity's warning about him.

Up close and personal like this, he seems less like the evil figure that I had envisioned and more like a really focused, intense guy. He may well mean us harm, but it's not in that cruel, Freddy Krueger way. It's something else. It's like the difference between being scared of a person breaking into your house compared to a bear passing by the cabin you're staying in. Both are terrifying, but you know the bear has no malicious intent. Even if it attacks you, it's because it's a simple creature that doesn't know any better. The guy breaking into your house, however? Evil dick. Him you have total contempt for.

Even so, I'm not that scared for now. I just have this feeling that we're going to slip out of this like we always seem to. I don't know. Maybe it's like after you dread something for a long time, as it's happening it doesn't seem that bad in a way, because at least the dread is over.

As we walk on, the land flattens out into total desolation. No trees. No signs of any life. Just a flat expanse of untouched snow. A tundra that seems to stretch on forever.

Am I excited to see where we're going? Maybe a little. Is this what Cromwell meant when he said you feel like anything is possible when Farber is around? I guess I can see it. Even when you're his prisoner, you feel like something massive is about to go down.

I watch gusts of wind flutter frozen powder this way and that. I think my body temp goes down a few degrees just from looking at it.

My arms, legs, and face are so numb now that the cold doesn't bother me that much, though. A dull ache persists everywhere instead of sharp pains in the coldest places like before. It's not pleasant, but it's not too bad. And my core stays reasonably warm from the aerobic exercise anyway, or at least I think that's what's happening. Maybe the chill is merely calming my thoughts before it shuts off the lights for good. I understand that hypothermia is a smooth talker. It soothes you right up until the end.

I don't know. Pretty sure if I keep moving, I'll be fine, though.

My thoughts sink below the surface level of sensory details again and forage around in the feelings part. Even if I'm mostly not panicking about my predicament, one bit of uneasiness still resides down there in the murky bits – a twinge of genuine, pants-shitting fear emitting from one detail: Cromwell's lack of eye contact. I don't like it. That's probably the one thing that makes me worry that this whole thing will turn out the wrong way.

I think back to his demeanor in his apartment. He seemed so much the type to be himself under any circumstances, to do so to a fault by annoying people with his honesty. There's a fine line between candor and obnoxiousness that I figured Cromwell crossed with gusto like it was a finish line on a regular basis. I just can't imagine him being too discrete about anything, you know?

And then he gave me that gesture to tell me to get out of the church when Farber made his triumphant return. So he was into helping me at that point.

Something has changed, though. He sure isn't helping me now. But is he playing it all cold to conceal his feelings from me or from Farber? Hard to say.

A creaking sound beside me shakes me back to reality. It's Glenn gasping almost under his breath, his eyes gone wide. I follow his gaze out into the snowy distance.

There's something there, a darker shade set in the white, maybe a structure of some kind. It takes my eyes a second to make sense of it. I see columns set in a circle with a platform in the center of them. It's hard to get a sense of scale, but it almost looks like a gazebo with no roof.

The men mumble behind us. I glance back to see Woods pointing and Farber nodding. I can't understand them, but I take it that they've spotted the gazebo as well. I look upon Cromwell for a while, but he stares at the ground.

I turn back and we walk on, the structure seeming to grow as we draw near.

"What is it?" I whisper.

"An altar," Glenn says.

CHAPTER 29

So the roofless gazebo is a little bigger than I thought. The marble floor forms a circle about the size of a basketball court. There's no snow coating it, not even a little, nor is there any white stuff on the matching marble platform in the center of it. I guess that's the actual altar now that I think about it. Anyway, it doesn't look like the snow has been cleared from these surfaces. It looks like there never was any there. I guess that's hard to say definitively, but that's what it looks like.

We walk toward the altar, our feet moving with ease in silence that is shocking after so long battling at the crunchity crunch out there.

"Sit," Woods says, pointing.

As soon as Woods commands Glenn and I to take a seat on the altar, I know two things: it's a matter of time before the cold freezes me solid now that I'll be sitting still on a stone slab, and we're probably about to perform some ritual which may or may not involve a human sacrifice of a guy with a consonant stuffed last name that rhymes with Throbdagger.

Yep. So things are looking up.

We sit.

"I don't suppose you guys have any blankets," I say.

No one even cracks a smile, so I learn right away that this is a tough crowd. Glenn elbows me in the ribs and shakes his head. He always gets uptight in moments like these, but I don't see how talking could make any difference now.

The hooded men look at each other and then back at me.

"You're just a kid," Farber says.

His voice sounds thinner than I had imagined. It's not squeaky or anything like that. Just kind of a normal, intelligent tone. I guess I figured him for a deep, thick voice like a lich lord or something.

"I don't know," I say. "I'm 27."

Air puffs out of his nostrils, and in the cold, it looks like smoke.

"That may be so," he says. "You're fully grown. You've existed for the time necessary to become a man. But you think and live like a child that knows nothing. Out here? This place? It has given you a gift that you don't know how to accept."

I don't say anything. He paces a little as he talks. Woods' eyes watch my face, a curious look to them. Cromwell only stares at Farber, his face expressionless.

"Because, like a child, you see the world only within a framework of achieving happiness," Farber says. "You try to reconcile how this gift will fit into your pursuit of happiness instead of seeing it for what it is."

He brushes a gloved hand on one of the pillars and turns his hand over to observe it.

"Only fools speak of happiness. Only children," he says. "Men speak of power. Fools see power as an idea to be interested in or disinterested in, perhaps even an inconvenience to their dreams of happiness. Men see how power is inevitable and concrete. If ignored, it doesn't go away. Someone will possess it one way or another. Someone will use it to bend reality to their will whether you're interested or not. Power and what it's used for are what's real. They're the only things that are real. Happiness, or a lack thereof, is the inconvenience to what really matters. Or at least that's often the case."

He looks at me again and tilts his head to the side. I can't decide if there's some sympathy in his body language. I kind of doubt it.

"A man with an absence of interest in power is like man with an absence of interest in breathing," he says. "It is obtuse, unnatural, unsustainable. It fails to grasp the primal, the essence of being human."

I say nothing. Whatever is left of the body heat in my legs drains into the marble through my hamstrings. The cold reaches up through me now, finally sinking into the core of my body.

"I'm right about you, aren't I?" he says. He spreads his arms out wide, upturned palms gesturing to the sky. "Heaven gave you these gifts. It brought you here. It showed you miracles. You. Out of everyone, it loved you. It wanted you. It chose you. And you've spent your days mulling how that fit into your happiness, have you not? Perhaps it even made you sad. Think about that. A miracle that made you sad."

He smiles, and for the first time I get just a glimmer of that demonic fervor I expected to find. Perhaps it's not one of his primary personality traits, but there's a little in there after all.

"Isn't that the most adolescent thing you can imagine? A grown man that has never experienced real hunger, never experienced real pain, never experienced much of anything at all, finds a way to make a gift a burden, a way to make a miracle a tragedy."

His smile fades. I just stare into his eyes. I try not to shiver because it makes me feel weak.

"You know, real suffering exists in the world. There are babies born that starve to death before they ever learn to walk or speak. Rape. Murder. The worst abuses you can imagine are happening somewhere right now. You know what can change those things? Power. Power is the only force that can change reality. Everything else is dreaming. Escape. Selfish, delusional bullshit. Awful teenage poetry scrawled in a notebook."

My primary interest at this point is smashing his face in so he will see that I understand how power works on one of the most primal levels - the "my fist shuts your mouth" level.

My hands are so cold. I bet hitting him would really hurt. It'd be worth it and all, but still.

"This place loves you. It's connected to you. I always thought it liked me best. I thought I was special, but it is different with you," he says. "Whether it's spiritual or energy we can connect to or a little of both, it connects with you the deepest of all. And you don't care. You could change the world, and you don't care."

He clears his throat, one of those disgusting bursts of phlegmy vibrations.

Gross.

"You got nowhere on your own," he says. "Why do you think you went through all of those rituals? Culminating with the fire in the well and your resurrection? I put you through a sped up version of all of the lessons I learned. I made you more and more powerful, because you were too dumb and too selfish to see what you had. You didn't even know what was happening. Never had a clue until after you were killed and reborn."

He goes to clear his throat again, but it turns into a cough this time. A hacking, wet cough that reminds me how frail he is. It's harder to tell with the robe and hood on.

When he resumes talking, his voice sounds a little raspy from the coughing fit.

"But you and your friend will be made useful in the end. One way or the other, you will serve power just as we all do, whether we want to or not. You will serve a force greater than yourself."

Farber looks over my head and nods. I see movement out of the corner of my eye, and then something heavy bashes into the back of my head.

What?

Not cool.

I'm falling over onto my side. The words, "brain not work right," occur to me as the darkness descends, but there's something important hovering at the edge of my fading consciousness. There's something I need to remember now before it's too late.

Yes.

I know what to do.

CHAPTER 30

I let myself pour out of that spot between my eyebrows like Amity showed me. That feeling comes over me again, like there's all of this pressure focused on that one area, like water spiraling down the drain just there, except up. This time I keep my eyes open for the duration of the process. I rise slowly, inching up but not quite out of my head yet.

Everything goes the rest of the way black, though.

Shit.

Did I not get out in time? Did unconsciousness beat me to it? I try to fight it, try to push myself back to the surface.

Am I still here?

My vision fades in, a yellow tint to everything at first, and I realize that the pressure is gone. I feel free. I float skyward in slow motion. I try to look down, to see what they're up to, but I can't move. My focus won't shift anywhere else. I can look only at the sky, a gray mass of cloud-like fluff that looks more poised to go black than I had been aware of until now.

The paralysis I'm experiencing fails to scare me, though. I suspect it won't last long. I think everything is still coming around, like rebooting a computer.

Cromwell strides into my frame of vision. He opens his robe and tucks a blackjack in his pocket. Never thought I'd get knocked out by one of those, especially out here on the astral plane. I guess you never know where your life will lead until you get there.

He kneels through me, which is a weird sensation. He's down there a while, fumbling about below where I can see, presumably checking on my body. I hear noises, something scraping or sliding.

My repeated attempts at moving finally find purchase. I swivel to see Cromwell with his arms looped under my arms. He drags my body away from me. My chin rests on my chest, bobbling with every step, my neck as limp as a piece of spaghetti.

"Leave him," Farber says.

Cromwell stops walking, lets my shoulders lean back into his knees. His forehead wrinkles up.

"But I thought..." Cromwell says.

"Leave him," Farber says again. "He can wait until we go back. We'll do this one here and the second on the other side. Doing one on each side should heighten the effects."

Cromwell eases my torso to the ground. He moves with care, but the back of my head thuds into the marble still, and the man maneuvering my body grimaces at this. He bites the middle finger of his glove to pry it off quickly and feels around the back of my skull. His fingers come back clear. I'm not bleeding. So things could be worse between Cromwell and me, I figure. At least he doesn't laugh at the thought of cracking my head open like an egg. It's a start.

I turn to find Glenn's body face down on the marble. I guess he got the blackjack treatment as well. His face angles away from me, so I begin floating over there to get a look. Before I even get close, Farber and Woods come along and stoop to hoist Glenn by his armpits and ankles. They shuffle toward the altar with him.

There's mumbling as they line him up parallel with the long side of the platform. Then they sway his body back and forth, counting aloud in unison:

"One.

Two.

Three."

On three, they toss his limp body onto the stone. He wobbles there, tipping onto his side and flopping face down, but now his visage points toward me. His expression looks solemn but fine, like he's deep asleep, perhaps having a mildly disturbing dream.

Only an unconscious human being lies face down with their arms pinned underneath them. It doesn't look right. His shoulders slump oddly, and his face appears to be pressed down a little too flat somehow, like without the arms positioned to support some of the weight, it all grinds the face into the marble. It reminds me of pictures I've seen of people gunned down in the street.

I inch closer, but I'm so slow. Farber steps forward and puts a hand over Glenn's eyes. He speaks, but it's all quiet, almost a whisper, and I can't make out the words. My progress reminds me of a turtle riding a glacier, but as I draw near I can make out a syllable here and there. I think Farber is speaking Latin.

He finishes his chant, and all three men bow their heads. I move forward in the silent moment, but I'm still a good 15 feet out.

And for the first time, I'm scared. All the way scared. This has never quite felt real, I think. Even now, it's off, but I get that something bad is happening. Something really bad. It never really sank in until this long, quiet spell fell upon us like a blanket, this elongated bit of pure anticipation, a last gasp of how things are that will soon be undone.

I know something permanent is about to happen. Something that can't be taken back. I know that my life will be divided into segments after this. One segment before this moment. One segment after. I know that it will change me. I can feel all of these things.

And I can do nothing to change any of it. I can only move closer and closer to Glenn's place on the altar at the speed of an inch worm.

The men stir, the moment of silence reaching its endpoint. From my vantage point, I can see only the back of Farber's hood. Cromwell and Woods face my direction, though. They look at each other, grave expressions etching hard lines on their foreheads and around their mouths.

Farber's head bobs. That is the sign. He gives no verbal command. He doesn't have to. He can speak without moving his lips. His legion acts at his slightest gesture, his bodily whim. He commands life and death with a wink, a nod, a wave of the hand.

Woods ducks down, fiddling with something underneath the altar. Stone grinds against stone, and then the sound cuts off. Did he open something? I can't see from here, but it sounded like something of that variety.

He reaches in with one hand and then the other, presumably pulling something free, but the marble platform blocks my view. He turns to Cromwell, extends both hands. Cromwell takes the offering. I get a momentary glimpse. I think I know now, but I could be wrong. I could be wrong.

Woods reaches in again, first with his left, then his right. Stone grinds on stone once more. He stands. Another glimpse, a metallic reflection flaring my way. I don't know. I could still be wrong.

And the men lean over Glenn like babysitters checking on a napping baby. They tilt their heads, their eyeballs running up and down his sprawled figure, sizing him up.

And I know. I already know. I should stop moving closer, but I can't. I should back away. I should disappear completely, just disintegrate into a cloud of dust and blow away over the tundra.

I do none of these things. I inch toward Glenn's face, my progress as slow and steady as ever.

Woods steps forward. He stands up a little straighter, raises his right hand into view. I wasn't wrong.

I can only watch now. I can only watch.

The first sword enters the left hamstring. The tip pierces the pant leg and glides through the meat, seemingly finding little resistance. There's a metallic clink as the blade meets the marble. A little blood comes, but not much. The sword plugs most of the hole.

Woods releases the hilt, and the sword stands on its own. It looks like some illusion from a magician's act, something you'd see in the circus, but it's real. I look on Glenn's face, expecting him to wake up screaming any second, but he doesn't move.

The second sword enters the small of the back, just off center, to the left of the spine. His jacket rides up, and the navy blue t-shirt pulls taut in the area surrounding the point of entry and then relaxes into wrinkles as the incision is made.

Now Cromwell steps up for his turn. He looks a little somber, though not as disturbed as you might imagine.

The third and fourth blades find homes in the lower back as well. They enter at odd angles compared to those placed by Woods, which both ran parallel to the spinal column.

Woods finds gaps between ribs to insert the fifth and sixth blades, and Cromwell does the same for the seventh and eighth, though he must also avoid the shoulder blades.

Number nine sinks into that ball of muscle that connects the neck and shoulders. And Woods pushes the tenth blade into the back of Glenn's neck. He works at it a little as this is toned and fibrous compared to the rest.

A sound like a single throaty snore comes from Glenn's throat as the metal penetrates his wind pipe. Woods unhands the hilt of the tenth blade, and we all just watch.

Ten blades stick out of Glenn's back. For now, he continues breathing. He lives. But it won't be long.

Am I in shock? I must be. I must be. I wait for the reality to sink in. Maybe none of this can be real until he is gone.

His breath rasps on, scraping in and out like he's inhaling steel wool instead of oxygen. The red spills out of him, the largest volume flowing from his neck, but it's slower than you'd think. It will take him a long time to bleed out.

He doesn't appear too upset. It is peaceful in that sense. His face shows no signs of pain. His lips still display the faintest downward curl at the corners like he's still walking through the same vaguely unpleasant dream as before. He has no clue how much worse reality has become. And I'm glad for that. I'm glad he doesn't know.

And I find parts of my brain rejecting all of this out of

hand. Wild animal parts that flail against this as a concept. How can this be the end of Glenn's story? How can he die? He is a large man, a strong man. He gets all pushy and takes what he wants from the world. He knows his way around life, knows what matters to him. He says, "What the fuck?" to the grocery store clerk that ignores him and elbows people in the back to fight through the crowd at the airport. He tried so hard to point me toward the light, tried so hard to help me see myself and my life with clarity.

He was never supposed to die. It doesn't make sense.

And I am close now. I am right next to him. Right next to his face.

Respiration inflates his chest. He doesn't stir beyond that. His features are calm and striking.

I'm not sure how long I watch him. It feels like a long time, but I can't say that with any certainty.

But his breathing slows down now, becomes more strained. The wind groans on the way in and rasps on the way out. The hesitation between each exhale and inhale grows longer and longer. And it's too long.

A final sigh emits from his lips and seems to shatter all of his bulk at once. He is smaller now.

Shrunken. Spent. Drained.

Forever.

CHAPTER 31

Please, God, erase me. Undo my creation like I was never real.

Just help me disappear.

I don't care how. I don't.

Burn me. Bury me. Cover me in dirt.

Just take me out of this place, this life.

I don't belong here. I never did.

CHAPTER 32

I wake. The sound fades in first. The quiet. The sound of the open air of the outdoors dampened by a thick shroud of snow. Muffled. A filtered version of how it's supposed to sound outside.

It is cold. It is a cold world.

I open my eyes to see the gray sky above me with columns of stone evenly spaced at the periphery of my vision. Glancing down at my body reveals my location: I lie on the marble slab where Cromwell left me. The memory of that image flashes across my mind, my head thudding against the stone and him ripping off his glove to check for blood or skull fracturing or whatever.

I blink and look back up. Is the sky going black before my eyes? It seems like it, it seems darker now, but I'm not sure.

I sit up.

The body still lies there, the swords sticking out of it. It looks posed, almost cheesy like something in one of those awful serial killer movies.

This is real, though. This is my friend. Or was. I want to cover him up. It feels like he's out in the open, exposed for everyone to see, and covering him, that will keep him safe. He looks all small now, defeated and deflated, but he's mostly the same, like he'll wake up any second now.

The cells that comprise Glenn's biological makeup are all still there for the most part. His brain is still there. His organs are still there. It doesn't make sense. All the pieces are still there. How can you turn those parts off and never be able to turn them back on? They are the same as they were before, mostly. They are the same cells, the same material. But the magical juice that made him alive is gone now. That's how it works.

He will never come back, and there will never be another Glenn Floyd.

I burst into tears. My face goes all red and hot. And I twitch in my chest and arms. I think the spasms come over me out of attempts to stop crying, out of feeling powerless and small and trying to stop it physically somehow. I try to squirm away from the overwhelming sadness and anger that racks sobs from my throat without my say so. I try to hold myself still and stop the water from pouring from my eyes.

I try these things, and I fail.

It's not fair.

Why? Why is he gone? Why does this happen? Why are we all brought here to die? Why would anyone bring us here to kill us all one by one? Who would want to hurt us like this? Why would anyone want that? What purpose could any of this serve? Why do we exist at all just to be wiped out?

Why would the universe work this way?

And consoling words erupt in my imagination.

"Death is a part of life."

Shut up. Stop trying to tell me how to fucking feel. My friend is gone. This one individual is gone forever. That the same fate befalls everyone doesn't make it any less real or any less tragic every single time. So shut it. Just leave me alone.

"He's in a better place."

Fuck off. You don't know anything. How do you know where he is? I don't need you to patronize me, talking like you know more than me when you don't know anything. Believe it or not, it doesn't comfort me to have people condescend to me, to have people talk to me in childish terms. Just because you're a coward that can't look at shit honestly, trying to put death in some box to make it seem smaller, trying to label it in some way to make it make sense to your dim brain so you don't have to think about it too hard, so you don't ever have to feel confused. But I am confused because I see it all for the mess it really is. I don't pretend I can spout some platitude that makes all the ugliness inside of me go away, all the ugliness in a universe that murders everyone and everything in time.

If you were honest with yourself, you would see it the same way. If you weren't scared to death of your own feelings, you would see how massive this is, you would feel how big it hurts. You wouldn't get all uptight. You wouldn't be so concerned about snuffing out my emotions, just as I don't care about extinguishing yours.

Nobody knows anything, so stop trying to boil it down into a bullshit slogan that will make you feel safe. It doesn't make you safe to dumb everything down like that. It just makes me think you're dumb.

Stop.

Just stop. Stop trying to police my feelings. Stop trying to tell me what I should think of what is going on. Stop forcing your bullshit on me. Stop giving me my own box and my own label so you don't have to think too hard about me either. So you can be comfortable like nothing is really real, like none of this is really happening.

Like you're so fucking cool, you can look down on everything. You can look down on what's real and what matters and what people really feel. You can laugh and laugh like what you pretend is so much better than reality, like you are apart from it all, way up above this pettiness.

But you are no different. Your body will betray you just the same. A car crash will drain your blood, or a cluster of damaged cells in your colon will turn cancerous, or your heart will pop in your chest while you watch reruns of Seinfeld one afternoon. The day will come. Your body will slide out of your control even though part of you was certain it would never really happen to you. You will be made small. You will be made powerless. And you will die, and we will plant you in the ground like all of the others.

And the people that care about you will be inconsolable, and other people will try to calm them down. 'Cause life goes on. And it's all part of God's plan. And they're so sorry for your loss.

And that's good enough, right?

So let's all get back to production and consumption already. There's a new show where Gordon Ramsay yells at chefs on tonight, and I want to eat a bunch of fish sticks and watch it without people crying in the background. And I want to finger fuck my smart phone all day without feeling anything real, if possible.

See?

See?

I was right, wasn't I? I should have just stayed alone. I

should have stayed away from everyone.

I should have disappeared.

"Jeff," a voice says.

I realize that I'm standing now. I see only blobs and blurs through the tears, but based on the voice I think it's Cromwell.

"What?" I say.

There's a pause. It suddenly feels very silent here. Awkward.

"Just be quiet for a minute, man," he says. "I'm sorry."

"OK," I say.

I feel embarrassment. Not so much that I care what these other people think. I feel embarrassed and vulnerable as I forgot they were even here. I forgot I was even here in a way. I got lost in my thoughts and felt alone.

So they want me to be quiet. Was I crying too loudly for their delicate sensibilities?

Wait.

I was having that hypothetical argument out loud, ranting at myself, I think. Yelling, I think.

But yeah... It's fine. It's really just as well.

Who fucking cares?

And then I'm crying all the way again. The red and hot and wet spread across my face, descending over me like a cloak of hurt that smothers me and blocks the rest of the world out. I twitch and flail. I try not to fight it, but I do. So I weep, and I strain against it involuntarily. I think the struggle makes the sobs more anguished, more frustrated.

Pain catches in my throat and tries to choke me before its music passes through my lips. This happens over and over. I feel myself sink down into the heat like I'm leaving reality and going somewhere else, a darker place, a wet place. And I have a memory of feeling this sensation before, when I was a toddler or maybe even an infant. I knew it then, what it feels like to descend into this inconsolable place, this wounded and helpless place.

And pictures open in my head of Glenn:

He pulls on the DAMN SEAGULLS trucker hat outside of the diner, his eyes a little paranoid looking as we head into our undercover work.

A black and white version of him squats in some bushes in the other world, talking to me through a mirror. He looks tired. His beard sprouts thick wires of hair, matted down in some areas and fluffed up in others.

He feeds the cats and guards the food from Leroy, his mouth stuck in a permanent half smile as he shuffles his feet to block the cat's advances repeatedly, like a blocker picking up a blitzing linebacker.

He shovels faux Australian food into his face at Outback, his mouth juicy, his eyes crazed with gluttony, his mustache sporting barbecue sauce like a loaded paintbrush.

And I am underwater now, submerged in some warm liquid that separates me from the rest of the universe. Does my body flood me in warmth like this to try to help me stop being sad? Is it supposed to comfort me? Is it trying to make me feel safe and warm?

I don't.

And I remember how I felt at the Outback with Glenn when I couldn't stay awake. I floated face down. That's how I described it then, that I floated face down through my life.

And now I am under. I am sinking. And hitting the bottom might be a relief. It really might.

I try to put my hand over my face, but it doesn't work right. I try it again, but something is wrong. It takes a second to figure it out. A piece of rope holds my wrists together. I can't get either palm flat to my face. So I just hold my two stupid hands in front of me, my thumbs leaning into my forehead like I'm praying into them instead of crying.

And voices are yelling, and I know somehow that they've been yelling for a while now. They sound far away and weird and wet like all of us really are underwater.

But I think they're yelling at me, barking commands, trying to make me do something.

Can't they see how much I don't care about any of that? I don't even remember what's going on here, exactly. Can't they see that? Can't they see I have other concerns at the moment?

I don't want to do whatever they want me to do. I don't even want to breathe.

Something thumps me on the back of the head again, but I don't mind. What difference does it make at this point, you know? I'll just take a little nap is all.

CHAPTER 33

I fall into the black again, just like I did after that black fog surrounded me in the alley. But I feel no fear this time. I do not scream. I do not wave my arms.

I hurt.

I feel the place where Glenn is supposed to be, the piece of my consciousness where he resides, and it's like something has been ripped out by the roots. Like if the dentist took pliers to your teeth. Like that, but bigger.

One person out of all of the billions that have walked the Earth, out of all of the billions of years the planet has existed. The idea that I would even meet and know that one person is so unlikely from that perspective. But I did. I knew him for part of that tiny fraction of time he existed. And he was funny and interesting and smart and an endless well of thoughts and feelings and dreams that were all his own. It was a miracle that he lived and breathed. A miracle.

And now he is gone for good. Forever.

One second he was alive, and the next he was dead. Every morning that I wake up for the rest of my life, Glenn will be dead.

And if we had just done things slightly differently, he'd still be alive, probably for many years. Just one different choice. If I had hidden instead of locking onto Farber's face. If we kept trying to talk to Amity via the sleep thing instead of cracking open the wall and taking the direct route. A million other things. Endless options we could have pursued. They would have averted this.

And he would still be alive.

The blackness is everywhere. It is everything. It is the only thing.

And that's fine.

I fall for a long time, the sinking feeling dominating me, filling me with that nausea you get when you think too hard, when you worry too hard, when you think about where every story ends, and why you're here, and why you bother to carry on, when you think about the broken pieces that can't be put back together again.

I try to remember the last thing Glenn said. He was quiet after we were in captivity. Did he even speak to me at the end there? I guess he told me not to run, but I don't even remember his words. I just remember the gist of him saying it, like it happened off screen.

Wait. I remember he looked scared and told me the weird shape in the distance was an altar. I think that was it. I think that was the last thing he said.

It doesn't seem right. No grand declaration of any kind. No goodbye. Just a random moment. A transient snippet of a conversation that would be forgotten under any other circumstances. It's too obscure of a moment to house his final words. It's not big enough.

I keep thinking I should tell him about all of this. Ask him about all of this. See what he thinks about all of this awful shit. But I can't, of course. I can't. I never can.

What a stupid world. Why would things work this way?

Something occurs to me just then. The alley appears in my imagination. My alley. I see the noose. I see the gray. I see the hooded figure creeping closer. And for the first time the parallel becomes clear to me.

I was brought to a place and killed over and over again, seemingly for no reason. That's like life, you know? We're brought into the world to be killed in a sense. We're all having this insane metaphysical experience that we don't understand, that we can never fully appreciate, and it ends abruptly and unexplained. We're all experiencing an incomprehensible miracle, the meaning of which forever eludes us.

Life is it.

Did something bring me to the alley to try to teach me that, or did my imagination reflect that into whatever energy that connects us all? You know, the thing in quantum physics Glenn talked about. The infinite energy that connects all of us and is somehow faster than the speed of light or whatever. Do my dreams transmit things to that place? Or does it transmit things to me?

Maybe it's both. Maybe it doesn't matter. That's all behind the scenes. Life is what happens on the stage.

It's part flesh, and it's part consciousness. We don't know how they fit together. Not for sure. When the flesh dies, do we die? Is Glenn – the energy, the consciousness – somewhere else now? Does he go somewhere else or does he flicker out?

I don't know.

But the life part for the flesh - that ends. It ends for everyone.

And the bottomless black nothing all around me brightens

ever so faintly. It shows what it's made of, just a little. The light comes up. The black dissolves.

And red surrounds me. The primal color. The red on the inside that spills out of us when you slice our skin. The red on the inside that we see flashes of in moments of wrath, moments of vengeance. The wet, hot red on the inside of all of us.

And I find a red purpose here in the blackest moment. I find a reason to not disappear just yet.

Because Riston Farber is red on the inside, and when I open him up, it will all drain out. He will end like all the rest.

CHAPTER 34

I bubble up to the surface slowly. My eyes pulse open and closed a few times, the sounds around me fading in and out in unison with the light and darkness.

First I see only the ground, snow-covered land. It rolls by beneath me like I'm walking, but my legs are still. I do hear the crunch of footsteps beating through the snow again, though. They're close.

I see motion out of the corner of my eyes, but it's blocked from my view, I guess by my torso? Ah, I see. My head sags down onto my chest. Pretty uncomfortable now that I think about it.

I tell my neck to lift my head. It doesn't seem to be in the mood to do that. It bobs up and back down twice before I can make the motion stick.

There. Now I see. Woods and Cromwell carry me, each with one of their arms hooked under one of mine in such a manner that there's a shoulder digging into each of my armpits.

I look around for a moment. The sky is going black. Was it real before? Is it blackening because of what they did to Glenn? Or are we just walking into a new place where it's dark out? Not sure. There's still a little light to see by for the moment, either way. It's a dusk type darkness, and the snow reflects however much light there is, so it looks quite a bit brighter still.

Black trees populate the landscape again, and they're not as sparse as they were earlier today. Branches of opposing trees cross like they froze amid sword fights. I take this to mean that we left the tundra some time ago. Even so, snow stretches as far as I can see.

I let my head loll back down. Why bother telegraphing that I'm awake? They'd only make me walk on my own if they knew. Let 'em carry me, I say. It doesn't feel so great to have collar bones grinding into that soft place under each arm, but I'll conserve some energy this way.

I watch the ground a while. I note that the snow here isn't as deep as the stuff we traversed earlier. I guess we must truly be on our way out of this winter wonderland.

So... yay.

The crunching seems to change somehow. Part of the sound shifts spatially, seems to move from behind me to the left to right next to me and then ahead. I tilt my head up just a little to see Farber stride out in front of the group now, leading the way. He's right in front of me, hood nodding and billowing a touch with each step.

Looking at him makes me want to spit. Heat crawls up over my shoulders, climbs my neck and grips my cheeks. Not the crying warmth this time. A hateful heat. Homicidal.

I watch the drapey bits of his dumbshit robe flap and waver. I watch the wobble of his upper carriage as each footstep grinds down into the snow. Something about his walk is pompous.

I take a deep breath and let the air out of my nostrils all slow. Clouds of steam coil out of my nose. It looks like I'm breathing smoke, which is more or less how it feels.

But I have to bite back my hatred. I have to push it down.

Not yet. It has to wait. I have to...

I can't take it anymore. I shoot mind bullets out of my eyes, and they rip through his hood, penetrating the back of his head, his skull exploding hard shards and pulpy bits everywhere like a cantaloupe meeting an m-80 and showering forth flesh and seeds alike. His body slumps to the ground, the shattered skull landing first, a red river splashing out onto the snow, a faint sizzling as the red melts a groove into the white, steam rising up from what's left of his head.

OK, not really.

I can see it in my mind, but it's not real. He still walks ahead of me, bouncing along.

Wouldn't that be great, though? Mind bullets. That's my dream power, I think.

Anyway, I know killing Farber won't be that easy. I know it will require patience. I'm prepared for that. I will bide my time. I will wait for the perfect moment. For now, I hold still like a sleepy spider waiting for something small and wiggly to find itself tangled in my web.

It's a matter of time. It always is.

I let my head sink all the way and close my eyes. Rest. Rest is what I need now.

CHAPTER 35

I dream that Glenn and I sit in his library, reading books. His glasses rest on the tip of his nose, his hands fold on his belly, and one of those huge war books sprawls on his lap. We don't speak, but I have a sense of relief that he's with me. I can breathe. I can let the muscles in my neck and shoulders relax. There's almost a deja vu quality to the sensation vibrating within me. Like I knew all along that he wasn't really gone. I knew it. He couldn't be. It wasn't real. Could never be real. It wasn't possible.

The universe makes sense again. The familiar order has been restored.

I have a hard time reading my book. My eyes won't take in the words, won't stay on the page. I keep wanting to look around the room, to take it all in, to keep it. The sunlight slanting into the window, making one tilted rectangle on the floor glow, the smell of the open books, like something old and important remembered, the chime of the clock, the feeling of companionship, of not being alone, the sense that we have no reason to worry, no reason to rush, like we have all of the time in the world to just sit and read. I want to keep all of it. Because this is how things are supposed to be.

CHAPTER 36

When I wake up, my back stings. I sit up from my resting place on the ground, the back half of my body numb, caked in snow. I try to stand, but it's hard when your hands are tied together, and you can't feel most of your body. The odor of pine trees lingers in the air. It smells like Pine Sol, only more real.

"He's up," a voice says. It's Woods.

"Good," Farber says from somewhere behind me. "Help him up, and let's move on."

Footsteps beat their way to me, and I'm scooped up. At this point these guys have their hands in my armpits more often than not. They're insatiable. Of course, I barely feel it this time out of numbness. I mostly just shake around and shiver and such. I can kind of tell something grips under my arms, a little pinch, but that's it. And I know I'm going up, hovering a moment, getting my dead feet under me.

I take a second to find my balance, my legs wobbling like a pair of Jello jigglers, knees buckling, again, three times. But the hands catch me, and I try again, and everything evens out a little. The ground feels solid again, like it did in the good old days, back when I was a warm blooded ape of some type that walked upright on two legs. Those were good times.

Once I'm steady on my feet, the mitts retract from my pits.

I feel so used.

A weird sensation comes over me. I try to get a handle on my state of mind, but I can't find anywhere to grip. It's all sludge in my cranium from what I can tell, the consistency of soft butter. Nothing to hold onto.

I do know this much: it's not quite right in a mostly pleasant way. My brain feels half asleep, and I think the other half is numb from the cold. It ain't so bad as it might sound, though. It really takes the edge off when you chill your brain like this.

I'm almost giddy, even. Almost.

Is drunk one of the stages of grief or something? Feels like that in a way. Feels like I drank a bunch of vodka mixed with Redbull. All of this energy burns in me, but my motor skills are terrible, and my thoughts are a little slowed down, dimmer than usual. I'm very motivated in a way, but if I were back in the real world, my aspirations would be to do something like spray paint my surname on the hood of a police car. With no pants on. A modest goal, I'd say, and very much a drunken one.

Cromwell and Woods busy themselves with ropes, strapping them around their waists. There's barely any light now, so I can't tell what they're doing.

"Let's go," Farber says.

His face stays angled away from me, which is probably for the best for both of us. Looking at him brings a loathsome feeling over me, that humiliated sensation that there are no words for; the one that drives men to kill each other for some kind of honor, some kind of pride.

And I know even now, in some way, that doing so will not satisfy me, it will not fulfill me. Even with my drunk brain I know this, but it's like there's nothing else to do, you know? There's nothing else. There's no satisfaction left to be had, no fulfillment, so I'll settle for this. Whatever it is.

As our walk begins, I glance back and see that Cromwell and Woods pull a sled. Where the hell did that come from? Has it been with us all this time?

A blanket covers its cargo. It's a big sled, too, about as long as a coffin and wider... As soon as that thought crosses my mind, I realize what it is.

"What are you doing with him?" I say.

I address Cromwell, but Farber answers me.

"Every man deserves a decent burial," he says. "We'll take him back with us."

I want to beat Farber's face in with a hammer. Just pound it until all that's left of his head is a bloody jelly. I know that on some level taking Glenn's body back is a good thing, an act of kindness for his family and whatnot. I know that. But when Farber's mouth opens, I want to close it for him. That's all.

We walk a long while, and no one talks. The snow stands less than two inches deep now, though still firm, and there are patches of exposed land here and there, frosted grass and dried-out dirt spots, all cracked and hardened by the cold. The trees grow denser and denser until we're walking in legit woods instead of a sparsely wooded field. Pines comprise the majority here, but there are plenty of those black, dead looking trees, too.

My limbs thaw out a little as I get my body moving and heart pumping, which basically means my arms and legs tingle and throb and get pricked by a few thousand of those really fat needles all over. Thankfully, my head doesn't suffer the same fate. My brain stays half frozen or whatever, that loopy, drunk feeling keeping the darkness at bay. For now.

Should I be more scared than I am? I have no sense of where they're taking me, though I have a pretty good idea that they intend to murder me in some spectacular fashion, to sacrifice me. It just doesn't seem real, even after all I've seen.

I wasn't too scared last time, and I was wrong. So yeah. I don't know what to do with this information, though. Should I try to whip myself into some frenzy? Can you fill yourself with fear with sheer willpower? And what would that accomplish?

Wait.

I'm getting an idea. I can feel it forming, can feel my mind churning out some shiny clump of new material.

Wait for it.

Wait for it.

Oh.

Yep.

Yep, that makes sense.

I should escape. That's the idea.

A sound plan.

Maybe I'm drunker than I thought if this is just occurring to me now. I don't know. Have I mentioned that I do not have a college degree? Not even close. I'm not proud.

We stop for a moment as they switch the ropes up. Farber takes his turn at pulling the sled, taking over for Cromwell. They pull ahead of us, blazing a trail. I'm thankful that the blanket lies flat, pulled taut over the top of the sled, not showing any outline or sense of silhouette.

We must be walking into warmer territory. I can't feel the difference, personally – it's still well within the boundaries of cold to me - but the snow is wetter here. Melty. My feet slosh through slushy spots as thick as split pea soup, and the exposed dirt no longer displays cracks. It forms mud pits. All soggy. I think the sky shines a little brighter now, too, though it's hard to be sure about this.

A hand grips my elbow and pulls me to a halt. I turn to see Cromwell, the gloved index finger on his opposite hand pressed to his lips to shush me without him making a sound. Now he yanks me forward, so we're still walking, just at a slower pace. Farber and Woods pull away from us, the sled dragging behind them.

Is he going to tell me something? Maybe he'll help me escape. That'd be pretty sweet.

I look at him, study his expression for a long moment, but his face shows no emotion. He stares straight ahead with some intensity like a cat watching a woodpile, waiting hours for the mouse that lives within to come out.

I trip then, stubbing my toe on a tree root and then slipping in the mud. I right myself just in time for Cromwell to club me on the back of the head again.

I flop down into the slush, eyelids fluttering, the world whirling around me, everything out of focus. Reality fades out slowly this time.

"Hold up. He's passed out again," Cromwell says.

And a few seconds later I do.

CHAPTER 37

I wake with my hands clasped in front of me, my fingers weaved through each other. Did I do that in my sleep?

And then I sense that the sounds around me are different. No snow. No more white blanket dampening everything, rolling off most of the high frequencies, softening and smoothing everything out. That's over. All of the world's bright and harsh and hard noises have been restored to their full glory.

Bony shoulders dig into my ribs once more, and the ground slides by below my dangling feet. They carry me. Again. Walking. Carrying. Knocked out. Revived. Snow to slush to grass. It feels like all of this has been going on for years. Forever.

It's brighter now. The light shines on the branches and pine boughs above us, casting a spiderweb of shadows onto the forest floor. There's still a touch of gray to the illumination. It looks like the morning, though I guess that doesn't really exist here.

So how did my unconsciousness happen upon me this time? I think back on it. Right. Cromwell bashed my skull again. What'd he do that for? Just felt like carrying me some more? All he had to do was ask. I thought we had the kind of captive – captor relationship where I didn't need to tell him that out loud. Communication issue, I guess. That's the only real problem in any relationship, isn't it?

Pine needles carpet the ground here, dried-out and orange. They pile on top of each other, matted up, extinguishing most of the foliage. Little clouds of gray billow up from beneath the orange layer every time Cromwell's feet make contact with it. This landscape proves much drier than my last stop.

My nose itches, so I bring my hands to my face and unknit my fingers to scratch it.

Ah. As soon as my hands detach from each other, the lash around my wrists almost falls off. It's very, very loose. I could pull my hands free of the rope if I wanted, though I will wait for the right moment. I'm smooth like that.

That must be what Cromwell was doing. Making an opportunity to loosen my bonds. I suppose braining me with a blunt object was probably the most fun and efficient way for him to do that. He couldn't slip me a sweet dagger on the sly or something less violent? Has this guy never heard of the old piss break as a diversion trick?

No, no. Apparently, his idea of being discrete is dishing out concussions. Blunt force trauma. Subtle.

Whatever. I shouldn't complain. In all fairness to Cromwell, I have a pretty thick skull, and I barely use my brain as it is. Both of these facts are well established, well understood. He knew what he was doing.

So now I wait. I look for my chance. I position myself to make my move.

I wiggle some, pretending like I'm just now waking up, and the men stop and set my feet on the ground. I figure I can't escape if they're toting me around, right? I've got to create some distance. I've got to walk on my own.

"If it happens again, you'll ride in the sled," Farber says.

No thanks. I'm happy to walk now, dickface.

We pick our way through the woods. More of the pines give way to oaks, maples and birches, and the pine needle flooring recedes with grasses and green leafy stuff stepping forward to fill the void. This is good. Much less visibility. Much better cover. Both excellent characteristics for those of us plotting a daring escape.

Now I'm antsy. I don't want to launch my escape pod too hastily as I may only get this one opportunity to get away. On the other hand, for all I know, our intended destination lies around the next corner. Farber might have the plastic sheets all laid out and ready to go in a serial killer style kill room just past that Douglas fir up there. So yeah. There's a real risk of waiting too long and screwing myself that way, too.

Decisions, decisions.

Of course, part of me wants to attack Farber now that I have the free hands to do it. I strangled him once. I could do it again. He wouldn't see it coming. That's for sure.

It'd be 3 on 1 most likely, though. Even if Cromwell harbors some sympathy for me, I don't see him jumping in to help me kill one or both of his friends. Seems unlikely. Maybe if I told him he'd get to hit someone over the head, he'd get so excited he wouldn't think about it too hard, but I doubt this. He could side with them and get another free shot at my skull that way. That's like the best of both worlds from his point of view.

Damn.

What should I do?

Think, Grobnagger, think!

We find a trail cutting through what is now incredibly thick vegetation and take it. Even on the path, branches grasp at my head and shake their tiny fists. Blades of various grasses smear their bodies against my jeans.

Worst lap dance ever.

We move in single file now, Farber leading the way with Woods right behind him, straining to drag the sled by himself at this point. I'm up third. I lag a little, dropping further and further back from the leaders to give myself extra distance from them. This is probably the perfect setup, the perfect chance to go for it. With Cromwell behind me, he'd be the first to see me veer off of the path, which could help me buy a little time.

I see it taking shape before it arrives, and the adrenalin courses all through me. Farber rounds a bend, moves out of view. Woods disappears into the wall of greenness as well, the sled trailing.

My heart pounds in my chest, blood thrumming in my ears, pulsing in my temples, my jaw clenched all tight.

Is this it? Should I do it?

Suddenly an arm loops through mine, hooking my left elbow and pulling me off the trail. I'm confused, being dragged through leaves and limbs and stems and stalks. A hooded figure pulls me along, zigging and zagging to avoid trees. Is Cromwell making a break for it with me?

No. This hood, while black, seems to have a red shimmer to it somehow. This person's frame occupies less space, too. Narrow shoulders. Slender waist. Much shorter.

We hit a little clearing, a straightaway through knee high grass, and she turns and smiles at me.

"Ain't no party like a rescue party," she says.

It's Amity.

CHAPTER 38

I shake my hands loose from the rope, though Amity still drags me along by the wrist. The forest remains a green blur around us. She's quite nimble, this one. She changes direction like a puma. I don't think I've ever seen a puma change directions, actually, but I bet they do so with a lot of class and style. Either way, she is very light on her feet. She moves like a ninja, all quiet and shit. I, on the other hand, crash through the woods, gigantic yeti feet tromping down ferns like the guy in the Godzilla suit destroying a miniature city.

I want to ask her about 50 questions, but it's difficult to do so while sprinting and puma leaping and gasping for breath and all. I suppose some of my queries could perhaps be unwise to speak aloud at the moment, too.

I mean, does she know? Does she know about Glenn? And should I tell her while we're in getaway mode? Probably not, right? It wouldn't help anything that I can think of.

And Glenn flashes in my head again, lifting his navy blue ball cap with his left hand and slicking his hair back with his right, splayed fingers working like giant teeth on a comb. He blinks and looks far away and pulls the cap back on.

No. Don't think about that now. Run.

I smash plants flat. I trample them. I squash them. I'll admit it. I can be a little rough with the plant life.

I hear running water now. The words, "a babbling brook," pop into my head, because my head is weird. Anyway, the water must be pretty close to be loud enough to hear over my yeti stomps. We run a while longer, take a hard right around a weeping willow, and the rushing stream appears before us, gashing a spurt of wet movement over a brown river bed that parts the green ground covering all around it.

Yep, the babbling brook itself.

We turn right again, running alongside the water. Maybe there is some biological response to seeing fresh water like this, but I think I feel better. Invigorated. Refreshed. The tension in my neck seems to dissipate. The fire in my lungs dies down to a smolder. The stabbing pain that feels like a knitting needle piercing my liver disappears entirely. Sure, I still half expect Farber to come round house kicking out from some bushes at any second, but I feel better about it.

The water smells fresh. This whole section of the woods smells alive. Awake.

Wait. I'm not great with directions necessarily, but I think we might be headed back in the direction we came from. Is that possible? I remember two pretty hard right turns. I guess that would do it, eh? Would be pretty ridiculous to run right into the dudes chasing us, right?

I tug on Amity's hand, doing the double jerk that is the universal hand language for pull over. But she's not having any of it. She yanks my arm a little harder and continues running, weaving, ninja-ing. Not so much as a glance my way.

So I keep up the best I can. Not because I'm ashamed that this girl is a superior athlete to me or anything like that. I do it because if I don't, I'm pretty sure she will rip my arm off.

The sound of the water gets louder and louder. The pitch seems lower, too, almost thunderous in the distance. The stream looks a little wider, for sure, perhaps a little deeper as well, but it must get really huge somewhere up ahead based on what I'm hearing.

Now we slalom through a cluster of sumac trees, young ones with trunks about the girth of cigars. They're packed together tightly. I try to take diagonal steps and contort my torso to avoid contact as much as possible, but it's not a huge help. Sticks scrape against me with each step. It's like running through a gauntlet that should be part of some TV game show. Each step seems to bring a new injury with it, thankfully minor. This step jabs my knee. That step rubs a patch of skin off of my forehead about the size of a quarter.

And my eyes water. And my mouth is all dry. And my throat burns, probably because the fire in my lungs packs a pretty good rage at this point.

The water is a never ending crash of thunder now, and I realize that there must be a waterfall up ahead, a pretty big one by the sounds of it. That suggests a cliff, which consequently suggests a possible detour ahead for us.

This is all too complicated for my liking. Couldn't we just find a nice spot to lie down, shrouded in all the cover the green supplies? That'd be cool. And how would they find us, honestly? These woods stretch out forever. They can't turn over every leaf or poke through every bush. They could search for days and never get within 150 feet of us.

You know what? Yeah. I vote for that. Let's lie down ASAP.

I consider how to broach this topic with Amity, especially without using words since I'm too busy trying to breathe to speak right now.

But just then her hand disengages from mine, and she turns to me and lips something at me, but I can't hear her. Then she splashes out into the stream and jumps over the edge of the waterfall where the river drops off into nothing.

CHAPTER 39

I stand on the bank of the river, too scared to even get close enough to the edge to peek over the falls. The loudness of crashing water vibrates the world. I feel it through my feet and rattling in my ribcage. Mist kicks up into the air all around here, a little spritzing my forehead, cooling me. So that's nice, at least.

Nothing is ever just simple, right? Remember my idea about lying down in the weeds? Now, what the hell was wrong with that? But no, no, let's hurl ourselves over a damn waterfall instead.

I think people underestimate how frustrating it can be to realize that pretty much everyone is more brave than you.

So what am I supposed to do? I can feel my eyebrows twitch as my brain works this out. My mouth hangs open, my lungs rapid fire huffing and puffing to try to get some wind in me.

I was pretty taken aback by this waterfall leap, right? Right.

OK. Just making sure.

I run it back. She turned to me just before she leapt off the edge of the world. She turned to me, and her mouth moved. She spoke one syllable, but I couldn't hear her over the roar of the water rushing over the falls. Did she whisper? Did she yell? I suppose it makes no difference. But I can still see her lips opening at the beginning of the word and then pushing together at the end. It ended with a p, I believe.

I watch her lip the word at me in my imagination over and over, and I try to read it. Ah, OK, it ends with an "mp" now that I think about it. By process of elimination, I believe I can narrow this down to "jump" or "hump."

Now, for me personally, it'd be a lot funnier if she turned and yelled "hump" at me just before plummeting off of these falls. I would like that quite a bit. Plus, she could be making plans for what we're going to do later. Also awesome.

But no, she was telling me to jump, I guess. Damn it. Everybody just assumes I'm like Indiana Jones or Tom Brady or something, but I am more like Marcia Brady.

My feet pad over the muddy banks, walking all slowly because part of me, maybe most of me, never actually wants to arrive at the edge and look down. I manage to really stretch this mosey out, kicking at pebbles, taking in all of the sights and sounds on the 20 foot route. I even strike up a small talk conversation with myself:

Boy, it's a nice day isn't it? The warm air, the sound of the falls, that little touch of mist in the air. Oh man, I'm telling you, a guy could get used to this. He could get used to it real quick.

But I don't feel like myself. It all comes off like I'm pretending, going through the motions of being alive. I haven't felt like myself since Glenn's death, I guess. Like the best I can do is disconnect from what's going on, detach from my surroundings, my reality. Things can seem funny again when I'm far away from it, when nothing is real. Is that the best it can ever be? Ironic detachment? Floating above the world with a layer of absurdity swathing everything.

I don't know. I may never feel like myself again.

I look over the edge, my toes nearing the point at which the ground shears off into a cliff wall at about a 90 degree angle. It's about 30 feet down, I'd say. A pile of jagged rock chunks occupy the place directly beneath me. It looks like the spot straight down from the falls is the place to jump. There's a rounded area there just beyond the splash zone where the water is fairly still. I assume it's deeper than the rest.

I don't see Amity, though. Maybe she took cover in the woods.

Well, I guess I should go for it. You only live once. Or twice, I guess, if you resurrect after an old man burns you alive in the bottom of a well. (Is that a thing that happens to people, or was it just something that happened to me the one time?)

I wade out into the wetness. It's a little over knee deep where I stand, but the river grows more shallow going toward the falls. The stream widens as it gets to the drop off, the water pulled thin as it passes over the rock corner and dumps off the edge.

I take a deep breath and let it out all slow. I never do shit like this. My fear is too big, always has been. Even as a kid, while everyone else possessed this false sense of immortality, I feared injury and death all of the time. I was the kid that couldn't make a tackle in football with my eyes open, didn't want to jump off of the roof onto the trampoline to see what happened, didn't think it was fun to get the 4 wheeler going full speed. I'm that tiny percent of scaredy cats that must be necessary to ensure that the entire species doesn't get wiped out by head trauma or eating poison mushrooms.

Another deep breath, the exhale flowing out of me, deflating my ribcage. The water refuses me a moment of silent reflection. It roars and crashes into the rocks and generally taunts me.

I close my eyes and block everything out for a moment. I picture myself soaring over the edge, long jumping like an Olympian, legs churning in the empty air, face all stoic like I've done this a million times before. Something about it is like a silent film.

I can do this. I have nothing to lose and all to gain. It's a leap of faith, or a leap to faith, as Randy said shortly before he covered me in gas and set me on fire.

See? I've made it through worse.

I open my eyes. The watery sounds fade back into my consciousness.

I run ten paces, my speed building as the water gets shallower and shallower. The edge comes up on me. I gulp in one last breath, hold it.

And jump.

CHAPTER 40

The bottom of the world drops out, and I fall into nothing, into empty space. Everything flicks into slow motion. My arms flail one time a piece in something akin to a swim move that I believe is some kind of recoil or follow through from the exertion of the lift-off jump itself. I seem to float at first, just ever so faintly dropping and without much velocity. Like I might just be able to do one of those astronaut jumps and nestle into a touchdown on the opposite shore.

That half nauseous, half exhilarated feeling bubbles in my stomach as the fall continues. It feels me sinking before it really happens, tries to brace me for it.

From there, the angle of my motion bends quickly to straight down. My descent picks up speed at an ever increasing rate. The air rushes against me, tears pooling in my eyes and draining from the corners.

Good news: I'm headed right for the deeper pool of water. Knowing I won't get chewed up by that mouth of jagged stones makes me feel a little better. I'll probably just hit my head and drown in this calm pool, which should be a much less painful way to go.

Good deal.

I don't churn my legs like I did when I imagined this jump. In fact, I straighten out a little more than I would like, feet pointed down. This isn't great. I think if you hit the water feet first with your knees locked, you can hyperextend that shit pretty badly, maybe even tear some ligaments. I try to not lock them, but it's hard to concentrate on things like this while also focusing on not pissing and shitting yourself in terror.

Falling faster and faster and I hit the water with a slapping sound and keep going, submerged, the shock of cold hugging against me, its embrace broken up only by the air bubbles rocketing past on all sides. And the sound cuts off as the water surrounds me, muted, deadened. Not silent – I can hear a muffled version of the waterfall that reminds me more of stampeding elephants now – but mostly sounds are turned inward. I hear my heart beat louder, and the sounds of swallowing saliva magnified. And I keep my eyes open during all of this, which surprises me. I'm more of a flincher, or I was, at least. I always was.

Momentum carries me down and down into the deep, the chill growing more intense as I go. The cold grips my torso in a way that makes it hard to breathe, like it's too chilly and my lungs just want to quit now and get it over with.

Looking up I can see the light illuminating those top layers of water, shimmering in the choppiness, an expanding ring of ripples my splash landing created. I can see where I need to go, maybe 15 feet up or so, but I'm powerless to get there, still going down, slower than before, but it's too much force to fight still.

But I can't panic either. I can't. If I waste energy fighting the momentum of the fall, I'll be much worse off. So I stay patient. I wait.

The sinking slows to almost nothing, a drift that's as much

sideways as descending. When my downward motion reaches its end, I hover there a second as the forces that pull me down and up negotiate their equilibrium. Then the weight lifts off of me, and a great lightness takes its place. I float upward just a touch, and I know it's time. I kick my legs and reach out with cupped hands now to help floating along.

Even with the kicks, rising to the surface takes longer than I'd like. I almost wish I had gotten to the sandy bottom so I'd have something to push off of. The light gets brighter. The surface grows nearer and nearer, but some part of me panics anyway. It remains convinced that I'll never get there, that I'll never bob up through the top, move back into the light, and draw fresh air into my lungs. It remains convinced that the liquid will hold me under in some suffocating hug, its arms surrounding me forever.

I breach the threshold, pushing face first through the surface and feeling the open air again. It's almost shocking for that roaring waterfall sound to click back on, to feel the air that seems to stretch out into the sky like it never ends, to be bombarded with daylight. I blink twice, and my lungs creak and hiss as the first breath gasps into me. Breath number two gets interrupted by a mouthful of water, which I thankfully catch and spit out right away rather than inhale. I taste a little sulfur in there, I think.

Yum.

I want this to be over. I want to swim to the shore and be on the land. But I tread water for a moment, trying to get my wind back before I make the swim out.

Patience. Maybe I am learning something. Maybe I am changing.

Maybe I will never feel like myself again because my self isn't some static thing. It changes with everything I do, every experience, every conversation. It rolls in and out like the tide, every wave unique. When I think about it that way, I don't feel quite as bad. It hurts me a lot, and I might never get over it, I might never heal, but at least I can say that Glenn taught me a lot of shit. He changed me for the better. That's something, right?

I swim to the shore and crawl up the mud that slopes along the bank to lie in the grass, rolling over onto my back and closing my eyes. My breath heaves in and out of me, and I shiver a little, though I'm somehow too hot and too cold at the same time. Clammy all over. I open my eyes and look up at the treetops, at the barrier of cloud hung above them.

And Glenn pops into my head, wielding a plate of jerked chicken with that cheesy rice and bean concoction. And then he's walking through his backyard, arms limp at his sides, his posture somehow like an overgrown toddler's.

There was nothing I could do, but I should have done something, you know? I should have done something. I should have. There was nothing I could do, but I should have done it anyway.

And my face clenches up, those balls of muscle hardening at the crook on each side of my jaw, and I know I was wrong. That shit I thought before about Glenn changing me? It didn't make this any better. Nothing makes it any better. Nothing makes it make any sense.

I burst into tears again. They rush down my face, and my chest spasms, and my body squirms on the grass without me telling it to, and strange noises rattle out of me that don't sound like me, and I know in my heart that nothing will ever make it better.

CHAPTER 41

When Amity finds me, I am under that blanket of wet, hot red again, plunging into the gloom inside of me, blocking out reality. I don't fully realize she is there at first.

I gurgle up to the surface, poking my head out of the internal world into a moment of clarity, seeing her silhouette, a dark shape against the light. I know what I need to do now, and it will hurt some more. For both of us.

Amity kneels on the line at the edge of the stream where the dirt gives way to grass. I swallow, and it's loud – a gulp and a click. I half sit up and rub my hand against my chest like I'm smoothing out some wrinkles before my big speech. I take a beat, our eyes locked. I wanted to gather myself, and I think I've done an OK job. I know how much worse this will be for her than it is for me, which is hard to fathom, but I know it's true.

I muster some gravitas. I don't know why, but it seems necessary.

But as I speak that flash of heat comes over me again. I sink into the darkness, the emptiness. I know the words are coming out of my mouth. I know from the outside it probably seems fine – the gravity is right, the empathy is right. But I am disconnected from it, plummeting deeper inside myself. It's like someone else does the talking, someone stronger than I am.

I tell her about the snow and the rope and the swords. All of it. And I ultimately succeed at dragging her down here with me, engulfing her in the sorrow and anger and powerlessness.

And we lie on the grass for a long time, and we rip our insides out and let the air touch them and let the mist touch them. We pour out our souls through our mouths and eyes without saying a word.

And the water just keeps thundering over the edge and clobbering the rocks below, totally indifferent.

CHAPTER 42

At some point I realize that we've just been lying still for a long time, and I think about how Farber is surely looking for us. It hadn't even crossed my mind in a long while.

I sit up. It's been so quiet that I almost expect to find Amity asleep. She is awake. She stares up into the heavens, a dead expression in her eyes. Redness still splotches her cheeks. Moisture still shines on the swollen eyelids.

"We should get moving, right?" I say, my voice sounding deeper than normal like I just woke up. "You know they're still looking for me."

She doesn't blink. The dead expression doesn't change at all, in fact.

"They won't find us," she says. "But we should get going anyway."

I pinch that place where my nose connects to my forehead and lift. I don't know why. I saw a guy doing it at a restaurant once, and I tried it. Seems to relieve some tension. Maybe it's some kind of pressure point or something.

"How do you know they won't find us?" I say.

She sits up, brushing away the dirt that clings to the backs of her arms.

"I know these woods a lot better than they do," she says. "Unless they decide to jump off the falls like we did, they'll never find us. They won't find an easier way down here. It doesn't exist."

I nod.

"Well, that's good," I say, though I consider saying, "clever girl," like that scene in Jurassic Park where the guy gets eaten by velociraptors. Probably should have gone with that. Damn.

I lift myself to one knee and stretch my back, arching my neck and rotating my core a little. My muscles fight this movement, wanting to remain rigid and motionless, but I won't allow such nonsense. I stretch them harder, putting some stank on it. They shouldn't have challenged me. I can be pretty coldblooded with this kind of stuff, pretty callous.

I stand. My calves give me a little pinch once my full weight rests on them. They are sore to a degree that I never really expected to experience here. Kind of weird. I bounce up and down on my toes a few times to try to limber those babies up.

Amity stands and rolls her neck a few times, scrunches her shoulders. She is so much shorter than me that it's hard to believe we are members of the same species. It must be about a foot and a half difference. The top of her head comes up to my nipples.

She mops at her top lip with the back of her tiny hand as if on cue to illustrate my point. She has those cute, little elf ears, too. Maybe that is her species: elf.

I believe we've already established that my species is troll, or maybe I'm some hybrid of troll and yeti. I could buy that.

Without saying anything, she walks into the woods. I follow. The plant life seems a touch more suffocating down here. Prickly stuff grabs at my shirt. Branches snap off of Amity, threatening me by shaking leaves in my face, almost daring me to take another step. The green smothers me. It grinds itself on me.

And then we hit a clear spot, and that's all over. We now trot on a reasonably well worn path, heading deeper into the woods where the shade gets thicker. The canopy above knits its leaves together tightly so only pinpoints of light ripple through when the air moves. It's like we're walking into the dusk.

The roar of the waterfall trails off into nothing as we move along.

"So where are we going?" I say.

"I know a place we can hide out for a while," she says. "There are a couple of apple trees, and a spring where the water doesn't have that sulfur taste."

"Do you need food out here?" I say.

"Not much," she says. "I think getting some water to drink once in a while helps keep your mind clear, though, and the apples always make me feel better."

"So a comfort thing more than a nutrition thing?" I say.

"Yeah, exactly," she says. "Anyway, we should be safe to stay there as long as we want. I figure if we wait long enough, they'll be gone, and we can get back to wandering around. Time is hard to judge out here, but Farber and his people don't seem to stay more than a couple days at a time or something that feels like that. Not sure what that translates to in the real world, but I think it's like 40 days or so."

I look down at myself as my brain digests her words. My feet kick up dust with every step, not clouds so much as puffs of gray that resettle on the ground as quickly as they appear.

"So you were planning for me to stay here a while?" I say. "Cause I was kind of figuring to get back as soon as possible."

"What for?" she says. "Farber is trying to kill you, right? You stick with me, and that will never happen. Not a chance he'll find us. It's peaceful out here, you know? There's a lot of interesting stuff to do. Lots of things I could show you."

"I don't know. There are matters back there that I need to take care of," I say.

"Well, it's your choice," she says. "But there's nothing back there that you'd miss. You know that, don't you?"

I think it over.

"I don't know if that's true," I say. "I mean, don't you want to go to your Dad's funeral or whatever?"

She stops walking, blinks a few times. When she starts going again, her gaze shifts to the ground. We walk in silence for a while, moving past sections of woods that are difficult to distinguish from the rest. The green is so dense above us and so sparse on the ground. The lack of light coming through leads to mostly dead leaves and barren trunks down here. There are a few ferns that must like the shade here and there, but that's it.

I'm glad to have this path to tell us where to go. Elsewise the woods grow intimidating as we walk in their shadows. Indecipherable. Claustrophobic. I feel a little lost, even though I know Amity knows it all inside and out.

She speaks again, and after the distractions, it takes me a second to catch up with the conversation.

"I can't go back," she says. "I don't make sense there anymore."

CHAPTER 43

The trees thin out in time and let some spots of light sift between the leaves and branches. My dread recedes as we move out of the shade, into the warmth. Daylight melts anxiety, I think, at least somewhat.

I watch Amity as we walk. Her body language is foreign to me: upright posture with a sense of power or athleticism in that section of the torso where the abs meet the ribcage. There's a bounce in her step, a sureness even in the way her arms go back and forth at her sides. She moves with a confidence that I'll never have. Not cockiness. Not arrogance. It's not something for show. It's no attempt to intimidate. It's genuine. You can see it.

Even her build exudes confidence. She is not one of those waif girls with little toothpick arms, nor does she look like a bodybuilder or anything like that. Her physique remains feminine. There's something strong about her, though. A toughness. An anger that flashes in her eyes sometimes and tenses up in her shoulders at others.

Am I saying that she seems like a tough elf? Yeah, I guess I am. She's about as tough as a girl that's about five feet tall can be, at least.

In any case, as a bona fide sissy, this assertive personality type always makes me uneasy. Like maybe I will say or do something wrong, and she will lash out or judge me harshly. Look, it's a matter of time before she turns on me. I've been around. I know this.

The path coils around a couple of bends, and the trees alongside us fall away. A grass field opens up ahead of us. It looks familiar. It looks a lot like that too-perfect grass field that led me to the tree. This field displays some imperfections, though – a few taller stalks gone to seed sprout here and there. They rasp when the wind blows.

That comprises another difference itself. The wind seems more legit here. It gusts and dies out just like the real thing. There was something very artificial about it on the way to the tree. More like breath than wind, or maybe more like a machine, even.

Still, the grassy expanse before us bears a strong resemblance to the other one. Maybe this is the way there? That question postures on the tip of my tongue, ready to dive out of my mouth. I push the urge down, though. Some part of me doesn't want to break up the silence yet.

It's neither an unpleasant silence nor an all the way comfortable one, but something about it feels right just now, so I leave it alone. Amity makes eye contact with me for a second, her eyes scanning back and forth across my face with a questioning look. I get a little nervous about what she might see. Just a little. Then, apparently finding some kind of answer there, she smiles at me, and I smile at her. We go back to looking at other things and maintaining the quiet.

See? It's nice to have a silent friend like this.

Blades of green swish against our pant legs as we move into the taller grass. It feels so strange to walk out into the open, no longer hidden amongst the trees. I look out to the horizon now rather than being encased in green leaves. The land just flattens out like it lied down here to nap for a bit and forgot to wake up. There's something satisfying about being able to see what's going on around you, even if I also get that twinge of vulnerability that comes with being exposed.

The air here must be warmer as it's not long before I feel the sweat collecting on my forehead, briny fluid draining from the corners of my brow. I wipe the back of my neck, not surprised to find more moisture. That sensation proves shocking in its own way. Not long ago, I trudged through knee deep snow, shivering. I woke up like a popsicle, caked in white powder, numb as could be from upper back to lower sack. Now I'm all greased up with perspiration.

It's a small astral plane after all.

We walk, grass all we can see in any direction. For a while, I could look back at the tree line to gauge how far we'd come, but the horizon swallowed that up some time ago. Now? Only grass. The wind gusts in our faces every so often, and the air feels cool as it glides across my skin. Something about it is just enough to keep this trek over a monotone green from becoming tedious.

"It's not far now," Amity says, squinting at me.

These are the first words spoken between us for what feels like days. Her voice sounds a little tired, just a touch of gravel to it, but it's nice. You forget how stimulating a human voice can be until the sound leaves you for a while. When it comes back, it makes your heart beat faster. It makes your eyelids flutter. It makes a tingle spread down your arms and throb in the palms of your hands.

I think about this before I answer her, though. Because maybe that's not true of all voices. Maybe it's true of her voice in particular. But I push the thought aside.

"You mean the place with the apple trees," I say.

She clears her throat. It's weird. When I do that, it sounds like some grotesque troll mating call, like tectonic plates of phlegm vibrate in my throat in such a manner that trolls happen to find arousing. When she does it, it sounds so small. Dainty. Trolls wouldn't find it stimulating, I think. They would just go, "Awww."

"No," she says. "You said you want to go back, so we're going to the tree."

"Oh, right," I say.

So I guess this grass field does lead to the other one. Good to know. But wait.

"So are you coming with me?" I say.

She shakes her head.

"I don't think so," she says. She looks far away for a second, and then she smiles. "I think I'm walking you home."

CHAPTER 44

The tree seems to take shape out of the mist all at once, its size still hard to believe even though I've seen the thing before. It remained invisible until we were quite close this time. After giving this some thought, I decide we're approaching it from a different direction, thereby changing the appearance of things pretty dramatically as it turns out. So it goes.

The mist douses us, though, just like before. So that hasn't changed a bit. The clots of moisture hang in the air, tiny droplets all over the damn place. We have no choice but to walk through them. We do that. I'm typically not a fan of sogginess, but this doesn't feel too bad. I was too warm much of the way, so it's kind of a relief.

Amity carries her robe, draping it over her arm. The fabric sways, and it glimmers when the light hits it right. Pretty fancy shit.

Her hair is a bit shorter than I realized now that it's out in the light and I can really see it. She wears a black tank top, visible with the robe removed. I try not to ogle her too much, but I am a disgusting troll, so what do you expect? Anyway, I have gotten the strong impression that I'm not her type, so it's not like that. I don't take as much joy in eyeballing girls that aren't into me, you know? I mean, I do it involuntarily and compulsively, but I don't enjoy it as much.

Sigh.

Not that she has been mean to me or anything like that. She's really nice, and I get it. I'm not my type, either. You know how those jerk-offs have those decals that say, "No Fat Chicks," on the rear windshields of their shitty cars? They should make those that say, "No Disgusting Trolls," so I'd know who not to approach. I can't speak for the other trolls, but I wouldn't be offended by that.

Anyway.

The tree's trunk takes up much of my frame of vision now. Pretty big. The clusters of roots jut out of the ground around us, but they're neither as big nor as plentiful as they were in the place where I met up with Glenn.

Shit. Don't think about him. Not now. There will be time later. Fight it, Grobnagger. Change the subject, right? Right. So, um...

"So what's with the tree?" I say.

"What do you mean?" she says.

"I don't know," I say. "Why does it... do the thing it does?"

She shrugs, cupped hands facing the sky.

"Well, um... What kind of question is that, really? I mean, why does anything exist?" she says.

I wait for her to go on. She doesn't. Is it just me, or do her and her dad get a lot of mileage out of rhetorical questions? I guess that quality can run in families.

"Why does anything exist?" I repeat back to her. "I don't know."

"Exactly," she says. "I don't know if there's a reason why the tree does anything, or a reason why this place is here, or why we're here. I figure in all likelihood, I'll never know these things, not the why part anyway."

"Doesn't that seem shitty, though?" I say.

"In a way," she says. "But I don't worry much about it. I am finding out how things work or at least fragments of that, and that is interesting enough for me. For all I know, there is no reason why, and that's OK."

We walk, and I think it over. I don't like it, but I don't say anything. I mean, she could be right, but I don't like it. I want to know why some day, not just how. It might be impossible, but I want it anyway.

"Nobody knows what they're doing," she says. "We all just make it up as we go, fashioning the pieces of information that we have into a reality. It's all a little bit make believe, you know?"

I don't know what to say. There is a fatalism to this girl that I love and hate. These words sound, to some degree, like something I might say, and even so, hearing someone else say them is painful in some way. I want to tell her that you can't let those things in, that you have to bludgeon these thoughts and keep them outside of you. But I say nothing.

The grass grows patchy underfoot, receding to dust. The tree stands within 200 yards now. We could sprint to it and be there within a few seconds, but I believe we will walk. As you may know, I'm no fan of unnecessary exertion.

But my mind flips into record mode again, like I know this chapter is ending, and as awful as it was, I feel weird about leaving it. The ache of vulnerability creeps upon me as I prepare to change settings, perhaps more so than ever. And who can I even trust now? Who can I talk to?

I picture Glenn doing that move where it looked like he was

clawing at his mustache, and tears come into my eyes. I mostly fight them back, but Amity turns to me right then, lips flattened against each other as she studies my expression again.

"You sure you don't want to just stay here?" she says.

"There's something I have to do," I say. "Maybe a couple of things."

She looks up at the tree.

"I understand," she says.

A new kind of quiet falls over us. I don't know what to make of it, but it's tense in a way that makes our feet scuffing in the dust sound really loud. Self consciousness takes hold in a way that makes breathing suddenly seem strange. I try to remember how to do it comfortably. My first attempts come out too shallow, almost panting, and then I overcompensate and do it too slow and deep.

"Well, make me a promise?" she says.

Before I can react, she pounces on me in a hug that pins my arms to my sides. I wriggle to get free enough to hug her back.

"What's that?" I say.

She leans back to look up at me.

"Promise me you'll come back," she says.

I nod.

"I promise," I say.

She stands on her tiptoes and closes her eyes to kiss me then. I stoop a little to make it work. Just a peck on the lips. I don't even know what to make of it. But I still feel the tingle on my lips and only that when I stumble along in a daze and touch the tree and everything disappears.

CHAPTER 45

A sandy brick facade masks the front of the building, and elegant gold lettering sparkles like this is some fancy bed and breakfast. It's not.

Pushing through the steel door, red carpet runs down the narrow hallway, and the cinder block walls are painted white. It's chilly here, and just looking at those concrete walls somehow makes it feel even colder. The florescent lighting yellows everything a little. Like a dead tooth.

Arrangements of flowers sit on every table, stand, ledge and any other flat surface. Some even arrive in standing baskets mounted on their own metal legs. The little clusters of mostly muted rainbows line the hall. Each a little different and all exactly the same. The odor of lilies, snapdragons, mums, roses, poms and all the others shift and congeal in the air. Every breath gulps in the smorgasbord of a perfume that is totally natural and somehow vaguely unpleasant.

The way vomit smells too sweet.

Turning right through the red velvet curtain and into the main chamber, the flowers now pile high to the left and right of the room's centerpiece along the front wall. Crammed, wedged and squeezed onto shelves, the baskets and ceramic pots jockey for position. Flowers floor to ceiling, and they just keep coming.

They flood the shelves, and the overflow splashes down onto the carpet. Waves of white lilies flow across the floor, crashing up against potted yellow roses and a sympathy cross made of white orchids with a border of deep green palms. A white gardenia topiary sinks between a couple of wreaths in stands. A pink everlasting love wreath made of roses and hydrangeas spills out into the aisle. Now even more flowers lurch onto the main floor, hug the wall farther out still, stretch for the doorway. More and more and more.

The plants seep slowly toward the rows of folding chairs, desperately reaching their stems out away from death.

CHAPTER 46

Why are you here?

You detach until it isn't even real. You're aware it's happening, but all true meaning has been removed. You watch it transpiring, and your mind records the sounds and images, but the feelings have all numbed away. The connection is bad somehow. Broken.

The casket sits in the front of the room like a big black Cadillac. The hood is closed, but what a beauty. A finely crafted product. All smooth and shiny. Sleek. The lines curve just right. You can picture it having a leather interior and pop-up nav screens. Dual zone climate control. Maybe even those Xenon headlamps that shine blue. Power everything. This is the Eddie Bauer edition of coffins. The Titan series. Top of the line. It beams luxury, comfort, and style, but you're not quite sure who the beneficiary is.

Sunlight glints through stained glass windows, casting red and blue and yellow streaks that stretch across the floor, painting stripes of color on the coffin. People walk by, paying their respects to the family, hugging, shaking hands, blue light smearing their faces.

The chatter permeating the room maintains a hush, a reverence.

Why are you here? You don't do this. You don't go to

funerals. You don't go to hospitals. You don't go out to eat or answer social calls of any kind. That is who you are. And the abortion unfolding in this room is why.

Because you saw what really happened. You saw the body slumped face down, blood seeping from a menagerie of holes. You saw this. You saw it.

Everything between you and Glenn ended there, didn't it? So who is this for?

Why are you here?

CHAPTER 47

And now the people huddle around the box, and the man in black speaks, and he points his finger in the book, and he points his pig nose at the book, and his voice quivers with veneration and quavers with deference, but his words ring vague, ring hollow, ring out the emptiness like a bottomless hole of black nothing in ourselves, in our culture, in our souls that can never be filled, cause this is the same goddamn shit he reads for all of them, for all of the heart attack victims or cancer dads or guys that got hit by a drunk driver or whatever, like if he sells it well enough with a shaky voice and puppy dog eyes it'll really mean something, like it's not some empty gesture, like this isn't just another assembly line pumping out their, "Hallmark card speech for a guy who died fairly young," product so everyone can try to feel OK about it, and the people stay huddled around the box, and they bow their heads and bob their heads and sigh their stupid fucking heads off at all of the appropriate moments, and they're sorry, sorry, so sorry for your loss, like whoops, sorry about that, my bad, y'all, like they just took out your blue piece in the board game "Sorry!" or some shit, and the people huddle around the box and clap each other on the shoulder and pat each other on the back and offer each other Kleenex to dab their stupid fucking eyes out with, and the man in black finishes up his routine, and he lifts his pig nose out of the book and shuts it and smiles a knowing smile shaded with just the right amount of sadness based on focus group testing, and the huddle breaks up now, and the people start to move on, and the box lowers into the ground, and the gravediggers will bring in the backhoe or whatever to cover him over with soil now, and golly, hopefully he'll rest in peace down there, like he's just resting, just taking a little cat nap inside of a fucking box forever, and like there's any peace in being a stiff, rotting corpse with 10 sword holes gouged into you, but it's all part of God's plan, and it all happens for a reason, and you don't go to funerals, so why are you even here, why would you do this to yourself, why are you here, why are you here, why are you here, why are you here, right? Right?

CHAPTER 48

And you stand a while over the hole in the Earth, the open mouth swallowing the casket. You stand while the others drift away. You stand because you don't know what else to do.

And you look down past the Astroturf draped around the edges like a terrible green rug. You look into the hard angles etched into the dirt. You look at the shine and curve of the box. You look because you're here.

And a hand grasps your hand, wriggles its fingers between yours, and it's Babinaux, and she looks at you, and you look at her, and you're not as alone as you were. And you know that people care about you, and you care about them, and that it's not all bad, even if it's a lot bad.

You stand together.

You look together.

And you don't have to say anything, and she doesn't have to say anything, and it's for the best this way. Because there are no words for these things inside of you, no turns of phrase that can do these feelings justice, no language to capture what it really means when someone was here and now they're gone.

There are no words, but it's OK, because words aren't your only friend anymore.

CHAPTER 49

I walk over the grass in the cemetery, feeling reconnected to myself, at least a little. I walk alone. Babinaux went off on her own at some point. I haven't seen her in a while. The sun comes out from behind clouds and glares off of the shiny bits on the newer, glossier headstones.

Yeah, the sun shines down like it's just another day, and I guess it is. Not for me, but in the general sense it is. Time holds us down and snuffs us out eventually. All of us. One at a time. The sun is indifferent to this notion.

I walk on a dirt path now. It's a straight shot to the gate that leads into the parking lot where Babinaux's car sits. I can see some movement in the lot, people milling around and talking, cars pulling out, people moving on. This party is over, I guess. The lot remains a ways off, though, and there's not a soul between the gate and me. Just a few of those gigantic pine trees and a lot of graves.

So I answer the question I keep asking myself as I walk this path:

I am here because it felt like the right thing to do. Not for other people. For me. I don't know why. At the moment it doesn't seem that it was a worthy course of action in most ways, but I think maybe it will later, maybe a long time from now. Eventually, I will be glad I did this... maybe. Hard to say.

I don't go to funerals. Remember that tirade? Way back before all of this even really got started, it felt like one of my core beliefs. I wasn't interested in forms of reality beyond what I feel, right? I didn't go to funerals. I didn't go to hospitals. I didn't go out to eat.

Well, here I am. I did it. So have I changed? Am I not who I thought I was?

I spit on the ground.

The soles of my shoes grind rocks into the dirt with each step. My feet are sore, tired, as are my eyes. Really, I suppose all of me is pretty worn out. Every muscle aches, every joint creaks, but I shuffle forward anyway, like a zombie pursuing brains.

Are Farber's men looking for me now? Did they know I would go to this funeral? Did they have the decency to let me do that before they continued their pursuit?

I don't know any of these things. Just thinking of Farber gets my jaw clenched, though. The skin between my eyebrows wrinkles. Blood throbs in the veins in my temples. Murder swells in my heart. I feel like smoke should come out when I exhale.

It doesn't.

In fact, my throat seems to close a little as I imagine the smoke. I cough once, and my chest constricts and seizes up. It won't expand no matter how many times I will it to. I bang a fist into my ribcage to try to jar something loose. When that fails, I bring my hands to the place where the neck and collar bone meet, fingers scraping and scrabbling at my flesh like I might be able to wrench something loose and fix it.

What is this?

I try to yell for help, but my mouth only emits wet sounds, guttural sounds like a cat purring underwater. I see my reflection in the glossy black gravestone next to me, my face gone red, bloated, strained.

I collapse there, writhing in the dirt flecked with bits of gravel, 15 feet shy of the gate where people just on the other side talk and laugh and enjoy the company of friends and relatives.

CHAPTER 50

When I wake, the odd bloat still surges in my face, that unnatural warmth and overfilled feeling, but I can breathe. I take in a deep lungful of air to celebrate this fact, finding it a touch on the humid side, almost like breathing in a mist. Too lazy to open my eyes just yet, I swing an arm out next to me to feel at my surroundings. My arm finds no resistance, though. It flails at empty space and returns to where it was – dangling beyond my head.

Oh.

Great.

I open my eyes, and I'm not surprised. I probably should be surprised, but I am not.

I find myself in the alley again – my alley - hanging upside down. It all looks to be in order – the water filled pothole I've fallen in many a time, the dumpster housing the dead dog, I even see the downspout I once climbed down at the far end. Those were good times, yeah? Little has changed. Perhaps the gray seems a touch grayer than I remembered, but it's close enough. It's all the same to me.

And that question echoes in my head one more time for good measure. I suppose it applies in so many ways now:

"Why are you here?"

AWAKE IN THE DARK

Want to read what happens to Grobnagger next?

For more information on the Awake in the Dark series, please visit http://ltvargus.com/awake4us

SPREAD THE WORD

Thank you for reading! We'd be very grateful if you could take a few minutes to review it on Amazon.

How grateful? Eternally. Even when we are old and dead and have turned into ghosts, we will be thinking fondly of you and your kind words. The most powerful way to bring our books to the attention of other people is through the honest reviews from readers like you.

COME PARTY WITH US

We're loners. Rebels. But much to our surprise, the most kickass part of writing has been connecting with our readers. From time to time, we send out newsletters with giveaways, special offers, and juicy details on new releases.

Sign up for our mailing list at:
http://ltvargus.com/mailing-list/

ABOUT THE AUTHORS

Tim McBain writes because life is short, and he wants to make something awesome before he dies. Additionally, he likes to move it, move it.

You can connect with Tim on Twitter at @realtimmcbain or via email at tim@timmcbain.com.

L.T. Vargus grew up in Hell, Michigan, which is a lot smaller, quieter, and less fiery than one might imagine. When not click-clacking away at the keyboard, she can be found sewing, fantasizing about food, and rotting her brain in front of the TV.

If you want to wax poetic about pizza or cats, you can contact L.T. (the L is for Lex) at ltvargus9@gmail.com or on Twitter @ltvargus.

TimMcBain.com
LTVargus.com

Made in the USA
Middletown, DE
13 July 2015